Every Bride
NEEDS A GROOM

Books by Janice Thompson

WEDDINGS BY BELLA

Fools Rush In

Swinging on a Star

It Had to Be You

That's Amore

BACKSTAGE PASS

Stars Collide

Hello, Hollywood!

The Director's Cut

WEDDINGS BY DESIGN

Picture Perfect

The Icing on the Cake

The Dream Dress

A Bouquet of Love

BRIDES WITH STYLE

Every Bride Needs a Groom

Every Bride
NEEDS A GROOM

A NOVEL

JANICE THOMPSON

Revell
a division of Baker Publishing Group
Grand Rapids, Michigan

© 2015 by Janice Thompson

Published by Revell
a division of Baker Publishing Group
P.O. Box 6287, Grand Rapids, MI 49516-6287
www.revellbooks.com

Printed in the United States of America

Library of Congress Cataloging-in-Publication Data
Thompson, Janice A.
    Every bride needs a groom : a novel / Janice Thompson.
        pages ; cm. — (Brides with style ; book 1)
    ISBN 978-0-8007-2399-6 (softcover)
    1. Dating (Social customs)—Fiction. 2. Man-woman relationships—Fiction.
I. Title.
PS3620.H6824E94 2015
813'.6—dc23   2014047669

The author is represented by MacGregor Literary, Inc.

15 16 17 18 19 20 21   7 6 5 4 3 2 1

To the real matriarch
of Fairfield, Texas: Eleanor Clark.
You have inspired me, reshaped my view of
the golden years, and given me hope that
I can continue to share my gift all of my
days, no matter my age.

And to the queen of country music,
the amazing Loretta Lynn.
What fun to name my chapters
after your song titles!

1

God's Country

It was very much like Norman Rockwell: small town America. We walked to school or rode our bikes, stopped at the penny candy store on the way home from school, skated on the pond.

Dorothy Hamill

That whole thing about being a big fish in a small pond is more than just a saying, at least in my neck of the woods. When you grow up in a sweeter-than-peaches town like Fairfield, Texas, you find yourself captivated by the love of family, friends, and neighbors. And don't even get me started on the church folks. They'll swallow you up with their bosomy hugs and convince you that you're the greatest thing since sliced bread.

If you're not careful, you'll start believing it too, especially if you're fortunate enough to be named Peach Queen like I was my senior year at Fairfield High. And why not? Why shouldn't a small-town girl like me allow a little lovin' from the locals to go to her head? Being a somebody in a small setting is a sure sight better than being a nobody in a big one.

Not that us small-town girls are unaware of the goings-on beyond our quaint borders, mind you. Oh no. I've had glimpses of life beyond the confines of my little town—say, on one of those housewives reality shows. But I can't picture it. Not really. I mean, who in their right mind would treat their friends and family members like that? And the language! If I ever took to swearin' like those potty-mouthed gals, my mama would stick a bar of soap so far down my throat I'd be gargling bubbles for days to come. No thank you. I may be twenty-four years old, but respect for my elders has been pounded into me. If I ever lost sight of it, my grandmother would be happy to remind me with a swift kick to my backside.

We small-towners aren't just taught respect, we genuinely care about our neighbors. It's not unusual for folks to linger in the checkout line at Brookshire Brothers grocery store to chat about the weather or discuss plans for the upcoming peach festival. And the investment at our local churches is stronger still. The big news there most often revolves around the various prayer lists, where the Pentecostals are interceding for Brother Sanderson, who has undergone a much-needed hip replacement, and the Baptists are shocked to hear that Bessie May Jenson, the congregation's oldest member, has recently suffered a gall bladder attack. This sort of news is always followed by a rousing chorus of "God bless 'em!" and "Don't stop praying!" from the prayer warriors.

And boy howdy, do those prayer warriors take their work

seriously. The Fairfield Women of Prayer—known to the locals as the WOP-pers—have pulled many a wandering soul back from the abyss. Take Levi Nash, for instance. Fairfield High's best-loved football hero tried to get involved with drugs his freshman year of college. Stress *tried*. Party-lovin' Levi never stood a chance, not with the WOP-pers beating down heaven's door on his behalf. Before he knew it, the dear boy, as they called him, had seen the error of his ways. He'd also transferred to a Bible college in the Dallas area, where he planned to major in theology. Go figure. No doubt the WOP-pers would pray in a godly wife for Levi and a couple of precocious kids to boot.

Yep, those prayer warriors clearly had an inside track straight to the Almighty. My grandmother—known to the locals as Queenie Fisher—insisted this had something to do with the fact that the WOP-pers didn't discriminate. They invited women from all of the local denominations to pray in one accord. Even the Presbyterians. Whatever that meant.

"There's something to be said for praying in unity, Katie," Queenie would say as she wagged an arthritic finger at me. "When you're out of unity with your fellow believers, you're prone to wandering."

And heaven forbid any of us should wander. Not that the temptation rose very often. Most of us wouldn't trade our small-town living for any amount of money. Okay, so my oldest brother, Jasper, talked incessantly about moving away to Houston, but Pop always managed to reel him back in by reminding him that he would one day manage our family's hardware store. That seemed to pacify Jasper, at least for now. And Dewey, my middle brother, had talked loosely about going to A&M but ended up at the local junior college, closer to home. This, after Queenie insisted she might just have a heart attack if a family member ever moved away. My grandmother had nothing to worry about where my youngest brother, Beau, was concerned. The way Mama coddled that boy, he would never leave home. Or learn to do his own laundry. Or get a job.

With the exception of my older cousin Lori-Lou Linder, no one in my circle had ever moved away to the big city. Who would want to leave paradise, after all? Certainly not me. Not now. Not ever. In my perfect small-town world, Daddy coached Little League, Mama directed the choir at our local Baptist church on Thursday nights, and Queenie sat enthroned as Fairfield's most revered matriarch. And that was precisely how I liked it.

I pondered my idyllic life as I drove to the local Dairy Queen on the last Thursday in April. After a full day's work at our family's hardware store, I was due a break, and what better place than my favorite local hangout? Besides, Casey would be waiting on me in our special booth, the second one on the left. If I knew him well enough—and I did—he would have my Oreo Blizzard waiting for me.

Waiting.

Casey.

Hmm. Seemed a little ironic that my boyfriend would be waiting on me for a change. How many months—okay, years— had I spent waiting on him to ask me to marry him? Seemed like forever. Oh well. Something as great as a marriage proposal to an amazing fella like Casey was worth the wait. Besides, I had every reason to believe it wouldn't be long before he popped the question. The signs were all there.

Any moment now I'd have a wedding to plan. Not that the lack of a proposal had slowed down my hoping and dreaming. I'd started mapping out my wedding at the age of six, when I'd first served as a flower girl. In the years since, I'd turned wedding planning into an art form.

A delicious shiver ran down my spine as I thought about

how wonderful my big day would be. I'd planned out every single detail, right down to the music, the colors of the brides-maid dresses, and even the flavor of the cake. Of course, all of it hinged on one thing: Casey's proposal. Which, I felt sure, would arrive any day now.

Just as I pulled into a parking spot at the DQ, my cell phone rang. I recognized my cousin's number. After turning off the car, I climbed out and took the call. "Hey, Lori-Lou!"

Her usual cheerful voice sounded from the other end of the line with a hearty, "Hey yourself! What are you up to today? Working?"

"Hmm? What?" I waved at Casey through the big plate-glass window at the front of the DQ, then pointed at my phone to let him know I'd be a minute. "Oh, yeah." I turned my attention back to my cousin. "Just wrapped up at the hardware store. We've been swapping out the window displays for the upcoming summer season. Now I'm meeting Casey at Dairy Queen for an Oreo Blizzard."

A lingering sigh erupted from Lori-Lou's end of the line. "I'm so jealous."

"Of what?" I leaned against my car but found myself dis-tracted by the pensive expression on Casey's face. Weird.

"A Blizzard sounds great in this heat." She sighed again. "It's sweltering outside and it's not even summer yet."

"Ah. It is hot."

"Our AC is on the fritz and we don't have the money right now to fix it. That's not helping things. But honestly? I'm most jealous because I can't remember the last time I had a minute to do anything fun with Josh like hang out at Dairy Queen."

"Aw, I'm sorry." And I was. Sort of. I mean, how bad could it be? The girl had a great husband and three adorable—albeit rowdy—children.

"You have no idea what it's like to be married, Katie," she said.

Gee, thanks.

"Well, married with kids, anyway. We never have date nights anymore. These three kiddos of ours are so—" The intensity of Lori-Lou's voice grew as she hollered out, "Mariela, stop eating your sister's gummy worms! Do you want to end up in time-out again?"

I giggled. "Nope. Don't want to end up in time-out again. And give that ornery little girl a hug from me. I miss her."

"Sure you do."

"No, really. I miss all of your kiddos."

"Stop it, Gilly!" Lori-Lou hollered. "If you smack your sister one more time, you're going to spend the rest of the day in your room." The shrill tone of her voice intensified further. "*Why* are you kids so out of control? You. Need. To. Calm. Down! You're going to wake up your baby brother!" This led to a lengthy period of time where I lost my cousin altogether. I could hear cries coming from the baby moments later. Lori-Lou finally returned, sounding a little breathless. "Sorry about that . . . You know how it is."

Actually, I didn't. But she happened to be offering me a living illustration. "Oh, no problem."

"Hey, not to change the subject, but has Casey popped the question yet?"

Ugh. She would have to go there. Again. And how had we transitioned from ornery kids to marriage proposals? I couldn't help the rush of breath that escaped. "Not yet, Lori-Lou. I tell you that every time you ask."

My gaze shifted back through the window to my boyfriend, who gave me a little wave. My heart soared with hope as I waved back. I could almost see it now—me walking down the aisle in a fabulous dress, Casey standing at the front of the church with his groomsmen at his side. Six of them, to match my six bridesmaids. Okay, maybe seven.

"Right, I know." My cousin's voice startled me back to reality. "But do you think it's going to happen soon? I have a special reason for asking this time, I promise."

"Oh? Well, he *has* been acting a little suspicious." I glanced through the DQ window once again and noticed that Casey had engaged the elderly store manager in conversation. "I didn't see him at all yesterday. He just sort of . . . disappeared."

"Very odd."

"That's what I was thinking. I have a sneaking suspicion he went into Dallas to pick out my ring." The very idea made my heart flutter. For years I'd worn my grandmother's antique wedding ring on my left ring finger. She's always called it my purity ring—a reminder to stay chaste until marriage. The idea of replacing it with a modern ring from Casey made me giddy with anticipation. *Where* would he propose? *How* would he propose? *When* would he propose? My imagination nearly ran away with me as I pondered the possibilities.

"Ooh, you think it's going to happen soon?" Lori-Lou giggled. "Well now, that's perfect."

I nodded, which was dumb, because Lori-Lou couldn't see me over the phone. "Yeah. Why else would he be gone all day? Casey never leaves Fairfield unless it's important."

"Good, because I wanted to talk to you about something that involves him. You read *Texas Bride* magazine, right?"

"Usually." I released a lingering sigh. "To be honest, I've been trying to lay off of bridal magazines for the past couple months. I guess you could call it a self-imposed fast. Since the proposal hasn't actually taken place yet, I decided not to get too caught up in the wedding stuff just yet, for my own sake and my family's. They're getting tired of hearing all of my plans, I think."

"Ah. Well, I wondered why you hadn't said anything about the contest."

"Contest?" That certainly piqued my interest.

"Yeah. They announced it a couple of issues back." Lori-Lou hollered at one of the kids, then stopped a toddler tantrum in the background. "The magazine is linking up with Cosmopolitan Bridal in Dallas. You know about that shop, right?"

"Of course. They have the most exclusive bridal gowns in the state."

"In the country," Lori-Lou said. "And here's the great part. *Texas Bride* announced that they're teaming up with Cosmopolitan Bridal to sponsor a contest. An essay contest. Deadline is May 1."

"May 1, as in tomorrow?"

"Right. By midnight. Then one month later, on June 1, they're going to announce the winner."

"Okay." I tried to figure out what this had to do with me. "What does this winner get, anyway?"

"Cosmopolitan Bridal is going to give away a couture gown to one lucky bride-to-be. And—drum roll—she also gets to be on the October cover of *Texas Bride*! Can. You. Believe. It?"

Whoa. No wonder Lori-Lou was so excited. "Sounds like the opportunity of a lifetime."

"Right? And I totally think you should enter. You would stand a great chance, since it's an essay contest. Your writing skills are amazing."

"You think?" I sucked in an excited breath and considered her words. In my wildest dreams I couldn't imagine winning a dress from Cosmopolitan. "Oh, Lori-Lou, this is . . ."

"The best news ever?" She giggled, then called out, "Gilly,

if you hit your sister one more time, you will never eat another gummy worm as long as you live!"

I did my best to ignore the ranting going on from the kids in the background as I thought this through. Every wedding dress at Cosmopolitan was a one-of-a-kind. Brides came from all over the country to have specialty gowns crafted for their big day, and they paid for it . . . to the tune of multiple thousands of dollars per gown. All of this per *Texas Bride* magazine.

"They're going to tailor a special gown for the winner," Lori-Lou added. "Can you even imagine?"

Oh, I could imagine, all right. The idea of walking down the aisle in an original Cosmopolitan gown made my head spin . . . in a good way.

"So, I have to write an essay? About what, specifically?" I glanced through the window of Dairy Queen once more and gave Casey a thumbs-up to let him know I was okay. He nodded and turned his attention back to the restaurant's manager. "By midnight tomorrow night? Do I email it or something?"

"Yes, there's an email address. Just write five hundred words about your dream dress and your dream day," Lori-Lou explained. "Easy-breezy, right? All of the essays are going to be read by Nadia James, and she's going to choose the one that she feels the strongest about. Or, as the contest entry says, 'the most compelling.'"

"Nadia James?" Whoa. Texas's most touted dress designer would read my essay? The very idea made my palms sweat. The woman was revered among brides across the continent, not just in Texas. "I'm sure hundreds—maybe thousands—of girls will enter," I argued. "And most of them will actually be engaged. You know?"

"I read the rules, even the fine print. There's nothing in there that says you have to have a date set or anything like that. It just refers to the entrant as the 'potential bride' and leaves it at that. You're a potential bride. I mean, c'mon. All single women are, right?"

Ugh.

"So, I think you're okay to enter," she said. "I honestly do."

"You really think I stand a chance?"

"Yep. It won't hurt anything to try. You can write a compelling essay. Give it a title. Call it 'Small-Town Wedding, Big-Town Dreams.'"

"'Small-Town Wedding, Big-Town Dreams,'" I echoed. Sounded about right, though I certainly had no aspirations of becoming a big-town girl.

"What have you got to lose?" Lori-Lou asked. "Wouldn't you like to win a gown from Cosmopolitan Bridal?"

The idea of wearing a designer gown on my big day seemed like something out of a fairy tale, not something likely to happen to a girl like me. Still, what would it hurt to write an essay? Maybe I could play around with the idea a little.

After having an Oreo Blizzard with my sweetie.

I waved at Casey and then said my goodbyes to Lori-Lou, promising her that I would at the very least pray about it. No harm in that. Surely the good Lord would show me what to do. And maybe, just maybe, I could throw in a "please let Casey pop the question soon" prayer while I was at it.

After all, what was a potential bride . . . without a groom?

2

Don't Mess Up a Good Thing

Everybody wants you to do good things, but in a small town you pretty much graduate and get married. Mostly you marry, have children, and go to their football games.

Faith Hill

In the Fisher family, we celebrated traditions that went back dozens, if not hundreds, of years. Springtime tea at Queenie's house, Christmas Eve service at the Baptist church, reinventing the front window display at our family's hardware store with the change of every season, and canning local peaches from Cooper Farms. These were the things I'd grown to appreciate.

The tradition I loved most took place every Friday night when the whole Fisher clan gathered at Sam's Buffet, the best place in town for good home-style cooking—outside of Mama's kitchen, anyway. I'd never known a finer location for barbecue, salad, home-style foods like macaroni and cheese, chicken-fried steak, mashed potatoes, gravy, and more. And the pies! Coconut meringue, milk chocolate, deep-dish apple, lemon meringue . . . Sam's always had an assortment guaranteed to make your mouth water. In the South, grazing around a buffet was something of a religious experience, and we Fishers were devout in our passion for yummy food.

Our weekly dinner routine usually kicked off with Queenie and Pop arguing over who's going to treat who—or would that be whom?—to dinner. Queenie always won. Pop, never one to offend his mother, sighed and conceded, then proceeded to order the buffet. We all ordered the buffet. Well, all but Mama, who, under doctor's orders to lower her cholesterol, ordered the salad bar. That happened one time, and one time only. From that point on she ordered the buffet and made healthier choices. Mostly. There was that one time when, stressed over losing her top soprano from the choir, Mama ate her weight in lemon pound cake. But we rarely spoke of that anymore. In front of her, anyway.

Not that anyone blamed my mother for giving in to temptation. Who could go to Sam's and nibble on rabbit food with so many other flavorful offerings staring you in the face? Not me, and certainly not my three brothers, who all chowed down like linebackers after a big game. The poor employees at Sam's probably cringed when Jasper, Dewey, and Beau came through the door, but they never let it show. Instead, they greeted our family with broad smiles and a hearty "Welcome!" then told us all about the special of the day.

As much as I loved Sam's, it wasn't the first thing on my mind when I awoke on Friday morning. I'd tossed and turned all night as I pondered Lori-Lou's suggestion that I enter the contest. Should I allow the lack of a groom-to-be to stop me from writing an essay? I needed to check out the fine print myself, just to put my mind at ease. And if I decided to go through with it, I'd have to get my act together . . . quickly!

I stopped by Brookshire Brothers and was relieved to find several copies of *Texas Bride* on the rack. The rules seemed simple enough and, just as Lori-Lou had said, only referred to the "potential bride," not an engaged woman. Still, I wondered if—or when—I would find time to write my essay, what with family dinner plans and all. An evening at Sam's with the family meant I wouldn't have time to carefully construct my entry until later that night. Hopefully I could press the Send button before midnight.

I read and reread the rules while I worked at the hardware store that afternoon. Pop never seemed to notice, thank goodness. I would get the usual ribbing about needing a fiancé if he saw me with a bridal magazine. I didn't need to hear that again. Besides, Casey would propose. Soon I would have a fiancé. But what would it hurt to give this contest thing a try in the interim?

Carrying the magazine to the restaurant that evening seemed a little over the top, but my mother and brothers were used to me daydreaming with a bridal magazine in my hand, so they probably wouldn't mind. Queenie would likely take it as a hopeful sign. And with Casey out of town—again—I was safe to browse the pages without putting him on the spot.

I pulled into the parking lot of Sam's Buffet in my '97 Cadillac DeVille—a hand-me-down from Queenie after she purchased the 2001 model—and noticed that my parents had just arrived. Mama bounded from her Jeep, nearly stepping into a pothole as she headed my way. I noticed her new hairdo at once and gave a little whistle.

"Mama! It's beautiful."

"Do you think?" She fussed with her hair and grinned. "There's a new girl at Do or Dye and she doesn't know a thing about my usual cut, so she just went at it like a yard guy with a weed whacker. Said this style was all the rage in Dallas right now. I guess that's where she's from." Mama ran her fingers over her hair. "I've never considered myself trendy."

Boy, you could say that twice and mean it. Mama's usual style was reminiscent of the early eighties. But this new do suited her. In fact, she looked downright beautiful.

My father approached, his expression a bit sour as his gaze traveled to my mother's hair.

"You okay over there, Pop?" I asked.

He shook his head. "Not sure yet. What do you think of Mama's hairdo?"

"I think it's gorgeous." I offered an encouraging smile. "She looks like Diane Keaton in that one movie, you know . . ."

"Oh, that one with Nicolas Cage?" Mama fumbled around in her purse, obviously looking for something. "I always loved that movie. So funny. Well, except that one part where I had to fast-forward because it was so, well, you know."

"It was Jack Nicholson," Pop said.

"Nicolas Cage, Jack Nicholson . . ." Mama pulled out a tiny compact, popped it open, and gave herself a look. "What's the difference?"

"Trust me, there's a world of difference." My father dove into a passionate dissertation about Jack Nicholson's performance in *One Flew Over the Cuckoo's Nest*.

"I don't know what that has to do with anything, Herb,"

my mother said. "Katie wasn't even talking about that movie at all. Were you, Katie?"

"Oh, no ma'am. I—"

"And this conversation about cuckoos has nothing whatsoever to do with my hair." She snapped her compact closed and shoved it back into her purse.

I bit my tongue to keep from saying something I shouldn't. I'd better get this train back on track. "Pop, I mentioned Diane Keaton because she wears her hair just like this." I pointed to Mama's new do. "And she's gorgeous, just like Mama."

"Humph." My father's nose wrinkled, and I could almost read his mind: *It's not your mother's usual style.*

And heaven forbid anything should change. Consistency was key in his life, after all. To my father, staying regular had less to do with the bottle of fiber on the kitchen counter and more to do with the day-to-day routine of everyday life.

"I think it's kind of nice to try something new." Mama looked at her reflection once more and giggled. "Would you believe that stylist tried to talk me into going blonde?"

"B-blonde?" My father's eyes widened. "Glad you didn't bow to the pressure."

"Hey, what's wrong with blondes?" I pointed to my long mane. "It's worked for me."

"And for your mama, back in the day." Daddy slipped his arm over her shoulder and pulled her close. "Your mother was quite a looker." He kissed her forehead.

"Back in the day?" My mother shrugged off his arm. "*Was* quite a looker? For those remarks, I might just have to go platinum to spite you." Her gaze narrowed and I thought for a minute she might throw her purse at him. Wouldn't be the first time she'd used the oversized bag as a weapon.

"Well, if you ever did I'd love you anyway. You were beautiful

then, but you're even lovelier now, Marie. Or should I call you
Ms. Keaton?" My father pulled her into his arms and planted
kisses on her cheeks.

My mother's expression softened like a chocolate bar left
sitting out in the sun. "Call me whatever you like," she said,
her face now lighting into a smile. "Just call me."

Mama gave him a playful wink, and before I could look
the other way, she kissed him square on the mouth. In front
of God and everyone. Well, not that anyone happened to be
looking. Our early arrival at Sam's always put us here ahead
of the dinner crowd. This to help Queenie, who struggled to
get around on her cane.

Queenie.

Strange that she hadn't arrived yet. I glanced around, curious. "Have either of you heard from Queenie?"

"Now that you mention it, no." Mama turned to look at
the handicapped parking spaces, which were all empty. "Odd.
She always beats us here."

"Oh, she probably stopped off at Brookshire Brothers on
the way." Pop waved his hand as if to dismiss any concerns.
"It's double coupon day. You know how careful she is with
her money."

Mama didn't look convinced. "Maybe, but I'm still concerned. If she doesn't show up in a few minutes I'll call her."

Pop laughed and led the way toward the door of the restaurant. "You'll be wasting your time. She's having the hardest
time getting used to that newfangled smartphone of hers. Says
it's smarter than she is."

"Nothing is smarter than she is," I countered.

"True." Both of my parents nodded. Queenie wasn't just
smart by the world's standards, she had the wisdom of the
ages wrapped up in that eighty-one-year-old brain of hers.

Just as we got to the door, my brothers rolled up in Jasper's new Dodge Ram. His tires squealed as he whipped into the parking lot from the feeder road. I knew Mama would give him what for the minute he joined us.

"Jasper Fisher!" She hit him on the arm with her overloaded purse as soon as he was within reach. "What if there had been a small child or elderly person in your path?"

"Mama, really." He pulled his baseball cap off and raked his fingers through his messy blond hair. "Ain't never run over anyone yet." He slipped his arm over her shoulder and gave her a kiss on the cheek. "But don't worry. There's still plenty of time to remedy that. Give me awhile."

Her eyes narrowed to slits. "Good thing your grandmother wasn't here to witness your driving skills or to hear you smart off to your mama like that. She would tan your hide."

"Wait, Queenie's not here yet?" Dewey yanked off his cap and looked around the parking lot. "That's weird."

"Very." Beau shrugged. "It just won't be the same if she doesn't show up. Who's gonna talk about hernias and hemorrhoids and stuff?"

"I volunteer." Dewey raised his hand. "I've become an expert after hearing her stories."

For a minute I thought Mama might smack him with her purse too, but she refrained.

"Are you sure Queenie's coming?" Jasper asked.

"Sure she's coming?" Mama, Pop, and I responded in unison. We'd never had Friday night dinner at Sam's without her—unless you counted that one time when she was hospitalized after having an allergic reaction to her titanium knee implant. And nothing had seemed right that night.

Mama glanced out at the feeder road. "I sure hope that old car of hers is working. I've been telling her for years that she needs a newer vehicle, but you know how she is about spending money."

I knew, all right. My grandmother was ultra-cautious when it came to the financial, unless she happened to be springing for dinner at Sam's. I also had my suspicions she planned to pay for my wedding dress when the day came. If I entered that contest and won, it would potentially save her a bundle. Just one more reason to write that essay.

"I doubt she's running late because of her car," Pop said. "That Cadillac of hers is in tip-top shape. Fred Jenkins up at the mechanic shop keeps it running smoothly."

"She's always been one to get folks to work hard," Mama said. "And Fred Jenkins tops the list."

"Think we could get her to light a fire under Beau here?" Pop slapped my youngest brother on the back, nearly knocking him off his feet.

"I'm hungry," Beau grumbled. "We gonna stand out here all night talking or get inside and eat?"

Minutes later we were seated at our usual table, eating our usual slices of yummy bread and fighting one another for our usual place in the buffet line. I'd just filled my plate with thick slices of barbecue beef and mashed potatoes when Queenie showed up, looking none too happy. She shuffled toward our table, her cane providing just the right balance to get her there.

"Well, thanks for waiting, everyone. Don't I feel special."

She might not feel special, but she certainly looked it. Soft white curls framed her perfectly made-up face, evidence that she'd made it to her usual Friday morning beauty parlor appointment. And the outfit! I thought I'd seen most of her ensembles, but this one surprised me. The blouse and slacks had a colorful springtime look—all flowery and pink. Beautiful, especially against her pale skin. Well, mostly pale. If I looked hard enough, I could see bits of foundation between the teensy-tiny wrinkly folds.

Unfortunately, one thing dampened her overall look—the sour expression on her face. And trust me, if Queenie wasn't happy, well, no one in the Fisher family was happy.

"We waited like pigs at a trough, Mama." Pop forced a smile, clearly trying to make her laugh. When she did not respond in kind, he rose and pulled out her chair.

"I raised you better than that." Queenie lifted her cane and pointed it at him as if to use it as a weapon.

He took it out of her hand and hung it over the back of her chair. "Well, we're happy to see you now, Mama. We're already prayed up, so grab a plate and dive in."

"Hmm." She eased herself down into the seat, which happened to be to the right of mine.

"You look fabulous, Queenie," I said. "Like something straight out of a magazine."

"Thank you, child." She offered a warm smile, the first sign that she might have forgiven us for starting without her. As the edges of her lips turned up, the wrinkles in her soft cheeks disappeared for a moment. Then her expression shifted and the wrinkles became visible once again. Fascinating. Who knew the human skin had that much elasticity?

"So glad you made it." I wiped my hands on my napkin and then reached to pat her arm. "We were getting worried."

"Blame it on the Methodists." She unfolded her napkin and draped it over her lap.

Mama looked perplexed. "The Methodists made you late?"

"Yes." Queenie gestured to the waitress, then turned back to Mama. "The Methodists are having their annual craft fair tomorrow. The whole church is flipped upside down. The

WOP-pers had no place to pray, and there's nothing more annoying to a group of prayer warriors than missing out on an opportunity to pound on heaven's door."

"But that was all taken care of in advance," Mama said. "You ladies were supposed to meet at the Presbyterian church this week. Bessie May told me that—"

"Nope." Queenie put her hand up as if to bring the conversation to a halt. "Decided to stay put at the Methodist church, even under the circumstances. I do not believe the Presbyterian church is an appropriate place to meet for prayer."

She turned her attention to the waitress long enough to ask for a glass of tea, no sugar. Queenie was the only one in the family who didn't take sugar in her tea. Her concerns about type 2 diabetes kept the sugar at bay.

I found myself distracted by what she'd just said. "So, the Presbyterians can join your prayer group, but you can't pray at their church?" I asked.

"Exactly." Queenie nodded and reached for a piece of bread from the basket in the center of the table. "Discussion ended, please and thank you."

"Probably best to change the subject." Pop gave me a "can it!" look, sticking a piece of sliced beef in his mouth.

"I do hope you've saved some of that barbecue for me, son. You know how I love it." Queenie took her fork and stabbed a piece of meat on his plate, then took a bite. "Mmm. That fixes everything."

"Even the brouhaha with the Presbyterians?" I asked.

She gave me a "let it go, Katie" look, but I couldn't get past her earlier comments. I wanted to ask, "What's your beef with the Presbyterians?" so we could get to the bottom of this once and for all. From the look on my father's face, though, I knew this wasn't the time or place to press the issue.

"Wait. I thought it was the Methodists we were mad at." Jasper looked up from his plate, his brow wrinkled.

"We're not *mad* at anyone. I'm just irritated because the Methodists made it difficult to pray." Queenie slapped his hand as he reached across her to grab a slice of bread from the basket in the middle of the table. "Discussion over. Now, let's all just get busy doing what we came here to do."

"Gossip about folks from other denominations?" Dewey asked.

Queenie scowled at him. "We don't gossip. We share our concerns. And if I can't share them with my own family, who can I share them with?"

"She has a point there, you must admit." Pop snagged a piece of bread and tossed it to Dewey, who caught it in midair. Queenie let out an unladylike grunt and shook her head.

The conversation shifted to baseball, and that inevitably led to Mama asking me why Casey hadn't shown up yet. "Where is that boy, anyway?" She glanced toward the door as if expecting my boyfriend to materialize. He usually joined us on Friday nights, as did Dewey's on-again, off-again girlfriend, Mary Anne. These days, Mary Anne was more off than on. I was secretly grateful for that. I'd never thought she was good enough for my brother, to be honest.

"He can't come tonight," I said. "I think he's working or something."

"I sure hope he's able to take some time off when you two . . ." Mama's voice lingered off, and she patted my knee as if she felt sorry for me. "I mean, *if* you two . . ." She shook her head and took a bite of her salad. "Isn't this the yummiest new dressing? I'll have to ask Gretel Ann what she puts in it. Mmm."

And that pretty much ended her conversation about Casey.

Not that I minded. She hadn't hurt my feelings, anyway. Folks were surely wondering why he seemed to be taking his time. But I didn't need to focus on Casey tonight. I had to whip together an essay guaranteed to catch the eye—and heart—of Nadia James, the dress designer from Cosmopolitan Bridal.

What could I say to win her over? Would I tell her about my small-town life? Convince her that the dress had to be perfect for a small-town-girl-goes-uptown-for-her-wedding-day event? Would I share the story of how Casey and I had grown up together and were destined to be man and wife from the time we were children?

Man and wife. Hmm. I caught a glimpse of my parents, who gazed at each other with genuine sweetness. One day that would be Casey and me. We'd sit next to each other at Sam's, elderly parents at our side, gabbing with our children about hernias and hemorrhoids. We'd talk about baseball and reminisce about Queenie's obsession with the Presbyterians.

One day.

In the meantime, I'd better wrap up this meal so I could get home to write an award-winning essay before the clock struck midnight.

3

For the Good Times

Listen to advice, but follow your heart.

Conway Twitty

I made it through the meal without overeating, something that rarely happened at Sam's. My thoughts were elsewhere this evening, firmly fixed on the essay I needed to write when I arrived home. My distraction must've raised a red flag with family members. Several times Mama glanced my way as if to ask, "What's up with you, girl?" I just smiled and opened my bridal magazine, scouring the pictures of dress designs. Oh, the dreaming a girl could do with so many options at her disposal!

About halfway into the dessert round, Jasper tossed a chunk of bread at me. It hit me on the forehead. "You okay over there, Katie?"

I picked up the piece of bread and popped it into my mouth. "Hmm?"

"Readin' that magazine again?" Dewey rolled his eyes.

"Mm-hmm." I didn't look up for long because a shabby chic gown on page 67 had caught my eye. Lovely. I could almost picture myself wearing something similar on my wedding day. Simple. Small-town. Country-ish, even. Add a nice pair of cowgirl boots and the ensemble would be complete. If I opted to go that route, anyway. I'd have to ask Casey's opinion on the whole shabby chic thing. He might not be keen on it.

Jasper stuck a huge chunk of dinner roll in his mouth, then spoke around it. "Want my opinion?"

"What's that?" I closed the magazine and looked at him.

"Run." He nodded. "As fast and as far as you can."

I pressed the magazine into my oversized purse and took a sip of my tea. "Puh-leeze. That's your plan, not mine."

"Yep, it's my plan, all right." He took another bite of bread. "But you would be wise to follow my lead, Katie." His expression grew more serious. "Live your life. Don't fret about getting married right now. Have fun. That's what I'm doing."

"You'll settle down someday, Jasper." Mama wiped her lips with her napkin, which smeared her lipstick all around her mouth. "Hopefully sooner rather than later." She glanced at me. "And don't you be discouraging Katie here. She needs a good man in her life."

Weird, the way she'd phrased that. Casey was a good man.

My grandmother nodded. "Yes, Katie should get married and settle down."

"Settle down?" Seriously? Could I get any more settled?

Queenie pointed at Jasper. "And you, young man, need a swift kick in the backside for driving like a maniac in the parking lot. I heard all about it from Missy Frasier, who pulled in right behind you. You scared the poor girl to death. She got so worked up telling me about it that she had to take a pill."

"But I . . ." Jasper hung his head and went back to eating.

Queenie turned to Beau. "You stay as sweet as you are, honey bun. You hear me? Don't ever break Queenie's heart by falling off the straight and narrow."

"Oh, no ma'am. I won't fall, I promise." Beau dropped some crumbs from his fork as he scooped another piece of cake into his mouth.

"Stick close to the family and you'll do just fine." My grandmother gave him a tender smile as she passed him a napkin. "There's no place like home, after all."

"Why would he want to move away?" Pop glanced up from his food long enough to pose the question. "His mama waits on him hand and foot. Does everything for him."

"Beau's my baby." Mama's face lit into the loveliest smile. "Can't help spoiling the baby."

This garnered a snort from Jasper.

And me. "He's twenty-two, Mama," I argued. "Twenty-*two*."

"Wouldn't matter if he was fifty-two. He'd still be my baby boy." She turned her attention to Beau. "Want Mama to slice up another piece of bread for you, honey?"

He nodded. "Yes, thank you, Mama."

She went to work carving out a large chunk of bread, which led to a loud groan from the others at the table. Beau was too busy staring at the bread to notice.

"Want me to butter this for you too, baby?" she asked him.

"Yep. Thanks. You're the best, Mama."

"Bless you for that, son. A mother needs to feel needed." Mama slathered his bread with butter, then addressed the rest of us. "See? Beau will never leave me. He's gonna stay put right here in Fairfield . . . forever."

"Not sure if that's a blessing or a curse," Pop whispered and then gave me a wink.

"Why would anyone want to leave? Small-town living is good for the soul." Queenie took a sip of her tea and leaned back in her chair, knocking her cane off in the process.

"Don't I know it." Pop rose and fetched my grandmother's cane, then hung it back on its perch. "Give me a small town any day. No rushing through traffic. No running late to catch the subway to work. No fighting the crowds on downtown streets."

"No stress." Mama passed Beau's slice of bread to him. "Well, other than the stoplight going out at Main and Elm, but we don't get a lot of cars through that intersection anyway, and Mayor Luchenbacher promised to fix it soon."

"I want to get the heck out of Dodge," Jasper said. "There's only so much of this good clean air I can stand. I still want to go to Houston and look for work there. It's the best place on the planet to find a job, and the cost of living is better than most anywhere else."

"Houston?" Mama paled as if she was hearing all of this for the first time. Which she wasn't. "Oh, but it's not safe in the city, honey." Her brow wrinkled. "So much crime."

"We have crime here too," Jasper said. "Didn't you hear that Bobby Jo Henderson got arrested for tipping cows in Doc Henderson's field?"

"He wasn't arrested. The sheriff gave him a warning. And that was just in fun."

"Try telling that to the cows." My father jabbed me with his arm, which sent my fork flying out of my hand, across the table, and onto the floor next to Widow Harrison at the next table. I hollered out a quick apology, but before I could remedy the problem myself, the waitress showed up.

"Saw the whole thing," she said. She passed a clean fork

to me and made her way to a nearby table to clear it for the next guests.

"I could never live in the city," Mama said. "You can't leave your doors and windows open."

"Oh, that reminds me." Dewey dove into an animated story about a skunk wandering into Reverend Bradford's house through the doggie door.

"Well, that's not commonplace," Mama argued. "And I'd rather have a skunk in my house any day than a burglar."

"I might rather have the burglar." Pop laughed. "Less mess to clean up afterward."

Mama rolled her eyes and muttered something under her breath.

"Hey, doesn't Aunt Alva still live in Dallas?" Beau licked the butter off of his fingers as he glanced Queenie's way.

You could've heard a pin drop at that question. My grandmother glared at him. "We don't talk about Aunt Alva." Queenie dabbed at her lips, smearing her lipstick in the process.

"Why not?" Beau looked perplexed.

I gave him a "shush" look. I'd never figured out the story about Queenie's older sister, but this clearly wasn't the time to ask.

"So, we can't talk about the Presbyterians and we can't talk about Aunt Alva." Dewey chuckled. "I guess that limits the conversation to Doc Henderson's cows and the criminal element taking over the city of Fairfield."

"Criminal element, pooh." Mama shook her head. "Such an exaggeration."

The expression on Queenie's face showed her relief that we'd switched gears from talking about Alva. "I still say it's safer here," she said. "You couldn't pay me enough to live in the city. We might have a problem with skunks, but those city folks have to worry about snakes."

"Snakes in the city?" I asked.

"Yes." My grandmother's eyes widened. "They're small. They get in tiny spaces. City dwellers have snakes in their homes and don't even know it."

"Only the kind you need to unstop your toilet," Pop said. "I can sell you one of those at the hardware store."

"Speaking of toilets . . ." Mama took a teensy-tiny bite of her lemon pound cake. "When you live in the city, you can't even flush your toilet without the folks downstairs knowing about it. Folks live on top of one another in condos and such."

"Kind of like we do at our house right now?" Dewey asked.

"Oh, that reminds me, I need to put a new handle on that upstairs toilet," Pop said. "It's been acting finicky."

Queenie rolled her eyes. "My point is, people are pressed in like sardines in the city. No space to move around or have privacy."

"Privacy?" Jasper snorted. "We have that here?"

"In theory," Pop said. "In theory."

"Good luck finding a Dairy Queen in the city," Mama added. "I hear they're not building them in metropolitan areas anymore."

This led to a lengthy discussion about ice cream, which caused Pop to say that he needed a piece of coconut pie. He returned moments later with a slice of chocolate pie in his right hand and a slice of coconut in his left. "Couldn't make up my mind," he said. "Oh, and Marie, they just brought out fresh lemon pound cake. You should have another piece."

"Oh, I shouldn't. I really shouldn't." Mama remained in her seat for a moment and then bounded to the dessert table.

"There she goes again," Queenie said. "Marie and her pound cake."

The conversation carried on long after Mama returned to

the table, but my thoughts were elsewhere. I couldn't stop thinking about the contest and the essay I needed to write. What should I say? Should I mention our quaint little town? The church sanctuary where I planned to say my "I dos"? Should I talk about Casey and how we met at the ballpark when I was running for cheerleader of the Little League team?

"You okay over there, Katie?" Queenie asked.

"Oh, yes ma'am. I'm just . . ." *Strategizing. Writing a letter in my head.*

"Thinking about that new window display at the hardware store, I'll bet." Pop winked. "I know how much you love that."

"Oh, I do." Changing out the displays was my very favorite part of working at the store. Well, that and the customers. But my mind was definitely on other things.

By the time I arrived home from Sam's, I'd sketched out the whole letter in my mind. I knew just what to say. I waited until the whole family was tucked away for the night before grabbing my laptop and composing the essay. It didn't take long to lay out my plea for the dream dress. After all, I'd been planning for my big day all of my life. I knew just how I wanted things to go.

The essay—all five hundred words—came together seamlessly. I pushed the Send button at exactly 11:17, just forty-three minutes shy of the midnight deadline. Whew! Talk about cutting it close.

I couldn't help but smile as I reread my essay after sending it in. It sounded pretty good. No, really good. If I didn't know any better, I'd say it was God-inspired.

God-inspired.

Just like my relationship with Casey. I smiled again as I thought about my fiancé. Well, soon-to-be-fiancé. If he knew I'd penned this essay, would it hurry him up? Would he tickle my ears with the question meant to make my heart sing? Would our happily ever after start sooner rather than later?

For the first time all evening it occurred to me that Casey hadn't called. I'd received a text early in the afternoon, but nothing tonight. Nothing whatsoever, not even our usual "Love you, sleep tight" text. I double-checked my phone, just to be sure. Nope. Nothing.

Oh well. He was probably at his house this very minute, scheming up a way to propose. And wouldn't he be thrilled to receive the news that I'd saved a bundle by winning the perfect gown?

If I won.

Oh, but I would. I knew it in my heart of hearts. This was my answer, my solution. I would win the dress, walk the aisle, and live out my forever with my small-town sweetheart. We'd raise our kiddos in Fairfield. Casey would coach Little League alongside Pop. I'd take over the choir at the Baptist church when Mama retired. And we'd all live happily ever after.

I hoped.

4

I've Got a Picture of Us on My Mind

The way I see it, if you want the rainbow, you gotta put up with the rain.

Dolly Parton

I spent the next couple weeks with my stomach in knots. Barely a day went by when I didn't wish I could un-press the Send button. Ugh. Every day I prayed Casey would propose. Every day he didn't. In fact, he seemed to be acting a little odd—evasive, even—whenever I dropped hints about our relationship, which really bugged me. But I couldn't beg the guy to marry me, now could I?

Instead, I went about my business, working at the hardware store, hanging out with Casey and my friends at Dairy Queen, and listening to my brothers ramble on about the goings-on in our little town.

Until Thursday evening, May 14, when I received a call from Queenie.

"Katie, I want you to come by my place in the morning for breakfast." Her words sounded more like an order than an invitation.

"But we're going to dinner tomorrow night at Sam's, Queenie."

"I know, but I need some time with you . . . privately."

Hmm. Seemed suspicious. Still, I knew better than to turn her down. "What time?"

"Seven thirty should be good for me. That way we can visit before you have to go to work. Sound agreeable?"

Sounded more like a business meeting, but I didn't argue.

I tossed and turned all night, unable to sleep. Worries consumed me. Had Lori-Lou told Queenie about the contest? Maybe that was why I'd been summoned into her royal chambers—for a lecture about how I'd overstepped my bounds. What if she told my parents? Then what? I'd look like an idiot.

I already felt like one.

When I did sleep, crazy dreams consumed me. In one of them, I wore a zebra-striped wedding gown, a wacky avant-garde number with huge, puffy sleeves. I walked the aisle toward Casey, who turned and ran in the opposite direction. I'd run too if someone walked toward me looking like a caged animal.

I woke up earlier than usual on Friday morning, determined to put the weird dreams behind me, though I couldn't get Queenie's breakfast invitation off my mind. No doubt she had ulterior motives.

I pulled up to her house at 7:30 on the dot and got out of my car. The front walkway was surrounded by the loveliest flowers, all pinks and yellows. Queenie had quite an eye for color. She had quite an eye for everything.

I didn't have to knock. She stood in the open doorway, arms extended. "Glad you could come, Katie-girl."

That made me feel a little better. I relaxed and did my best to give a genuine smile. "G'morning, Queenie." I slipped into her warm embrace and received several kisses on my cheeks. As her soft skin brushed against mine, I thought it felt a bit like velvet.

She took me by the hand and led me inside her spacious, comfortable home—the same one I'd grown up loving. We passed by the photographs of our various family members—including the second cousins twice removed—to the breakfast table, where a spread of foods awaited. Pancakes. Bacon. Orange juice. Yum. I settled into a chair and she blessed the food, then we dove right in.

I had a feeling this visit wasn't really about the food, at least not completely. We made small talk and nibbled for a while, but I could sense something coming around the bend.

After she finished up her first cup of coffee, Queenie rose—slowly, using her cane—and walked to the coffeepot for a refill. "You want more, honey?" she asked.

I shook my head. "Nah. Better not. I'll take one to go when I get ready to leave for the store."

With a shaky hand she refilled her cup, then turned to face me. "I do hope you can give me a few more minutes before you leave. There's something I want to talk to you about."

Ah. I knew it.

I rose and helped her with her coffee cup. She hobbled back to the table and took her seat, then lifted the hot coffee, her hand still trembling. "Let's talk about that boyfriend of yours, Katie."

"Casey?"

She gave me a knowing look. "Well, yes, Casey. Unless there's some other boyfriend out there I need to know about."

"Nope. No one." I smiled and tried to look confident.

"Honey, I get the sense that you're itching for a proposal. Am I right?"

"Well, I'm not sure *itching* is the right word, Queenie, but yes. Isn't that the idea?"

The long gap in conversation made me a little nervous. Queenie stirred her coffee, which was weird, since it didn't have any sugar or cream in it.

Maybe I'd better build her confidence with another speech. "I'm pretty sure he's going to propose any day now. I think he went to Dallas to order my ring a couple weeks ago, then went back yesterday to pick it up. Maybe it had to be sized or something like that."

"You sound pretty sure of yourself. And of him. Has he given you any clues, other than his disappearing act?" She put the spoon down and stared at me intently. Too intently, really. Made me nervous. I could never keep my emotions hidden from Queenie. She could read me like a book. No doubt she was scanning a few pages now.

"Just a few suspicious comments about plans. And the future. He's always talking about his future. Career stuff. The kind of house he'd like to one day live in. Pretty sure those comments are meant to tease me."

"Could be." She sipped her coffee. "Some men are just a little slow to bat, honey." Her nose wrinkled, and I wondered if maybe her coffee was too hot. "Not sure why he's taking his time, but I suppose that's a good thing. Kind of reminds me of that Loretta Lynn song 'You Wouldn't Know an Angel if You Saw One.' I sometimes wonder if he sees what's right in front of him."

"Yeah, I wonder too." I couldn't help but smile as she mentioned one of my favorite songbirds. "I love Loretta Lynn."

"Me too." Queenie sighed. "Always have, from the time I was young. We have a lot in common."

"Oh?"

"Well, sure. We're both small-town girls. She's from Butcher Holler, I'm from Fairfield."

"What else? Is there something you're not telling me? You own a guitar? Write songs when no one's around?" I took another nibble of my food and leaned back in my chair.

"Hardly." Queenie shrugged. "But we do have one key thing in common. Loretta and her husband Doo married impulsively." As soon as she'd spoken the words, my grandmother clamped a hand over her mouth. "I'm sorry, honey. I didn't mean to say that. Not out loud, anyway."

"Are you insinuating that you and Grandpa married impulsively?" I asked.

She brushed some crumbs off the edge of the table. "I loved your grandpa. He was truly one of the best men I've ever known. But yes, I guess you could say I did marry him impulsively. And things weren't always a bed of roses, if you know what I mean. We had our share of obstacles."

"Like Loretta and Doo."

"Yep." My grandmother took another sip of her coffee, and for a moment I thought I'd lost her to her memories. She put the cup down and smiled. "You remember that story about Loretta? The one where she accidentally put salt in the pie instead of sugar?"

"Of course. The pie was for some sort of contest, right?"

"Yep. She worked so hard to bake the best pie to impress the fellas. Her sweetie bought the pie and took a big bite. Only, it tasted like salt, not sugar."

"I remember." What this had to do with Queenie's comment that she'd married impulsively, I could not say. "What are you getting at, Queenie?"

"If it's meant to be, it'll be, whether you put salt in the pie or sugar. If he loves you—if he really, really loves you—any obstacle can be overcome. That's how it was with Grandpa and me. We got past the salt. And if it's meant to be with you and Casey, you'll get past the salt too, and the rest'll be sugar."

"You think?"

"I really don't know for sure, but I know someone who does." She pointed heavenward. "Only he knows who we're supposed to end up with. But that's part of the adventure—finding out his will, then getting in the stream."

"Hmm." I didn't feel very adventurous at the moment. And for whatever reason, Queenie's story about the pie left the weirdest salty taste in my mouth. "So, do I just come out and ask him if he's going to marry me?"

"No." She picked up her cup and nearly dropped it. "Don't even bring yourself into it. Whenever he gets to talking about his career, the home he'd like to live in, just listen. Let him talk. Ask for details about *his* plans. *His* future. Ask where he sees himself in five years. Or ten years. Or whatever. Might be hard, but leave yourself out of it for now." She took another swig of coffee and adjusted her position in her chair. "He needs to know that you care as much about his plans as your own. You see?"

"Yes, I get it. Sort of a nonthreatening way to bring up the subject of our life together." I grinned in spite of myself. "Makes sense."

"I suppose you could look at it that way." Queenie's furrowed brow didn't bring me much comfort, but I managed to remain positive anyway. "Point is, the conversation might just add a wee bit of sugar to the pie, if you catch my drift. And I have it on good authority that Casey likes pie."

I rose and gave her a kiss on the cheek. "You're always loaded with great advice, Queenie. Thanks so much."

"Mm-hmm." She nodded and attempted to stand. I reached to help her. After a few moments of awkward silence, she glanced my way, her eyes glistening with tears.

My heart skipped a beat as I analyzed the pain in her expression. "Queenie? You okay?"

She reached for my hand and squeezed it so tight that it hurt. "Just promise me something, honey."

"Anything."

"Promise me you'll make the best possible decision for your future happiness. And pray. Ask God's opinion. Don't just jump willy-nilly into something because it feels right in the moment. Really, truly seek the Lord and ask his opinion. If you think that Casey's approach is too calculated, think again. It's better to think things through from start to finish before jumping in."

"Well, of course. Do you think I'd do something without thinking it through? I'm more levelheaded than that." *I think.*

"I want you to pray it through. Look for answers, not just in your heart but in your head. If you ask the Lord's opinion, he'll be happy to give it. Problem is, most of us just move along with our emotions leading the way and live to regret it later."

The sadness in her eyes made me curious. "Queenie, is there something you're not telling me? Do you think Casey and I shouldn't . . . well, get married?"

"I didn't say that, honey. I just want God's best for you. If you ask him, he'll tell you what to do."

Her words lingered in my thoughts long after we parted ways. Did my own grandmother really think I shouldn't marry the man of my dreams? What was up with the hesitations?

I pondered all of these things as I drove to the hardware store. Once I arrived, Pop put me to work, sorting through a new shipment of door hinges. Exciting stuff. I dove right in, my focus still on Queenie's words. Perhaps she had a point. If I focused on Casey, if I cared more about his plans than my own, then perhaps God would open the door for those plans to include a happily-ever-after for me too.

5

Ten Little Reasons

You do sing about what you know about. And I grew up in a small town, and I grew up in a place where your whole world revolved around friends, family, school, and church, and sports.

Kenny Chesney

In the weeks leading up to the June 1st contest announcement, I could barely sleep. Most nights I tossed and turned, designing wedding gowns in my head. Every second or third day I'd go into a panic, wondering what I'd do if I actually won the dress. On the in-between days I convinced myself there was no way I'd win, not with thousands of entries. By the time I received my proposal, which seemed to be taking longer than I'd imagined, the whole contest thing would be behind me, just an elusive dream.

On Monday morning, June 1, I drove to the hardware store and found it teeming with customers. Mrs. Raddison needed a new faucet for her kitchen sink. Reverend Bradford browsed the lawn and garden aisle, looking for a connector for his water hoses. And Brother Mitchell, my favorite Sunday school teacher from early childhood, had finally decided to spend "the big bucks," as he called it, on a new power drill. Pop was busy unloading a new shipment of fertilizer, so I waited on the customers and then headed to the front window to continue my work on the summer window display.

I'd just hung up a banner advertising the sale on fertilizer when my cell phone rang. I pulled it out of my pocket, stared at the unfamiliar number, and answered with, "H-hello?"

"May I speak to Katie Fisher?" a female voice said from the other end of the line.

"Th-this is she."

"Katie, this is Madge Hamilton, assistant to Nadia James, from Cosmopolitan Bridal."

My heart sailed directly into my throat, making it impossible to respond. I finally managed a shaky, "Yes?" Maybe they called every losing entrant as a courtesy. Right?

"I am delighted to inform you that you've won our *Texas Bride* contest." Her voice sounded chipper. Light. "Your essay was chosen from over four hundred entries."

For a minute I thought I might faint. I'd pictured this call a hundred times but hadn't really believed it would take place. In my imagination, sure. But in real life?

"W-what?" I nearly lost my balance.

Pop meandered down the aisle nearby, his eyes wide as he saw me bump into the window. "You okay over there, Katie-girl?"

I nodded, then eased my way down into a seated position. "I'm sorry. What did you say again?"

Pop must've thought I was talking to him. He hollered out, "I said, 'You okay over there, Katie-girl?'"

The woman on the other end of the phone laughed. "I said you've won the contest. But I can tell you're in shock, and I don't blame you. It's a lot to take in, I'm sure."

"That's putting it mildly," I managed.

"Putting *what* mildly?" Pop asked as he took a few steps in my direction. I pointed to the phone.

He shook his head and whispered, "I've told you not to talk on that thing at work, Katie Sue. Very unprofessional."

I turned my gaze out the window to avoid his glare.

"This is quite an honor," Madge said. "Trust me. Hundreds of girls would love to be in your place right now."

She went on to say something about how my essay had touched Nadia James's heart to the deepest level, but I only heard about half of it.

"I . . . I'm sorry," I said when I finally found my voice again. "Did you just say that I"—my voice squeaked—"w-won?"

"You did. What a compelling essay, Katie. Small-town girl with cosmopolitan wedding plans. We all read it and loved it. You have some serious writing skills, by the way. Are you a writer by trade?"

"Oh, no ma'am. I work at a hardware store."

"Oh yes, that's right. I remember reading that now. Well, you have quite a way with words. And the way you described your fiancé, well, it just swept Nadia off her feet. You two must really be in love."

"Yes ma'am." I swallowed hard as I realized she'd called him my fiancé. "Only, Casey isn't actually—"

"We can't wait to hear the details of the proposal. It'll make a terrific addition to the *Texas Bride* article."

Ack. "I, well . . ."

"So, we have a dress to design," she said. "And fittings will need to start soon because Nadia will be leaving for an internship in Paris."

"She won't be in Dallas anymore?"

"Only for the next week or so. Then she'll leave for an exciting year in Paris. Her son Brady is taking over the shop in her absence. He—well, he'll be here to supervise as our seamstresses work on your gown." Why the woman sounded hesitant, I could not say. "Anyway, the point is, this will be a rushed job because Nadia is leaving soon. When can you come to the shop for your first fitting?"

"Oh, I . . ." Hmm. Go to Dallas? Wasn't it more important to talk Casey into marrying me first so that I could show up with a ring on my finger?

"It's important to get going on your dress design before Nadia leaves. And we have to think of the time frame for your big day. What date have you set for the wedding, honey? I don't remember that part from the essay."

That's because I didn't mention a date.

Should I fess up? Tell her that I wasn't exactly engaged— only almost engaged?

"Oh, never mind. I can hear that you've got something going on in the background there. We can talk about your wedding plans later."

I didn't have a chance to get a word in edgewise because she continued to fill my ears with instructions. She buzzed through a list of details that included an interview and photo shoot with *Texas Bride* and several dress fittings.

"I see that you live in Fairfield. Hmm. You're an hour and a half from our shop. I'm not sure that's practical."

I'd do anything to have the dress of my dreams. But how could I manage going back and forth to Dallas for fittings? Pop would flip if I left in the middle of a shift at the hardware store, and Mama would have a conniption if I missed choir practice, but maybe I could work around those things. Bessie May drowned out the rest of us altos, anyway. I'd never be missed.

"We really need to go ahead and set up an appointment for your first fitting," Madge said. "Ideally, we would need to get your measurements as quickly as possible—say, by next Monday?"

"Next Monday?"

"Yes. If you come sooner rather than later, it would give Nadia time to draw the sketches before she leaves. Then we'll need you to come and go while the dress is being made. Is that doable?"

"How long will it take?" I asked.

"At least a month or so. Maybe longer. But we need to get the ball rolling. Let's just say one week from today at noon for the consult, shall we? Does that work for you?"

"Well, I'll do my best—"

"Great. We look forward to getting to know you and making the dress for your big day."

She ended the call in a hurry, but I was grateful for the reprieve. I needed time to think. To plan. To get my heart beating normally again.

For a good ten minutes after the call ended, I stared at the phone in total silence. Maybe I'd just dreamed this whole thing. Surely I hadn't won the contest.

I headed to the stockroom at the back of our store and began pacing, my emotions shifting from disbelief to an undeniable sense of excitement. Surely God had just opened a door for me. This was all a sign that Casey was going to pop the question. Hopefully soon.

My roller coaster of emotions continued as I began to pray

about all of this, thanking God from the bottom of my heart for giving me such an amazing opportunity. Then I lit into one of my favorite worship songs, which must've alerted my father. He stuck his head in the door, eyes wide.

"Someone having a church service in here?"

"Yep. Just having a little praise and worship."

"Next time invite me to join you. Mama says I have the best baritone voice in town." He lit into an off-key rendition of "What a Friend We Have in Jesus," and I giggled as he disappeared back out into the store.

After a while I calmed down a bit. I couldn't share my news with Pop, but I did feel the need to tell someone. Only one person made sense. I picked up my cell phone and pushed the button to call Lori-Lou.

After three rings I half expected it to go to voicemail, but she answered, breathless. "Katie? That you?"

"Yes. I have such exciting news. I—"

"I'm in the bathroom. Hiding. From the kids."

"W-what?"

"It's the only privacy I can get around here. Hold on a minute. One of the girls is beating on the door." Her voice grew shriller as she hollered out, "Mariela, if you bang on that door one more time, so help me, you're going to be grounded from now until you leave for college." The noise level escalated and then she returned. "Okay, what were you saying?"

I could barely remember. The image of her hiding in the bathroom served as a deterrent and affected my ability to think clearly for a moment. "Girl, you're not going to believe the call I just got."

"Ooh, tell me!"

I'd just started to when I heard a loud flush, followed by water running. "Speak up, Katie. It's loud on this end."

Ew.

"I won the dress!" A nervous laugh surfaced, though I tried to press it down.

"I'm sorry, what did you say? The water was running. I thought you said you won the dress."

"I did! I won the dress!"

The squeal from her end of the line nearly deafened me. I had to move the phone away from my ear.

"Oh, Katie, that's the best news ever!" She lit into a lengthy conversation about the style of the gown, asking me a thousand questions along the way. Finally she paused. "So, um, I hate to bring up the obvious, but does this bride have a groom yet?"

"Well, not officially, but I'm 99 percent sure Casey's going to pop the question soon. He's been back and forth, going out of town and then returning. The boy has a ring in his pocket. I know he does. He even asked me some weird questions the other day about the cost of apartments. Isn't that odd?"

"Perfect sign. Well, hurry him along. You know those people at the bridal shop are going to be asking a lot of questions."

"They already are. But just so you know, no one else has a clue about any of this. Not my family. Not anyone. I mean, Queenie knows that I'm hoping for a proposal, but she . . ." I hesitated, unsure of how much to share with Lori-Lou. "She wants me to be 100 percent sure. She doesn't want me to jump into something."

"Jump into it?" Lori-Lou laughed. "How many years have you and Casey been dating again? A dozen?"

"No. I'm only twenty-four. That would mean we started dating at age twelve. We only made it official when we were seventeen."

"Well, that's almost eight years, girl. Besides, you've known him since you were twelve. No one will think you're jumping into anything. Besides, someone needs to make a move. The people at Cosmopolitan Bridal are going to announce it to the world in just a few months, Katie Sue."

"Trust me when I say that no one in my inner circle reads *Texas Bride*, so I think we're safe there. And other than you, I don't have any friends or family in the Dallas area, so no one will hear those radio announcements anyway."

"Wait . . . doesn't Queenie have a sister who lives here?"

Ack. I'd almost forgotten about Alva—the family's black sheep.

"Well, yes. Alva's there. But what are the chances she would find out and say something to Queenie? They don't even speak."

"True, that." A shriek followed. "Mariela! How did you get that door unlocked? Mama needs her privacy!" This escalated into an argument between mother and daughter. I could tell I'd lost my cousin altogether, so I said my goodbyes.

After I ended the call with Lori-Lou, I went back to work on the summer window display and pondered my situation with Casey. He needed to know about the dress. If I showed up at the bridal shop next Monday without an engagement ring, I'd have a tough time answering questions about how my wonderful fiancé had proposed, now wouldn't I?

I had to talk to Casey about our future together as a couple. And I had to somehow get him to pop the question.

6

A Dear John Letter

Of emotions, of love, of breakup, of love and hate and death and dying, mama, apple pie, and the whole thing. It covers a lot of territory, country music does.

Johnny Cash

After a stressful afternoon of trying to balance work with my frazzled emotions, I managed to talk Pop into letting me off early. By four thirty I was in my car, driving through the heart of town to Casey's house. If I knew my guy—and I did—he was just arriving home from work. Changing into his jeans and cowboy boots, no doubt, then heading out to work in the yard for his mama. Such a great son. Such a great guy.

Underneath the brilliant late-afternoon sun, the whole town seemed brighter, happier than ever. Banners hung along Main Street, advertising next month's Fourth of July parade. Folks strolled from building to building, store to store, chatting and hugging like the old friends they were.

What a blissful place to live. What a fantastic place to marry and raise a family. No wonder my parents had opted to stay here all these years. We lived in paradise.

When I turned right at the next corner, I saw Reverend Bradford shopping at the local bookstore. He waved as I drove by and I returned the gesture. He turned his attention to Mr. Finkle, the store owner, who patted him on the back and gestured for him to step inside the store.

As I drove past Tu-Tu-Sweet, our local bakery/ballet studio, I caught a glimpse of a faux wedding cake in the front window, one I'd never seen before. I made a mental note to stop by tomorrow to check it out. I'd have to start shopping for wedding items soon. Well, as soon as I had a date set. To my left, flags flew over the courthouse, the sunshine causing the white stripes to shimmer in the breeze. All in all, a picture-perfect day to broach the happily-ever-after question with my sweetheart.

Mayor Luchenbacher stood in front of the courthouse, gazing up at the American flag. He gave me a frantic wave, and I rolled down the window to holler, "Good afternoon!" I didn't dare slow down for a conversation. He'd have me signing up to coordinate the Fourth of July parade again. Hopefully I'd be too busy planning for my big day to head up the festivities this year.

The radio station blared out a familiar worship song, and I leaned back against the seat as I drove, the words sliding off my tongue. Words of joy. Hope. Faith. They made my heart sing all the way to Casey's homestead.

When I pulled up to the Lawson home, I sighed with pure joy. I'd always loved this expansive property with its traditional picket fence. Gorgeous. I could see myself living in a place like this someday. Our children would run and play in the yard. Our dog—probably a Lab—would romp around with the kids and then take a dip in the pond out back. Someday. Then again, from what Casey had shared, he might be more interested in getting something new. Maybe we'd build a small house on the back acreage. That might be nice. We could have our own space and still be close to the family.

Before getting out of the car, I checked my appearance in the rearview mirror. A quick lipstick touch-up was called for, and then I climbed out of the car, adjusted my twisted blouse, and headed to the front door, where Casey's mother greeted me with tilted head and wrinkled brow.

"Well, Katie Sue. Didn't know you were coming over."

"Neither does Casey." I giggled. "Just wanted to surprise him. Is he here?"

"Yes. He's . . ." Her words drifted off. "Well, let me get him for you, honey. C'mon in." She gestured for me to come inside. "You want a glass of sweet tea? There's a fresh pitcher in the fridge. Help yourself."

"Oh, yes ma'am." I followed her down the front hallway of the house, taking in the country-chic décor. Some might consider it outdated, but I was enamored by the simple, rustic environment. Homey. That was the word. And nothing made a girl feel more at home than homey. The wood paneling in the living room put me in mind of the eighties, but even that brought comfort. Familiarity.

I made myself at home in the kitchen until Casey joined me a couple minutes later. My honey walked into the room looking as handsome as ever. His dark hair was a bit more tousled than usual, and those gorgeous blue eyes flashed with intrigue when he saw me standing in the middle of his kitchen, swigging a giant glass of sweet tea. I couldn't help but wonder about the basketball shorts and faded T-shirt, though. He usually wore jeans and button-ups around the house, even on the most casual day.

I let out a whistle. "Hello, handsome. Love seeing you like this."

"Thanks. Different, right?" The edges of his lips curled up in a smile. "And hello yourself. Didn't know you were coming."

"Exactly." I snuggled into his arms and gave him a kiss on the cheek. "That's what makes it so fun. Thought I'd surprise you by stopping by. That okay?"

"Sure. But you look like you have something on your mind."

"O-oh?"

"Yep. I'd know that look anywhere." He gave me an inquisitive look. "Is your mama trying to get you to talk me into singing that bass solo next Sunday morning? I tried to tell her it's out of my range."

"Nope. She never said a word about it."

Casey looked half relieved, half perplexed. "Ah. So, is it your dad?"

"Oh no. Not that. I—"

"Does he need me to come and move that shelf unit to the back of the store? I've been promising to do that for weeks now but haven't had time."

"Nothing like that." I tried to figure out where to start this delicate conversation. "I, um, just have a lot on my mind today. I just wanted to ask you—"

"Something big going on at the store? Or is Queenie still upset with the Methodists?"

"Presbyterians. But I really came by to—"

"She's mad at the Presbyterians too?" he asked. "Wonder how she feels about the Lutherans. And the Charismatics."

"Pretty sure she's okay with the Lutherans, but I wouldn't place any bets on the Charismatics. Anyway, that's not why I came by, I can assure you."

"Dewey in trouble again? Mary Anne break his heart?"

"Well, yes, but that's not it either." I took a seat at the breakfast table and he sat down in the chair next to me. I gazed at him, wishing I could work up the courage to come out and ask him about his intentions. Still, a girl could hardly pop the "are you ever going to propose?" question.

"You've got something on your mind, Katie." He poured himself a glass of tea, then leaned back in his chair. "Might as well spit it out. No offense, but you've never been very good at hiding your emotions, especially when you're upset."

"Well, I just woke up this morning thinking about . . ." *Marrying you. Duh.* "Thinking about the future."

"The future?" He took a swig from his glass. "Like, years-from-now future or tomorrow future?"

"Both, actually." *And thanks for playing along.* Maybe this would be easier than I'd guessed. "Casey, I just wondered if maybe *you've* given any thought to, well, the future." I mustered a smile and prayed he would take the hint.

An odd expression overtook him and a moment later he nodded. "Katie, I think about the future every day."

"Really?" A hopeful spark ignited within. "Me too. So let's compare notes, okay?"

"O-okay."

"Where do you see yourself in five years?"

"In five years?" He rolled his eyes. "Out of this town, for sure."

"W-what?" In all the years I'd known him, I hadn't heard

him talk about leaving. "You mean, like, the outskirts of town? In a different house? Different property?"

"No. I mean, like, *way* out of town. Another state, even. If a man's gonna have a career—a real career—it's going to be in someplace bigger than Fairfield, Texas."

"But I thought you planned to live here someday. On this land, I mean."

"That's my parents' plan for me. They've said it a thousand times. And I've done my best to play along because I didn't want to hurt their feelings. Heck, I even thought I could talk myself into it. But I'm not really into all of that, Katie. I thought you knew that. Sometimes I think my father loaded me up with ideas that were really his, not mine. I want something bigger than a few acres of land and a garden. You know?"

No, I didn't know. My response was stuck in my throat, however, and refused to dislodge itself.

He rose and paced the kitchen, finally coming to a stop in front of the refrigerator, where he turned back to face me. "Katie, I'm glad you asked me about the future, because there's something I need to talk to you about. I've been praying about this for days. Just didn't know how to come out and say it, but you've given me the perfect segue."

"Oh? Have I now?" I tried not to let the little giggle in my heart escape. Oh, hallelujah! He was going to propose right here, in his kitchen! Perfection! I'd always joked about getting engaged on a random weekday. What a story to tell our kiddos: "Mama got her proposal on a Monday afternoon over a glass of sweet tea at your grandma's kitchen table, the one that was passed down from one generation to another." Lovely!

"Just say it, Casey." I smiled. "Won't hurt a bit, I promise."

He nodded, walked over, and stopped right in front of me, taking my hand. My left hand. With his free hand he reached into his back pocket. My heart skip-skip-skipped, and I wanted to sing a funny little ditty just to celebrate this glorious moment. He pulled out a small box, just the right size for a ring.

Praise the Lord! Thank you, Queenie! Your suggestion worked like a charm. We're talking about the future now, aren't we?

"Katie, you're the sweetest girl I know. So understanding."

"Th-thank you. I feel the same about you." *But this would be better if you dropped to one knee. That would make for a better story.*

My sweetie's smile lit the room, and I stared into his handsome face, a face lit with joy as he spoke. "You asked about my future, and I honestly believe it's going to be great. Better than great, actually."

"Me too!" This time the giggle escaped. "I can see it now."

"I can too." A contented look came over him. "And I like what I see. A lot."

A delicious sigh wriggled its way up inside of me as I whispered, "So do I."

"And because I'm so sure the future's going to be bright, I need to show you something that might come as a bit of a surprise."

Maybe not as much of a surprise as you think. I've been prepping for this for years!

His hands trembled as he opened the box, revealing . . .

Huh?

Instead of a ring, the box held a strange-looking pin. Weird. Casey pulled it out and held it up in front of me. "Can you read the inscription on this?" he asked.

I squinted to get a better look. "Chesterfield Oil and Gas?"

Weirdest. Proposal. Ever.

"Yes." He nodded and gazed at the little pin in his palm. "Chesterfield Oil and Gas. In Tulsa."

"O-okay."

He paced the kitchen and finally came to a stop in front of me once again. "Katie, I don't know any way to tell you this other than just coming out and saying it. I've been offered a job in Tulsa at Chesterfield Oil and Gas. They want me to start next month. I've been trying to figure out a way to tell you for ages now, but there just didn't seem to be the right opportunity . . . until now."

"W-what?" My heart felt like a stone. "What are you saying? You're . . . you're leaving?" How had we jumped from proposal to rejection in less than a minute? Surely I'd misunderstood.

"It doesn't have to be forever," he said. "But a great company with potential for financial advancement? I can't get that here in Fairfield. You have to admit it. This is a dead-end town."

"A dead-end town?" My heart felt as if it had been personally attacked. How could he say that about the place I loved so much? "I've never heard you say anything like that before. *I'm* here. In Fairfield, I mean."

"I know. And I'm not asking you for a long-distance relationship here, Katie. I've given this a lot of thought, and I know that's not what's best for the two of us."

Ooh, got it! He planned to propose but wanted to give me a heads-up first that we would be living elsewhere. Likely wanting to gauge my reaction. Well, I'd offer a brave smile and face the "do we really have to move away?" question later. Surely he would change his mind. Maybe the Texas heat was getting to him. He would come to his senses soon.

"So, you don't want a long-distance relationship?" I asked.

"No." He opened his hand and looked at the Chesterfield Oil and Gas pin. "I know it wouldn't work for either of us." He rolled the pin around in his hand, then looked my way, his nose wrinkled. "To be honest, Katie, I . . ." His voice lowered to a hoarse whisper. "I . . ."

"You . . . ?" *What?*

Any bit of lingering hope withered as I saw the somber expression in his eyes.

"I just feel like I need to focus on my work right now. My future with the new company is hanging in the balance. I need to play it safe. Be fully on board. That way they won't question my loyalty. You understand, right? You are, as I said, the sweetest, most understanding girl in Fairfield."

"Wait." In that moment, I had the strangest out-of-body experience, the one where you feel like you're dreaming. The one where you hope—no, pray—you're dreaming. "Are you breaking up with me?"

His expression contorted and his eyes filled with remorse. "We don't really have to say it like that. I know this is hard to hear, but I think we should step back for a few months. Maybe reassess at Thanksgiving when I come home for a visit."

"Thanksgiving? That's months from now."

"Yeah. Mama said she'd kill me if I didn't come home for the holidays."

"So your parents know? They've known you're moving away?"

He nodded.

"Great. Everyone knows but me." Only, I knew now, didn't I? And now . . . well, it pretty much changed everything.

I couldn't say what happened next because I found myself in a somewhat catatonic state. I vaguely remember knocking over the glass of sweet tea and leaving it to run down the edge of the table. I sort of remember stubbing my toe on the leg of the kitchen table as I fled from the room. And I'm pretty sure I remember nearly tripping down the steps as I bolted from the front porch.

Still, when I reached the car, as I stared back at the large ranch-style home, I had to believe the whole thing had been a terrible dream. I'd wake up soon, and Casey and I would laugh at how real it had all seemed.

Or not.

I couldn't stop the tears as they flowed down my cheeks. I didn't want to. My entire world had just come crumbling down around me. Every fantasy, every plan . . . vanished.

Thank you very much, Chesterfield Oil and Gas.

A humming noise from inside my purse got my attention. I glanced down at my phone as it buzzed and realized I'd missed another call from Cosmopolitan Bridal. I listened to the message, recognizing Madge's voice right away.

"Something I forgot to mention," she said, her voice sailing along in the same chipper fashion as before. "We'll be counting on you to be available not just for fittings but for press engagements, radio interviews, and that sort of thing. Hope this isn't too much of a distraction from your wedding plans."

Wedding plans?

What wedding plans?

As I pushed the button on my phone to end the message, I leaned back against the seat and dissolved into a haze of tears.

I had the gown. I had the church. I had the guests. The only thing missing from this wedding . . . was the groom.

7

Somewhere Between

I would rather wake up in the middle of nowhere than in any city on earth.

Steve McQueen

Just two days after I learned that I'd won the dress of my dreams, my would-be fiancé packed his bags and headed north to Oklahoma to look for an apartment. He might not be leaving for good just yet, but it sure felt like it. Looked like he was eager to get his new big-city life started.

I received the news through the grapevine—i.e., the WOP-pers—who made it their mission to pray the dear boy back home again. No doubt they would do it too, though frankly, I didn't care if I ever saw him again.

Okay, I did care. A lot. But how could I live with what he'd done to me? Talk about humiliating.

I went back and forth in my thinking—from wanting him to come home to wishing I'd never see him again. Mama seemed the most perturbed of all. On Thursday morning as we wrapped up breakfast, she stormed around the kitchen, her temper evident to all.

"I'm just so shocked." She shoved some dirty cups into the sink. "Did anyone see this coming?"

Dewey and Beau shook their heads, but Jasper gave her a knowing look. "No, but it's inevitable, Mama."

"Inevitable?" I put my hands on my hips and glared at my brother. "Explain what you mean by that."

"Not inevitable that he would leave you," Jasper said. "It's just inevitable that folks would want out of this town. I've tried to say it for years, but no one listens to me. Maybe now they will."

"But why?" Mama looked flabbergasted. "I just don't get it. I had no clue he wanted to leave."

"Me either." Dewey shoveled cereal into his mouth. "Weird."

"It's not weird that he wants to earn a decent living," Jasper countered. "There's no money in Fairfield, you know. No real money, anyway."

"Sure there is." My father reached for his wallet and opened it, revealing a couple of twenties and a five-dollar bill. "You just have to work hard to earn it, like any other respectable town. Money doesn't grow on trees, you know."

"Unless you happen to work for an oil and gas firm in Oklahoma," Jasper said. "In which case it grows on trees, under oil rigs, and in the air around you." He leaned my way and muttered, "Which is precisely why I've got to get out of this town and find a real job."

I pondered my brother's "get out of this town" comment all day. Maybe, all things considered, that was my answer. I needed to, as Jasper would say, get the heck out of Dodge. If I left Fairfield for a week or two, I could put this whole ugly breakup with Casey out of my mind. And maybe, if those WOP-pers were worth their weight in salt, Casey would be here waiting on me when I returned. I hoped.

As if operating under heavenly orders, Lori-Lou called me that very moment. I hated to share the news with her but had no choice. I couldn't muster up any enthusiasm, answering with a somber "Hey."

"Hey yourself." Lori-Lou sounded like her usual chipper self. "You doing okay, Katie?" Before I could answer, she plowed ahead, her voice more animated. "Your mama called Queenie, who told all of the WOP-pers, so naturally my mama found out. She called me this morning and said that Casey, well . . ."

"Yeah." I sighed. "It's true. I should've told you but didn't know how."

"Oh, Katie. My heart is broken for you." She turned to fuss at one of the kids, then returned. "I want you to come here. Stay with me. It'll do you a world of good."

"Ironic. I was thinking the same thing. Getting away from Fairfield for a while might be just the thing to get me over this hurdle."

"Yes, I really think it'll be relaxing and—Mariela! How many times have I told you not to run around the house naked? Put your clothes back on this very moment!"

Hmm. Maybe staying with Lori-Lou wouldn't be very relaxing after all. But it would provide a break from my current plight.

"Please come," she implored. "Stay at my place. We're getting the AC fixed this afternoon, so wait until the morning to come, but plan to stay with me a couple of weeks. It'll do you good to get away from Fairfield, and maybe we can figure out what to do about the dress while you're here."

"The dress. Ugh. I'm supposed to be at Cosmopolitan Bridal on Monday for my first fitting. They called about two minutes after I got my heart broken."

Lori-Lou groaned. "Well, I know it's probably the last thing you want to deal with, but what are you going to do about the dress? Have you given it any thought?"

I had, of course. In fact, I'd thought about that contest dozens of times over the past three days. Shame washed over me every time. No way could I go to the bridal shop now, not with my would-be fiancé leaving me in the lurch. What would I say? How could I face them?

Lori-Lou interrupted my ponderings. "Remember that scene in *Coal Miner's Daughter* where Doo got jealous because Loretta was more successful than he was?"

I sighed. "Lori-Lou, you've been spending entirely too much time with Queenie. She's rubbing off on you. And I don't know what this has to do with me coming to Dallas."

"Oh, everything! I've been thinking . . . maybe that's what's happened with Casey."

"Wait . . . what? Are you saying that Casey is jealous of me? I'm not successful by any stretch of the imagination."

"But don't you see? You're everyone's little darling. You've won every award that Fairfield has to offer, right down to Peach Queen. You're golden."

"Golden?"

"Everything you touch turns to gold."

"Puh-leeze. I work at a hardware store."

"And everyone adores you. Don't you see? You're a big fish in a small pond. Casey looks at how loved you are, how you've won over so many people just by being you, and he feels like he can't compete with that."

"So I should stop being lovable?"

"Of course not. That's not my point."

I didn't have time to ask her what her point was because the kids interrupted once again and she had to end the call. Still, I couldn't stop fretting over her words all afternoon. Was Casey really jealous of me? If so, why? I'd certainly never done anything—deliberately, anyway—to provoke that.

Casey.

My heart grew heavy as I thought about him. With Casey in Oklahoma, I didn't know how I could keep up appearances in Fairfield. Folks were already questioning . . . everything. Clearly everyone in Fairfield had heard about his leaving. If I ever doubted that, my questions were answered when I worked the cash register at the store that afternoon.

Mrs. Jamison patted my hand as she paid for her toilet handle. She leaned in to whisper, "Sweet girl. Don't give up. I'm sure there's a fella out there for you someplace." Then she patted my hand again. Lovely.

Mr. Anderson was loaded with sage advice as he paid for his door hinges. "I say give the guy time to figure out who he's gonna be when he grows up. It's just a phase. Went through something myself before I married Mrs. Anderson. He'll come back . . . eventually."

Mrs. Keller had the best advice of all. "Don't focus on what you've lost," she said as she hefted a huge bag of fertilizer onto the counter so I could scan in the price. "Focus on what you didn't know you had."

"What I didn't know I had?" I scanned the fertilizer and then lifted it to my shoulder to carry it out for her.

"Sure. You've heard the old saying, 'If God closes a door,

somewhere he opens a window'? There's a whole future out there for you that you haven't even discovered yet. Don't worry about what hasn't happened. Set your sights on what's gonna happen. It's an adventure, you know." She gave me a little wink and then held out her arms. "Now, give me that bag. Do I look like a lightweight to you?"

She didn't, actually. I just couldn't think clearly because of what she'd said.

An adventure? In Fairfield? With 99 percent of the population reminding me every few minutes of my heartbreak? Who had time—or energy—for that type of excitement?

By the time I'd ended my shift at the store, I knew what I had to do. A phone call to Cosmopolitan Bridal was in order, right this very minute. I made my way to the restroom so that I could have some privacy, then called Madge's number. Her voicemail kicked in after the fourth ring. When I heard her businesslike voice, it stopped me in my tracks. I couldn't leave a message. No, news like this had to be delivered in person.

I'd drive to Lori-Lou's tomorrow, get settled in, then head to the bridal shop first thing Saturday morning. I'd cancel all plans for the dress. It was the least I could do, all things considered. If I let them know quickly, then some other lucky bride could walk the aisle wearing her Nadia James couture gown. My heart ached at the idea of losing the dress, but doing the right thing was definitely more important. I'd come clean. Tell them everything. Afterward I'd settle in at Lori-Lou's place for a few weeks so that God could mend my broken heart.

When I arrived home from work that afternoon, I gathered the courage to tell Mama—not about the gown, but about visiting Lori-Lou. I found her in the kitchen making our usual Thursday night dinner, meatloaf. I explained my plan of action, doing my best to hold back the tears as I thought about leaving.

"Wait, you're going where?" Mama looked up from mixing the meatloaf, her brow furrowed.

"To Dallas to visit Lori-Lou."

"But Pop needs you at the store. You can't leave, honey."

The moment I heard those words, my heart twisted inside of me. As much as I loved being part of a tight-knit community, the words "you can't leave" made me want to. Leave. Soon.

"Mama, I work harder than anyone I know, and I never take a vacation. Well, unless you count those four days I worked at church camp as a counselor, but that was hardly a vacation, especially when you consider the fact that I spent a full day in the ER with one of the campers who broke her ankle. I'm due a little time off, and under the circumstances . . ." My words drifted off as I pondered my recent breakup with Casey.

"Say no more." Mama's eyes misted over. "You need to get away to deal with your heartbreak."

Something like that. I also needed to rehearse my "I can't go through with this" speech for the fine folks at Cosmopolitan Bridal. But I couldn't tell Mama any of that. In some ways, that relieved me a little. If I didn't go through with the wedding gown thing, my parents would never have to know I'd entered that stupid contest in the first place. That fact brought me some degree of comfort.

"Well, I have a perfectly lovely idea," Mama said after a moment of quiet reflection. "While you're in Dallas, why don't you go on over to Dallas Baptist University and see Levi Nash? He'll be tickled pink to see a familiar face."

"Mama, surely you're not suggesting anything by that."

"Well, heavens, no. He's a good boy, though, that Levi. And his faith is stronger than ever, thanks to the prayers of the WOP-pers."

"What does that have to do with me?"

"Oh, nothing. Only, he's a great catch. That's all."

"Mama!"

"Just saying, just saying! There are other fish in the sea besides Casey." She gave me a look and then walked into the other room, muttering something about how she'd learned that lesson personally. Weird. Had my very own mother just suggested that I date someone else right after having my heart broken? Crazy.

Pop didn't take the news about my leaving as well as Mama. When I told him that I planned to go to Lori-Lou's for a few weeks, he went into a panic. Well, not exactly a panic, but his version of it. Mama told him about halfway into our family's usual Thursday night dessert—chocolate pudding. I held my breath. My brothers all stopped eating—my first sign they were taking this seriously—and stared at Pop.

"That's impossible." My father pushed his pudding dish away and gave me a pensive look. Clearly he didn't believe Mama's words.

"She needs to get away for a while, Herb," Mama argued. "Katie is twenty-four years old. If she wants to go to Dallas for a couple of weeks to stay with family, we can't stop her. Besides, it'll do her a world of good."

"Weeks?" He groaned. "I can't believe you're saying this, Marie. Wasn't it just a month ago you sat at Sam's Buffet, listing all of the reasons why folks are better off in a small town? Now you want our daughter to go to the city—where they have snakes in the kitchens and neighbors living on top of one another? Where folks share their plumbing with total strangers? That's okay with you now?"

"Oh, Herb, get over it." Mama rolled her eyes. "It's just a couple of weeks. What are the chances Katie would have to deal with snakes in that length of time? Besides, she's already dealt with one far worse than the reptilian variety."

Pop looked genuinely confused. I felt a little confused myself.

"That Casey Lawson is a snake of the worst kind." Mama's jaw clenched. "Getting my girl's hopes up and then dashing them with his impulsive move to Oklahoma." She mumbled something under her breath that I couldn't quite make out.

"Now, Marie, we've known Casey since he was a boy," Pop countered. "He's a good kid, and his parents are pillars in the community."

"Even if they are Presbyterians." Jasper slapped the table and laughed.

I couldn't help the little sigh that erupted. As mad and disappointed as I was with him, I knew Casey was a good kid. Er, man. He would make things right eventually. I knew he would.

Just like I would make things right with the folks at Cosmopolitan Bridal.

"I can fill in at the store for Katie while she's gone." Mama's words interrupted my train of thought. "It'll be fine."

In that moment, I truly believed it would be. That same feeling lingered as I packed my bags later that evening. It stuck with me as I drove to Dallas the following morning. My feelings of hope didn't dissipate until I entered the messy three-bedroom condo that Lori-Lou and her husband shared with their children. At that point, with rambunctious kiddos swarming me, their shrill voices echoing off the Sheetrock in the small space, I wondered if perhaps I'd made a mistake.

"Aunt Katie, Aunt Katie!" Four-year-old Mariela jumped up and down, then wrapped her arms around my right thigh.

The youngest, Joshie, wrapped himself around my left ankle and tried to ride it like a pony. This left little room for Gilly, the two-and-a-half-year-old, but that didn't stop her. She attempted to propel herself into my arms, nearly knocking me over in the process.

"Well, hello, strangers." I laughed and then knelt down to give them all hugs. "I'm going to be your roomie for the next couple of weeks."

"What's a roomie?" Gilly asked.

"It means she's going to stay with us." Mariela put chubby hands on her hips and spoke to her younger sister in a know-it-all voice. "Maybe forever!"

"Yes, I'm staying with you," I said. "But not forever." When Mariela pouted I added, "But Aunt Katie is going to have a lot of fun with her babies. Pinkie promise!" I held out my pinkie and she grabbed it with hers.

"I hope so." Lori-Lou chuckled. "Let me start by apologizing. I'm so sorry you have to share a room with the baby." My cousin's nose wrinkled. "But he's the quietest of the three, if that makes you feel any better. And I'm pretty sure these two girls would drive you crazy if you bunked with them."

"I'll do just fine," I said. My words were meant to convince myself as well as Lori-Lou. "And I'm sure the blow-up mattress will be comfortable." *I hope.*

I couldn't help but smile at the kids. Mariela looked adorable with her cute little pigtails and freckled nose. She had that impish look that rotten children often have, the one that says, "I'm secretly up to no good." Still, no one could deny her outward beauty. Gilly, on the other hand, made me laugh just looking at her. For one thing, her shirt was inside out. And her socks didn't match.

"Please ignore the way she looks." Lori-Lou gestured to Gilly. "She didn't start out the day looking like this. She's changed clothes four times already."

"She looks cute," I countered.

"Hmm." Lori-Lou pointed at her daughter's feet. "See those socks she has on?"

I glanced down and nodded.

"One of them is mine," Lori-Lou said. "The other one is the baby's. And you don't even want to know whose underwear she's wearing. Worst part is, she's not potty trained, so she won't be wearing the underwear for long. They'll be sopping wet in a matter of minutes. I've never seen a kid go through as many panties as this one."

Okay then. Welcome to the big city, Katie Sue. This is what you've been missing.

Still, baby Joshie was adorable. I swept the little one into my arms and held him close . . . until I realized he had on a stinky diaper. Then I passed him right back to his mother.

Lori-Lou bounced him on her hip as if he didn't smell at all. "Josh has a couple of vacation days coming. He says he'll watch the kids so we can have some girl time." My cousin's eyes flooded. "I love that man. He's so great."

Terrific. True love. Nothing like a little salt in an open wound.

Lori-Lou must've realized she'd struck a nerve. "I'm sorry, Katie. But if it makes you feel any better, we spend about half the time arguing about, well, everything. The man drives me out of my ever-lovin' mind, but I love him. I really do."

Well, wonderful. While I wasn't pining away for Casey, I'd enjoy listening to my cousin and her husband argue. And then watch them kiss and make up. Perfect way to get over a breakup.

She shifted the baby to her other hip, and the stench from his diaper permeated the room. "Anyway, I hate to bring up a sore subject, but what did you decide to do about the wedding gown?"

Was she kidding? What else could I do? "I can't go through with it. Not now."

"You're going to tell them?"

I sighed and nodded. "Don't have any choice. I was hoping you'd go with me tomorrow. What do you think?"

"Tomorrow?" She hesitated. "I think I'd better make sure Josh can watch the kids. Otherwise we'll have a fiasco on our hands if we have to take these three into the swankiest bridal shop in town."

"In the state," I corrected her.

"In the country." She laughed. "Which is precisely why I can never, under any circumstances, take any of these three— Mariela! Don't you dare use those markers on my new coffee table! We've talked about this a hundred times." She raced across the room and grabbed the markers from the four-year-old, who burst into tears. About three minutes into the emotional tirade, Lori-Lou glanced my way. "Sorry!" she hollered above the din. "Welcome to my world, Katie."

Some welcome. And some world. But this would be my home for the next two weeks, and I'd better learn to love it. At least here no one would break my heart.

8

Who Was That Stranger

A city is not gauged by its length and width, but by the broadness of its vision and the height of its dreams.

Herb Caen

Spending the night on an air mattress turned out to be quite the adventure. Add to the discomfort a crying child just three feet away, and it made for a sleepless night. Mostly sleepless, anyway. I did doze off a couple of times. One of those times I dreamed about Casey. Sad, sobering dreams. Bittersweet. I also thought about the fact that I'd missed the family's Friday night gathering at Sam's Buffet. Bummer. As much as I needed to be away from things, I still felt homesick, especially when I thought about the coconut meringue pie.

I awoke on Saturday morning with that horrible feeling you always get just before doing something you don't want to do. The sound of the children's voices rang out from the kitchen, but they paled in comparison to the argument going on between Josh and Lori-Lou over the AC repair bill. I didn't mean to eavesdrop on their conversation, but in such a confined space I didn't have any choice. Lovely.

A few feet away from my air mattress, baby Joshie slept in his crib. I would've let him continue to doze, but the smell leaking from his diaper was enough to prompt me to wake him. Ick.

After I rose and slipped on my robe, I picked up the baby from his crib and made my way out to the kitchen, holding him at arm's length.

"Well, good morning, sunshine." Lori-Lou laughed when she saw me.

Mariela lunged at my legs, almost knocking me over in the process. Lori-Lou reached for the baby and said something about taking him for a quick bath before breakfast. The two of them disappeared from the room before I could say, "Hey, who's watching the other two?"

I spent the next fifteen minutes debating the finer points of cereal eating with Mariela and trying to figure out some strategic way to get a Cheerio out of Gilly's left nostril. I'd never seen anyone stick cereal up their nose before, so this caught me totally off guard.

My cousin's husband came into the kitchen a few minutes later, matter-of-factly tugged the Cheerio out of Gilly's nose, yawned, and poured himself a cup of coffee.

"Welcome to reality, Katie."

His version of it, maybe, but definitely not mine.

"One day"—Josh gestured around the messy kitchen—"this could all be yours."

"Once she finds the right man, anyway." Lori-Lou's voice sounded from the hallway. She stepped into the kitchen with the baby, wrapped in a towel, in her arms.

"So, let me get this straight." Josh leaned against the counter and took a swig of his coffee. "You two are spending the morning at a bridal shop where Katie has won a multi-thousand-dollar dress that she's not going to be wearing?"

"Something like that," I said. And then sighed. "I'm not keeping the dress."

"She's keeping the dress." Lori-Lou gave me a "we're going to talk about this" look.

"No. I'm not." I shook my head and sipped some of my now-cold coffee. "This is a moral decision. What would Jesus do?"

"Jesus wouldn't need a wedding dress, but I suppose that's irrelevant." Josh seemed to drift off in his thoughts for a moment, then added, "He wouldn't keep the dress. No way."

"But she'll never have another opportunity to have a dress from Cosmopolitan," Lori-Lou argued. "And she won the contest fair and square. Nadia James loved her essay. That was the determining factor, not the wedding date."

"Or the need for a groom?" Josh's right eyebrow elevated.

"There will be a groom." Lori-Lou glared at her husband. "Someday."

I groaned at that comment. Right now I didn't care if I ever found a groom. Weddings were highly overrated, after all.

"Might even be Casey. He'll come to his senses." My cousin passed the baby off to her husband and then poured herself a cup of coffee. "Wait and see."

"Could we end this conversation right here?" I stepped toward the door leading into the hallway. "I'm not taking the dress. Conversation over. I don't care how much it's worth—it's not worth it to me to do anything deceptive."

"Amen. Preach it, girl." Josh shifted the baby to one arm so he could continue drinking his coffee. "I'll be here taking care of the kids while you two swank it up at the froufrou wedding place."

"Swank it up? Froufrou?" Lori-Lou smacked herself in the head. "You've been watching those wedding dress shows, haven't you, babe?"

"Maybe." He crossed his arms at his chest. "What's it to you?" This was followed by a belly laugh. "Anyway, do the right thing, Katie. Don't take the dress."

Lori-Lou grumbled about this as we headed down the hallway to our respective rooms to get dressed. She continued to fuss several minutes later when we got into my car.

"I get Josh's point," she said. "But I totally disagree."

"Lori-Lou, I don't have any choice."

"Sure you do." She pointed to the stop sign ahead. "Turn right up here. Then left at the next light. We're about ten miles away from the store."

"Remember that scene in *Coal Miner's Daughter* where Doo takes Loretta out to a big piece of property and shows her the house he plans to build for her?" I made the right-hand turn and kept my eyes on the road.

"Of course. Turn left up here." Lori-Lou gestured and I eased my way over to the left lane.

"In that scene Loretta and Doo have been married awhile and she's had some measure of success, and he takes her up to this piece of property where he's already laid out a plan for a house."

"I remember, Katie."

"Point is, he doesn't consult with her, just goes off on his own and makes the plans without involving her."

"Right. She got mad."

"Very. I mean, she was thrilled that he wanted to build a house, but mad that he set out on his own to do it without her input."

"I can't imagine Josh going out and doing something like that without asking me." Lori-Lou grunted. "For one thing, our bank account isn't quite big enough for a down payment. We've been saving, but it's so hard with kids."

She carried on about their poor financial state, but I didn't hear half of it.

Lori-Lou let out a squeal and pointed to my right. "Oh, slow down. I think we're coming up on Frazier."

I slowed down and she gestured for me to get into the right lane. "I didn't mean to get you all worked up about that," I said. "I guess my point was, sometimes we get ahead of ourselves. And that's what I did with Casey."

"You wanted to build a house but forgot to ask Casey if he wanted to live there?" she asked.

"Something like that. Not a literal house, but—"

"Stop! It's right up here. See the sign?"

In the distance I saw the beautifully scripted sign reading COSMOPOLITAN BRIDAL. My heart quickened and then felt like it had turned to lead. I could avoid the inevitable no longer. What I wanted—what I needed—was to get this visit to Cosmopolitan Bridal over with.

We pulled up to the store's parking lot, and Lori-Lou's cell phone rang. She spent the next ten minutes bickering with Josh about how to discipline Mariela for coloring on her younger sister's arm with a marker. I spent those ten minutes praying for the courage to tell Nadia James that I could not—would not—allow her to make me a wedding dress.

Lori-Lou ended the call and glanced at me with an exaggerated sigh. "He's so totally hopeless."

"What do you mean?"

"He's clueless when it comes to dealing with the kids."

"He's on a learning curve, Lori-Lou."

She snorted. "Hey, he's had those three kids the same length of time I have, and I've figured it out."

I didn't want to argue with her, but she clearly didn't have it all figured out. Did any parent ever?

"Okay, you ready to go inside?" she asked. "This is about as close to heaven as we're gonna get in this lifetime."

"I . . . I guess." Right now, it felt a little more like purgatory. If I could just get past this "tell them what happened" part, my stomach could stop churning.

We got out of the car and crossed the parking lot to the gorgeous double doors. Lori-Lou pulled open the one on the right, and we stepped inside Cosmopolitan Bridal for the first time. The place was teeming with customers, many of whom wore expensive clothes and carried designer purses.

I stared up, up, up at the chandeliers hanging from the high ceilings above. Wow. Candelabras graced the walls to our left, and the tapestries on the windows were crafted from the most gorgeous fabrics I'd ever seen.

"Whoa," Lori-Lou said. "Check out this place, will you?"

"Welcome to Cosmopolitan Bridal," an older woman behind the counter called out to us. "I'll be with you shortly." She turned her attention back to an existing customer and I turned back to examine the room. Man, what a place!

I couldn't help but notice the intoxicating scent of some sort of air freshener wafting around us. It certainly wasn't the Lysol spray Mama used to mask the odor of the kitty litter box in our upstairs bathroom.

Lori-Lou let out a soft whistle. "We're not in Kansas anymore, Toto."

"You can say that twice and mean it."

"We're not in Kansas anymore." She giggled. "Check out that display. Do you think those are real diamonds on those branches?"

"Surely not." They looked like diamonds, though. Everything in the place looked expensive. Right away I felt overwhelmed, and not just because of the mission set before me. I'd always been intimidated by folks with lots of money, although I'd never really voiced that thought aloud. The kind of people who came into this shop had money. Lots and lots of money. I had no money. Well, not much, anyway.

"Chin up," Lori-Lou whispered. "You have every right to be here."

I glanced at her, wondering how she'd known my feelings.

"You're an open book, Katie." She nudged me with her arm. "Always have been. Just enjoy being here, okay? Who knows when we'll ever see a place like this again."

"True."

I took a few steps toward a row of white gowns, my head high, my shoulders back, with the most confident expression I could muster.

Distracted by a mannequin to my right, I paused. The wedding dress on it made me forget all about being intimidated. The gown drew me in and made my knees all rubbery, in a good way. Well, until I saw the price tag. "This dress is $6,700," I whispered to Lori-Lou.

"Wow." Her eyes grew large as she reached over to look at the tag for herself. "That's more than we paid for the used van we're driving. If I bought that dress I'd never come up with the money for a down payment for a house."

"No kidding." I made my way from aisle to aisle in the shop, completely mesmerized. I'd never seen so much white in all of my life. White taffeta, white silk, white tulle. Oceans and oceans of white. The mannequins, taller and slimmer than most I'd seen in department stores, were adorned in the gowns Nadia James had become famous for. Each was patterned after a female great from days gone by. I stopped to look at the Audrey Hepburn, then shifted my attention to the Grace Kelly. Wow. I couldn't believe the detail in both.

On and on I went, looking at the various gowns. The Doris Day caught my eye, as did the Ann-Margret. The one that puzzled me most was the Petula Clark. I'd never heard of her. Neither had Lori-Lou, apparently. She stared at the dress and shrugged.

Off in the distance a gorgeous blonde—probably a couple years older than me—walked to the cash register to talk to the older woman. I stared at the tall, stately woman with her fashionable hairdo, expensive clothes, and over-the-top heels.

"Look, Katie." Lori-Lou jabbed me with her elbow. "A real live Barbie doll." She giggled and leaned over to whisper, "I wonder if there's a Ken doll around here someplace."

Yep. There was a Ken, all right. He appeared from behind the row of gowns to our left. A handsome specimen of a man—tall with dark hair and just enough of a five o'clock shadow to make him gorgeous. I stared into the most beautiful eyes—after I got past the solidly built Adonis-like physique. The guy had to be at least six feet three. Okay, six four. Except for a slight limp, he moved with confidence and a bit too much speed for his delicate surroundings. The phrase "bull in a china shop" came to mind at once.

As he rounded the corner, a swatch of wavy dark hair fell casually on his forehead. He brushed it back with his hand. Something in his handsome face felt familiar, like I'd seen him before. Then again, he had that familiar Greek god look—firm features, confident set of his shoulders, perfectly placed smile.

And it didn't hurt anything that the guy's skin was bronzed, as if he'd spent the last few days on the Riviera, not holed up in a bridal shop. But judging from the fact that he ended up behind the counter talking to the older woman, he worked here. Fascinating. I couldn't take my eyes off of him. Didn't want to.

He glanced at me, his beautiful blue eyes sparkling as he gave me a nod and said, "Welcome to Cosmopolitan Bridal."

Lori-Lou stopped cold and grabbed my arm, moving us back a few feet. "Y-you know who that is, right?" Her words came out as a hoarse whisper.

"He looks vaguely familiar." I gave the guy another look. Yep. Familiar. But why? "Do you know him or something?"

"Know him?" Lori-Lou clamped a hand over her mouth and then pulled it back down. "Katie, don't you ever get out? That's Brady James, point guard for the Dallas Mavericks."

"Ah. Basketball." That explained it. "I remember now. He's one of Casey's favorite players. I think I've watched him play a time or two."

"*Was* one of Casey's favorite players. He blew out his knee four months ago. Happened on live TV, right in the middle of a playoff game. I feel really bad for the guy." Lori-Lou shrugged. "Wonder what he's doing in a bridal shop. Weird, don't you think?"

Suddenly something Madge had said made perfect sense. "Oh, wait. I get it now."

"Get what?" Lori-Lou asked.

"Madge told me that Nadia's son was taking over the shop when she left for Paris."

"Seems a little weird that a pro basketball player is in the wedding biz, though. He's definitely not the type. I once knew a guy who liked taffeta but always suspected there was more to that story."

I gave Brady James a second look and tried to analyze him through that filter. Nope. No way. This guy was all guy, all six feet five of him. Or six six. He seemed to be growing taller the more I stared at him. Or maybe I just felt small in his presence. He certainly commanded the room.

Stop staring, Katie. It's not polite.

But how could a girl help herself? A specimen like this didn't come along every day, especially not in a bridal salon. Staring up into that handsome face, I almost forgot why I'd come to Cosmopolitan Bridal in the first place.

Almost, but not quite.

9

You're Lookin' at Country

When you take a flower in your hand and really look at it, it's your world for the moment. I want to give that world to someone else. Most people in the city rush around so, they have no time to look at a flower. I want them to see it whether they want to or not.

Georgia O'Keeffe

Brady James looked at us again, and a welcoming smile lit his face. I felt my cheeks grow hot. Had he noticed me staring? He headed right for us, but I wanted to run for the door.

"Oh. No. You. Don't." Lori-Lou spoke through clenched teeth. "Don't take a step. You're going to face this like a man."

"Face this like a man?" Brady asked as he drew near. "Well,

if I must." When he chuckled, his eyes sparkled with merriment, which only made him more handsome and forced me to stare even more. "What am I facing?"

"Oh, I was talking to Katie Sue here." Lori-Lou nudged me with her arm, then looked at him with a smile too broad for comfort. "This is Katie. She needs to face life's situations like a man."

Brady gave me an inquisitive look. "Not exactly your usual opening line, but I'm thinking this has something to do with a wedding? Or a wedding dress?"

"Yes. A wedding dress. I've come to talk to you about a dress," I managed.

A boyish smile turned up the edges of his lips. "Well then, you've come to the right place. I'm Brady. What can I help you with?"

Get it together, Katie. You look like a goober standing here.

"I, um, spoke to a woman named Madge. On the phone, I mean. Yesterday. No, maybe the day before. I can't remember." *I've been busy getting my heart crushed, so the days are getting mixed up.* "Anyway, she doesn't know I'm coming today. She's expecting me on Monday. Maybe it would be better if I talked to her alone? Would that be okay?" My sentences came out sounding rushed. Staccato. Breathy.

"Of course. I'll get Madge for you. If anyone knows how to take things like a man, she does." He leaned so close I could smell his yummy cologne. "Brace yourselves, ladies."

Oh, I needed to brace myself, all right. My heart felt more vulnerable than ever as his arm brushed against mine. When he pointed at the middle-aged woman with dark red hair, I drew in a deep breath and willed my erratic heartbeat to slow down. I had to jump this hurdle so I could get back to the business of recovering from my heartbreak.

Just. Get. This. Over. With.

"Madge is one tough cookie." Brady waggled his brows.

"Ooh, cookies." Lori-Lou licked her lips. "When we're done with all this, let's go grab some lunch, Katie. I never get to have lunch without my kids."

"How did we transition from wedding dresses to cookies to lunch?" I asked.

Brady shrugged. "Not sure, but cookies do sound good. I'm pretty sure one of the girls brought in some homemade chocolate chip cookies just this morning. They're in the workroom out back." He grinned and then walked across the room toward Madge. I couldn't help but notice that he favored his left knee. Poor guy.

I gave the older woman another look to see if she really looked as tough as he'd described her. Broad shoulders. Button-up blouse over black slacks. Sturdy. Plain. Completely different attire from the glitzy blonde chick. Yes, Madge looked somewhat out of place in this swanky joint, but she barked out orders from behind the cash register like she owned the place. Well, until Brady approached her, then she appeared to melt like butter. A smile lit her face, replacing the stern expression.

"There's a little song I sing with the kids," Lori-Lou whispered as she gestured to the woman. "'One of these things is not like the other.'" My cousin shook her head. "That's what comes to mind when I see that Madge lady working here. She just doesn't seem to fit the place. Looks like she'd be more at home working at Fanny's Fine Fashions in Fairfield."

"Oh, I don't know. I think there's room for every kind of person in the wedding biz," I said.

Madge walked our way and my heart rate picked up.

Here goes nothing.

"Can I help you ladies?" she asked.

I offered a slight smile. "Yes. You're Madge?"

"Last time I checked." She put her hands on her hips. "What can I do for you?"

"Oh, I'm Katie Fisher. You called me the other day, remember? I'm the one who—"

"You won the contest!" The woman let out a squeal and grabbed my arm. "Well, why in the world didn't you just say so? You're early, kid! Didn't expect to see you until Monday. What brings you here today?"

"Well, see, that's the thing. I came today because I happened to be in Dallas with my cousin Lori-Lou here."

"Good to meet you." Madge grabbed Lori-Lou's hand and shook it. "Member of the wedding party? I know a maid of honor when I see one!"

"Actually, Lori-Lou is married."

My cousin grinned. "So, I guess that would technically make me—"

"Matron of honor!" Madge clasped her hands together. "Well, no time to waste. C'mon in and meet the crew. We've got a lot of work ahead of us. Nadia's in her office behind the shop, so I'll let her know you're here. She'll be thrilled you're early! That'll give her a couple of extra days for the design."

So much for thinking the woman was as tough as nails. Looked like she had a soft spot for contest winners, which only made my plight more pitiable. Or terrifying.

At this point, a couple of other girls came out of a back room, joining the blonde. After Madge introduced me as the contest winner, all three started applauding. Oh. Dear. Then they took to chattering. One of them appeared to be speaking another language, but I couldn't quite make it out, what with so many voices overlapping. Beyond them, Brady James glanced at me with intrigue in his eyes.

Madge continued to gush over me, and seconds later Brady joined us.

"Wait . . . you're the one who won the contest? Why didn't you tell me? I would've introduced you to Madge and made a big deal over you being here. She's been so excited to meet you. We all have."

"Well, thank you, but that's the thing. I don't really want to—"

"And my mom. She's in back," Brady said. He reached to straighten a veil on the mannequin to my right. "She's going over some paperwork in her office right now, but I'm sure she'll be thrilled you're here. Did she know you were coming?"

"No. I didn't tell anyone." And I certainly hadn't planned on a reception like this. How could I tell them now that I wouldn't be taking the dress? They were treating me like the queen of Sheba.

"Shame on you for not warning us that you were coming in early." Madge patted my arm in a motherly fashion. "We would've called the press. At the very least, I would've brought my camera."

"Ooh, I have a great camera on my phone." The blonde grabbed her phone and started snapping photos of me. "Do you mind?"

"Well, actually . . ." Ugh. I could just see it now: *Jilted Fairfield bride-to-be shows up at Cosmopolitan Bridal to make a fool of herself in front of pro basketball player and his . . . mother?*

Not that I was ever really a bride-to-be. And that reminded me that I had to tell Madge I wouldn't need a wedding gown.

"I'm sure Madge and the girls would love to show you around while you're waiting on my mom." Brady gestured to the three young women standing nearby and introduced them as Twiggy—*Really? Twiggy?*—Crystal, and Dahlia, the one I'd seen earlier with Madge.

Dahlia had one of those rich accents from . . . maybe Russia? No, Sweden. Hmm. I couldn't really tell, but she definitely wasn't from Fairfield. Her platinum blonde hair reminded me of one of those gals from the older Hollywood housewives show. Her face was a perfect oval. Her cheekbones high and exotic. Not a wrinkle around those beautifully made-up eyes. I'd be willing to bet she'd had work done, but no telling where. Every feature was picture perfect.

Twiggy, thin with a short reddish-blonde pixie cut, seemed really nice and bubbly. She held herself with confidence. And judging from the way she sashayed when she walked, she'd done some time as a runway model before taking on this job at the bridal shop. Maybe that's where the name had come from. A stage name, perhaps? And the dress she wore showed she knew her stuff when it came to fashion.

Then there was Crystal, who drew me in at once. Her freckled nose and dirty blonde hair put me in mind of someone I knew quite well—myself. And when she opened her mouth to speak, the thickest Southern accent tumbled out. If I had to guess, I'd say Crystal was from South Carolina. Or Alabama. Or Georgia.

Turned out I was right on the last count. She hailed from Georgia. Looked like we had another thing in common: peaches. All of this I learned in only a couple minutes of knowing her. And the fact that she had a passion for fashion, as she put it.

The three girls seemed giddy and fun as they took photos of me and then shared about their various jobs at the shop, but Madge was all business. "I'll show you around until Nadia is free." She turned her attention to Brady and smiled. "Sound agreeable?"

"Sure." He shrugged. "Not sure it'll take very long."

"Are you kidding?" I glanced at the racks on my right. "I live, eat, sleep, and breathe wedding gowns. This is like heaven to me." I glanced around the room. "Everything is so . . . white."

"Just how you pictured heaven, then?"

"Well, close." I released a happy sigh. "Just waiting for the angel choir to chime in."

"My pitch is terrible," Madge said. "So don't count on me for any angel action."

Brady laughed and gave her a hug. "Well, enjoy yourselves, ladies. I'll let Mom know you're here. If anyone needs me after that, I'll be in my office."

I still couldn't quite figure out what a pro basketball player was doing with an office at a bridal shop, even a shop owned by a family member. Had he traded in his running shoes for gowns and veils? Very odd. I tried to picture the look on Casey's face should he see his favorite player seated behind a desk at a bridal salon, but I couldn't. No doubt he would cringe at the very idea. Then again, what did it matter what Casey thought?

Madge's words interrupted my own thoughts. "We'll start with existing gowns so you can see Nadia's work," she said. "It should inspire you. She's going to be creating yours from scratch, you know, based on your favorite movie or TV star."

"Or singer," Twiggy chimed in.

"Yes, or singer." Madge nodded. "Point is, you get to choose the person who inspires you, and Nadia will take it from there."

"She does such a spectacular job of capturing the look and feel of that person in the gown," Crystal said. "Have you seen the Katharine Hepburn gown? It's like you've stepped back in time."

"I'm sure they're all great," I said. "But I really need to tell you that . . ." My words trailed off. I couldn't seem to spit out the rest.

"Oh, it's okay, honey," Madge said. "No need to spill the whole story right off. You need time to think it through, I suppose."

"Time to choose the best parts of the story for the *Texas Bride* interview," Crystal added.

"In the meantime, I'll show you the inner sanctum. Nadia's design studio." Madge leaned close to whisper, "Almost no one gets to go in there, so you have to promise not to share what you see until that reporter from *Texas Bride* comes to interview you. It's all top-secret information until then. Got it?"

"Got it," I echoed. "But that's really why I've come. I have something I need to tell you that's kind of a secret too."

"Ooh, inquiring minds want to know." Madge laughed.

"Katie's *great* at keeping secrets." Lori-Lou gave me a "please don't spill the beans until after she's shown us around the shop" look, and I obliged by closing my mouth and trailing on Madge's heels.

I elbowed my ornery cousin and mouthed the words, "I *have* to tell them."

She gave me a bemused smile, followed by a wink. Goofy girl. Did she not understand that I couldn't go through with this?

We saw the gowns, many of which took my breath away. I'd never seen so many designs in my life—everything from frilly to simple to over the top. Many were Nadia's, but the shop featured designs by a host of well-known designers, including one of my favorites from the Galveston area, Gabi Delgado.

After touring the gowns, Madge took us to the studio in the back where Nadia designed her line of wedding dresses. Long tables stretched the expanse of the room, with sewing machines and fabrics in abundance. I'd never seen so many bolts of satin and tulle in my life. And the trims! I could've spent hours just looking through the shimmery bolts of loveliness. They took my breath away. I wanted to finger each one and dream of the possibilities for where they might end up. Brides from all over the globe would likely find these lovely bits attached to their gowns.

"Want to see the fitting rooms?" Madge's words interrupted my ponderings.

"Hmm?" I couldn't imagine why fitting rooms deserved a stop on the tour, but why not?

She led the way to a row of closed doors and opened the first one to reveal a spacious changing area unlike any I'd ever seen before.

"W-wow." I'd been in a few fitting rooms in my life, of course. Department stores at the mall in Dallas, for instance. And Fanny's Fine Fashions in Fairfield. The one and only fitting room at Fanny's was spacious—well, spacious enough for Fanny, who'd been aptly named, to fit inside. The curtain in front of it offered a wee bit of privacy. Stress *wee bit*.

This room, however, outdid anything I'd ever seen. I stared in awe and muttered "Wow!" once again. It was octagon shaped, mirrors covering every side but one. A cushioned round bench sat in the center of the room. All in all, this room was the ideal place to don a wedding gown. And speaking of gowns, a beautiful ruffled one hung on the hook near the door. Brilliant. Shimmering. Luscious. I could almost see myself walking the aisle in something like that.

Only, I wouldn't be walking the aisle anytime soon, and I needed to let these fine people know right away. I had to speak my mind, no matter how difficult. This seemed like as good a place as any. I swallowed hard, ready to dive in.

Lori-Lou must've figured out my plan to spill the beans—probably my wrinkled brow and strained silence. At any rate, she headed off to the ladies' room. Coward.

Alone in the changing room with Madge, I finally worked up the courage to share my story. "Ms. . . . Madge, I need to let you know something. I didn't come today to start the fitting, or even to talk to Nadia about the dress."

Madge fussed with the ruffled gown, straightening the hem. "Oh, but you must talk to her today. She's leaving town soon."

"Well, I came to tell you that . . ." *Suck it up, Katie. Say the words.* "I cannot, under any circumstances . . ." *Deep breath! Forge ahead!* "Go through with this."

The woman's broad smile faded in an instant as she turned her attention away from the dress and to me. "I-I'm sorry. What did you say? You can't go through with the initial consult *today*, you mean? Or not at all?"

"Not at all. But more than that—I can't go through with any of it. Not just the consult, but the whole thing. No dress. No . . . wedding." I shook my head and glanced in the mirror, noticing the dress on the hook in the background had created an optical illusion. Almost looked like I was wearing it. Weird.

Okay, what was I supposed to be saying again? Oh yes. I faced Madge head-on and tried to calm my shaky voice. "I've just gone through a, well, a . . . a breakup."

"A breakup?" Madge's eyes widened. "With your fiancé?"

"Well, sort of. I mean, I . . . we . . ."

At this point Lori-Lou pressed her way back inside the changing room. "What she's *trying* to say is, the wedding's off."

"The wedding's off?" Madge repeated.

"Actually . . ." I released a painful sigh. "It was never really on."

10

I'm Living in Two Worlds

I was from a small town, and nobody really expects you to leave, especially before you graduate. That doesn't happen.

Taylor Swift

Did you say the wedding's off?" Madge's eyes widened as she dropped down onto the cushioned round bench. "The wedding's *off*?"

Good grief. Did she have to keep saying it aloud? Wasn't I hurting enough already? "What I'm trying to say is, it wasn't really on to begin with." I plopped down onto the bench next to her. "I mean, I *thought* Casey and I were getting married. I would never have entered the contest otherwise. But it wasn't official. And now it's . . . impossible."

"Impossible?" Madge echoed. She leaned forward and put her head in her hands. "Impossible. The wedding's impossible."

Do you have to keep repeating everything?

"At least impossible for now," Lori-Lou interjected. "Casey is moving to Oklahoma."

"Well, that's no reason to break up. I hear Oklahoma is nice." Madge lifted her head. "Maybe you'll still marry him and move there? You think?"

"Oh, no ma'am." I shook my head. "I'll never live anywhere but Fairfield. Can't picture it. And to be honest, I really think it's over with Casey." As soon as I spoke the words, my heart twisted inside of me. In all the years I'd known and loved Casey, I'd never pictured myself saying that. Or thinking it. Yet something about voicing the words felt strangely freeing.

"Are there any other guys in Fairfield you could marry?" A hopeful look sparked in Madge's eyes. "Anyone special come to mind?"

"W-what? No." I shook my head. Was she kidding?

"Guess I'm grasping at straws." Madge groaned. "It's just that Nadia's only got a narrow window to take care of all this before leaving for Paris. This is so important to her. It's a chance for her gown to be featured on the cover of *Texas Bride*. That's such an honor. If I have to tell her that she's not making the dress for you . . ." Madge shook her head. "It will crush her. Your name has already been announced, after all, and the reporter has set the date for the interview and photo shoot. This is a huge deal to her. Really, to all of us."

"Surely some other bride could take my place."

"No." Madge rose and paced the room. She hesitated at the dress and fingered the lace around the neckline. "The contest is over. You have no idea how complicated it was to put together. We can't possibly start again."

We sighed. All three of us. I happened to catch a glimpse of our trio of expressions in one of the full-length mirrors. Somber. Pitiful.

Then Madge turned away from the gown and snapped her fingers. "Perfect solution. Here's what we're going to do, Katie. You're going to let Nadia make you the wedding dress of your dreams. You'll appear on the cover of *Texas Bride*, the October edition. And I'll work double time to run interference so that no one around here is any the wiser."

"I just can't do it, Madge." I rose and took a couple of steps in her direction. "I can't lie to Nadia. It's not right."

"I'm not asking you to lie, and I won't either. We just won't mention that you're not getting married. Yet." With a wave of her hand she appeared to dismiss the matter. "I'm sure you'll get married someday."

I sighed again.

"Technically, it doesn't matter anyway, don't you see? There was nothing specific in the rules about a wedding date or even an engagement. So let's just let it go, okay? Skip the wedding part. Just take the dress."

"I . . . I . . ."

She gave me one of those stern looks that I often got from my mother. "I'm simply asking you to let Nadia James make you a wedding dress. That's all. I'm not saying you have to wear it this year. Or next. Or ever. Maybe you'll get old like me and give up on the idea of a wedding altogether."

Gee, thanks.

"But if you do find the right fella, you'll have the perfect dress hanging in your closet. Nadia will get her moment in the sun when the dress appears on the cover of *Texas Bride*, and you'll have the dress of your dreams."

"Or when Casey comes to his senses." Lori-Lou reached

for her phone, which beeped four or five times in a row. "Still thinking that could happen."

Ugh.

Her phone beeped again, and she groaned.

"What in the world is going on with that phone?" Madge asked. "Some sort of emergency?"

"I'm sorry. It's just that my husband doesn't know how much water to mix into the baby's formula. And I think my oldest daughter locked herself in the bathroom and can't get out." Lori-Lou responded to the text, then shoved the phone in her purse. "Sorry for the interruption, but the man is hopeless. Completely and totally hopeless. But I love him anyway."

I had just opened my mouth to continue the debate with Madge when I heard Brady's voice from outside the dressing room. "You ladies okay in there?"

Madge opened the door a crack and waved her hand. "Yep. Now go away, Brady. We're talking business in here. Besides, I thought you were going to your office."

"Haven't made it that far yet." He leaned against the door frame, his towering presence a little intimidating. "Just wanted to let you know that I talked to Mom. She's ready to see Katie now."

"Perfect." Madge nodded.

"If you ladies are talking business, don't you think it involves me? I am managing the store now, remember?" His words sounded a little strained, as if he'd had this conversation with Madge before.

"Sure, sure, kid." She waved him away. "Whatever you say. Just give me a minute with the ladies and then we'll head back to your mom's office." Madge closed the door in his face. "Poor guy. I know this isn't the life he would've chosen for himself." She took a seat on the bench once more and sighed. "It took Nadia weeks to convince Brady that he should take over the shop while she's in Paris. He agreed to do it, and he's settling in well. But I daresay he would rather be back out on the court. When his leg is ready, I mean. Until then, he's on our team."

Lori-Lou glanced toward the closed door. "I'd say he's a great team player. That's what they do. They stick around and pick up the slack. They don't care about the glory. If there's a need, they meet it, injured or not."

"That's Brady, all right. The boy's a real gem." Madge lowered her voice. "And it's not like he can play right now anyway. He's only three months out from his knee surgery, and the doctor says he might need another one because it's not healing properly."

I felt for him. Taking over his mother's wedding dress shop was probably the last thing he wanted to do. And here we were, excluding him from a conversation that involved the shop.

"He's the one in charge once his mom leaves for Paris." She chuckled. "Well, in theory, anyway." She leaned against the door, her voice growing louder. "If you ask anyone who works here, I run this shop."

"I heard that, Madge." Brady's voice sounded once more from outside the door.

"We have to tell him," I whispered. "That I don't need the dress, I mean."

"No way." Madge shook her head and lowered her voice to a hoarse whisper. "We'll go out there and smile and meet with Nadia. And we will not—under any circumstances—say a word to Brady. Not yet. The boy's nervous enough already. Let's don't rock the boat."

I agreed to keep my mouth shut, at least for now. When we exited the dressing room, I found Brady standing in the hallway. His blue eyes pierced the distance between us. "I was getting worried about you ladies."

"Nothing to worry about." Madge patted him on the back. "Now, you take it from here, Brady. Introduce Katie to your mom. I've got to get back up to the counter." She headed to the front of the store, mumbling under her breath something about how her work was never done.

Brady seemed to have resigned himself to the fact that he was now my tour guide. He looked at me. "So, you saw everything?"

"Yeah. All but your mom's studio, of course."

"She's going to meet us there in a couple minutes." He looked around as if trying to figure out what we should do next. The poor guy really looked lost. I could picture him shooting hoops, but not trimming out wedding dresses or talking brides into petticoats for their gowns.

He led the way to the back of the shop and turned to face me. "Do you know anything about my mom?"

"Do I?" I couldn't help the smile that followed. "Are you kidding? I've been following her designs for years. She's famous, you know."

"So they tell me."

"You goober." Lori-Lou jabbed me with her elbow. "Brady is famous too."

"Oh, I've heard all about you from Casey," I said. "I think he was watching the game when you . . ." I pointed to his knee. "Anyway, he was watching that night. Everyone in town talked about it."

"Which town?"

"Fairfield."

"So I'm famous in Fairfield, eh?" He led us through the workroom at the back of the store to a door that read STUDIO. "Well, that's good to know. But my mom's reach is a little farther than that. She's headed to Paris, which is why I'm here managing the shop."

"Working for Madge." Lori-Lou gave him a funny smile.

I expected Brady to smirk, but he actually grinned. "Madge definitely calls the shots around here, but don't ever tell her I told you that. We couldn't manage without her. I don't mind admitting she's the boss of, well, everything."

"She seems really . . . businesslike."

"All business, but she's really a marshmallow on the inside," Brady said. "Anyway, Mom's doing an internship in Paris for a year. That's why I'm at the shop. I'm—"

"You're filling in for your mom?" Lori-Lou asked. "Must be quite a gig after basketball, right?" She laughed. "From dribbling to walking the aisle. Quite a shift."

"Yeah." His gaze shifted to the carpet and then back to us. "Look, this isn't my idea of a dream job. In fact, it's not a job at all. It's a family business and one that someone has to run while she's away."

"I'm sorry, Brady." Lori-Lou's voice softened. "I was just kidding with you. I guess I don't really know you well enough to do that. Yet."

"Nah, it's okay." He shrugged. "It's just all new to me." His face lit into a smile. "Everyone's excited about the contest, which makes the transition easier. It's been months in the making, and Mom couldn't wait to meet the winner. Brace yourself, okay? I'm sure she'll ask you a million questions about your wedding plans."

"O-oh?"

"Yes. At some point she'll want to know your theme and color choices. Also your fiancé's tuxedo preferences."

"My fiancé?" The words stuck on the roof of my mouth, kind of like peanut butter. *Madge, I'm going to blow this! I have to tell him.*

"Sure. She wants to provide the tuxedo too," Brady said. "Didn't you know that? I thought Madge would've told you."

"She didn't. We, um, didn't really have a chance to talk about all of that."

"It was all spelled out in the contest entry form," Brady explained. "He'll have to come for a fitting in a few weeks. And the bridesmaids too."

"Bridesmaids?"

"Ooh, yes, yes!" Lori-Lou raised her hand. "I get to be in the wedding party, right? Matron of honor? Isn't that what you said out there?"

I glared at her.

"I've always dreamed of being a matron of honor. This will be quite a privilege, let me tell you." Her nose wrinkled. "But my figure's not what it used to be. You can thank three ornery kids for that."

Brady turned his attention to her. "Do you think you'll be able to find something off the rack? We have more choices than most bridal stores, so I'm hoping the bridesmaids can find something that will work with the overall theme." He turned back to me. "You did say you had a theme, right? Most brides do these days."

"Well, I've always loved shabby chic," I said. "But honestly, I think I should tell you that—"

"That we'll definitely be able to pick something off the rack." Lori-Lou smiled. "You've got oodles of options."

"Oodles of options. That's a new one." He grinned, and for a moment that handsome face of his looked magazine-cover ready. Yummy. If I told him the truth about my wedding—or lack thereof—I'd wipe that gorgeous smile right off his face. Maybe I'd better wait awhile to do that. Besides, what would Madge say? I'd only known the woman a few minutes, but I had a feeling she could take me down in a hurry.

"This is your special day, Katie." Brady gave me a warm

smile. "My mother wants to do everything she can to make it the best it can be." He reached to take hold of the handle on the studio door. "It doesn't hurt that the press will be there, you know. Great advertisement for the shop and for her designs."

"Wait, press? At my wedding?"

"Sure. Didn't you read the entry form at all?" His brow wrinkled in concern.

"Katie's just distracted," Lori-Lou said as she glanced down at her phone once again. "You know how hectic things can be during times like this."

Times like this? I glared at her again.

"Well, the point is, my mom wants all of this to be perfect for everyone, and not just because of the press. She loves what she does and wants everyone to be happy."

He opened the door and gestured for us to enter. I took a couple of steps inside Nadia's studio and fell in love with the place all over again. Seeing the dresses done up in the store was nothing in comparison to this. The fabrics, lace, and embellishments still took my breath away.

"Wow." I couldn't seem to manage much else.

"Wow, wow!" Lori-Lou echoed as she stood frozen in place. Except for the incessant beeping from her phone, the whole room was silent.

"Mom's pretty fixated with fashions from days gone by," Brady explained as he led us to the sewing area.

"I read all about it in *Texas Bride*," Lori-Lou said. "The article said her work has prompted a revival in the industry."

"That's true." Brady nodded, and I could see the look of pride in his eyes as we talked about his mother.

"I just know that brides can't get enough of her gowns," I added.

"They're coming from out of the woodwork." He laughed. "Not just from Texas, but all over the US and beyond."

"Vintage is in." Lori-Lou stopped at the cutting table to run her hand over a swatch of satin. "Wow. Wow."

"You ladies give me a minute to let Mom know you're here. She's anxious to meet you, Katie." Brady smiled and headed off to a room marked OFFICE.

Moments later Nadia James entered the sewing room. I couldn't help but gasp as the lovely woman moved in our direction. She had to be about Mama's age, but talk about polar opposites. Where Mama was short and slightly round, Nadia was tall and thin. Mama's short gray hair was naturally curly. Nadia had obviously taken hours to perfect her platinum locks.

Lori-Lou nudged me with her elbow and mouthed "Wow" once more. I felt like echoing the word myself. Nadia was the sort of woman who looked as if she belonged on the cover of a magazine. Gorgeous. Other than on television, I'd never seen anyone so well put together. And well preserved to boot. Her perfectly bobbed platinum hair held my attention, but the perfection didn't end there. High cheekbones. Excellent skin. And the makeup! Man, talk about flawless.

We didn't get a lot of women like this in Fairfield. Well, unless you counted Frenchie at Do or Dye. She'd gone away to beauty school a duckling and come back a swan. Rumor had it she'd gone under the knife, but the supposed plastic surgery had only changed her appearance—in particular, her nose. Her sparkling personality remained the same.

Speaking of sparkling, the older woman now standing in front of me sparkled with glitz and glam. No wonder folks gravitated to Nadia for her vintage gowns. She shimmered to the core. Well, maybe it had a little something to do with the crystals on her blouse. And that necklace! Were those real diamonds? Surely not.

Brady gestured to her with a broad smile on his face. "Ladies, let me introduce you to my mother, Nadia James. Mama, this is Katie Fisher, our contest winner."

I gave her a closer look and saw the family resemblance. Both were tall. Both had sparkling blue eyes. Both had that "just been in the sun" bronzed look about them. Most of all, they both seemed confident and kind. Approachable. All it took was one look at the sincerity in this amazing woman's eyes for me to know I had to come clean about my non-wedding, no matter what Madge had insisted.

"I . . . I . . ." I swallowed hard, knowing I was about to wipe that sparkle right out of her eyes with my terrible news.

Courage, Katie. Courage.

11

For Heaven's Sake

You aren't wealthy until you have something money can't buy.

Garth Brooks

Nadia extended her hand with a warm smile. "Katie, I'm so glad to meet you," she said. "I've looked forward to this day for ages."

I took hold of her hand—wow, soft—and shook it. "Nice to meet you." The intoxicating aroma of expensive perfume wafted in the air between us. I didn't know much about such things, but I could tell money when I smelled it.

"For some reason, I thought you were coming Monday, not today." Nadia tucked her hair behind her right ear.

"Her plans have been a little . . . loose." Lori-Lou typed

something into her phone, then glanced up at our hostess with a whimsical smile.

Nadia glanced at my cousin, her thinly plucked brows elevating slightly. "And who have we here?"

"Oh, this is Lori-Lou," I said.

"Katie's matron of honor," Brady explained.

"Yes, matron of honor. Because I'm married with children." Lori-Lou giggled. "Otherwise I'd be a maid of honor. I mean, you know . . ." Her words drifted off as I glared at her once again.

"Wonderful to meet you!" Nadia fussed with her hair. "Well, as I said, I wish I'd known you were coming this morning, ladies. I would've called the news stations. They could've sent a camera crew to greet you. Hope you don't mind that it's just me."

My heart quickened. "Oh, I'm relieved, actually. Can't imagine being greeted by the press. You see, I don't want my parents to know about this."

"Don't want your parents to know?" Nadia's face contorted, then she snapped her fingers. "Oh, I get it! You want to surprise your parents with the gown? This is even better! We'll let them know at the last minute, when your photo appears on the cover of *Texas Bride* magazine. How's that? I'll be flying back in from Paris for a charity event that week prior, so it's the perfect time for the big reveal. I don't mind holding off with the media. Makes perfect sense, actually. We'll stir up excitement in the week leading up to the reveal. Create a sense of anticipation."

Anticipation. Now there was a word I knew well.

"My parents live in Fairfield," I explained. "They rarely pay attention to Dallas news, especially wedding stuff. It's the furthest thing from their minds."

"Don't folks get married in Fairfield?" Nadia asked. "Weddings aren't a big deal?"

"Well, sure, they're a big deal. But in Fairfield we all get married in our local church or at the civic center. There's a gazebo at the park that we sometimes use for photos. Most of the girls I know got married in gowns that they bought at Fanny's or online."

"Fanny's?" Nadia looked confused.

"Online?" Brady echoed.

"You're in the big city now, Katie." Lori-Lou laughed and shoved her phone in her purse once again.

Nadia took me by the arm and patted it as she led me to her work area. "Yes, here in Dallas we do it a bit differently, especially at Cosmopolitan. Weddings are all about the gown. And the veil. But mostly about the gown." Nadia released a girlish giggle. "We are dedicated—and I do mean completely dedicated—to giving the bride the experience of a lifetime. A girl only gets married once, you know." A sad look came over her. "Well, in theory, anyway."

"Oh, I know Cosmopolitan is the best."

"It's wonderful to make brides feel . . . wonderful." Nadia glanced at her watch. "I wish I had time to visit with you awhile, Katie—to hear your story—but I have an appointment with another bride in less than an hour. Would you mind if we went ahead and took your measurements right away, instead of waiting until Monday? That way I can spend the weekend thinking through a plan. It'll give me a head start, which is always nice."

I shook my head. "No. I mean, no, please don't." I felt my face grow warm as I looked at Brady.

"Oh, right, right." She glanced at her son. "Do you mind, honey? We need some privacy. And would you mind fetching Madge for me? And Dahlia too. I'll need her help with my sketches."

Brady shot out of the room quicker than a player making a three-point shot in the fourth quarter of the game. I turned to face my benefactor, determined to tell her the truth before Madge arrived. "Nadia, I'm so grateful for this. You have no idea."

"Oh, sweetie, I do." Her eyes filled with tears. "I was a young bride once too." In that moment, the strong features in her face softened. "I married young and had nothing. Absolutely nothing. It would've meant the world to me to win a dress like this, so I understand."

"Well, thank you, but what I meant to say was—"

"Ooh, your ring!" She reached for my left hand and lifted it. "It's gorgeous! Antique?"

"Yes. It was my grandmother's."

"I love it. Keeping things in the family is so nice. I'm sure your fiancé was thrilled for the opportunity to slip it on your finger."

"Well, actually, he—"

"Nadia!" Madge's voice sounded from the open doorway. "You need me?"

"I do." Nadia released her grip on my hand. "And Dahlia too."

"She's with a customer right now." Madge walked our way. "Princess Bride."

"Ah." Nadia nodded as she looped the measuring tape around my hips. "Got it."

"Princess Bride?" I glanced up as Nadia reached around me to measure my bust. *Awkward!* "An actual princess?"

"No." Madge rolled her eyes. "In this case she happens to be the daughter of some oil sheik in the Middle East. Spoiled rich kid. Princess attitude, but none of the grace. We get a lot of 'em in the store, trust me."

"Ooh, this I've gotta see." Without any other warning,

Lori-Lou shot out of the workroom door and back into the shop. I felt sure she'd return with some whopper stories.

"These Princess Brides are accustomed to getting what they want when they want it, with never a thought for cost. Daddy has deep pockets." Madge smirked and reached for a notepad.

Nadia glanced over at her and flashed a warning look.

Madge clamped her mouth shut. "Anyway, how can I help?"

"I'm taking measurements. You write everything down." Nadia glanced up at me with a smile. "Hips are thirty-four inches."

I did my best not to groan aloud.

"Now, while I measure, let's talk styles," Nadia said. "What sort of design are you looking at? French bustle? Trumpet skirt?"

"Hmm?"

"I was thinking with your figure, maybe a modified sweetheart neckline? What do you think?"

"Sweetheart?"

"Something light. With an airy feel. Maybe a dropped waist? Ruffles?"

"I . . . it sounds wonderful."

Nadia appeared to be thinking. "Maybe I should have asked what famous person we're patterning this gown after. You have someone special that you like from days gone by?"

"Oh, lots of famous movie stars." In that moment, however, I couldn't think of a single one. Nadia began a lengthy discussion about the various movie stars she'd patterned dresses after in the past. Her favorite, it turned out, was Grace Kelly.

Several minutes into the conversation, Dahlia entered with Lori-Lou on her heels.

"Wow, Katie! You should've seen that bride out there. She was . . . wow." Lori-Lou gave Dahlia an admiring look. "Great job reining her in, girl. Impressive."

"Thank you." Dahlia giggled. "I left her in Twiggy's capable hands. She's great with the Princess Brides."

"So you get that a lot?" Lori-Lou sat in a chair across from me and watched as Nadia measured the circumference of my neck.

"Girl, we see all sorts." Madge looked up from her tablet to join in the conversation. "You wouldn't believe what we go through with the various brides that come in."

"What do you mean?" Lori-Lou looked confused.

"Well, there's the organized bride who knows what she wants, down to the style of dress and type of fabric," Nadia said. She looked at Madge. "Neck size is 13.5 inches."

"Got it." Madge wrote down the number.

"There's the spoiled rich girl bride who just wants a designer gown because it's going to make her friends jealous," Dahlia added. "You just saw one of those for yourself."

"There's the 'I'm so clueless I don't know what I want' bride," Madge said. "And then . . ." She shuddered. "Then there are the really tough cases."

"Tough cases?" I couldn't help myself. I had to ask.

Nadia stopped measuring me long enough to explain. "Sure. Brides whose parents just went through a divorce. Brides who've just lost a family member. Brides who want to be happy about their upcoming wedding, but just can't seem to focus because of what they're going through on the perimeter. Those poor girls can't help that they're going through trauma, so I do my best to wrap my arms around them and talk them through."

"We have other tough cases too." Madge chuckled. "You gonna tell her about the double Gs, Nadia?"

"Double Gs?" I asked.

Nadia's cheeks turned a lovely crimson shade. "The double Gs are the large-chested brides. Hard to fit, but just as deserving as every other bride-to-be. We get them in every shape and size around here, trust me. Short, tall, curvy, rail-thin . . . and we somehow manage to fit every one. But you . . ." She gave me a reassuring smile. "You are the ideal shape. Perfect for a magazine cover in every conceivable way." She pulled the tape taut and then turned to Madge. "Bust size thirty-five inches."

I suddenly felt more than a little intimidated. "I'm sorry. I hope you'll forgive me, but I feel so out of place right now."

Nadia put the measuring tape down. "Why, honey? Have I done something to make you feel uncomfortable? I sure hope not. Maybe we've rushed into this? Perhaps I should've waited until Monday after all. I just thought that it would be nice to get this part over with, but I didn't mean to make you feel uncomfortable or rushed."

"I'm just not used to . . ." I gestured around the room filled with hundreds of thousands of dollars' worth of materials. "This."

Nadia followed my gaze. "Being fitted for a couture gown, you mean?" she asked.

"Well, that, and all of this. I'm just a small-town girl. This is very . . . new to me."

"You'll get used to being pampered." Nadia gave me a motherly smile. "We want to make you feel like a real princess."

"Accept it, Katie." Lori-Lou glared at me. "It's a gift."

"Sounds nice, but . . ." I said the only thing that came to mind. "Mrs. James, do you happen to know anything about Loretta Lynn?"

"The country-western singer? Sure."

"Well, if you recall, she left her little hometown of Butcher Holler for the first time with her new husband, Doo. They drove all over creation trying to get radio stations to play her song and eventually ended up in Nashville. Remember?"

"It's been a long time since I saw the movie about her life, but I think I vaguely remember what you're talking about. They took a road trip?"

"Yes. They left Butcher Holler and set out for new places," I explained.

"An adventure," Lori-Lou added. She reached for her phone as it beeped again.

"Wait. Butcher Holler?" Dahlia looked back and forth between us. "Is that a place?"

"Of course it's a place." Madge clucked her tongue. "You don't know Loretta Lynn's real-life story?"

Dahlia shook her head.

"Quite the tale," Madge said.

"Well, anyway, I feel kind of like Loretta Lynn right about now," I said. "A fish out of water. That was my point."

"Dallas is your Nashville, in other words. Got it." Madge slipped an arm over my shoulders. "You'll be okay, kid. And we promise not to make you sing, if that makes you feel any better."

As she released her hold on me, I shrugged. "Dallas is still close enough to home to feel familiar, but big enough to intimidate me. And this shop . . ." I gestured to the room. "All of this pretty stuff—it's way outside my norm. We don't get a lot of niceties like this where I come from. It's out of my element."

"But Loretta Lynn eventually felt at home in Nashville, especially on the stage at the Grand Ole Opry." Madge gave me a knowing look. "It could happen to you too. Like Nadia said, we'll turn you into a real princess."

"Yes." Nadia clasped her hands together at her chest. "You'll be a couture bride in no time."

I put my hand up in protest. "No thank you. Don't want to fit in. Just call me a misfit and send me back home where I belong. When the dress is finished, I mean."

"Oh, but like I said, you've got the perfect physique for one of my gowns," Nadia said. "And look at that gorgeous face of yours. I love everything about it, right down to the freckles and blonde hair. Between you and the dress, this is going to be the prettiest cover *Texas Bride* has ever seen. I can't wait."

I sighed, unsure of what to say next.

"Now, you've given me such a lovely idea." A thoughtful look settled on Nadia's face. "When you mentioned Loretta Lynn, actually. It occurred to me I've never patterned a dress after her."

"Ooh, perfect choice," Madge said. "Frilly but simple. Small-town girl goes to the big city."

"I can see it now." Nadia dropped her measuring tape and reached for a sketchpad. "What do you think, Katie? Would you like the idea of having a Loretta Lynn–inspired gown?"

"Well, Queenie would sure love it. She's always quoting Loretta Lynn."

"Queenie?" Nadia, Madge, and Dahlia spoke the word in unison.

"My grandmother. The matriarch of our family. She's nuts about Loretta. She'd be tickled pink." *Of course, she has no idea I'm here and no idea I'm getting a gown at all, but she would be thrilled. After killing me.* Okay, Queenie wouldn't really kill me—I hoped—but this whole thing would certainly be enough to send her into a tizzy.

"Glad you like the idea," Nadia said. "I guess we'll dive right in. Let me tell you how I work. First, the bride chooses her inspiration—in this case, Loretta Lynn. Then I craft a look specifically for her, with all of her inspiration's elements. We're going for something that says Katie and Loretta, all at the same time. Make sense?"

"Well, sure, but . . ." Did I actually *say* I wanted a Loretta Lynn gown?

"A bride has to trust her designer." On and on Nadia went, talking about her plan for my life. My soon-to-be-married life, anyway. Not that I was soon to be married. Should I mention that? Just about the time I'd worked up the courage, she slipped the measuring tape around my waist and pulled it snug.

"Oh, I'm sure anything you do will be brilliant," I managed as I sucked in a breath to make myself as small as possible.

"Twenty-six-inch waist," she said.

"I remember when I had a twenty-six-inch waist." Lori-Lou sighed. "I think I was twelve at the time."

That got a laugh out of Dahlia.

"We'll start with sketching some designs," Nadia said as she slipped the measuring tape around my upper arm. "I hope you can come back Monday to look over the final sketches before I have to get on the plane to Paris. I'll leave Dahlia here to work on the sewing. That okay with you?"

"Oh, whatever you think," I said. "I'm easy."

"Come around eleven on Monday, if you can. At that time I'll give you my suggestions for fabrics, trims, and so on. The fabric, I always say, is as much the inspiration for the gown as anything else. People underestimate the role that a good satin or crepe plays."

I was underestimating it even now. Then again, with a measuring tape looped around my arm, who had time to think of satin or crepe?

"We'll have to sign a contract for the gown at that point."

"A contract?" I felt panic well up inside of me.

"Oh, no money will change hands, so don't fret over that. Just a standard contract to say that you'll give Cosmopolitan Bridal credit for the gown when you wear it." The measuring tape slipped out of her hand. "When did you say your wedding was again, Katie? I can't remember the date."

"Oh, I . . ."

Madge threw a warning look my way. "Katie hasn't settled on a date yet, Nadia, which gives us plenty of time. Isn't that wonderful?"

"It helps." Nadia looked relieved at this news. She picked up the measuring tape from the floor. "But we do have the impending deadline of the photo shoot on July 15, so we'll have to move quickly. Just five weeks to design this dress and get it made. I don't usually work this fast, but I feel sure I can do it with Dahlia's help." She gave her assistant an admiring smile.

"Happy to be of service. This one's going to be fun." Dahlia's rich Swedish accent laced her words.

"Can we do it?" Nadia asked.

"Even if I have to stay and work nights." Dahlia gave her a confident look. "You can count on me."

"Thank you, sweet girl. I know I can. And I know this one means as much to you as it does to me."

"Oh, it does." Dahlia's eyes misted over. "I'm so excited I can barely think straight."

Yippy skippy. One more person who would hate me if I backed out.

"The article is set to go live in *Texas Bride* the first week of October." Nadia slipped the tape around my arm once more, then adjusted it. "I'll trust that the finished product will be exactly what you had in mind, Katie." She turned to Madge and said, "Upper arm is nine and three-quarter inches."

Lovely.

"I remember when my arm was nine and three-quarter inches." Madge made a funny face as she wrote down the number. "I was in kindergarten."

That got a laugh out of everyone in the room, especially Lori-Lou, who snorted.

"I think we're going to be good friends, you and me." Madge nodded at my cousin.

The ladies carried on and on, talking about the idea of using Loretta Lynn as an inspiration for my so-called wedding gown. I could tell that Nadia was growing more excited by the moment. How could I possibly burst her bubble? Clearly my news would crush the woman. And Dahlia too.

No, I'd better keep my lips sealed for now and pray about how to open them later, at a more opportune time. Maybe I could send Nadia an email once she went to Paris. Perhaps that would be for the best. Until then, I'd sit here and listen to them ramble about fabrics, ruffles, and lace.

After wrapping up the measurements, Nadia took a seat and started making some initial sketches. "This is just for fun, you understand. The finished work will come later. Initially, we just consult, gab, dream dreams, come up with ideas."

Only, I wasn't really coming up with any ideas. Not that she happened to notice. Nadia kept sketching and gabbing.

"It takes at least five or six fittings before we're done. While I'm in Paris, Dahlia will be your go-to girl. And you can always talk to Brady. He's . . ." The edges of Nadia's lips turned up in a smile. "He's been a great asset to the store."

This time Madge snorted.

"Anyway, he'll be here to help you with . . ." Nadia's nose wrinkled. "Actually, he's not much help with the design part."

"Or the sewing part," Dahlia added.

"Or the management part," Madge threw in.

"But he's great with public relations." Nadia put her index finger up in the air. "And he'll be in charge of coordinating things with the people from *Texas Bride*, so he's your go-to guy, Katie."

"Got it. Brady's my go-to guy." I could almost picture the

tall basketball player as my go-to guy now. I'd go straight to him and share the news that my wedding was nothing but a farce. Then he could go to his mother and share the news with her. Perfect.

"At any point, we'll get this done." Nadia continued to sketch out her ideas. The simplistic design drew me in at once. Apparently Lori-Lou loved it too. The two of us stood over Nadia's shoulder, watching the magic take place.

"Wow, that's great, Nadia," I found myself saying. "I love the sweetheart neckline. And the ruffles are just right."

"Very Loretta Lynn, but not over the top," Lori-Lou chimed in.

"Thanks." Nadia looked up from her sketchpad, her eyes brimming with tears. "Have I mentioned how excited I am about this one, Katie?" She reached out to grab my hand. "This is really a dream come true, for all of us. Your happily ever after is playing a role in *my* happily ever after. I'm going to have a dress on the cover of *Texas Bride*, and you're going to get the gown of your dreams. It's all so . . . perfect." Her voice quivered.

Yes, indeed. It was all so perfect. Unless you counted the part where the whole thing was based on a half-truth.

"It's an answer to prayer," Nadia whispered. "Truly."

Lori-Lou nudged me with her elbow and I glared at her, then settled my gaze on the sketch once again. Wow, this woman really knew her stuff. Watching the design come together made me think, if only for a moment, that maybe, just maybe, I would really get to wear this dress. Someday. Yes, perhaps after all I'd get to have my happily ever after. Until then, however, I'd have to wait for the perfect opportunity for my go-to guy to get to work fixing all of this for me.

12

Somebody's Back in Town

A city is a state of mind, of taste, of opportunity. A city is a marketplace where ideas are traded, opinions clash, and eternal conflict may produce eternal truths.

Herb Caen

I somehow managed to make it through the rest of the week-end. Sunday morning was spent at Lori-Lou and Josh's church, a place unlike any I'd ever visited. They called the large metal building with its massive parking lot and drum-infused music a megachurch. No doubt Mama would've called it a rock and roll concert and would've scheduled an appointment with the pastor forthwith to change the structure of the service to include more hymns and fewer flashing lights.

Still, I found myself clapping along and connecting with the lyrics of the songs, particularly the third one, which had a resounding faith theme. Even the sermon seemed to fit my situation. The pastor took his text from Proverbs, specifically focusing on lying. Ironic, since I'd agreed not to come clean with Brady or his mother about my wedding . . . or lack thereof.

I hardly slept on Sunday night, what with the baby fussing for hours due to teething issues. Monday morning came far too soon. Josh took off for work, and Lori-Lou spent the morning on the phone with several of her friends, trying to find a sitter, but to no avail. With no other choice but to take the kids with us, we headed back to Cosmopolitan to meet with Nadia one last time before she left for Paris. I still felt a little guilty about agreeing to Madge's plan. I'd rather just come clean before Nadia left the country, but what could I do? Madge intimidated me—perhaps as much as Queenie.

Queenie.

I sighed as I thought about my grandmother. I wondered if she was still mad at the Presbyterians. Boy howdy, she would've had a field day with the megachurch folks.

Lori-Lou didn't seem to notice my concerns as she drove us to the bridal shop. She gabbed on and on about a rental house Josh had found online while the kids hollered at each other in the backseat.

"It's going to be perfect for us, Katie," she said above the noise from the children. "With an extra bedroom we can use as a playroom." She pursed her lips. "I remember the days when we would've killed for an extra room to use as an office. Now every square inch of the house is covered in toys. Getting married and having kids changes everything."

Gee, thanks. Another crushing reminder of my current state of singleness.

As we pulled into the parking lot of Cosmopolitan Bridal, the most horrifying odor emanated from the backseat. Mariela let out several squeals in a row. "Ew, Mama! The baby's stinky!"

"Baby's stinky!" Gilly repeated.

"My nose isn't broken, thank you very much. I plan to change him in a minute, right after I call your daddy about the house." Lori-Lou rolled her eyes.

Me? I rolled down the window.

My cousin shook her head as she glanced my way. "You have a lot to get used to, Katie."

"Don't think I'll ever get used to that."

The minute she put the car in park, I bolted. She hollered, "Chicken!" out of the open window. I didn't hear the rest of what she said, though, because I barreled through the front door of the bridal salon lickety-split.

Brady greeted me with a huge smile as I entered the store. In fact, I very nearly ran him down. Not that a five-foot-two girl could run down a six-foot-something basketball player, but I did manage to startle him a little. As I landed against him, I felt his muscles ripple underneath his white shirt. I did my best to still my quickening pulse but found it difficult.

"Well, hello there," he said as I took a step backwards.

Hello there, Mr. Go-To Guy.

"Mom said you were coming back today. Good to see you." He reached to steady me as I lost my balance and nearly toppled into him again. From the twinkle in his eye, I got the feeling he really was happy to see me. But he wouldn't be if I told him my news, would he? He'd be booting me out the door.

"Hi. Good morning. Is your mom ready for me?"

"Almost. She told me to offer you a cup of coffee when you got here to stall a few minutes. I think she's made some progress on the design since Saturday, but probably won't have the final details until she's had more time to pick your brain. She wants you to be happy."

"Oh, I'm sure I will be." *If I can just get past feeling so guilty.* "I'd love a cup of coffee." I stifled a yawn. "Long night. The baby kept me up. Teething."

"Baby?"

"Oh!" I clamped a hand over my mouth. "Not *my* baby. My cousin's."

Brady nodded. "Ah. The gal with the cell phone?"

"That's the one."

"She's not with you today?" He glanced toward the door as if expecting her to materialize.

"She is, actually." I gestured to the parking lot. "She just needed to . . . well . . . get some last-minute work done while she was still in the car."

"All work and no play, eh? Sounds a lot like my mom. And me too, for that matter." As if to prove the point, he readjusted the mannequin with the $6,700 dress on it.

I stifled another yawn.

Brady laughed. "C'mon, sleepyhead. I'll lead you to the coffee machine. That way you'll be fully awake when you approve your wedding dress design. Otherwise you might okay something you don't really care for."

As Brady took his first few steps, I couldn't help but notice that he still favored his left knee. I followed behind him as he led the way to the workroom at the back of the store. All the while I wrestled with guilt, the pastor's sermon on lying replaying in my head. A guy this sweet didn't need a fake bride stringing him along. Wouldn't it be better to go ahead and tell him now? Why oh why had I agreed to go along with Madge's plan?

After filling a cup for me, he offered me cream and sugar.

I took both. "That's what I like," he said. "A girl who's not afraid to dump a few calories into her coffee."

"Hey, what's coffee without the good stuff?" I gave it a good stir and took a little sip. "Ooh, hot." I stirred it again. "I work long hours, so I need my caffeine."

"I'm a workaholic myself, so I get it," he said.

"Looks like we have a lot of things in common then." I took another little sip of my coffee. Mmm. Sweet.

"Oh? We have a lot in common?" He quirked a brow as he reached for another cup to fill. "You play basketball too?"

"Ha. Very funny." I looked up at him. Way up. Of course, I had to get past the strong athletic physique first. Not that I minded the side trip before settling my gaze on those gorgeous blue eyes. "I work for my parents too. We own a family-run business. So there's one thing we have in common. Besides liking sugar and cream in our coffee, I mean."

"What kind of family business?" He filled his cup and then dumped in three packets of sugar and a ton of creamer.

"Hardware store."

"Oh, that's right. I remember reading it in your essay. I feel like I learned a lot about you. Great writing, by the way. You should think about adding 'professional writer' to your résumé." He stirred his coffee and then tried to take a drink. He pulled the cup away from his lips at once. "Gets me every time."

I laughed. "You okay?"

"Yeah. I've had worse injuries, trust me." He glanced down at his left knee and winced.

Poor guy. I decided to change the subject. "Anyway, working for the family is . . . different. There's no way out, though. If I ever left the hardware store, I don't know how my dad would survive without me. He depends on me for so much."

"Totally get that." A wistful look came over Brady. Just as quickly, his sadness seemed to lift. "So, what does one do in a hardware store? Besides waiting on customers, I mean."

I thought through my answer. How could I make the hardware store sound glamorous? "I, um . . . sometimes I do the window dressings. And I rearranged the lawn and garden section last week. I like putting things in order. Well, in the order that makes sense to my mind."

"I like to put things in order too. I guess you could say I'm calculated in my approach. Did you happen to notice the shoe display at the front of the store?"

"Of course. I saw at least five or six pairs that I'd love to own."

"You just proved my point. See, they weren't selling. It occurred to me that brides don't come into a bridal salon looking for shoes. They're an afterthought. Brides come in looking for a gown, but if we're savvy, we put the other things they'll need in strategic places so they'll have to trip over them on the way out. That's how I decided to put the shoes where you saw them."

"Right." I'd hardly given any thought to wedding shoes until seeing the display. Not that I needed wedding shoes. "Wise move on your part."

He shrugged. "Just trying to think like a bride." A grin followed. "Not that I'm good at that part, but you get the idea. I'm giving it the old college try."

Madge walked into the workroom at that very moment. She grinned as she listened in. "Brady's going to make a lovely bride someday. And he'll know just where to find the perfect heels to make his ensemble complete." She patted him on the back and then looked at me. "Good to see you again, Katie. Nadia will be with you shortly."

"Oh, I know. Brady told me."

"Brady. Right. Keep forgetting he's the manager now." Madge elbowed him and smirked. "He'll always be Nadia's little boy to me. All six feet four of him."

Well, that answered the question about his height, anyway.

Madge took a couple of swigs from a cup of coffee, then tossed the rest in the trash and left the room.

"Working for family is a dream come true." Brady rolled his eyes. "Anyway, that's my take on it. What about you? What do you love about the hardware store?"

"I love the customers. Love 'em."

"What else?" He took another sip of his coffee.

I thought about it for a moment before answering. "Honestly? I love the designing aspects. Laying out the specials. Decorating for holidays. Making sure people are . . . I don't know . . . entertained?"

"Entertained by a store?"

"Well, I like to make sure the window displays are entertaining. Eye-catching. And I guess you're right about the writing. I write most of the copy for the store. Put together ads for the local paper. That sort of thing." I glanced down at my watch.

"Getting anxious?" Brady asked. "I could see if Mom is ready for you now."

"No, I'm actually just wondering about Lori-Lou. She's been in the car a long time."

"On the phone." We spoke in unison and then laughed.

"It's part of her anatomy," I added.

"Let's go back to the front of the store then," Brady said. "Maybe she's already come inside and is looking for us. But we'll have to finish the coffee first. No food or drinks in the store. Too dangerous."

"Oh, I'm sure." I did my best to take a few more sips of the

125

coffee, but it was still too hot for comfort. I ended up tossing what was left in the trash can by the door. Brady did the same. What a waste of good cups of coffee. Still, I understood his point about not having food or drinks around the dresses. I could only imagine the possibilities for disaster.

He led the way out of the workroom, glancing back at me as we made our way into the shop. "Hey, speaking of phone calls, I had one this morning from the *Texas Bride* reporter, Jordan Singer. He was just double-checking the date for the interview."

"July 15, right?"

Brady looked concerned. "Well, that's the photo shoot part. We need five weeks to pull the gown together. But the interview will come first. Didn't Mom mention that he's going to be here next Monday—June 15—to interview you?"

"Next Monday?" *Oy vey.* "No. Pretty sure I would've remembered that. I thought he would interview me at the photo shoot. And that brings up something very important I need to talk to you about. Do you mind if we speak privately, Brady?"

To my left, Madge cleared her throat. We looked at her, and she put her hand on her neck and mumbled something about having a cold. Then she flashed me a "don't you dare" look.

At that very moment, the front door of the shop flew open and Lori-Lou stumbled inside, baby in her arms and two squabbling kids at her side. The wind must've done a number on her hair. She looked a fright. Not that anyone could make out her face underneath the mass of windblown locks, in any case.

As soon as Crystal, Twiggy, and Dahlia saw her enter, they all gasped.

"Oh no!" Crystal put her hands over her eyes. "Anything but that!"

"What?" I asked.

126

"Incoming Mama Mia!" Twiggy whispered.

"Cleanup on aisle four!" Madge threw in. She reached into her pocket and came out with a walkie-talkie, which she raised to her lips.

"Mama Mia? What's that?" I tried to follow her gaze but only saw my cousin and the kids. "Code word for the mother of the bride?"

"No." Dahlia shook her head. "A testy mother of the bride is called a Mama Bear. Sometimes known as a Drama Mama if she's making the bride overemotional during the fitting."

"But . . . Mama Mia?" I asked.

"A bride with small children. In this case, three. And she's bringing them with her."

"Oh, that's no bride-to-be." I laughed. "That's my cousin Lori-Lou. You met her on Saturday, remember? She tried all morning to get a sitter but couldn't."

"That's Lori-Lou?" Dahlia seemed stumped by this. Well, until my cousin brushed the unruly hair out of her face and stopped hollering at Mariela.

"She might not be an incoming bride, but she's still a Mama Mia," Twiggy whispered. "You can't deny that she's a mama."

Crystal nodded. "Every time we get one of those, we feel like pulling our hair out by the time they're gone."

"Code pink and blue," Madge said into the walkie-talkie. "Code pink and blue."

Brady flew into gear, moving the mannequin wearing the $6,700 gown and other merchandise up out of reach. Madge went to the jewelry case and closed the glass panel on the front, then got on her walkie-talkie again and radioed the news to a teenage boy in the back of the store, who headed our way and started pulling the shoe rack up out of reach.

Lori-Lou didn't seem to notice any of this. She'd decided

to pacify her children with some M&Ms. Perfect. Just the solution in an ocean of white satin and crepe.

Twiggy sighed as she looked my way. "We get at least two of these a day. I adore kids—in theory, anyway—but they wreak havoc on the place."

"You wouldn't believe the thousands of dollars small children have cost us over the years." Madge shuddered. She shoved the walkie-talkie into her pocket.

I'd have to remember to tell Lori-Lou later. Right now she was busy giving Gilly a juice box. Grape. Lovely. I could see it now—all over the ivory silk gown directly to the child's right.

"What is it about mamas?" Madge asked. "So many are preoccupied."

"They don't pay attention to their little *dah*-lings." Crystal's Southern accent thickened. "So those precious children just run a-*mock*."

"That's amuck, Crystal," Dahlia said.

"Amock. Amuck. It's all the same thing. They *tay*-uh the place up and Mama Mia is ob-*liv*-ious. Then when she's gone, we all have to work double time to put the place back ta-*gay*-thuh."

"Remember the kid with the chocolate bar?" Twiggy visibly shivered. "I'll never forget that."

"Four hundred dollars just to get the stains out of that taffeta dress." Dahlia's eyes moistened. "I worked for weeks on that dress, only to see it covered in chocolate like a kid's T-shirt after a day at the circus. Horrible, horrible." A lone tear trickled down her left cheek.

"If Nadia sees the kids with the M&Ms, we'll have to call in a therapist," Twiggy said. "Someone needs to talk to Lori-Lou before any damage is done."

I raised my hand. "I'll do it. She's my cousin, after all." I'd just gathered the courage to say something to Lori-Lou when the door of the shop swung open and an older fellow, mostly bald, stepped inside. Tall and thin, he seemed especially out of place in a bridal gown shop. And judging from the expression in his eyes after he pulled off his sunglasses, he felt a little out of place too.

"Ugh." Madge slapped herself on the forehead. "Just when I thought it couldn't possibly get any worse, the devil himself has to show up."

"The devil?"

"Well, a distant cousin, anyway." Madge turned to the others, eyes wide as she said, "Alley-oop!"

Brady, who'd been hyper-focused on Lori-Lou and the messy kids, startled to attention. "Shoot." He raked his fingers through his hair and groaned. "Here we go again."

I watched as the older man took a few steps in our direction, his focus on Brady. Unfortunately, he didn't happen to see that Gilly had taken up residence on the floor directly in front of him. The poor guy tripped right over her. This led to blood-curdling screams from the toddler and a look of hatred from my cousin, who'd only seen enough of what had happened to think the man had deliberately hurt her child.

Gilly continued to wail, the older fellow groaned and grabbed his foot, and Lori-Lou carried on like a Mama Bear. Or would that be Drama Mama?

Then Mariela burst into tears. The baby started crying too, probably scared by all the noise.

I started to rush toward them, but Madge took hold of my arm. "Let it be, girl."

"But—"

"Let it be. That old guy's got it coming to him. A little time on the floor will do him good."

"Really? What did he do?"

"He won't leave our Brady alone, that's what. Tries to wear him down. Get him back in the game before it's time. He's a barracuda."

"Leave him alone? Huh?"

I watched as Brady helped the older man to his feet, then went over and comforted the children.

"I really wish that old fart would give our boy some space. Brady doesn't need to be rushing back onto the court, no matter how popular he is with the fans. He needs time to recover, physically and emotionally. The doctors agree, which is why they've placed him on medical leave."

"Is that . . ."

"Stan is Brady's agent. And he's all business, trust me. Never gives Brady a minute just to . . . be."

Stan now stood aright, but I could tell from the way he favored his foot that he'd been injured. Madge and Dahlia headed over to Lori-Lou and offered to take the kids in the workroom to have their snacks. With the wailing behind us, I was finally able to focus on Stan and Brady as an agent-player duo. The older man reminded me of a fellow back in Fairfield—Mr. Harkins, who worked at the bank. I couldn't help but stare at Stan's shiny bald head and his somewhat crooked nose. What really got me, though, was his voice. He might look scrawny, but he came across as authoritative and strong.

"See there, boy?" The fellow slung his arm over Brady's shoulder. "You're in fine shape. You came to my rescue, just like you've done a thousand times for the team."

"You were on the floor, Stan." Brady chuckled. "Taken down by a three-year-old."

"Two-year-old," I added as I took a few steps in their direction.

"Taken down by a two-year-old."

"Still, you're missing my point." Stan pulled a hankie out of his pocket and swiped it over his sweaty head. "Point is your knee must be healed or you couldn't have moved so fast. I'd say you're nearly ready to get back in the game."

"I'm in the game, Stan." He gestured to the shop.

The older fellow swiped his head again, then shoved the handkerchief in his pocket. "I refuse to believe you've traded in your Mavericks jersey for a wedding gown. Please tell me it ain't so."

"Well, when you put it like that, no. Of course not. But I'm where I'm supposed to be for now. I've tried to tell you that before." Brady gave him a pensive look and I suddenly felt like an intruder. I stepped aside and pretended to look at one of the wedding gowns.

"It takes time to heal." Brady spoke in a hoarse whisper.

"Well, sure, but remember, my boy, men who take their time come in second. You've never come in second. Besides, the fans are clamoring for you. You wouldn't believe the calls I'm getting. And the owner of the team wants to make sure you'll be back next season." Stan gave Brady an imploring look. "You are coming back, right? I mean, this wedding biz thing is just a temporary assignment while the knee heals. Right?"

"My mother's going to be in Paris for a year, Stan."

The older man paled. "But you're under contract."

"I know." Brady's face contorted. "But I'm also on medical leave."

I wanted to interfere at this point but knew better. How dare this old coot come in here and start shoving Brady around? Not that anyone could shove a six-foot-four fella around, but still . . .

"Look, Stan, I'd love to stand here and chat all day, but Katie here has an appointment with my mom soon." Brady nodded toward me, and I took a step in his direction.

"Katie?" Stan's gaze narrowed as he looked me over. "Great. Another distraction."

I had no idea what he meant by that but didn't comment.

"If you'll forgive me, I need to help a customer," Brady said.

I watched from a distance as Brady dealt with a bride whose temper had gotten the better of her. Someone had obviously taught the boy some serious negotiation skills on the court, and they transferred over nicely to the bridal shop. Stan muttered something about needing a cup of coffee and disappeared into the back room.

I turned my attention to the wedding veils while watching Brady in action out of the corner of my eye. A few minutes later, the bride left with a smile on her face and a discount on her dress.

Stan reappeared, coffee cup in hand, at the very moment Brady headed my way. "Sorry I can't stay and chat, Stan." Brady narrowed his gaze as he saw the open coffee cup. "But Mom's waiting and her time is limited. Excuse us." He pushed past his agent and gestured for me to join him. As we headed to the back of the store, I glanced one last time at the bald-headed man, who'd pulled out his hankie once again.

"What just happened out there?" I asked.

Brady shook his head. "Don't worry about it. It's mine to deal with."

"Hmm." The older guy clearly had him rattled, but I'd better not say anything else. For that matter, I'd better not come clean about my issues anytime soon. Looked like Brady James had enough on his plate for one day. Right now I'd be better off just following along behind him and keeping my mouth shut.

13

I Keep Forgetting
That I Forgot about You

The nice part about living in a small town is that when you don't know what you're doing, someone else does.

Immanuel Kant

My visit with Nadia went better than expected. I got so drawn into her design, so overwhelmed by her kindness and love toward me, that I totally forgot I wasn't getting married. We talked for nearly an hour and I gave her idea after idea, all of which she took to heart.

We went back and forth by email until Thursday morning, at which time she presented me with a rough draft of my gown, one that simply took my breath away. I could see myself—really see myself—walking down the aisle in that. Obviously she could see it too. After promising to email me the final design before passing it off to seamstresses, she hopped on a plane for Paris and left me in Dahlia's capable hands.

The following morning I headed home to spend time with the family. My parents' thirtieth anniversary party was scheduled for the next day, and I needed to be there for them.

Mama thought I was coming back for good. Pop likely did too. But I had to return to Dallas so I could figure out how to deal with the guy from *Texas Bride*. With a Monday morning interview scheduled, I had to think quickly.

I couldn't tell my parents that, however, so I prepped myself to tell them that I needed more time with Lori-Lou and the kids. I arrived in Fairfield on Friday evening just in time to have dinner at Sam's. I ate my fill of coconut cream pie and shared funny stories about my time in Dallas, excluding all of the parts about the bridal salon, of course.

I couldn't help but notice Jasper giving me odd looks. He managed to catch me alone at the dessert bar and leaned in close to whisper a very unexpected question. "What's this I hear about you hanging out with Brady James?"

"W-what?" I stared at him, completely stunned. "Who told you that?"

"Josh. Queenie emailed him to check up on you, and he said you and Lori-Lou were all gallivanting with a pro ball player."

"Oh no." I dropped my pie plate and Jasper caught it on the way down. "Does Mama know?"

"No way. Queenie only told me because she wanted to know who Brady James was," Jasper said. "I think she was hoping he was some sort of secret love interest."

"No way!" I shook my head. "I barely know the guy."

"Well, maybe you should take a minute to tell her how you came to spend time with him. Josh said it had something to do with wedding gowns? Didn't make a lick of sense to me." Jasper grabbed an extra slice of pie and headed back to the table.

I couldn't get past what he'd said. So Queenie knew I'd been at a bridal salon, and she knew about Brady? Why oh why had Josh told her all of that?

I made my way back to the table and did my best to make it through the meal. I could feel my grandmother's eyes on me and knew a conversation would follow. Sure enough, it came in the parking lot, after everyone else had left for the night.

"Something you want to tell me, Katie?" she asked. "About a certain fella you've been seen with in Dallas?"

"It's nothing like what you think, Queenie."

"You've been spending a lot of time in a bridal shop, Josh says. Is there a reason for that?" She gave me a pensive look. "Still holding out hope that Casey will change his mind?"

"No, it's not that at all." To be honest, I hadn't spent as much time thinking about Casey as she might've thought. All of the hustle and bustle of the past week had pretty much taken precedence. That, and a houseful of unruly toddlers.

My grandmother reached to take hold of my hand, and her eyes moistened. "Can I ask you a question, Katie, and answer me honestly."

"Sure, Queenie." *Oh. Help.*

She gave me a thoughtful look, her soft skin wrinkling in concern. "Do you think maybe you're not really in love with Casey?"

"W-what?"

She squeezed my hand. "I'm going to venture a guess that you've been so excited thinking about your wedding that you haven't really had adequate time to think about the groom. Is that why you're still shopping for wedding items, even though he's gone?"

"Queenie! Of course I've thought about the groom. I . . . I love Casey."

"You hesitated."

"No, I do. I've loved him since we were kids. Everyone knows it. Mama knows it. His mama knows it. You know it."

"But do you know it? I mean, do you really think you're in love with Casey, or are you just in love with the idea of a big wedding with all the trimmings? Is that why you won't give up on this idea?"

I clamped my lips shut before saying something I might regret. How dare she suggest such a thing? Sure, I wanted a big church wedding. And yes, I'd collected enough issues of *Texas Bride* to paper our house. But did that mean I didn't love Casey? Of course not.

"I'm just asking you to pray about it, honey." Queenie attempted to shift her weight, but her arthritis must've gotten the better of her. She almost tumbled right into me.

"I-I have. I've had plenty of time to pray. And to think."

"And?"

"And . . ." I sighed. "I have to confess, I've always wanted a big church wedding. That part is right. But I was in love with Casey."

"Was?"

"Am. I am."

"You hesitated again." She pulled me into her arms and planted a kiss in my hair. "Remember what I said that day at my house. Be methodical. Don't dive in headfirst. Take your time. God has big things for you, sweetheart. Maybe even bigger than you dreamed for yourself."

"Yes ma'am." I returned her hug, then thought about her words as I drove home. I pondered them as I climbed into my bed—ah, how wonderful to sleep in my own bed! And I even dreamed about weddings that night. Oddly, I didn't see Casey in my dream. He was nowhere to be found.

When I awoke Saturday morning, the whole Fisher clan was in an uproar, preparing for my parents' anniversary party at the church. I'd never seen Mama so frazzled. Or Pop, for that matter. He'd actually closed down the hardware store for the day. This probably wouldn't be a good time to tell them I planned to go back to Dallas for another week. I'd have to do that after the party.

We ran into a situation when we prepared to leave the house. "Katie Sue, there's something you need to know." Mama stood next to my car with a concerned look on her face. "The party has been moved to the Presbyterian church, which has raised all sorts of problems with Queenie."

"Wait. Why isn't it at our church?" I asked.

"There was a flood three days ago. Well, not technically a flood. A toilet overflowed in the women's restroom and leaked under the wall into the carpet of the fellowship hall. The whole place smells like a sewer."

"Ew."

"Yeah. We tried to get the Methodist church at the last minute, but they're doing a community outreach today and have over a hundred elementary school children on the premises."

"That might be a problem."

"Right. So obviously, that left us with the Charismatics and the Presbyterians." Mama's gaze narrowed. "I weighed my options. I really did. But in the end, I went with the Presbyterians."

"Mama, are you saying Queenie won't come to her own son's anniversary party just because of where it's located?"

"She'll come, if Bessie May has to drag her kicking and screaming. But she's not happy."

"But this isn't about her. It's about you and Pop."

"Right. Your father tried to tell her that, but would she listen?"

"I talked to Queenie last night. She never mentioned any of this."

"He didn't call her until this morning. If we'd given her time to think about it, she would've left town."

"I just don't understand her issues with the Presbyterians. It's the strangest thing."

I pondered this dilemma as we drove to the church. The fellowship hall at Fairfield Presbyterian was a lovely room, even larger than what we boasted at the Baptist church. And with the WOP-pers doing the decorating, the whole place was festive and bright, just perfect for an anniversary celebration. Still, 10:00 a.m. came and went and the guests arrived in droves, but no Queenie.

For whatever reason, the WOP-pers took it upon themselves to spend the first forty-three minutes of the party focused on my love life, or lack thereof. They somehow involved my mother in the conversation, which only made things more awkward.

The women gathered around me like chicks around a mother hen. Bessie May slipped her arm through mine and patted me like a small child. "Have you been enjoying your time in Dallas, sweet girl?"

"I have."

"Have you had a chance to visit with a certain handsome young man while there?" Bessie May giggled.

My heart lurched as an image of Brady James flitted through my mind. Had Queenie told my mother that I'd met the handsome ball player?

"We've been sending up prayer after prayer that the Lord

would send him a godly wife," an older woman named Ophelia said with a wink. "And it's occurred to us that perhaps you are it!"

"Wait . . . who?" I asked.

"Why, Levi Nash, of course." A faint humor lit Bessie May's eyes. "You haven't figured that out yet?"

"Levi Nash?" I shook my head, unable to process her words. "Are you serious?"

"I believe she is serious, Katie," Mama said. "The WOP-pers have been praying for Levi for quite some time, as you know. He's walking the straight and narrow now."

"And you all"—I gestured to the group of women—"believe Levi is the perfect fella for me?" When they nodded, I turned to face my mother. "Mama! I can't believe you of all people really think that. Levi and I have nothing in common."

"You both love the Lord."

"Well, yes, but if that's grounds for matrimony, then I could marry millions of single men across the continent."

"Ooh, that reminds me of a show I watched on television where a fella married seventeen wives." Bessie May fanned herself with her hand. "I can't believe he got away with that. I do believe he went to jail in the end, if that counts for anything."

"That wasn't my point, Bessie May," I said. "And I guess I should go ahead and say that I plan to go back to Dallas for the next week or so to spend more time with Lori-Lou."

"Poor thing." Ophelia patted me on the arm. "That Casey Lawson really did break your heart, didn't he?"

"That snake." Mama's eyes narrowed.

"That scoundrel." Bessie May shook her head.

"A wolf in sheep's clothing," Ophelia chimed in.

Before I could come to my almost-fiancé's defense, Mama clasped her hands together at her chest. "Well, forget about him, honey! I happen to know that Levi is back for the summer, serving as an intern at the church. Maybe you can connect with him while you're home. He's heading up the youth department now, you know."

"Interning?" I asked. Crazy to think that the guy who'd once wreaked havoc in the youth group was now heading up the whole thing, but whatever.

"Yes. And if you're in Dallas too long, you won't get to connect with him. Do you really have to go back?"

I thought about the interview with the reporter and made up my mind in a hurry. I'd have to go back, if for no other reason than to let Brady know the truth. In fact, I should probably call him today just to put him on alert so that the reporter wouldn't show up.

I didn't have time to say anything else, though, because Queenie arrived. Turned out she'd been in the parking lot for a good fifteen minutes, unwilling to come in the door. Go figure. Reverend Bradford, the Presbyterian pastor, greeted her with a smile, but she huffed right past him and went straight to the food table.

After filling her plate, she took a seat at a table on the perimeter of the room. I walked over and sat beside her, ready to get to the bottom of this.

"Okay, Queenie, enough already. What's your beef with the Presbyterians?"

"Hmm? What?" She glanced my way, the soft wrinkles in her brow deepening.

"You know what I mean. Whenever you talk about how the WOP-pers allow all denominations in their group, you always add the words 'even the Presbyterians,' as if they're somehow different from the rest."

Her cheeks blazed pink. "Do I? I didn't realize."

"Mm-hmm. And Mama said that you had every intention of coming to the party today until you found out it was going to be held here, at the Presbyterian church. Why should that make any difference?"

"Well, the Presbyterians are godly folks, just like all the rest. I suppose . . ."

"You have a problem with their doctrine?" I asked.

"Oh my goodness, no. Nothing like that. I don't claim to be a theologian. Denominational doctrines aren't my specialty. To be honest, I always get a little confused where all of that is concerned. If they're Jesus-lovin' people, well then, they're all right with me."

"Okay, then what is it? Why do you always hesitate when it comes to the Presbyterians?" I glanced up and noticed that Reverend Bradford was waving at us from across the room. I responded with a little wave, but my grandmother ignored him. "Don't you like Reverend Bradford?" I whispered. "Is that it?"

"L-like him?" Her face grew redder still and she reached for a napkin, which she used to fan her face. "Who said anything about liking or disliking Paul Bradford?"

Very. Odd.

"So you don't like him?" *And why did you call him by his first name?*

"I never said that either." She attempted to stand, but her arthritis kicked in. "I've been told he's a fine pastor. Just fine. I'm sure he's very good at what he does." She glanced up at him and her cheeks flamed again. "Whatever that is. Now, if you don't mind, I have more important things to do, please and thank you."

"Queenie . . ." I stood and helped her up but didn't release my hold on her arm. "There's something you're not saying. What is it?"

"I believe they need to adjust the thermostat in here," she said. "It's so hot I could fry an egg on this table. Don't these Presbyterians know anything about how to cool a building?"

"No, it's perfectly comfortable. Now, let's talk about Reverend Bradford. Why did you say—"

"You two are talking about Paul Bradford?" Bessie May sidled up next to us and gave Queenie a funny look. "I thought you gave up talking about him fifty-some-odd years ago, Queenie."

"W-what?" I looked at my grandmother, stunned. "Gave up on him?"

"You're a silly old fool, Bessie May." Queenie's eyes narrowed to slits. "And if you know what's good for you, you'll . . . Stop. It. Right. There."

"Just saying, it's not good to hold a grudge. Even against the Presbyterians." Bessie May leaned toward me and cupped her hand next to my ear. "It's not really the denomination as a whole, you see. It's just one very ornery fella who broke her heart back in the day."

A little gasp escaped as I turned to my grandmother. "Queenie?"

She put her hand up. "I forbid you to discuss this further. Let it go."

Bessie May giggled and then moved toward the food table. "Aptly put, my friend! Let it go. Let it go."

My grandmother released a groan. "Honestly! That woman is filled with enough hot air to fill the *Hindenburg* and is equally as dangerous. Maybe more so."

"But Queenie—"

"No." She glared at me. "This conversation has ended. You just forget you heard any of that, all right?"

I doubted I could ever forget it but offered a lame nod. I couldn't say which bothered me more—the fact that this conversation centered on a man other than my grandfather, God rest his soul, or the fact that my grandmother seemed to hold a grudge against an entire denomination because of one man. The idea of my grandmother having her heart broken by any fella really set my nerves on edge, but . . . a reverend? No one messed with Queenie Fisher, even a man of the cloth.

I scurried over to the food table to chat with my father, who was filling his plate. "Pop, I have a question."

"Sure, kiddo. What's up?"

I lowered my voice to a whisper. "What in the world happened between Queenie and Reverend Bradford?"

My father nearly dropped his plate. I had to reach out to help him steady his hand. "Who told you about Reverend Bradford?"

"Bessie May."

My father shook his head. "That's one story best left untold, Katie."

"But Pop—"

"Your grandfather was an amazing man. Best dad I could've asked for. I sincerely doubt Reverend Bradford"—my father spit out the words—"would've made my mama half as happy. So let's just let sleeping dogs lie, Katie."

Okay, I had no idea what dogs had to do with this. And all that stuff about making my grandmother happy? Maybe I was reading too much into this. Still, I couldn't seem to let go of the fact that my grandmother had some sort of secret from her past. And a broken heart to boot.

I decided to bypass my dad and go straight to the one person who could—and probably would—give me the gritty details. I found Bessie May at the dessert table, reaching for a slice of my parents' anniversary cake.

"Okay, Bessie May," I said. "Fess up. What happened between Queenie and Reverend Bradford?"

"E-excuse me?"

"I have to know the truth. It's not fair that I only have bits and pieces of the story."

The fork in her hand began to tremble. "Well now, Katie Sue, we're talking about a tangled web here. And I'm not sure I'm the right one to be telling this tale."

"You're exactly the right one. Please, Bessie May. I want to know."

She set her plate down on the edge of the table. "Did you ever see *Coal Miner's Daughter*, Katie?"

"Is this a trick question?"

"Alrighty then. Remember that scene where Doo cheated on Loretta?"

"Which time?"

"Good point." Bessie May paused. "Well, anyway, after one of the many times, Loretta went back to the tour bus and wrote that song, 'You Ain't Woman Enough to Take My Man.'"

"I remember it clearly."

"Loretta was angry. Very, very angry."

"Right." I stopped to think through what I'd just heard. "Are you saying that Reverend Bradford *cheated* on Queenie?"

Bessie May reached to clasp her plate with her left hand, but her right hand went straight up in the air. "I didn't say that. If anyone asks . . . I. Did. Not. Say. That." She lost her grip on the cake plate and down it went, straight to the floor.

I leaned over to pick it up, but Reverend Bradford came straight for me. Oh dear.

"I'll take care of that, Katie," he said with a smile. "You just help Bessie May get another plate, okay?"

"O-okay."

I went to work doing just that but leaned in to whisper to Bessie May, "When you say cheat . . ."

"I did not say cheat. You did."

"Okay, but when you say cheat, do you mean, like . . ." This time I almost dropped the plate.

"Heavens, no. He's a reverend. A man of the cloth. But his heart was all twisted up with two different gals at once. One of them, Queenie, pretty much climbed on the proverbial tour bus and wrote 'You Ain't Woman Enough to Take My Man' so the other gal would know to back off. But the other gal didn't back off." Bessie May glanced at Reverend Bradford as he drew near with a rag in one hand and a mop in the other. "You get my drift?"

I wanted to say yes but still felt confused. Very, very confused.

"The, um, man in question . . . married the other gal—er, girl?" I whispered as I glanced down at the good reverend, who now worked cleaning up Bessie May's mess.

"Nope." Bessie May grabbed me by the arm and pulled me over to a nearby table. "In the end, he didn't marry either of them." She chuckled. "Ain't life strange? Just when you think you've got everything figured out."

Right now I couldn't figure anything out. Mostly this conversation. One thing I did understand: Queenie's heart had been broken by Reverend Bradford years ago. And her broken heart had obviously never mended—thus her beef with the Presbyterians. Thank goodness Reverend Bradford wasn't Baptist. Queenie's bitterness might've changed our entire family's denominational leanings.

Still, it seemed really, really odd that my grandmother had all of these skeletons in her closet. She'd done a fine job of keeping her emotions to herself.

Or maybe she hadn't. I glanced across the room and watched

as she sat alone at her table, eyes fixed on Reverend Bradford as he worked. He glanced up and caught her gaze, then gave her a little wink.

Alrighty then. Maybe the skeletons in Queenie's closet had a little life left in them after all. And maybe, just maybe, I would get to watch them make their way out into the open.

14

Why Can't He Be You

I grew up in a small town where everyone wanted to be the same or look the same and was afraid to be different.

Kate Bosworth

I spent the rest of the weekend in Fairfield, then headed back to Lori-Lou's on Sunday night. I arrived just in time to learn that she and Josh had put an offer on a house.

"Oh, Katie, it's perfect." Lori-Lou clasped her hands together in obvious delight. "Very little money down because it's one of those . . ." She looked to Josh for help.

"Repo," he said. "The bank repossessed the house from the owners when they got behind on the mortgage."

"They're letting it go for a song. And the very best part?" She released a squeal. "The mortgage will actually be less than our rent here. And we'll have double the space. Isn't God good?"

"We haven't exactly been approved for the loan yet," Josh was quick to add. "And we'll have to count every penny to come up with the down payment. But I think we can make it." He gave her a kiss on the forehead and before long the two of them were smooching. Ugh.

I'd wanted to give Josh a piece of my mind for telling Queenie about my trip to Cosmopolitan Bridal, but he seemed so happy about the house possibilities that I decided I'd better wait. Besides, who could blame him for not standing up to Queenie? From what I'd been told, the only person who'd ever tried and succeeded was Aunt Alva, and none of us had seen her for years.

One particular conversation couldn't wait any longer. I had to let the people at the bridal shop know about my lack of wedding plans before the reporter arrived. Madge would be upset, but I had to risk that. I called Brady's direct line at the store but got his voicemail. Great. I'd have no choice but to wait until morning. Maybe I could catch him in time, before the reporter arrived.

Lori-Lou wasn't able to go with me Monday morning because she and Josh had an appointment with their Realtor, so I drove myself to Cosmopolitan. Pulling up in the '97 Cadillac was a wee bit embarrassing. Hopefully no one would see the old girl. She sputtered to a stop and I got out, straightened my twisted blouse, and then drew in a deep breath, ready to get this over with. I walked inside the store and found it strangely quiet.

Madge saw me right away and headed toward me. "Katie, I'm glad you're here. Dahlia has put together a pattern for your gown and wants to show it to you after your interview."

"Well, actually, about the interview . . ." I shook my head. "Don't you see, Madge? I can't go through with it. This whole thing has reached a ridiculous point."

"No it hasn't. You're overthinking it."

"I'm not overthinking it. I'm being realistic. If I don't tell

Brady, it could come back to hurt him and the shop, and ultimately his mom. I don't want to be responsible for that."

"I'm telling you, you're overthinking this. There's nothing in the contract about a wedding. And I'm begging you to let Nadia have her moment in the sun. Please don't ruin this for her."

My heart softened toward Madge as I noticed the tears in her eyes. "Why is her career so important to you, Madge?"

Madge swiped at her eyes with the back of her hand. "She's like a sister to me, a sister that I never had. We're as opposite as two people can be—kind of like you and Lori-Lou. But I'll go to my grave looking out for her."

"Don't you think—and this might just be a guess—that she can handle whatever fallout occurs if I tell her?"

"Probably. But I don't want anything to mess up her time in Paris. She's worked too hard for this. Let's just let it ride, shall we? You won the contest fair and square and you got the dress. It also won't change the fact that Nadia James is a woman of her word. She gave you what you won."

"Talking about Mom?" Brady's voice rang out from behind us. "Are you having some concerns about the design of the dress, Katie?"

"About the design?" I turned to face him. "No. Not at all."

"Good." A boyish smile lit his handsome face. "Because Jordan Singer will be here in half an hour. I'm glad you came when you did. I wanted to go over some of the interview questions with you before he arrives. Do you mind?"

I would've responded, but his gorgeous eyes and broad smile held me captive and I forgot what we were talking about. One thing was clear—for a guy who didn't want to be in the wedding gown biz, Brady James was starting to look at home at Cosmopolitan Bridal. Peaceful, even.

Well, peaceful until the door to the shop opened and his agent walked in.

"Roll out the red carpet, folks." The familiar bald-headed fellow took a deep bow at the waist. "It's Stan the Man, showing up for round sixty-three of his never-ending pep talk with his favorite player. Maybe this time I'll be able to pound some sense into that thick head of his."

"Oh, joy." Madge groaned. "Stan the Man. Just what I needed to make my morning complete."

"Hey, I heard that, Madge." Stan gave her a playful wink. "And I'll take it as a compliment, thank you very much. One of these days you're going to see that it's me and greet me with the respect I deserve."

"Or not," she said.

"Admit it, Madge-girl. You love this crusty old soul."

"You've got the crusty part right," Madge muttered under her breath. "And the old part too."

"I heard that. And I'd be willing to bet we're the same age, so guard what you say. If I don't show up to annoy Brady, he'll settle into his life here at the bridal whatchamacallit and end up pushing petticoats for a living. We can't have that."

"Stan, really? Petticoats?" Brady shook his head.

"Someone's gotta keep your career afloat, my boy. Anything I can do to convince you that you should get back to the business of playing ball."

"Well, maybe we can talk later. Katie and I need to go over the Q&A for her interview."

"Ah yes, the infamous Katie." Stan sighed as he looked at me standing next to Brady. "The distraction."

"Stop it, Stan." Brady gave him a "cut it out" look and I did my best to ignore him. "She's practically a married woman."

Oh boy. Now what?

"Well, that makes me feel a little better, as long as you're not the groom. Gotta keep you focused on my game, son."

"Katie's our contest winner. She's getting married . . ." He looked at me. "When did you say the wedding is going to take place?"

Before I could say, "Never," Stan groaned. "Marriage is an institution, I tell ya. And it's one I was happy to escape from."

"You need to get married and settle down, you old coot." Madge gave him the evil eye. "Finding a good wife would do you a world of good."

"I found a wife once. Lost her a couple years later in the shoe department at Macy's. She never turned up again. Last thing I heard, she was draining some other sucker's pocketbook dry. Good riddance, I say."

"Nothing like true love." Brady chuckled. He glanced at his watch. "I hate to interrupt this inspiring conversation, but Katie and I really need to—"

"Don't ever get married, son." Stan nudged him with his elbow. "You'll be in a lot better shape if you stay single and free, like me."

Brady's smile shifted to a more thoughtful look, and he seemed to forget all about the upcoming interview. "No, I want a wife and family someday. I've been praying for the right person to come along." He shrugged. "Just haven't found her yet. But she's out there."

"Well, stop looking," Stan said. "You're still young. Live your life. There's plenty of time to be tied down later."

Interesting. Stan's little speech reminded me of what Jasper had said that night at Sam's.

"Tied down?" Fine wrinkles appeared on Brady's forehead. "Huh?"

"Yeah, you know." Stan rolled his eyes. "The old ball and chain." He nudged Brady again and gave him a knowing look.

"Puh-leeze. How would you know?" Madge balled up her fists and planted them on her hips. "Doesn't sound like you were tied to your wife long enough to know anything about it."

"I've been a confirmed bachelor ever since she took off. Er, ever since I ditched her at Macy's. Nothing wrong with the free and easy life."

"Nothing except for years of heartache, loneliness, and pain." Madge grimaced. "But who am I to say?"

"Point is, I can do what I want when I want, and no one is any the wiser." Stan scowled at Madge.

She pursed her lips and crossed her arms. "Whatever you say, oh wise one."

"That's more like it. Now, don't you worry about me, and don't you dare put any ideas into this boy's head. I'm married to the game, and Brady here is too." Stan slapped Brady on the back, but I could tell that move didn't go over very well.

"Basketball makes for a lonely bedfellow in the long term." Madge wagged her finger in Stan's face. "You can't cuddle with a basketball, you know."

"I beg to differ." Stan chuckled. "I've done it many a time. Besides, a basketball doesn't argue with you or spend your money on expensive shoes. And doesn't keep you up nights talking about nonsensical things like hot flashes."

"My mama has hot flashes," I chimed in. "She takes special vitamins for them. They help a lot."

Stan looked at me. "Great news, kid. If I ever find my ex, I'll tell her."

Okay then. No more getting involved in this conversation.

"I'm not sure I'd agree that basketball is the be-all, end-all," Brady said. "It's just a game."

At that statement, you could've heard a pin drop. Stan turned almost in slow motion to face his favorite player. His eyes narrowed as the punctuated words, "What are you saying, Brady?" came out.

"Saying it's just a game. Like any other game. It plays itself out. As my mama would say, it's non-eternal."

"Are you saying there's no basketball in heaven?" Stan stood as stoic as a Greek statue. "'Cause if you are, I might just have to reconsider where I'm going when the final quarter is over."

"Good grief." Madge slapped herself on the forehead. "Of course there's no basketball in heaven. And no women in high-heeled shoes from Macy's."

"But there is a Clinique counter, right?" Dahlia popped out from behind the rack of gowns where she'd been working. "'Cause I can't imagine going for all eternity without my makeup."

"Not sure how we got from basketball to makeup," Stan said. "But that's the problem with women."

"What's the problem with women?" Madge glared at him.

"First they're spending your money on heels, next they're headed to the makeup counter. It's a never-ending financial dilemma."

"Enough, folks. Enough." Brady shook his head. "But going back to the earlier conversation, I do plan to get married someday. Looking forward to it. Now, if you don't mind, Katie and I really need to—"

"He just hasn't found the right girl yet," Madge interjected. "Some people get so distracted that they don't see what's right in front of them." Her words were directed at Brady, but I had the weirdest feeling she was also trying to get some sort of subliminal message through to Stan. Odd.

He didn't seem to notice. The old coot mumbled something

about basketball, and minutes later he and Brady were em-
broiled in a dispute over a recent game. Go figure.

"Men." Madge shook her head. "You can't live with 'em
and you can't live without 'em."

Stan paused from his conversation with Brady to look at
Madge. "Strange. That's what I've always said about women."

"And there you go." Dahlia went back to work straightening
the row of white gowns. "The battle between the sexes rages
on, and no one comes out a winner."

"Some folks must," I said. "I mean, this is a bridal shop.
You see plenty of brides come through here. People must be
getting married and settling down. So surely there are still
some people interested in marriage, right?"

Everyone in the room turned to stare at me, their silence
deafening.

Oh boy. Why did I have to go and say that?

"Well, duh, Katie." Dahlia gave me a perplexed look.
"You're one of them."

"Sure, sure." Stan patted me on the arm in fatherly fashion.
"You're about to enter a life of marital bliss. We all have a lot
to learn from you. Right?"

Yeah. Like how to ditch a would-be fiancé in a hurry. I could
certainly teach lessons on that.

"Katie's a great teacher," Madge said. "I've learned so much
from her already." She gave me a penetrating look, one meant
to shut me up.

"I'm sure you're going to be one of the lucky ones, Katie."
Dahlia sighed. "You're going to marry . . . what's his name
again? . . . and live happily ever after."

"Casey," Brady said. "Her fiancé is named Casey Lawson.
It's in the essay."

Dahlia's eyes took on a dreamy look. "Well, you and Casey

are going to have a blissful life in Fairfield and raise 2.5 children and live in a house with a white picket fence."

"I'd pay money to see the 2.5 children." Stan elbowed Madge.

Madge, God bless her, managed to turn the conversation around, and before long we were talking about basketball once again. She gave me a "whew!" look, but I could read the warning in her eyes. No point in upsetting the apple cart, as Mama would say. I didn't want to spoil things for Nadia, after all. And with the reporter from *Texas Bride* coming soon, I'd better mind my p's and q's. Looked like I couldn't get out of the interview, no matter how hard I tried. Not with all of these people surrounding me, anyway.

A couple of minutes later, Twiggy and Crystal entered the shop from the workroom. Crystal glanced up as an elderly woman came barreling through the front door, fussing and fuming about the weather.

"Incoming tornado," Dahlia whispered. "Brace yourselves for a storm, ladies."

I was bracing myself for a storm, all right, but not the kind she had in mind. My storm involved a hurricane of emotions that had whirled out of control when Brady mentioned Casey's name. I bit back the tears, but Brady must've noticed. His compassionate look calmed me down at once. He mouthed the words, "You okay?" and I nodded, forcing a smile.

"Let's get back to work, shall we?" Madge gestured to the woman at the front of the store. "Someone needs to greet our guest."

Twiggy and Crystal headed off to do just that. I brushed the tears from my eyes and, for the first time, could see the woman more clearly.

"Oh no."

I didn't mean to speak the words aloud, but what else could

I do? The woman who fussed and fumed as she crossed from the door to the shoe counter was none other than Aunt Alva, black sheep of the family. She hadn't yet noticed me, so I ducked behind a mannequin and tried to steady my breathing.

Madge gave me the oddest look. "Um, you okay back there?"

"Someone you know, kid?" Stan added.

I whispered, "It's my great-aunt Alva."

Brady smiled. "That's great, Katie. Do you think she'll stay long enough to add a few thoughts to the interview? She knows your fiancé, right?"

"Well, she knew Casey when he was a boy." I felt the tops of my ears grow hot. "But we haven't exactly . . . I mean, she doesn't know him these days."

Madge glared at me.

Brady leaned in close, his breath soft against my cheek as he whispered, "Are you telling me that your aunt doesn't know you're engaged?"

"Um, something like that. Remember, I told you and your mom that all of this is top-secret information."

"Well, you said your parents didn't know, that you planned to surprise them. It's the whole family? No one knows you're getting the gown?"

Another glare from Madge put my nerves on edge.

"Gonna surprise 'em, eh?" Stan laughed. "That's one way to tell the family. Land yourself on the cover of a national magazine wearing a Nadia James original and see their heads roll."

"Keeping it from the extended family complicates things, for sure." Brady released a slow breath. "Guess that means we can't include your aunt in the interview." He scratched his head. "Or even tell her about the dress?"

"I don't know if she knows about that. If Lori-Lou told her, I'm going to . . . going to . . ." I groaned. "It's complicated."

"Sounds like it. But why not tell them? Your parents will probably be thrilled to save the money, right? I mean, wedding gowns are expensive."

"Right. I'm just, well . . ."

"So you're scared?" Brady's brow wrinkled in obvious confusion. "Scared of your family's reaction to the dress? Or to the engagement? That's why you're keeping it all a secret?"

"I'm just terrified . . . period."

Boy, if that didn't sum it up, nothing did.

Brady shook his head. "I'm. So. Confused."

"Me too, and I don't even know any of these people." Stan shrugged and peeked out at my aunt. "Why are we hiding behind a mannequin again?"

Madge squinted her eyes. "Get over it, girl. You don't have to tell your aunt about the interview. Just make nice and maybe she'll go away. Then again, that's been my approach with old Stan the Man here, but he doesn't seem to be going anywhere."

"I heard that," Stan said.

The two of them headed off to the counter, bickering all the way.

Brady glanced at me. "Katie, I'm just trying to make sense of this. You don't have a wedding date. Your family doesn't know you've won the contest. And the interview is supposed to be a secret. Is there anything else I should know?"

"Yes, actually, there is."

I'd just opened my mouth to add, "My fiancé isn't even my fiancé," when something—er, some*one*—interrupted me.

Aunt Alva let out an unladylike whoop and then hollered, "Katie Sue Fisher! *There* you are! I had a feeling I just might find you here."

15

Girl That I Am Now

A city is more than a place in space, it is a drama in time.

Patrick Geddes

Nothing—and I do mean *nothing*—could've prepared me for running into my great-aunt at Cosmopolitan Bridal. I hadn't seen the woman in years, after all. Why here, of all places? And why now?

Surely Lori-Lou was behind this. Or Josh. Only, Josh didn't really know Alva, did he? And Lori-Lou hadn't spoken to her in years.

So. Odd.

I sucked in a deep breath and worked up the courage to "face this like a man," as Lori-Lou had said. Looked like I was doing a lot of that these days. Brady and Stan disappeared into the workroom, and I headed toward my aunt.

"Aunt Alva!" I tried to steady my voice. "What in the world brings you here?"

"Katie Sue Fisher, as I live and breathe!" She extended her arms, and a broad smile lit her chubby face. "That's a fine how-do-you-do when we haven't see one another in years. I'd say a handshake is in order if you're not the hugging sort."

"Oh, I'm definitely the hugging sort."

She swept me into her arms, which totally threw me. Queenie's description of Alva was a cold, mean woman, not one who grabbed near strangers and pulled them into bear hugs. I had a lot to process during the thirty seconds that her sagging bosoms held me in their grip. Nothing about this seemed remotely normal. Or expected. Or within the realm of possibility.

She finally released me, and I did my best not to let the relief show on my face as I took a giant step backwards.

"Now I'll answer your question, Katie Sue." My aunt brushed a loose hair off my cheek with her index finger, a gesture I knew well from Queenie. Weird. "You wanted to know how I came to find you here?"

"Yes ma'am."

"Can we sit down someplace so we can chat?"

Madge must've overheard that last part because she suggested the spacious fitting room, the one with the cozy padded bench in the center. A couple minutes later I found myself closed inside with my aunt, who eased her ample frame down onto the bench.

"There, that's more like it. Now, where were we?"

"You were telling me how you knew to look for me here," I said.

"Right, right. Well, it's the strangest thing. I got this new smartphone. Tried to figure it out looking through the contacts list, and I accidentally telephoned someone."

"Oh?"

"Lori-Lou. Haven't talked to her in years, but there she was on the other end of my phone. Now, don't be mad, Katie . . . I'm sure she didn't mean to let it slip, but she said something about you being in town. I was floored. Thought you'd stay rooted in Fairfield forever."

"Well, I haven't moved here, Aunt Alva. I'm just here for . . ." I released a sigh, unable—er, unwilling—to complete the sentence.

"I know why you're here. She told me all about that contest. So, you're engaged?"

Ack. "She told you I'm engaged?"

"Well, she let it slip that you were in town to be fitted for a wedding gown. What else could I deduce?"

"I see."

"She refused to tell me which bridal shop, but you know me . . ."

Actually, I don't.

"I'm not the sort to give up easily. I'm like a dog following a skunk down a hole. Or would that be up a tree? I'm not really sure where skunks go when they're running from dogs."

I cleared my throat.

"Anyway, I called every shop in town. When I tried this one, I talked to some woman named Twiggy—do you suppose that's her real name? When I told her I was family, she clued me in that you were being fitted for a gown here."

"I see." I'd have to remember to talk to Twiggy later. So much for keeping things a secret.

"I couldn't come right away, what with my knee giving me fits and all," Alva said. "But once I got past all that, I got in my car and came on up here to have a little chat with that

Twiggy gal and ask when you might be coming in next. Just happened in on a day you were here, which is just peachy." She clasped her hands together, a gleeful look on her face. "So tell me about this fella of yours. I vaguely remember hearing you were dating the Lawson boy."

"Oh?" How in the world could she have known that? Was Aunt Alva spying on us? "Casey's a great guy. He's really sweet." *When he isn't breaking my heart.*

"When's the wedding? I don't suppose I'll be invited, but it's good to know what's going on in the family anyway. Keeping up from a distance is a sure sight better than not keeping up at all, at least that's my philosophy."

"Well, I'm afraid you won't be the only one who doesn't get to go to the wedding, Aunt Alva." I took a seat on the bench next to her.

"Figured you wouldn't want me there." She let out a little humph.

"Oh, it's not that. Not at all."

My aunt gave me a pensive look. "Is it because he's Presbyterian?"

"W-what? How did you know that Casey is Presbyterian?"

"I have my sources. I still know folks in Fairfield, you know. Bessie May and I talk every now and again."

"You do?" But she was Queenie's best friend. How in the world . . . ?

"Is that why I can't come to the wedding?" Alva asked. "Because it's at the Presbyterian church?"

"No." I shook my head. "If there was going to be a wedding, it would be at our church."

"What do you mean, *if*? Are you saying there's no wedding at all?"

I lowered my voice, just in case anyone happened to be

standing on the other side of the door. "The whole thing is a giant fiasco, trust me."

"But you won a contest. That Twiggy girl said you're getting a free wedding dress. Isn't that right?"

"Well, yes. In theory."

"Here you are in the bridal shop. You must be here for a reason." She paused. "Do you mind if I ask why you're getting this gown made up if you don't plan on wearing it?"

"I'm going to wear it for the photo shoot one month from today, and then one day I'll wear it at my for-real wedding."

"Which isn't taking place at the Presbyterian church. But at least there is a for-real wedding, right?"

"Not really." I rose and paced the little room. "It's complicated. And why in the world is everyone so hung up on the Presbyterians?"

"Define *everyone*."

"You. Queenie." I hesitated. "Though I guess I've finally figured out why she is. But why you?"

"Humph. This conversation just took an interesting twist. And for the record, I've always had a special place in my heart for the Presbyterians, so if you do decide to get married, feel free to invite me if you have the service there."

Ironic. Alva would come, but Queenie wouldn't.

Not that I was getting married. I needed to make that very, very clear.

I sat down and reached for her hand. "Alva, I'm sorry to tell you the wedding is off." I sighed. "I'm not marrying Casey."

"You're not marrying him? For real?"

"For real."

"Do the folks back home know?"

"They know that Casey and I have parted ways. He moved away to Oklahoma."

"You poor thing. I understand what it's like to be alone. I truly do." Her eyes flooded with tears.

Interesting.

"But the big question is, do the folks back in Fairfield know you're here at this bridal shop, getting a wedding dress, even though you're not marrying the Lawson boy?" She crossed her arms.

"No. That part they don't know."

Crazy. I'd only been with my long-lost aunt five minutes and had already told her the very thing I hadn't yet been able to share with Brady.

Ironically, Brady rapped on the door of the fitting room at that very moment. "You ladies okay in there?"

I opened the door and saw him standing there with Stan at his side.

"Aunt Alva, this is—"

"Brady James." My aunt took one look at the ball player and almost hyperventilated. Her eyes practically bugged out of her head. "I-I-I know who he is."

"You're a basketball fan?" Stan stepped inside the fitting room.

"A fan?" She unzipped her sweater to reveal a Mavericks T-shirt underneath. "You never met such a fan! I would have season tickets if I could afford them. But at least I can watch the games on TV. Wouldn't miss a one!"

"See there, Brady?" Stan gave him a knowing look. "Told you the fans were clamoring for you."

"We're clamoring, all right." Alva's girlish giggle filled the room. "Come over here, young fella. I want to ask you a few questions about that game with the Spurs. Then we'll talk about your knee. But first, let me show you something I think you'll be very, very interested in."

Brady hesitantly stepped into the fitting room. The four of us fit easily in the large space, but it felt more like eight or twelve, what with all of the mirrors reflecting our images every which way.

My aunt rolled up the hem of her slacks, showing off mismatched trouser socks. She kept rolling until we saw a whiter-than-snow kneecap. "I've got a titanium knee myself." She patted it and laughed. "Got it six months ago."

"Really?" I said. "Weird. That's the very thing Queenie has."

A deafening silence rose up between us. Alva turned to face me. "If you don't mind, I would like to avoid that subject altogether."

"Titanium?" Brady asked.

"Knees?" Stan chimed in.

"Queenie." Alva glared at me. "Now, with that behind us, let's talk shop. That Spurs game was a complete fiasco, but I guess I'm not telling you anything you don't already know. So let's skip right on over to your injury. I want to know every detail about your surgery, Brady James. And most importantly, when will you be back on the court? I don't think I can last a season without you. My heart's not strong enough for that."

"Amen!" Stan said. "Preach it, woman."

She stood without rolling down her pants leg. Wagging a bony finger in Brady's face, she took to preaching, all right. "Things just won't be the same next season if you're not there to raise my blood pressure." Her cheeks flushed red. "Well, you know what I mean. With your plays." She shook her head. "Anyway, it won't be the same without you."

"Told you." Stan nudged him.

"The orthopedist did the best he could, under the circumstances," Brady said. "And the goal is to get me back on the court by the time the season kicks off." He must've caught his image in the mirror, because I saw him glance down at the reflection of his bad knee. "Honestly? It still bugs me . . . a lot. I feel like it could go right out from under me sometimes."

"A feeling I know well." She took a step, nearly losing her balance. Brady helped her take a seat once more, and she started rolling down her pants leg.

"I heard on the news that you were running some sort of shop. This is it?" She stopped fussing with her pants and stared at him. "My favorite player plays around with wedding gowns on the side? That's kind of . . . odd."

"My point exactly." Stan put his hand on Alva's shoulder. "Thank you for putting words to what I've been trying to say for weeks." He faced Brady. "See? Do you get it now? The fans are having a hard time and folks in the media are having a field day with your transition from the court to the . . ." He waved his arms around. "Fitting room."

"Can't say I blame 'em!" Alva laughed and slapped her titanium knee. "Ouch."

"They can't get over the fact that my boy Brady here is in the wedding gown business."

"So what?" I offered Brady what I hoped would look like an encouraging smile. "He's multifaceted."

"He's multifaceted, for sure." Madge appeared in the open doorway. She stepped inside the fitting room with the rest of us. "You should see him behind a sewing machine. The boy can whipstitch like nobody's business. And he's becoming quite the expert with veils."

Stan put his fingers in his ears. "Make it stop! I can't take it anymore. I've gotta get this boy back out on the court before he slips off to a place where he's irretrievable."

That got a laugh out of Madge. "Don't worry about him,

Stan. He's still got the love of the game in him. I think he dreams about basketball."

"Praise the Lord." Alva attempted to stand again. "Thought for a minute there I was going to lose my favorite player." She poked a finger in Brady's chest. "I've heard of fellas falling in love with girly things. Never dreamed you were one of those."

"Well, for pity's sake." Madge laughed. "It's not like that."

"No, it's nothing like that." Brady sat on the bench. Alone. Poor guy.

No doubt he missed basketball. With so many people hounding him, it had to be tougher still. Didn't anyone hear him say that the knee still gave him fits?

"I'd be heartbroken if you quit for good." Alva's downcast expression confirmed what she'd just said. "Please promise you won't."

Brady stood and flinched as his knee buckled. "I'm not quitting, I promise."

"Can I get that in writing?" Stan asked.

Brady groaned.

Alva's gaze narrowed. She looked back and forth between us. "I'm trying to get all of this straight in my head. Brady is here, in a dress shop, because of his knee." She turned to face me. "And you're here, in a dress shop, because you won a contest."

"That's right," Brady and I said in unison.

"Well now, I have a suspicion there's more to this story. Much more." Alva nudged me. "And the answer is staring me in the face. Well, technically, he's so tall he's staring at the top of my head." She looked back and forth between us. "I see now why everyone around here is being so secretive about everything and why it's all so hush-hush."

"Wait . . . secretive?" Brady looked confused.

"Of course." My aunt clasped her hands together and squealed. "It's so obvious when I see the two of you together. I've put the puzzle pieces together. Katie told me all about the fiasco with the fella from Fairfield."

"Fiasco?" Brady looked at me, wrinkles forming between his brows.

I felt the blood drain out of my face but couldn't muster up a word. Not a word.

"And now it's as plain as the nose on your handsome face. My sweet niece is really secretly engaged . . . to you!" Alva pointed at Brady. "Do I have it right? Is that why it's all so top secret?"

"W-what?" Stan paled and I thought he might have to be revived. He sat and put his head into his hands. "I knew it. I *knew* she was a distraction."

"W-wait, what? No!" Brady shook his head. "I'm so confused."

"I might just have to reconnect with the Fisher family if Brady James is a member." Alva's face lit into a smile. "Those ladies up at Curves are going to be green with envy once they hear that the Mavericks' point guard is my nephew by marriage." She giggled. "I can't wait to tell them."

Brady glanced my way, and I could read the panic in his expression. Still, to his credit, he said nothing else.

I felt panic rise up inside of me as well. "Aunt Alva, you can't tell them that!"

"Okay, okay, I won't rush to tell anyone right away. You two want your privacy. I get that." She poked her finger in Brady's chest again. "But you'd better take good care of this girl. I've known many a man who said he'd love and cherish a woman, only to drop her like a ball dribbling down the court. If I hear you've done anything to break Katie's heart, I'm coming after you faster than a long shot in the last two seconds of the game. You hear me?"

"I, um . . ." Brady looked at me, concern in his eyes. "I wouldn't deliberately hurt anyone. But honestly—"

"Good. Because I've known far too many women who were mortally wounded over a love spat." Her eyes clouded over, and she used the back of her hand to swipe at them. "Well, you two didn't come to talk about all of that, though I'm glad you've let me in on your little secret."

"Aunt Alva, we don't have any secrets. Honestly."

"Well then, it makes me feel very special that you've included me. It's been years since anyone in the Fisher family"—she spat the words—"felt the need to include me in anything."

An awkward pause followed, and I tried to gauge Brady's reaction. Oh boy, were we going to have a lot to talk about after this.

"I, um, think we'd better get out to the front of the store," Brady said. "I'm guessing Jordan Singer is here by now."

"Jordan Singer?" Alva's nose wrinkled. "Who's that?"

"He's the reporter for *Texas Bride*, and he's about to interview Katie, since she won the dress."

"The one she's going to wear when the two of you get married." My aunt giggled. "Oh, this is perfect. Absolutely perfect!"

Brady took off so fast it made my head spin. Stan turned and glared at me. If I hadn't been so dumbstruck, I would've hollered, "It's not true! None of this is true!" but I couldn't seem to get my brain and my tongue working in unison.

Madge stood in total silence, eyes wide as saucers.

Aunt Alva slipped her arm through mine, and we followed the men back into the store. She chatted all the way, going on and on about how wonderful it would be to have a pro basketball player in the family.

And Brady? Well, I could tell that he had located the reporter by the businesslike tone in his voice when he addressed the man standing near the counter. "Perfect timing, Jordan," Brady called out. "C'mon over and meet our bride, Katie Fisher."

"*Our* bride." Aunt Alva elbowed me. "*Our* bride. I get it now, Katie. I get it." She said something about how her life would be complete once I married the pro ball player, but I missed most of it. I pretty much missed the interaction between Brady and Jordan Singer too.

Right now, one thing and one thing only held me captive—the sight of my three brothers sauntering through the front door of Cosmopolitan Bridal.

16

Holding On to Nothin'

I think growing up in a small town, the kind of people I met in my small town, they still haunt me. I find myself writing about them over and over again.

Annie Baker

If someone had asked me, "Where's the last place on earth you'd ever imagine seeing your brothers?" I might've gone with "a high-end bridal shop in Dallas." I'd seen them in a variety of places over the years: on the ball field, chugging Mountain Dew in front of the Exxon station, swallowing down barbecue at Sam's, giving themselves brain freezes at Dairy Queen . . . but never, ever in an ocean of white taffeta and tulle. And certainly not surrounded by experts in the wedding business.

And yet, I couldn't deny the fact that Jasper, Dewey, and Beau stood at the front door of Cosmopolitan Bridal looking like small-town deer caught in the headlights of a big-city BMW.

"Ooh, incoming country boys." Crystal giggled.

"*Handsome* country boys," Twiggy echoed.

"What have we here?" Dahlia stared at my three brothers. "Not sure what we ever did to deserve these three, but I pray they're not grooms-to-be."

"They're not." I swallowed hard. "They're my brothers."

"Your brothers?" The ladies spoke the words in unison.

"Yep. My brothers."

"Well now." Alva rubbed her hands together. "Plot twist."

It was a plot twist, all right. I tried to envision Jasper, Dewey, and Beau through the eyes of the bridal shop staff. Three burly boys in jeans, plaid shirts, cowboy boots, and baseball caps. They looked as out of place as fish out of water.

Just when I thought the day couldn't possibly get any more interesting, Beau gave me a friendly wave and called out my name. "Yoo-hoo! Katie Sue!"

Dahlia looked at me, eyes wide. "You should've warned a girl."

"I had no clue they were coming."

"I just can't believe I'm looking at Jasper, Dewey, and Beau." Aunt Alva shook her head. "They look nothing like the little snot-nosed boys I remember. Last time I saw them was in a photograph your mama sent me years ago. They were hanging upside down from a tree in your side yard. I do believe one of them was hiding from your father because he was in trouble."

"Not much has changed then." I returned Beau's wave and tried to figure out what they were doing here.

"Well, I'll be." Alva chuckled. "I knew they'd be all grown up, but those fellas look like men, not boys."

"Oh, they're men, all right." Dahlia fussed with her hair as my brothers drew near.

I watched as the girls greeted my brothers and welcomed them to the shop. Dewey, known to our locals in Fairfield as a bit of a player, took one look at Dahlia and froze in place. Now here was a side to my middle brother that I'd never seen before. Player, yes. Womanizer, yes. Frozen in place by a gal he'd just met? Never. She greeted him with that thick Swedish accent of hers, and it appeared to hold him spellbound.

Behind Dewey, Jasper stood in a similar statuesque pose. I'd seen my oldest brother smitten before, but when he clapped eyes on Crystal, he couldn't seem to see straight. Or walk straight.

The one who surprised me most, however, was Beau. He might be twenty-two, but all of Mama's babying had pretty much kept him away from the dating scene. I'd secretly wondered if he would ever take any serious interest in the opposite sex. But unlike the older boys, he didn't seem frozen at all. In fact, his fluid movements in Twiggy's direction caught me completely off guard. And when he sidled up next to her with a twangy "How do you do?" the shock was apparently enough to de-ice Jasper and Dewey. They startled to attention and greeted the ladies.

I did my best to make proper introductions, but no one seemed to notice I was even there. Well, no one but Aunt Alva, who whispered, "Do the boys know you're engaged to Brady James?" in my left ear. I shook my head so hard that I almost gave myself whiplash.

I'd just started to respond when I noticed Brady still standing by the counter with the reporter. He signaled for me and Madge to join them. My brothers must've thought they were invited too. They looked at Brady and Jasper gasped.

"Doggone it, it's true!" Jasper took several steps toward the ball player. "You're Brady James."

"I am." Brady gave him a warm smile. "And you are . . . ?"

"My brother Jasper," I said.

"Oh, family." The reporter grabbed his tablet and turned it on. "It'll be great to have additional input for the article."

"Article?" Jasper looked perplexed by this. He turned his attention back to Brady. "See now, Josh said you were workin' at the bridal shop, but I didn't believe it. Had to see it for myself."

From behind the counter Stan let out a groan. "See, Brady? No one can believe it."

"Let me get my brothers in on this action." Jasper called for Dewey and Beau, who turned their attention from the girls long enough to acknowledge Brady. Before long all three of my brothers had engaged him in an intense conversation about that infamous game with the Spurs.

When Jasper stopped for a breath, I tapped his arm. "Are you saying you guys drove all the way to Dallas just to meet Brady?" I asked.

"I would've driven twice as far," Alva interjected. She stuck out her hand to Jasper. "Howdy, boy. I'm your aunt Alva."

"Aunt Alva?" My brother stopped in his tracks and looked her over. "Whoa."

"Whoa is right. Wouldn't have recognized you for anything," she said.

"That's strange, because I definitely would've recognized you. You look just like Queenie, so I'm pretty sure I would've figured it out in a hurry."

"Just like her," Dewey agreed.

"Spittin' image," Beau added.

"I'd appreciate it if you'd stop bringing up her name." Alva's expression soured. "But listen here, boys, your timing stinks.

Your sister here's got a big interview with this reporter." Her nose wrinkled. "'Course, I probably wasn't supposed to say that out loud, with everything top secret and all, but she's gonna talk to him about that wedding dress she's getting."

Jasper looked at me. "You're getting a wedding dress? But why? I thought you and Casey were . . ."

"Tsk, tsk. Don't go there." Alva gave me a wink. "It's all top secret." She laughed and slapped Jasper on the back. "Only, now you boys are in on it. And I don't mind saying I'm relieved I'm not the only one who knows. Having a ball player in the family is going to be the best thing that ever happened to any of us, don't you think?"

"Wait." Dewey pulled off his baseball hat. "Having a ball player in the family?"

Madge coughed. "There's been a huge misunderstanding. Fellas, let me offer you some homemade peanut butter cookies, baked by Crystal this very morning. They're in the workroom. Alva, why don't you come with us so you and the boys can catch up on old times?"

I cringed as my aunt left with my brothers. No telling what she'd say to them. I'd be dead in the water before this day ended. Jasper, Dewey, and Beau would tell my parents everything. And Queenie . . . I shuddered as I thought about how she would respond if she heard any of this.

"Katie? You ready for the interview?"

"Hmm?" I looked at the reporter.

"I'm assuming from what I've just overheard that your fiancé is a ball player?" Jordan asked. "Is that right? Casey plays ball?"

"Oh yes. Casey has always played ball." At least I didn't have to fabricate that. "Baseball. From the time he was a kid."

"Got it." Jordan looked around the shop as he shifted his tablet under his arm. "Well, let's find a place where I can interview you. Would you mind if Brady stayed with us? I have some questions about the shop's role in the contest, if you don't mind."

"I don't mind a bit." In fact, having Brady there felt strangely comforting. We would have a lot to talk about when this day ended, no doubt, but at least he kept silent for now. Still, he gave me the strangest look as we walked back to the studio. Poor guy. He probably wondered how—or why—he'd gotten stuck in the middle of my family drama. He was probably also wondering why my aunt assumed we were a couple. I couldn't figure that part out myself.

Right now I just wanted to run straight out the front door. Instead, I tagged along behind the guys, through the work-room, where I saw my brothers eating peanut butter cookies and flirting with the girls. I gave Aunt Alva a warning look as I passed through the room, and she waved in response and gave me another wink. I followed behind Brady and Jordan until we reached the studio, where I took a seat at Dahlia's work table.

I glanced down at the sketch of the Loretta Lynn dress and sighed. Off to my right I saw the fabrics for my gown, already cut, with the ruffles started. "Oh, look!" I grabbed one of the pieces and examined it. "Dahlia's been working."

"She's moving fast on this one," Brady said. "The photo shoot is just a month away."

"To the day," Jordan added. "July 15."

"It's going to be the prettiest dress ever." No sooner had I said the words than my eyes filled with tears. I didn't deserve a dress like this. And I certainly didn't need a dress like this, what with being single and all.

"I can tell you're emotional." Jordan reached for his camera. "Do you mind if I get a quick shot of you as you hold the fabric? And the sketch too? The passion in your eyes will translate better to the page if I can capture it on film first."

I didn't have time to say, "Please don't," before he started snapping pictures.

Afterward he took a seat and reached for his tablet. I did my best not to let my nerves get the best of me, but I couldn't stop thinking about Aunt Alva, couldn't stop wondering what she might be telling my brothers right about now.

"I have quite a few questions for you, Katie," Jordan said. "Do you mind if I record our conversation?"

When I shook my head, he pressed a button on his cell phone and set it on the table between us. Then he reached for his tablet once again and turned it on. "Okay, first question: what is it about the wedding dress that matters so much?"

"Oh, wow." I stared at the reporter and tried to put it into words. "It's so hard to explain, but it's a magical thing." My gaze shifted back over to the fabrics and ruffles near the sketch of my gown. "Kind of like Cinderella getting her ball gown from her fairy godmother. When you've got just the right dress, you believe that anything could—and will—happen. Happily ever afters. The perfect ceremony. Anything. Everything."

"It all comes down to a dress?"

"Not the dress specifically, but the feeling you get when you're in the right one."

Brady smiled. "My mom always says when a girl has the right dress, she's capable of just about anything."

"Well, I happen to be married to a dress designer myself," Jordan said. "Have you heard of Gabi Delgado Designs?"

I gasped as the realization hit. "Of course! You guys live in Galveston, right?"

"Right."

"She's done a lot of great gowns, but I especially loved the one for the bride who was having twins."

"Bride having twins?" Brady looked perplexed.

"Technically, she was already married." Jordan laughed. "Bella Neeley and her husband D.J. recently renewed their wedding vows, and Bella was almost eight months pregnant at the time. They're good friends of ours."

"Well, that dress was amazing. I'll never forget it." I gazed at Jordan. "If you're married to a dress designer, then you get it, right? The right dress is like . . . like . . ."

"Finding the right person?" he tried.

"Well, finding the right guy is a lot more important than finding the right dress." I swallowed hard at that statement. A wave of guilt slithered over me.

"Sorry to interrupt." Madge's voice sounded from the doorway. "Your aunt wants to know if you want to meet her for lunch when you're done. She and the boys are going to a Mexican restaurant around the corner."

"I have to get back to Lori-Lou's to watch the kids," I said. "She and Josh are getting a new house."

"Gotcha." Madge nodded and then looked at Jordan. "Just for the record, I heard that last question. I've met many a bride who'd found the right dress but had the wrong guy. Even the best dress in the world can't fix that."

"Some of them get married to Mr. Wrong anyway?" Jordan asked. "Just so they can wear the dream dress?"

Madge shrugged. "Just saying I've witnessed it firsthand. Once that dress is tucked away and preserved, the bride's still stuck with the wrong fella." She gave me a knowing look. "Nothing worse than that. Don't ask me how I know."

Some sort of subliminal message, maybe? Or did Madge have a story?

"Anyway, I'll tell your aunt that she and the boys should go on to lunch. Just hope the girls don't decide to take off with them." Madge turned away from us, muttering something under her breath, then added, "Gotta get back to the front of the store. Someone's gotta keep this place running while everyone else is busy flirting."

"Flirting?" Jordan looked back and forth between Brady and me.

"Just ignore her," Brady said. "Next question?"

"Well, let's get back to you, Katie." Jordan tapped the front of his tablet and it sprang to life again. "Tell me what you like most about the Loretta Lynn gown, then tell me how it makes you feel when you see yourself in the gown that Nadia made just for you."

"My favorite things about the gown? That's easy. It's not as fussy as some of the wedding dresses I've seen. I mean, if you think about Loretta Lynn, she comes from a simple background in Butcher Holler. I'm from a simple background in Fairfield. So having a fussy dress would've been too much. On the other hand, Loretta Lynn's style has always been ruffly and sweet. Look at the dresses she performed in during the eighties. Everyone wanted to look like her because she was so delicate and pretty. But in a nonthreatening way."

"A nonthreatening beauty?" He laughed. "You'll have to explain that one."

"Just saying she never had to try too hard. So many women— even brides—try too hard. They don't look like themselves on the wedding day. They're so overly made-up, so fussy, that people don't recognize them when they walk down the aisle. I want people to know me, to know that I'm the real deal. Genuine."

The moment those words were spoken, I had a revelation. I wanted people to know me. Me. Not the dress, but the girl inside the dress. Simple. Unpretentious. Genuine.

Only, I hadn't been very genuine, had I? I'd made this all

about the dress. The day. The event. Really, I needed to make it about me. And the groom.

Not that I had a groom, but if I did . . .

Jordan continued to pepper me with questions, but I couldn't get past what I'd said. Nothing about me had been genuine, at least not since my arrival in Dallas. And now look at the mess I'd caused—Aunt Alva thought I was marrying Brady, my brothers couldn't figure out why I was hanging out with a pro basketball player, Stan thought I was a distraction to Brady's career, and Mama and the WOP-pers were likely praying I'd come to my senses and marry Levi Nash and have a houseful of babies.

Eventually Jordan shifted gears to get Brady's input. I sat like a schoolgirl with a crush as I listened to the handsome basketball player answer each question with confidence and poise. This guy might not be a pro in the wedding world, but he certainly knew how to handle the press. I had the feeling he knew how to handle a great many things. And his obvious love of the Lord came through with every answer. I found myself completely drawn in as he spoke, hanging on every word, every syllable. When he glanced my way I felt my cheeks grow warm.

Careful, girl.

I cautioned my heart to steady itself. The idea that it had fluttered in the first place alarmed me a little. But who could resist someone with this sort of charm and grace? I had a feeling the WOP-pers would change the direction of their prayers if they could meet this guy face-to-face. In the meantime, I'd just sit here and listen to his heartfelt words and allow my heart to flutter all it liked.

17

You Lay So Easy on My Mind

If you don't like the road you're walking, start paving another one.

Dolly Parton

When I arrived back at Lori-Lou's condo, I found her awash in tears. The baby had screamed all afternoon due to teething pain, Gilly had overflowed the toilet in the hall bathroom by shoving dirty panties down it, and Mariela had colored on the kitchen wall with Lori-Lou's new craft markers.

My cousin was on her knees on the floor, scrubbing the wall, tears streaming down her face. "We'll never get our de-

Library name: DCPL
User ID: 50006477

Title: Every bride needs a groom : a novel
Author: Thompson, Janice A.
Date due: 6/2/2018,23:59

Title: Summer house : a novel
Author: Thayer, Nancy, 1943-
Date due: 6/2/2018,23:59

posit back now. We need that money to put down on the new house." She leaned her head against the wall and cried some more. "How are we ever going to make a fresh start if we can't move to a place with a lower payment?"

"I'm sorry, Mama!" Mariela started wailing too. After a while I felt like crying myself.

My cousin finally dried her eyes and looked up at me with a sigh. "I'm sorry, Katie. I know this isn't much fun for you."

"Don't worry about it. Please."

A strained smile turned up the edges of her mouth. "How did it go at the bridal shop? Did you have your interview?"

"I did. It went okay. Oh, and Aunt Alva was there. And my brothers."

"Aunt Alva?" Lori-Lou paled. "Oh, yikes."

I gave my cousin a pensive look. "Anything you want to tell me?"

She threw the rag into the sink. "Look, it wasn't my fault. She caught me at a vulnerable moment. One minute we were talking about her new phone, the next she was wheedling family information out of me." A sheepish look followed. "Will you forgive me?"

I couldn't help the feelings of emotion that escaped as I said, "I already have. But you're not going to believe what happened. For whatever reason, she thinks I'm engaged to Brady James."

"Engaged to Brady James?" Lori-Lou quirked a brow. "Now there's a thought."

"It was the biggest mix-up ever. But just for the record, it turns out Aunt Alva's pretty great. A lot like Queenie, actually. It's so sad that they don't speak because they'd have a lot to talk about. It's weird how much they have in common."

"Okay, but let's go back. Did you say your *brothers* turned up at the shop too?"

"Yes. And we can blame your husband for that. Josh is the one who told Jasper about Brady James, so he came to see for himself."

"To meet his favorite player."

"Turned out Brady wasn't the one who ended up captivating the boys," I said. "I think they're twitterpated."

"Twitterpated?" She took a seat at the breakfast table and reached for her coffee cup.

"Dahlia, Twiggy, and Crystal."

"Ooh. Wow, that was fast."

"No kidding. And get this—the last thing I heard, Aunt Alva took all six of them out to lunch at a Mexican restaurant. Weirdest thing ever."

"Going out to lunch sounds wonderful." Lori-Lou sighed. "Doing anything grown-up sounds wonderful. Shoot, I'd give my right eye just to go grocery shopping by myself." Her eyes flooded with tears.

"I'll make you a deal, Lori-Lou. Tomorrow morning I'll watch the kids and you can go to the grocery store alone. Take all the time you need."

"Seriously?"

"You bet. As long as you promise to buy some of those kiddy yogurt things I loved so much."

"You know those are for toddlers, right?"

"Who cares? I loved 'em."

This got a smile out of my cousin, one of the first I'd seen all day. We ended up having a great conversation after that, but it was interrupted by a phone call, this time on my cell. I glanced down and saw *Cosmopolitan Bridal* on the screen, so I answered it right away, thinking Dahlia must be calling about my dress. A male voice greeted me instead.

"Hey, Katie, this is Brady James."

For whatever reason, my heart skipped a beat when I heard his name. "Brady." I released a slow breath and tried to figure out what to say next. I needed to address what had happened today at the shop, after all. "Hey, listen, about what my aunt Alva said today . . . I hope you don't think I told her any of that? She's just . . . confused."

"Well, she's getting up there in years. It happens."

"True."

"I won't lie, it kind of threw me that she thought we were a couple, but my grandmother got like that in her golden years too. If she ever says it again, should I just play along? That's what people say you should do with folks who have memory loss. It stirs up trouble to argue with them."

"I don't really know what to tell you about that," I said. "To be honest, I don't know her well enough to speculate."

"Well, I'm calling with an idea. After you left today, Jordan and I went to lunch. He thinks you're really great, by the way, and he loved your answers to his questions about the dress."

"Aw, really?"

Out of the corner of my eye I caught a glimpse of Lori-Lou staring at me. Nosy poke! I turned away from her to focus on Brady.

"Yeah, and he suggested we go ahead and scope out a place for the photo shoot. Someplace that jives with the theme of the dress, so definitely country-western. I was just trying to put together some ideas for places when my mom called, asking how the interview went. She's been a little anxious, since she's so far away."

"Oh?" My heart quickened as soon as he started talking about her. Maybe Madge had told her the truth about me.

"I told her it went great and she was thrilled. But she loved the idea of settling on a place for the photo shoot. She suggested some practice shots."

"Do we really have to do that?" I asked. "I've never been very photogenic."

"Are you kidding me? That gorgeous hair? Those freckles? That great smile?" He cleared his throat. "Sorry. Anyway, I'm guessing you're very photogenic. Why are you so hard on yourself?"

"I . . ." I couldn't find the words to explain. If I told him about the rejection I was currently facing, he'd know everything. And if he knew everything . . . Hmm.

Maybe that would be a good thing. Maybe I'd be off the hook and wouldn't have to go through with the photo shoot after all.

"I was thinking of the stockyard," Brady said. "Ever been there?"

"Once, several years ago. They have a cattle drive?"

"Every day at eleven. My mother thought it might be fun to photograph you there, since your wedding is going to be country chic. That's the theme you said, right?"

"Well, it's what I like, sure. And it matches the Loretta Lynn dress."

"Perfect. What about your fiancé?"

I felt sick as Brady spoke those words. "What about my fiancé?" I asked.

"Doesn't he like the country chic thing?"

I sighed. "I kind of think Casey is burnt out on country living. He's more of a big-city kind of guy at the moment." *Tulsa, to be precise.*

"Oh, interesting. Well, the stockyard is perfect for both of you then. It's in Fort Worth, right in the heart of the city, but it's still got that country flair. Do you think maybe Casey would like to join us there? It would be great to meet him in person before he comes in for his tux fitting. And who knows? Maybe Jordan will want to get him in the cover shot. You never know."

"N-no." I shook my head. "He, um, he's actually out of the state on business right now."

"Oh, bummer. Well, I guess I'll have to meet him later on."

"Guess so."

"So, back to my original idea. What are you doing tomorrow?"

"Tomorrow?" I looked at Lori-Lou. "Sorry, but I just volunteered to watch the kids in the morning."

"Ah. I was hoping to steal you away to find the perfect spot."

"Steal me away?"

"He wants to steal you away?" Lori-Lou's eyes widened. "Ooh, this is getting good."

I shook my head and put my finger to my lips, hoping she would shush before Brady heard.

He didn't seem to notice. "If you're free in the afternoon, that works for me. I'd like to take you up to the stockyard to see if we can find some spots for the photo shoot. Would that be okay?"

Lori-Lou mouthed, "Is. He. Asking. You. Out?"

I shook my head and responded with, "Of course not!"

"Of course not?" Brady sounded dejected. "You don't want to go?"

"Oh, I wasn't talking to you, sorry." I narrowed my gaze at Lori-Lou as she tried to interject something else. "Maybe I can work it out."

"You can!" Lori-Lou reached for my phone and turned on the speaker button so she could listen in. "You totally can."

"I'd love to go with you, Brady." I pulled the phone out of my cousin's hand.

Lori-Lou let out a squeal. "I know! Let's all go! It sounds like the perfect way to spend the day."

"I'm sorry? Was that you?" Brady sounded confused.

"It's me, Lori-Lou," my cousin responded in a singsong voice. "I don't really need Katie to babysit. She was just being nice. I'd rather go with you guys to the stockyard. It's one of my favorite places."

"That's great," Brady said.

"The kids will love the stockyard. And I've got a great eye for photography. I'll help you two find the perfect spot, and I'll even snap the pictures."

"The kids?" Brady appeared to hesitate. "So, everyone's coming?"

"Sure! We'll make a day of it. And like I said, I'm great with the camera, so maybe we can do some practice shots. Maybe I can bring my wedding dress for Katie to wear. It'd swallow her alive, but oh well."

"No thank you." I shook my head. "Let's skip the dress."

"Whatever." Lori-Lou sounded hurt that I'd rejected her dress, but I couldn't picture myself showing up in public wearing someone else's gown.

"Brady, I'd love to go," I said. "And it sounds like we're bringing the whole crew. You okay with that?"

"Sure."

I couldn't tell if he was just being polite or really wanted Lori-Lou and the kids there, but we went ahead and set our plans in motion, agreeing to meet in the back parking lot— wherever that was—at 10:15 the next day.

I could hardly sleep that night as I thought about meeting up with Brady. Doing so would finally give me the perfect opportunity—away from Madge—to tell him that I couldn't go through with the photo shoot or take the dress. He would be disappointed, sure, but maybe he would understand my situation if I presented it carefully.

The following morning Lori-Lou awoke not feeling well.

On top of that, her car wouldn't start. I offered to drive, which meant we had to transfer car seats into my Cadillac. Mariela was particularly whiny and not thrilled with the idea of going to the stockyard. By the time we reached the parking lot, I realized why. The poor kid lost her cookies—er, breakfast—all over the backseat of my car. Minutes later, her mother joined her.

Just about the time Brady arrived, Lori-Lou had put in a call to Josh to come and take them all back home. She made profuse apologies to Brady. His response? Ever the gentleman, he offered to chauffeur them back to her place.

"No, you guys will miss the cattle drive." Lori-Lou leaned against my car, looking a little green around the gills. "We'll be fine."

"You sure?" he asked.

"Yeah. We always recover from these things quickly, trust me." She proved it by getting sick once more, right in front of us. Lovely.

Josh showed up about fifteen minutes later to cart his sick family home. Turned out he had the bug too. They left moments later, kids crying, Lori-Lou holding her stomach, and Josh looking like he needed to crawl under the covers.

This left Brady and me alone to clean out my car—ick!—and tour the stockyard without the others. I didn't mind that part one little bit. From the look of relief on his face, he didn't either. We started on the far end of the venue, near the parking lot. Just about the time we made it to the first row of shops, we realized the cattle drive was about to begin. People began to gather along the edge of the street to wait. A young man approached Brady and tapped him on the arm.

"Hey, you're Brady James!"

"The one and only." He flashed a welcoming smile.

"I've been praying for you, man. How's the knee?"

The two of them engaged in a conversation, which ended with the total stranger praying for Brady right then and there. Well, after he asked for Brady's autograph.

On and on the people came, each with a request to sign this or that. I couldn't help but admire Brady as I watched him in action with his fans, who approached him as if he were a long-lost friend.

Long-lost friend.

As I gazed up at Brady's kind face, as I took in the joy in his eyes while he talked to total strangers about his life, I realized I felt like I'd found that very thing . . . in him. And as he looked my way, offering a boyish smile, I had the feeling he'd found a friend in me too. Why that felt so good, I could not say. After all, I had lots of friends in the little town of Fairfield. But having one in the big city made me feel more at home than I would have dreamed possible.

In fact, I felt so at home that I might just have to stay for a while.

18

My Past Brought Me to You

You can be the moon and still be jealous of the stars.

Gary Allan

A familiar old-school country song blared from the overhead speakers as the crowd along Main Street thickened. Brady's fan club dissipated, likely overwhelmed by the noise and chaos. We were finally left to ourselves.

"You want to watch the cattle drive?" Brady asked. "I think you'll like it."

"Sounds like fun." We eased our way into a spot near the street. Unfortunately we landed right next to an overly romantic couple. They started out holding hands. A few minutes later they were smooching, right there in broad daylight. Awkward.

The crowd continued to press in around us, which pushed Brady a bit closer to me. I didn't mind. His yummy cologne tickled my nostrils. At least I thought it was his cologne. With people packed in like sardines, who could tell?

I glanced up at him to find that his gaze was already on me. He looked away, his cheeks turning red. Of course, that might have something to do with the heat.

"Brady, I wanted to apologize for yesterday. I know it was all so . . . chaotic. You guys probably aren't used to that kind of family drama at the shop."

"Oh, we see our share of drama, trust me. That was a little different, though. Your brothers seem pretty nice."

I couldn't help but snort at that one.

"Having your family around is a real blessing, Katie. But I'm not telling you anything you don't already know."

I looked up at him and smiled. "My brothers are a pain in the neck, but I adore them. Even Jasper. He's a challenge because he's always wanting to leave home."

"Leave Fairfield?"

"Yeah. It's hard on my parents to hear him talk like that."

"So they don't think anyone will ever want to leave?"

I shrugged. "Most people adore our town. They get so rooted that the idea of going anyplace else seems ludicrous. You know?"

"I've only ever lived in the big city, so I guess I can't really relate to that part. But life is an adventure."

It was an adventure, all right, especially if you happened to be a six-foot-four pro basketball player in a large crowd. Another round of folks wanting autographs showed up just then. Brady willingly obliged, and even answered a few too-personal-for-comfort questions about his knee. Man, did people get in his business, or what?

When the last of the autograph seekers turned away, I felt free to respond to what he'd said about life being an adventure. "My dad isn't all that adventurous," I explained. "He runs a hardware store. But what he lacks in adventure, he makes up for in loyalty."

"Loyalty to family is important." A thoughtful look settled into Brady's eyes. "If I ever understood that, it's now."

"True." I thought about my parents, my brothers, and Queenie. "But how will you ever know what you're truly called to do if you're only ever doing what family members tell you to do?"

I saw what could only be described as tenderness in his eyes as he responded, "I'm the only son my mom has. The only child at all. She needs me. And I'm going to be there for her, even if it hurts."

"Does it?" I asked. "Hurt, I mean."

"Wedding gowns aren't my first love," he said. "But they're growing on me." He gave me a little wink and my heart fluttered.

"Ha. Well, you're being more adventurous than you know because you've stepped outside of the box. Outside of your comfort zone."

"True, that."

"The problem with my family is that they never step outside of their comfort zone. My dad is as regular as a clock. And he doesn't seem to be able to function without me." I pulled out my phone to prove my point. "I've had three texts from him just since we got here, asking random questions about where things are in the store. Sometimes I wonder who's the parent and who's the child. He depends on me for so much."

"Yep. I get it. Trust me."

Brady and I both grew quiet. Not that anyone around us

would notice our silence. The music continued to blare, and at the end of the road I could see a flurry of activity.

A voice came over the loudspeaker announcing the start of the cattle drive. Seconds later, the whole atmosphere came alive with excitement as cowboys on horses led the cattle down the middle of Main Street.

"Just like something straight out of the Old West," Brady called out above the din of horses' hooves clip-clopping along the road and cows making that strange lowing noise.

I nodded, then turned my attention to the animals passing by. This would be the perfect place for a photo shoot. If I happened to be getting married. Which I wasn't. Still, I could see myself wearing the Loretta Lynn dress in this setting, with cowboys on horses in the background and longhorns lumbering by. Obviously Brady could see it too. A couple of different times he leaned over to give me ideas for how and where we could get some great shots.

When the cattle drive ended we walked through an area with quaint shops, including a large old-fashioned candy store. We stopped inside and I squealed when I saw the taffies. "Ooh, I have to buy some of these. I love them."

"Here, let me get them for you, Katie. I love 'em too. We can share."

I felt my cheeks grow warm as he grabbed a bag and handed it to me. "Fill 'er up, kid."

I did. In fact, I put so many taffies in the bag that he ended up handing me a second one. When we reached the register, the clerk engaged Brady in a lengthy conversation about basketball while he paid for the candy. As they gabbed . . . and gabbed . . . and gabbed . . . I nibbled on taffy. Okay, more than nibbled. I ate four pieces. Brady didn't seem to mind.

When he wrapped up the conversation with the store clerk,

Brady signed a couple more autographs for two little boys in the store, and then we walked back outside. He reached into the bag to grab a piece of taffy, unwrapped it, and popped it into his mouth.

I found myself mesmerized by him. "Okay, I just have one question, Brady James."

"Yeah?" He gave me a curious look. "What's that?"

"Are you always this nice?"

"Nice?" He gave me a funny look. "I'm just being myself."

A flood of emotions washed over me as I thought about how humble he was. "Well, don't ever stop. I mean it. You're a great guy, whether you're playing basketball or helping a girl find the perfect wedding dress."

"Right now I think I'd rather be helping the girl out than playing ball. Not sure my knee's ready just yet."

"Right." I sighed. "I feel for you. I really do. I wish your agent was more understanding. I know it's none of my business, but I wanted to give him a piece of my mind yesterday."

"Stan." Brady shook his head. "That guy wears me out, but I know he's got my best interest at heart. He's totally in my business, but then again, I pay him to be. That's what agents are for."

"I know what it's like to have people in your business, trust me. My family doesn't know the first thing about boundaries. Well, all but Aunt Alva. She puts the word *distant* in the phrase *distant relatives*."

"What do you mean?" He popped another piece of taffy in his mouth and gestured for me to sit on a nearby bench.

"I mean, until yesterday I hadn't seen the woman in years." I took a seat on the bench and he settled into the spot next to me. "Since I was a kid."

"Wow. Well, she's definitely something, isn't she?" He

grinned and tossed the taffy paper back into the bag. "I liked her, though."

"Me too. But I think she might be a little delusional. She's a big fan of yours, that's for sure."

"That's what makes her delusional?" Brady quirked a brow.

"No, silly." I jabbed him with my elbow. "I just think she's hoping you'll marry into the family so she can get season tickets to the games." I gave him a playful smile.

Goodness. Was this guy easy to flirt with, or what?

"Good to know I still have a few fans out there. But I guess the only way we can convince her I'm not your fiancé is to let her see you marry the real one. That ought to do the trick, right?"

"Right." Perfect opportunity to segue into the truth. "Since you brought up Casey, there's something I need to tell you about him."

"Oh, I already know. Madge told me."

"She—she did?"

"Yep. She told me that he's a ball player. Or at least he used to be. Baseball, right?" When I nodded, Brady lit into a lengthy story about how he'd played Little League as a kid. At some point along the way I got caught up in his story and gave up on trying to tell him the truth about Casey. On and on Brady went, talking about what it was like growing up with a dad who loved sports.

I wasn't sure how to broach the subject, but something he said made me curious, so I dared to ask. "What's your dad like now? Does he come to your games?"

"My dad . . ." Brady's words trailed off, and I could read the pain in his eyes. "He passed away when I was twelve. Killed in a car accident."

"Oh, Brady." My heart skipped a beat and I felt like a heel for bringing it up. "I'm so sorry. I had no idea."

"Please don't be sorry." He gave me a sympathetic look. "My memories of him are all good. He was a great dad. The kind of guy who laughed—in a good way—at everything. Positive, upbeat guy. And a dreamer too. Always reaching for the stars and telling me I could do the same."

"Sounds a lot like his son."

If I didn't know any better, I'd say Brady's eyes misted over as I spoke the words. "That's quite a compliment. Thank you."

"You're welcome." I grew silent for a couple of minutes as I pondered the depth of emotion I'd seen in his eyes. "Did your mom start her business while he was still alive?" I asked after a while.

"No." Brady shook his head. "She started about a year after he passed away. I think she did it to fill the time, but also to bring in income. Started with a couple of friends asking her to make their gowns, and it kind of went from there. Her big break came about ten years ago when a local designer saw one of her gowns and approached her about doing a show with him. Next thing you know she had her own line. Then she had a write-up in *Texas Bride*. Then Madge came to her and offered to help fund the shop."

"Whoa, whoa." I put my hand up. "Madge funded the shop?" No way. Simple, frumpy Madge?

"Yep." Brady chuckled. "You probably would never have guessed that, right? She doesn't come across as a woman with a lot of money. Not pretentious at all. But she's definitely the pocketbook behind the project."

"Wow."

"Trust me, the shop has done so well that Madge's investment has been paid back several times over. Both women have done very well for themselves."

"I'd say."

"And Mom has helped a lot of other people along the way. Dahlia was in a pretty low place when she came to us. Crystal too. Her parents had just passed away in a house fire, and she'd moved to Dallas to try to get past the pain. She had worked in retail but never a bridal shop, so hiring her was a bit of a stretch."

"Wow, Brady."

"Yeah, my mom has always known how to love people through hard times. It's a gift."

I paused to absorb everything I'd just learned. "I'm sure your dad would've been so proud of her."

Brady grew silent, and I could see his jaw tense as emotion took hold. "He was always the first to sing her praises. And I have no doubt he'd be crooning day and night if he could see all that she's accomplished."

"He'd be so proud of you too." I reached to put my hand on Brady's arm . . . his very, very muscular arm. "Was he a basketball fan?"

Brady's eyes took on a faraway look. "You have no idea. From the time I was a kid we shot hoops together. Every time I aim for that basket—whether I'm in front of a huge crowd or just on the court by myself—I picture him standing next to me, telling me I can do it." He grew silent. "Only, now I can't do it."

"Because of your knee?"

Brady nodded. "Yeah. I mean, the doctor says I can go back in time, but right now it just seems impossible."

"What would your dad say?"

He appeared to be thinking. "He would tell me to pray about it and then wait on God's timing. He'd remind me of the Scripture about how with God all things are possible."

"And that would be true," I said.

"Right. Point is, my dad was a great guy, and he would've been very proud of the fact that I've made a name for myself as a player." Brady's cheeks flushed and he quickly added, "A *basketball* player. Not a *player* player."

"Of course." I couldn't help the giggle that escaped.

Brady grew more serious. "But he would have been more proud that I've stepped in to help Mom here so that she can fulfill her dreams in Paris. He was so proud of her and wanted her to shine. I can't help but think he's smiling down on me as he watches me"—Brady shrugged—"get swallowed up by a world of taffeta and tulle."

"You're getting more and more comfortable in that world, and that's okay. Maybe he would want you to know that."

"Yep. I am feeling pretty comfortable." He slipped his arm across the back of the bench, and I fought the temptation to lean into him. Brady wasn't the only one who felt comfortable. Why I felt so at home around this guy, I couldn't say. He towered above me—my five-foot-two frame completely dwarfed by his six-foot-four one—but he always seemed to make me feel ten feet tall.

And right now, as we stuck our hands in the taffy bag at the exact same moment . . . as our fingers touched, sending tingles all the way down to my toes . . . ten feet tall felt just about right.

19

My Shoes Keep Walking Back to You

I'm a romantic, and we romantics are more sensitive to the way people feel. We love more, and we hurt more. When we're hurt, we hurt for a long time.

Freddy Fender

Our morning at the stockyard stretched across the lunch hour. Brady insisted on buying me lunch at a barbecue place that turned out to be almost as yummy as Sam's. The conversation went really well until the end of the meal when he brought up Casey.

Brady took a swig from his glass of tea and then leaned

back in his chair. "Tell me about your fiancé, Katie. Where did you meet him?"

"Is this for the article?" I asked. "Because if it is, I'd rather not."

"No, not for the article." He gazed at me from across the table, a pained expression on his face. "I'm not all business, you know."

"I-I know." I gave a deep sigh. "I'm sorry, Brady. I have a lot on my mind today."

"Like what? Stressing over the photo shoot?"

"Not really so much that."

"Your wedding?" Brady grabbed the bill, then pulled out his wallet.

"No, trust me. Not that."

"It's coming together like you'd hoped, then?" He gave me an inquisitive look as he placed a credit card with the bill.

I shook my head. "I'm not saying that either."

"Is there anything I can do to help?"

"You and your mom are doing a lot already. Too much, really."

"Never too much for you, Katie." As Brady spoke these words, he reached across the table as if he wanted to take hold of my hands. He stopped just before touching me. "I-I'm sorry."

"Sorry for what you've done for me?" I asked.

"No. Not at all." He pulled his hands back and passed the bill off to the waiter, who'd appeared at his side. "You've been really easy to do for. And I'm glad—really, really glad—that you're the one who won the contest. We wouldn't have gotten to know you any other way. So I'm grateful."

There was a genuineness in his voice that touched me to the core. For whatever reason, his kindness stirred up emotions in me that I hadn't felt before. In that moment, I knew what I had to do.

"Brady, there's something I need to tell you. It's really important."

"Of course. What is it, Katie?" I could read the concern in his eyes, which did little to squelch the gnawing in my gut.

"It's about my wedding."

He put his hand up. "I might work in a wedding shop, but I need to give a little disclaimer that I stink at wedding stuff. So if you're looking for my advice or my input, it's probably going to stink. I might just ruin your big day."

"Oh, trust me, you're not going to be the one to ruin my big day." I sighed. "It's too late anyway."

"Too late? What do you mean?"

The waiter returned with the check and Brady glanced at it, took his credit card, and signed the receipt.

"Brady, I just feel like I should tell you that—"

His cell phone rang, and he groaned as he glanced down at it. "I'm sorry, Katie. It's my mom. She knows we're out looking for the perfect site for photos, and I think she's anxious." He shrugged and answered the phone. Seconds later, the two were engaged in a lengthy conversation about various places at the stockyard that would be good for pictures.

A short time later Brady ended the call and then leaned my way. "I haven't been very good company, I'm afraid. And I guess that call doesn't really prove what I said earlier, that I'm not all business."

"It's okay," I said. "It really is."

We could talk later. Or not. Why I felt like baring my soul to this handsome basketball player, I could not say. I barely knew the guy. Still, he deserved to know the truth. Maybe if I could get him to understand my situation, he could help me figure out a plan to let his mother know before the photo shoot.

"I promise not to ruin the rest of the afternoon with business stuff. Where would you like to go next?"

"You're not ruining my day at all, Brady. I've really enjoyed being with you." And I had. More than I'd imagined. "And I know the perfect place we can go. My country girl roots are about to be exposed."

"Oh?" He rose.

"Yep. It's the perfect place." I stood and faced him. "The petting zoo."

"The petting zoo?" He chuckled. "Now, that's a first."

"Do you mind? I'd love to."

"Don't mind a bit."

His leisurely manner continued as we walked down Main Street toward the pen where the animals were kept. At the entrance we bought some feed for the goats and then went inside the covered area.

"We're the only adults in here." Brady laughed as he looked around. "That's a telling sign, don't you think?"

"Maybe, but it doesn't matter. I love animals. I miss them." I knelt down in front of the first cage and dumped some of the feed into my palm, then passed it off to a baby goat.

"Whatever you say." Brady followed my lead and tried to do the same, but a goat snatched the feed cup straight out of his hand.

"Ha. Looks like you're not as fast in the pen as you are on the court."

"Hey now."

"I'm serious. When you hang out with animals, you've got to think quick."

"Obviously." Brady stuck his hand inside my cup and grabbed some feed, then passed it off to a baby goat, which licked his hand clean. "See there? I'm a fast learner."

"You're good with animals." And people. No one could deny this guy was great with people.

I knelt down for some time, the weirdest emotions rippling over me as I tended to the goats. I was struck by feelings I hadn't experienced for a while—homesickness, and heartsickness too. A lump rose in my throat.

"Casey has goats," I whispered.

"Casey?" Brady tried to dump more of my feed into his hand but missed. It landed in a clump on a goat's nose. "Oh yeah. The fiancé."

I sighed. "The fiancé. Only . . . not."

"Not? He doesn't really have goats, you mean?"

"Oh, he has goats. Four of them." Tears sprang to my eyes. "I miss them."

"The goats or the fiancé?" Brady set the feed cup down on a post and stared at me.

"All of them." Being around these animals had stirred up far too many emotions. When I shut my eyes I could see myself standing on Casey's property. Running in the field. Playing hide-and-seek as kids. The scents, the noises of the animals in the background. All of it melded together in my memory, in my heart. And in that moment, though I could never have predicted it, tears flooded willy-nilly down my face.

"Let's get you out of here." Brady's voice startled me back to reality. "I think the scent of the goats is getting to you." He helped me stand and then slipped my arm through his to walk me out of the petting zoo, back to Main Street. I didn't say a word the whole time. I couldn't, not with all of the sniffling going on. We finally came to a stop at a lamppost near the parking lot. Brady reached into his pocket and came out with a handkerchief, which I used to blow my nose.

"I don't know what happened back there, Katie," he said.

"But we're not coming back to the stockyard for the photo shoot. This place is obviously too emotional for you."

"I'm sorry. I really am. I just don't think I can do it, Brady."

"The photo shoot, you mean?"

"No. Well, yes. The whole thing. All of it. The dress, the photo shoot, the—" I stopped myself before saying anything else. "I tried to tell Madge, but she wouldn't listen. This isn't what you think it is. I'm not who you think I am."

He stared into my eyes with the sweetest, kindest expression on his face. "I know exactly who you are. You're Katie. From Fairfield." A little wink followed as he added, "Enamored by goats."

"Right. But the rest of it . . . it's not what you think."

"Katie, I've had the strangest feeling all along that you don't like the wedding dress design. Is that it?"

"Oh, I totally love the design. It's not that at all."

"You're not happy with the way the interview went yesterday?"

"The interview was a farce."

"A farce?" He shook his head. "Explain."

"It was a farce. I'm a farce. The wedding . . . is a farce. And the fiancé?" I pinched my eyes shut. "He's the biggest farce of all."

"Wait. Are you telling me that you're not really engaged to Casey Lawson?"

My nerves really kicked in now. I shook my head. "I . . . I'm not engaged to Casey Lawson."

"He broke your heart?" Brady's jaw twitched. "If he did, I'll hunt him down and—"

"It's not like that." I paced the sidewalk. "I mean, he did break my heart, but not today. It was a couple weeks ago. Before I ever met you."

"Huh?" Brady's confusion was evident by the expression on his face. "What are you saying?"

"I'm saying that he broke up with me right after I found out I'd won the dress. The engagement was off—really, it didn't even exist at all. I was never going to marry Casey."

Brady scratched his head. "Of course you were going to marry him."

I put my hand up. "Let me rephrase that. In my imagination I had the whole thing planned out. The entire wedding was strategized from beginning to end. I could tell you anything you wanted to know about my big day, but I couldn't tell you anything about what my life would be like after that. I planned for one thing and one thing only . . . and it didn't happen."

"It's really not going to happen? Is that what you're saying? No wedding?" Brady's expression shifted from concern to frustration. "Please tell me this is some kind of sick joke so that I don't think you were just taking advantage of my mom."

"I never wanted to take advantage of her . . . or you. And I do hope to get married someday." I glanced at his face. The clenched jaw clued me in that he was angry. Who could blame him? "I'd love to wear the dress your mom designed for me. But it's not going to happen anytime soon. Casey . . ." The tears came in earnest now. "Casey took off for Oklahoma."

"Oklahoma?" Wrinkles formed between Brady's brows.

"Where the wind comes sweepin' down the plain." I gave a deep sigh. "And I'm just plain stuck being a wannabe bride with an MIA groom." My voice began to quiver again. "Only, I didn't know he was going to be MIA. I was sure Casey was the one. So sure that I made plans as if he'd already popped the question."

"Wait. You're saying he never did?" Brady raked his fingers through his hair.

"Not technically. But don't you see? The point is, I was so busy planning for my fairy-tale wedding that I overlooked my very real life." Tears came with abandon now as I felt the release of my words. "I'm an idiot. I wanted the wedding. I wanted it so bad that I entered the contest thinking it was inevitable. Only, it wasn't. And . . . he wasn't. And . . . we weren't. Nothing was inevitable except the part where I came out looking and feeling like a fool. I wanted the dress. I wanted the church. I wanted the invitations."

"Wanted it so much that you didn't mind putting my mom on the spot?" A flash of anger sparked in his eyes.

"Trust me, I never wanted to hurt her. I came that first Saturday just to tell her I couldn't go through with it. But something—someone—stopped me."

"Someone?" He gave me a knowing look. "Let me guess. Madge?"

"Yeah."

"So, no wedding and no groom . . . but she still wanted you to take the dress?"

"You've got the picture. She didn't want to get your mom worked up before leaving for Paris. She thought it would be better to let sleeping dogs lie."

"Do you mind if I ask what you planned to do with this dress if you weren't going to wear it?"

"I don't know." I squeezed my eyes shut and willed myself not to cry. "Sometimes I think the whole wedding thing was just a big fantasy, something I dreamed about but was never meant to have."

"You wanted the wedding, or you wanted the groom?"

A lump rose in my throat and I tried to speak around it. "I wanted him too."

"Wanted . . . as in past tense?" For whatever reason, the

hopeful look in Brady's eyes gave me the courage to speak my mind.

"Wanted. Past tense." I paused. "Casey is a great guy. He would've looked great in the tux. And he would've been smashing in the wedding pictures. And if you want the truth, I'm sure he would've made a great dad to our kids, even if he is a Presbyterian."

"Wait. What does being Presbyterian have to do with anything?"

"I have no idea, really, but it factors in. Ask Queenie."

"Well, if I ever meet her, I will."

"Point is, he wasn't the right guy for me. The wedding was never supposed to happen. It's so obvious now. I had to come all the way to Dallas to see what I couldn't see in Fairfield. I was just blinded by . . ."

"The idea?"

I sighed. "Too many years reading bridal magazines."

"Don't let Jordan Singer hear you say that!" Brady rested his hand on my shoulder and smiled.

"Jordan Singer." I hesitated. "The photo shoot. I-I can't do it. You see what I mean? How can I go on the cover of a bridal magazine wearing a dress that was never meant for me?"

Brady didn't respond for a moment. Instead, he started pacing. And pacing. And pacing some more. His expression shifted several times—from confusion to frustration to resignation. Finally he came to a stop in front of me, a more peaceful look on his face.

"Okay, it's clear we've got some things to figure out. But maybe Madge was right. Maybe you should still take the dress." Brady shrugged. "Just because the fiancé wasn't the perfect fit doesn't mean the dress won't be. And just because the wedding isn't pending doesn't mean you're not going to someday be a beautiful bride. I say you put on the wedding dress, hold your head up high, and march into that photo shoot with a smile."

"You sound just like Madge."

"Well, for once I agree with her."

"You do?"

"I do. So what if the timing isn't right? Take the dress anyway. It's yours. We want you to have it. I want you to have it."

"You've been too good to me, Brady. You've gone above and beyond." I tried to swallow the ever-growing lump in my throat. "This has nothing to do with Cosmopolitan Bridal. Or your mom. Or you." I put my hand on his arm. "You've all been nothing but wonderful. But I can't take this dress, Brady. I can't."

"You can and you will. Jordan is coming back with a photographer on July 15. Dahlia's working like crazy on the dress to meet that deadline. Don't let her work be in vain, okay? You're going to put on that dress and look like a million bucks."

"But that's the point. I might look like a million bucks in a dress that I don't deserve, but I'll feel like a loser. If Casey saw me standing there, dressed in that gorgeous Loretta Lynn gown, he'd—"

"He'd feel like an idiot for letting you go."

Brady's words threw me for a loop. They also gave me the first bit of encouragement I'd felt in quite some time.

"You think?" I whispered.

"No, Katie." Brady grabbed my hand and gave it a comforting squeeze. "I don't think. I *know*."

20

*M*iss Being Mrs.

As a remedy to life in society I would suggest the big city.
Nowadays, it is the only desert within our means.

Albert Camus

Two weeks after our trip to the stockyard, I learned that Dahlia had made enough progress on the dress for me to come in for my first official fitting. When I tried to argue the point with Brady, he reminded me that I'd won the contest fair and square and had every right to try on the dress because it was meant for me. So I showed up on the last Tuesday in June to take a peek at the Loretta Lynn gown in its earliest stage of production.

Dahlia brought it to the front of the store, where she placed it on a hanger for all to see. She hadn't added any of the ruffles or embellishments yet, but from what I could see, it was shaping up to be the prettiest gown in the place. Exactly my taste. Was it really meant for me? My heart said yes, but my conscience debated the issue.

"You want to try it on for me, Katie?" Dahlia asked. "It's going to look great on you."

Before I had a chance to respond, however, Dahlia was distracted with a customer. "Ooh, incoming Barbie Bride," she whispered.

"Barbie Bride?" I glanced up at the front of the store and saw a gorgeous brunette entering. She looked like a runway model. By now I should be used to all of these labels that Dahlia and the others placed on their customers, but I was not.

"Check out the hair, the makeup." Dahlia whistled. "She's practically perfect in every way."

"Practically perfect in every way is Mary Poppins, not Barbie," I argued.

"Well, physically perfect. You know the type I'm talking about." She gestured to her chest. "Curvaceous. Buxom."

"Buxom?" Crystal giggled. "Is that a *re*-ul word?"

"Of course it's real." Twiggy rolled her eyes. "Don't you see any buxom women in Atlanta?"

"Duh." Crystal pointed to her own chest and we all laughed. She headed off to wait on the new customer, who'd come into the shop for a tiara. Ironic.

"I'm sure you see a lot of Barbie doll types come through the bridal shop," I said after she left.

"Maybe not as many as you think," Madge said. "Mostly we just get normal-shaped girls. With hips. And bellies. And saggy boobs. But you know the interesting part? Put those girls in a wedding gown and they look perfect."

"Speaking of perfect, let's get you in that gown, Katie. Okay?" Dahlia clasped her hands together and grinned. "I can't wait to see it. And we have to take pictures to send Nadia. She called this morning and gave me specific instructions on the angles of the photos. She wants to see my seam work. Do you mind?"

"As long as no one else sees the pictures, I guess it would be okay." I would flip out if anyone from home saw me in the gown.

The thought had no sooner flitted through my mind than the front door of the shop opened and who should walk in but my brother Jasper. Again. He took one look at Crystal, who was working at the front counter, and headed her way. I stood transfixed, watching all of this take place. He clearly hadn't noticed me or, if he had, was ignoring me.

"There's one of those handsome brothers of yours," Dahlia said. "Come back for another visit, I see."

"Looks like it. Give me a minute, Dahlia. I want to talk to him before I try on the dress, okay?"

"Sure."

I walked up to the counter and stood next to Jasper. He continued to gab with Crystal but didn't seem to notice me. I cleared my throat. Nothing. I coughed. When Crystal headed off to tend to a customer, he finally looked my way.

"Hey, Katie. What are you doing here?"

"I could ask you the same thing. Jasper, you do realize this is a bridal shop, right? A place where women come to buy their wedding dresses?"

"Well, yeah. I can see that." He glanced around with a horrified look on his face. "Promise you won't tell Mama I was here?"

"Only if you make the same promise."

"Trust me, mum's the word."

Mum—er, Mom—was the word, all right.

"And if you happen to see me in a wedding gown, you won't ask any questions?"

"Wedding gown? Are you getting married? To Casey?" My brother's expression hardened.

"I didn't say that."

"Then what Alva said is true? About you and Brady being engaged?" He leaned against the counter.

"Definitely not. He's a great guy, but I'm just getting to know him."

"Then I'm confused. You're going to wear a wedding dress?"

"Yes. I'm going to be modeling it for a magazine cover."

"Oh, okay. Why didn't you say so? They're paying you to model gowns now?"

"Um, no. But close." I decided to change the subject. "Isn't Pop missing you at the store?"

"Told him I was coming into Dallas to pick up some supplies. Nothing unusual about that. I come to Dallas all the time to get supplies for the business. You know that."

"Well, yes, but—"

"Beau is holding down the fort until I get back."

"Beau?" I laughed. "Beau? Working?"

Jasper nodded. "I know, it's hard to believe. But something's grabbed ahold of him over the past several days. He's a changed man. I've never seen him act so . . . responsible."

"Um, Jasper?" I pointed to the door, where Beau and Dewey stood side by side. "Looks like you might want to rephrase all of that."

"No way." Jasper slapped himself on the forehead. "He promised he'd cover for me at the store. Pop's gonna flip."

I took a few steps toward my brothers but didn't get to

them fast enough. Twiggy beat me. She offered to show Beau the latest order of tuxedos, fresh in from Paris. Like Beau gave a rip about tuxedos. Still, my youngest brother trotted off behind her.

Jasper had been right about one thing—something had definitely grabbed ahold of Beau. Her name was Twiggy.

And Dewey? He'd come to Dallas for one reason and one reason only . . . and she happened to be standing next to me. I watched as Dahlia's face turned the prettiest shade of crimson when Dewey talked to her. Good grief. I needed to get this train back on track, and quick.

"Dewey, I hate to be the bearer of bad news, but Dahlia and I have to take care of something in the back."

"You do?" Dewey looked perplexed by this. "Like what?"

"Oh, don't worry about us," Dahlia said. "You just look around the shop and I'll be back out in a few minutes. Don't go anywhere, okay?"

"Oh, I won't." Dewey gave her a little wink and she giggled.

We had just turned to walk back to the studio when the door to the shop opened again. Dahlia stopped in her tracks, eyes widening in obvious terror.

"What is it?" I asked.

"Sybil. Incoming." Madge's voice sounded from behind us. She reached for her walkie-talkie and whispered the words again: "Sybil. Incoming."

"Sybil?" I asked. "Her name's Sybil?"

"Um, no." Madge shook her head. "Her name's Francine Dubois. But she's definitely a Sybil."

"I don't get it."

Dahlia pulled me behind a rack of gowns, her voice lowering to a hoarse whisper. "Did you ever see the old movie *Sybil*? The one about the girl with all of those personalities?"

"Don't think so."

"You never knew what she was going to do. She was . . . c-c-crazy." Dahlia could barely get the word out.

"Crazy as a loon," Madge added. "The crazy ones are harder than all the Drama Mamas and Princess Brides put together. They . . . well, you'll see."

"Not sure I want to stick around to see," I said.

"Too late." Dahlia turned me around to face the door. A fairly normal-looking woman stood near the entrance of the store. She pulled off her dark sunglasses to reveal finely plucked brows and heavily painted eyes. Crystal headed her way, offering assistance.

I shrugged. "Seems okay to me."

"Just. Wait," Dahlia whispered as she gestured for me to move out from behind the rack. "Give it ten minutes."

Fortunately—or unfortunately—it didn't take ten minutes. Judging from the minute hand on my watch, it took exactly four. Miss Sweet as Sugar flipped out on Crystal at the four-minute mark, completely changing personalities. At the five-minute mark, she began to weep uncontrollably. At the seven-minute mark, she'd dried her tears and was inviting all of us to her ceremony. At the nine-minute mark, she threatened Madge with a lawsuit.

"Oh. My. Goodness." I wanted to run for the door, afraid of what might come next.

Fortunately, Madge appeared to have a special anointing for dealing with the Sybil bride. She not only managed to talk the emotional nightmare down from the ledge but also gave her a discount on a pair of shoes. But the one who really seemed to know how to handle her best, ironically, was Brady. He somehow got her redirected when she lost it, and had her smiling by the time she left the store.

Wow.

When the Sybil incident ended, Dahlia and I were finally free to head back to the fitting room. Even as she helped me into the Loretta Lynn gown—what there was of it so far, anyway—I could tell that Dahlia would rather be out in the store, visiting with Dewey. Thankfully, my oohs and aahs must've brought her back to reality.

"You like?" she asked.

"Mm-hmm." I stared at my reflection in the mirror. Even without the embellishments—the lace, the crystals, the ruffles—the gown looked amazing. Dahlia still had a bit of work to do to get the bust to fit, but she assured me that would not be an issue. She reached for her phone and snapped several photos of me in the gown, which she planned to send to Nadia right away.

I gave a little twirl and examined myself in the mirror. The length of the train was just perfect—not too short, not too long. I could see myself walking down the aisle in this dress. Someday. If I ever found a groom.

Stop it, Katie. Just smile and say thank you. That's what Madge would want.

So I smiled. And said thank you.

Dahlia looked as if she was about to respond when Madge showed up at the fitting room door. "I hate to bother you, but we have an incoming 9-1-1."

"Oh dear." Dahlia looked my way, her eyes wide. "Do you mind, Katie?"

"Well, no, but what in the world—"

Dahlia took off in a hurry, with no explanation whatsoever.

"9-1-1?" I turned to Madge. "Are you calling for an ambulance?"

"Oh, no, honey. That's not what I meant at all. A 9-1-1 is an overly emotional bride. In this case it's a sweet girl whose father passed away just a couple of months ago. He won't be there to walk her down the aisle, so the dress fitting is going to be an emotional roller coaster for the bride and her mother. Dahlia knows just how to handle it, trust me. She's been through this dozens of times. One of the services we provide is counseling. It's not on the résumé, but we do it."

"Wow, Madge." Tears sprang to my eyes as I thought about that poor bride and her situation.

"People think the wedding gown biz is all glitz and glam, but they don't see the hard parts." Madge took a seat on the cushioned bench. "We're half counselor, half wedding gown expert, half BFF."

"That's three halves," I said.

"Yep. Which is why it takes so many of us working together to accomplish anything. But you know what? I'm grateful for open doors."

"Open doors?"

"Sure." Her eyes filled with tears. "I never married. Never had kids to pour myself into. When these brides come in, the Lord opens a door for conversation, and sometimes—if I'm not feeling like a sourpuss—he uses me to offer a bit of encouragement."

"Oh, Madge." I slipped my arm over her shoulder. "You're a softie inside of that hard shell, aren't you?"

"Shh." She put her finger to her lips. "Don't give away my secret. Around here, folks think I'm a drill sergeant."

"One with the sweetest disposition in town." Brady's voice sounded from the hallway outside the open fitting room door.

"Better get back to work, boss." She rose and saluted him. Brady pulled her into an embrace and planted a kiss on her forehead.

"I should be the one saluting you, you know. You've got that drill sergeant act down pat."

"It's just an illusion, my boy. Just an illusion."

She headed to the front of the store, which left me alone with Brady. It felt a little odd to be standing here in a wedding gown now that the other ladies had ditched me. I couldn't even figure out how to get out of the crazy thing without their help. Not that I wanted to. I felt like a princess, and all the more when I saw the admiring look in Brady's eyes.

"You look amazing, Katie. Gorgeous."

His flattery tickled my ears and made me feel a little giddy. Just as quickly, I felt like a traitor. I pictured myself standing in Casey Lawson's kitchen as he broke up with me. The emotions of that moment flooded over me even now, and I felt the sting of tears in my eyes.

"You okay, Katie?" Brady's voice shook me out of my reverie.

"I . . . I think I'm just emotional. Hearing about that 9-1-1 bride really got to me. You guys are a lot more than a bridal shop, Brady."

"Agreed." He nodded.

"I think Madge opened my eyes. This is a ministry for all of you. It's a place to reach out to people who are going through stuff."

"That's my prayer every single day, that God will bring exactly the right people here so that we can bless them. Most of the time they end up blessing us too. Like you, Katie."

"Me?"

"Sure. Everyone has loved having you here, and you've definitely brought out the softer side of Madge." He gave me a knowing look. "Maybe you should be in the wedding business."

"You think?"

"I do!" Madge's voice sounded from outside the door. "You'd be great at it, Katie."

"See what I mean?" Brady chuckled. "Underneath that

crusty exterior is a marshmallow." He leaned so close that the scent of his yummy aftershave caused my nostrils to flare. "But don't get her worked up or you'll see a completely different side of her."

"Oh, trust me, I've seen that side too. She's a tough cookie. But she reminds me of Queenie. The image she puts out there is one tough mama. On the inside, though, she's like a flower, unfolding one petal at a time."

"Madge? A flower?" Twiggy entered the room, all giggles and smiles. "That's a good one, Katie."

"Hey, I heard that." Madge popped her head in the door. "And just so you're aware, folks, I come in this place every morning smelling like a rose. A tea rose, I mean. It's my perfume." She stepped inside the room and started fussing with the laces on the back of my dress.

"How do you guys do it?" I asked.

"Do what?" Madge, Twiggy, and Brady said in unison.

"The people part. Working in the wedding business isn't just about dresses, is it?"

"It's about people," Brady said.

"And there are people of every sort who come through that door," Madge added.

"True," Twiggy said. "There's the Dollar Store Bride—that's the one who doesn't have the money but really wants the dress."

"And the Ninja Bride—ready to take out anyone in her way," Madge chimed in.

"The Flighty Bride," Twiggy continued. "She can't make up her mind about anything."

"The Dieting Bride." Madge groaned. "She's the one who really wears a size 14 but insists she'll be a 10 by the time the wedding arrives, so she refuses to order a dress in the proper size."

"And then there's the Not-Quite-a-Bride Bride." Twiggy sighed. "Those are the worst."

"Not-Quite-a-Bride Bride?" I asked.

"Yes. It's always the same. They come into the shop looking for a dress, but when we press them for a wedding date, they fumble around."

My heart jolted.

Twiggy giggled. "Can you imagine? Shopping for a wedding dress with no groom? These girls are so desperate to get married that they show up alone—or with a friend, even—to try on gowns that they hope they'll one day wear. If they find the right guy. I feel a little sorry for them, really."

The compassionate look Madge gave me drew Twiggy's attention my way.

"Huh?" Twiggy gave me a curious look.

I glanced at my reflection in the mirror and suddenly felt ill.

"Katie?" Twiggy looked concerned. "Are you okay?"

I shook my head. "I . . . I think I should've eaten some breakfast. I'm just a little woozy."

"She needs some air." Madge began to fan me using one of the store's brochures.

"Maybe Dahlia tied the laces too tight," Twiggy said. "You've got such a tiny waist. I'm sure she just wanted to emphasize it."

"Don't." I put my hand up. "Don't emphasize anything."

"O-okay." She stepped toward me and loosened the laces. "Sorry about that."

"No, you've done nothing to be sorry about. It's all me. Every bit of it." I couldn't stop the sudden rush of tears.

Brady took one look at me and ushered the other ladies out of the room. Once we were alone, he turned my way. "Katie? What's happening?"

I stared at my reflection in the mirror. With Brady standing next to me, we looked like a wedding cake topper. The image was more than I could bear.

"I have to get out of here. I. Need. To. Get. Out. Of. This. Dress."

"I thought we agreed you were going to keep it. Don't you like it?"

"Yes." I turned to him, feeling heartsick. "I love it. That's the problem. I love the dress. I love this store. I love these people. I love everything. But it's not right, Brady."

"Not the right fit?" he tried.

I shook my head. This guy just didn't get it, did he? "The only thing that's not a good fit here is me. I don't belong here. This isn't the right time. Or place. Or situation. You know that. I told you—Casey's gone. The wedding isn't happening. And the last thing I want to do is hurt your mom when she finds out."

"Then let's tell her." He shrugged. "Let's go ahead and get it over with. She'll probably take a day or so to get over it, but she'll figure out a plan that we can all live with. And then you can relax and just enjoy the dress."

"You think she'll want me to keep it if she knows the truth?"

"I do." He smiled. "That dress was meant for you. I believe it with everything that's in me. And if you don't take it, nothing will be the same. Don't you see that?"

Yes. The dress was meant for me. And it fit beautifully. Only, I didn't deserve it. Right now I just wanted to get out of it, put back on my jeans and T-shirt, and run from this place once and for all.

21

I Don't Wanna Play House

I love my small town, and I love going back there and support-
ing the community. But I could not have stayed there. No way.

Jeremy Renner

I somehow managed to stay put in the fitting room but
couldn't seem to control my emotions. I could read the
concern in Brady's eyes and felt compelled to say something. Anything.

"I'm the Not-Quite-a-Bride Bride. That's what Twiggy
called me."

Brady shook his head. "No. Technically she didn't call you

that. Not you personally, anyway. But I might need to talk to the girls about using code names like that. I don't suppose it's very flattering."

"Tell them I've come up with a new one for girls like me." I yanked off my veil and handed it to him. "The Phony Baloney Bride."

"Phony baloney?" He gently laid the veil on the bench. "There's nothing phony about you, Katie. In fact, you're more real than most of the girls I've known put together. You look like the real deal in this gown, and you will be, in God's timing. That's all I've been trying to say. The dress was meant for you, no matter when you wear it."

I sighed. "I'll pray about that, Brady. I will. If you think I should do the photo shoot, I'll do it for you. And for your mom. And Madge. And all of the wonderful people I've met here in the city."

An awkward silence followed after I said the word *city*. In spite of what Mama had told me that night at Sam's, I hadn't seen one snake since I moved here. Weird.

"So . . . question." My hands began to tremble as I worked up the courage to broach the subject on my heart. "Have you told your mom yet? About my situation, I mean."

He shook his head. "I started to, but Madge reminded me this is fashion week in Paris. I'm going to give it a day or two and then give her a call."

"Ah."

"Don't fret, Katie. It's going to be fine. I know my mother better than anyone. She's going to agree that you should keep the dress, so stop worrying. Promise?"

"I guess. You don't think she'll be mad?"

"No. All that matters to her is a lovely young woman on the cover of *Texas Bride* wearing her gown."

"Lovely?" I didn't mean to say the word aloud, but there it was.

"Yep." Brady smiled. "I don't mean to sound biased, but I see a lot of brides come through this place, and you're going to be the most beautiful one yet. Not just on the outside either."

"O-oh?" His compliment caught me off guard.

"You're always thinking of others. That's a beautiful trait, Katie. We don't see as much of that here as you might think. Most brides are pretty self-focused. Sorry to be so blunt, but they are. You're not like them . . . and I like that." He grinned. "Anyway, I'm going to get out of here and let you get changed."

"Yeah, I need to go soon anyway. Aunt Alva is expecting me for dinner tonight."

"Are your brothers going too?"

"No. They have to get back to Fairfield. Pop is waiting on them at the store, I'm sure."

"Well, have fun. Tell Aunt Alva I said hello."

"I will. And by the way, I plan to tell her that we're not really engaged, so you're off the hook. You don't have to marry me after all."

"Well, that's a relief." He gave me a playful wink. "Might be awkward, marrying someone I just met."

"I know, right?" My heart fluttered a bit as I took in his whimsical smile.

With Dahlia's help, I spent the next several minutes getting back into my jeans and T-shirt. I said my goodbyes to my brothers, who seemed sad to leave. I thanked Dahlia for her work on my dress and then waved goodbye to my new friends—even Stan, who'd just arrived for his daily pep talk with Brady. I walked out of the store to the parking lot, deep in thought about the day.

When I climbed inside my car and tried to start it, nothing happened. I tried again. Nothing. I rested my head against the steering wheel and ushered up a prayer for mercy. My day had been hard enough already. Still, the car didn't start. As much as I hated to go back inside, I had no choice.

Brady met me at the front of the store and I explained my predicament.

"I don't mind giving it a look," he said.

"Betcha he can figure it out," Madge added. "He's always loved stuff like that. From the time he was a boy."

"Tinkering with things makes me happy." Brady shrugged. "What can I say?"

"Say you'll get back to the business of tinkering with a basketball." Stan raked his hand over his bald head. "Did I really just use the word *tinker*?"

"You did." Madge laughed. "And I'd pay money to hear you say it again."

"Tinker." Stan busted out with a belly laugh, and before long we were all laughing. It felt really good, especially after the emotions from earlier.

Brady followed me outside to my car, making small talk all the way. I found his conversation comforting. It felt good to know I had someone to call on, what with my brothers being gone and all, and Brady didn't look as if he minded a bit. In fact, if one could gauge from the expression on his face, he wasn't upset at all.

"Pop the hood for me, Katie."

Brady opened it and then spent the next ten minutes oohing and aahing over a variety of meaningless things underneath. I stood next to him and listened as he carried on, but couldn't make sense of half of it.

"Looks like you've got a loose belt here." He pointed down at it. "And these hoses are shot. In this heat you'll need to make sure you replace them. They're cracked."

"I have a cracked hose?"

"More than one. Can't believe this old thing is still running."

"It's not at the moment. Remember?"

"Right. I'm also guessing your battery's dead. How many miles did you say this car has on it?"

"Two hundred and fourteen thousand. But trust me, it comes from a long line of people who keep going even when they should give up."

Brady gave me a curious look at that one.

"So, I guess I need a new battery." I sighed. "And some hoses. Where do I find all of that?"

"Do you have AAA?"

I shook my head.

Brady glanced over as a customer pulled into the spot next to my car. "Well, let's start with the battery. That's the most critical thing right now. I'll take it out and we'll go to the store and get another one, then I'll put the new one in for you. Madge won't mind keeping an eye on things. We'll be closing soon anyway."

"You would do all of that for me?" I could hardly believe it.

"Well, of course."

"Do you think it will take long? I'm supposed to be at Aunt Alva's house in less than an hour."

"Can you call her?"

I nodded and fumbled around for my phone. Less than a minute later her voicemail kicked in. "Weird. Maybe she didn't hear the phone ringing?" I left a message and then ended the call and pressed the phone back in my purse.

"Hmm." Brady appeared to be thinking. "Well, here's another idea. We'll just load up your stuff in my truck and I'll take you over there. Then I'll come back here and take care of the battery after we close up shop for the night."

"That's too much to ask, Brady."

"It's not." He closed the hood. "I want to help you, Katie. Please. Just let me tell Madge I'll be gone for the rest of the day."

I offered a lame nod, and before I could say, "What sort of movie hero are you?" we were in his truck, headed to Aunt Alva's house. I had a doozy of a time finding the place. Her directions, it turned out, were a bit skewed. Brady was a good sport about it, though. He didn't complain once, even though we had to turn around several times. Instead, he made light of it and we ended up laughing.

By the time we arrived at Alva's house, she was standing on the front porch waiting for me. When she saw us pull up in Brady's truck, she started waving. Brady got out and came around to my side to open my door for me.

My aunt approached with a smile as bright as sunshine. "Now, that's what I like to see. A true gentleman. Your skills on the court are great, Brady, but I'm more impressed by the fact that you're a Southern gentleman."

"Why, thank you, ma'am." He gave a deep bow at the waist and then laughed.

"I hope you're staying for supper," Aunt Alva said. "I've made lasagna."

"Oh, I wouldn't want to impose. Just brought Katie over because her car broke down."

"Yes, I left a message on your phone, Aunt Alva."

"My phone?" She fished around in her pockets but came up empty. "I can never for the life of me remember where I put that goofy thing."

"Well, anyway, he came to my rescue." I couldn't help but smile as I said those words aloud. "So he really is a gentleman."

"Well then, I insist you stay for dinner as a thank-you for rescuing my niece. My cooking skills aren't what they used to be—mostly because of my vision going south—but I gave it the old college try. So c'mon inside and you can tell me all about how you rescued this niece of mine."

I felt my cheeks grow warm as I glanced at Brady.

"Are you sure?" he asked.

"As sure as you were in the final ten seconds of that game with the Rockets. Remember that? You took a long shot from the opposite end of the court, and what happened?"

He grinned. "I can't believe you remember that."

"As if anyone could forget!" My aunt recounted all of the details of the game and then paused for breath. "What were we talking about again? Oh yes, dinner. I do hope you'll stay, Brady. Please? You're practically a member of the family now. Not that being a member of this family means much, but I guess that's not the point."

"About that, Aunt Alva," I said. "Brady and I aren't engaged. I think you misunderstood."

"You're . . . you're not?" Her smile faded. "Well, cut off my legs and call me shorty. I felt sure you two were getting hitched."

"No. It's kind of a long story," I said.

"Well, we'll have plenty of time over supper to talk. Maybe by dessert we can get this boy to pop the question." She slapped him on the back. "So c'mon in, Brady."

As if he'd want to stay now.

Still, he offered a genuine smile. "I just hate to impose."

My aunt put her hands on her hips as she glared at him. "You ready to bolt just 'cause I said my cooking's not what it used to be?"

"Oh, it's not that at all. Just didn't know if you really wanted me to stay or if you were just being polite." He directed his words to her but looked at me. "And I need to work on Katie's car tonight."

"I can probably take care of my car in the morning," I said. "Maybe you could just take me to Lori-Lou's tonight after dinner?"

"Sure." He nodded. "Happy to spend more time with two of the sweetest ladies in town."

"Why, thank you very much." Alva ushered us through the front door. She led the way into the dining room and we took our seats. "I made a homemade lasagna. Got the recipe from my favorite show on the Food Network, *The Italian Kitchen*. Have you ever seen it?"

"Oh, sure. The one with the elderly Italian couple?" Brady nodded. "It's one of my favorites. I love the way they argue with each other while they cook. Lots of fun."

"I don't get a lot of company around here, so it's fun to cook for other people."

We spent the next hour and a half eating, laughing, and basically having the best time I'd had in ages. I couldn't believe how well Brady and my aunt got along. More than that, though, I couldn't believe how kind Alva turned out to be. From all of Queenie's stories, I would've pictured her as an ogre, not a sweet, lonely woman with a penchant for pro basketball.

As I nibbled on my dessert—a yummy tiramisu she'd made just for me—I gazed tenderly at my aunt.

"What's up, sweet girl?" she asked. "Do I have something in my teeth?"

"No, nothing like that." I giggled. "I just wanted to thank you for the dinner. It's been such a great night."

"Really great." Brady grinned and sipped from his coffee cup. "I've loved every minute."

"Me too," I said. "Aunt Alva, it's been so great to have time with you. I didn't realize how much I missed you until I started spending time with you again."

"That's the way of it, I suppose." She leaned back in her chair and took a sip of her coffee.

I knew my next words were risky but felt they were necessary all the same. "You know, everyone in the family misses you." I drew in a deep breath. "Especially Queenie."

"She'll go right on missing me then."

Ouch. Maybe I'd overstepped my bounds. Brady glanced my way and I could read the concern in his eyes, but I felt I needed to keep going. "Alva, you know that my grandpa Joe passed away four years ago, don't you? Queenie has been living alone ever since. It's been a hard time for her, especially since her surgery."

"I . . . I heard. I still pick up a few things through the grapevine. Bessie—"

"May." We spoke the word together and I smiled. "Well, I guess it's a good thing that she's kept in touch. Is that how you knew about Casey and me dating?"

She nodded and her gaze shifted to the ground.

"Aunt Alva, I'm glad you're staying connected to the goings-on back home."

"This is home now." Alva's jaw clenched.

"But Fairfield will always be—"

"The place where no one needed the likes of me. But never mind all that. If you've come to give me what for, I guess I can take it, but I don't have to like it."

"Not at all. Like I said, I just came because I've missed you and I truly enjoy being with you."

Her expression softened. "Well, thank you." She dabbed at her lips. "Please forgive me, Katie. There are some topics that are still hard to discuss."

Brady finished his coffee and glanced at his watch.

"It's late," I said. "I suppose we should be getting back."

"I'll walk you out." Alva led the way out of the dining room and into the living room. I noticed a black-and-white photograph on the end table. "Alva, is this you and Queenie?"

"I don't know why she expects everyone to call her that." Alva rolled her eyes. "She always thought she was the queen, but I was the oldest sister, you know."

"You still are," I said. "Her sister, I mean." I picked up the picture frame and gazed into the faces of the two girls. "How old were you when this was taken?"

"I don't know. I think maybe I was seven, she was five? Something like that."

"Well, it's darling. You were both so precious."

"Humph. I've never been precious a day in my life."

I couldn't help myself. I threw my arms around her neck and gave her a kiss on the cheek. "You *are* precious," I said. "And don't ever forget it."

Her eyes flooded with tears. She extended her arm for Brady to join the circle, and moments later the three of us stood in an embrace. My heart did that strange pitter-pat thing as he slipped his arm over my shoulders and pulled me close. For a moment I could hardly breathe. Then again, Alva had pretty much swallowed me up in her bosom, just like that first day at the bridal shop.

When the hug ended, Alva clasped her hands together. "Ooh, I have the most wonderful idea. You should stay here with me tonight, Katie."

"Stay here?"

Brady glanced at me. "I think this is the perfect solution, Katie. Stay here with your aunt, and I'll fix your car in the morning and bring it to you."

"Perfect!" Alva gave a little squeal. "We'll have a slumber party. I've got a lovely spare bedroom. It's just sitting there, as empty as can be. I'll loan you a nightgown, if you need. Even have a spare toothbrush."

"Well, there you go." Brady laughed. "The house comes equipped with a spare toothbrush."

Aunt Alva gave me a wink. "If you enjoy your time, maybe we could extend things a little."

"Extend things a little?"

"Sure. What would you think about coming here to stay for a week or two? However long you're in Dallas? Just rest your heart and your head on the pillow in that guest room of mine. No noise. Just quiet. I'll leave you to yourself as much as you need."

"Oh, Aunt Alva." I reached over and gave her another hug. "That sounds wonderful."

"You think Lori-Lou will mind?"

"I think she's preoccupied with the kids and moving plans. She's got to be tired of me. The air mattress is taking up precious space in the baby's tiny bedroom. She trips over it just to get to his crib."

"Then it's settled. Can you call and tell her?"

"I guess I'd better let her know I'm not coming back to her place tonight anyway." I glanced at Brady. "Want to hang around until I've told her, just in case the plan changes?"

"Sure." He took a seat on the sofa and offered a smile so sweet that it convinced me he didn't mind sticking around one little bit. And judging from the warmth that filled me as I gazed at him, I didn't mind it either.

22

Shoe Goes on the Other Foot Tonight

Some of God's greatest gifts are unanswered prayers.

Garth Brooks

I gave Brady a warm smile as I punched Lori-Lou's number into my cell phone.

"H-hello?" She sounded a little breathless. Odd.

"Am I interrupting something?" I asked.

"Um, no. Nope. No." She giggled. "Nothing. Nothing at all. Stop that, Josh! Not now."

Ew!

"I'll make this fast. I'm calling to let you know that I'm staying overnight with Aunt Alva."

"Okay. Weird, but okay." She giggled again. "Josh, stop it."

"Lori-Lou, I love you. You know that."

"Of course I know that. But I have a feeling you're about to challenge that notion in some way. What's happening?"

"Your house. It's so . . ."

"Chaotic?"

"Well, yes."

"Loud?"

"That too."

"Impossible to navigate because of the toys?"

"Boy, if that ain't the truth." Josh's voice sounded from the other end of the line.

"I'm not saying that I'm not grateful for the time I've spent with you," I added. "But Alva has asked if I would stay with her. She's got a great guest bedroom."

"And a spare toothbrush," Brady called out.

"Wait," Lori-Lou said. "Was that Brady James I heard?"

"Yes."

"He's at Aunt Alva's with you?"

"Yes. Long story."

"Mm-hmm." She chuckled. "Well, it's a story you're going to share when we do see each other again. You'll have to come get your stuff, right?"

"Right. I'll come by tomorrow morning after Brady fixes my car."

"He's fixing your car?" She laughed. "Katie, I turn my back on you for five minutes and you have a thousand adventures without me."

"Not deliberately."

"Right, right." She dissolved into giggles again and then ended the call. Probably for the best.

I turned to Brady and smiled. "Well, that's behind me. Looks like you're free to go now. If you want, I mean."

"Wish I could stay, but I'd better get back so I can figure out the car thing." He stood and gave Alva another hug before turning to me. "Walk me out?"

"S-sure." For whatever reason, my heart started that little pitter-pat thing again.

"I'll be clearing the table," Alva called out as she headed out of the living room. "Take your time, you two. Take your time." A little wink followed. For pity's sake. Did she think I needed to be spending time alone with Brady James?

Hmm. The idea wasn't altogether unappealing.

I followed him outside to his truck. "Brady, I can't thank you enough for everything you've done for me."

"Happy to be of service." His warm smile convinced me that his words were genuine.

"Your kindness to me has proven Mama wrong. She said that people in the big city are impersonal and rude. You've been anything but."

"I can't speak for all the people in Dallas." He reached out and slipped his arm over my shoulders. "But spending time with someone like you makes it easy to be friendly. You bring out the best in people." He gave me a hug and then stepped back. "Anyway, you and Alva have a great time at your slumber party. I'll call you tomorrow morning when the car's ready. Then I'll come and fetch you."

I nodded, realizing for the first time just how much I wanted to be "fetched" by this sweet guy.

"And while we're talking about making calls, I think I'll go ahead and call my mom in the morning before I come. I'll fill her in."

"Ugh. She's going to hate me."

233

"Pretty sure she could never hate you. I can't imagine anyone feeling that way about you, Katie. Don't worry, she's pretty clever. She'll come up with a new slant for the *Texas Bride* article, I'd be willing to bet. It'll all work out."

"I hope so."

"I know so."

As he spoke those last words, I had no doubt whatsoever. If Brady knew so, I could know so too.

I watched as he got into the big, manly crew cab of his truck—the one with the extended bed and huge black tires—and drove away. My heart didn't slow down until I was back inside Aunt Alva's house again. I walked through the living room and dining room and into the kitchen, where I found her washing dishes by hand and singing a funny little song. She looked up as I entered and then tossed me a dishrag.

"Might as well join in, Katie Sue."

I stepped into the spot beside her, feeling completely at home in this kitchen. Out of the corner of my eye I gave her a closer look. I saw soft, wrinkly folds of skin on her face, which was the same ivory color as Queenie's but with the addition of some minuscule age spots. The wrinkles traveled like tiny ripples down to her throat, and when I let my gaze wander down her arms, I found them there too. Her soft hands played with the bubbles in the sink, in much the same way I'd seen Queenie do. The two ladies even shared the same style in clothes—floral tops and solid-colored slacks. Even Alva's shoe style felt reminiscent of home.

So many things about this woman reminded me of Queenie. The flashing eyes that spoke of stubbornness and authority. The pursed lips. The strong, charismatic voice. The authority in her stance, despite the stooped shoulders. If I didn't know any better, I'd almost think that Alva and

Queenie were twins. The similarities were mind-boggling, to say the least.

My aunt stopped and gave me a closer look. "Something's happened to you, Katie Sue."

"What do you mean?"

"I mean you look . . . different." She waggled her brows.

"Do I?" I sighed and then dried a plate that she passed to me. "I have no idea what you mean by that."

"Sure you don't." She laughed. "Girl, I wouldn't blame you. No one would. There's nothing like a handsome man to knock a girl off her feet." For whatever reason, her smile faded in a hurry, and she got right back to the business of doing dishes.

"Aunt Alva . . ." I looked up. "Have you ever felt . . . confused?"

"Yep. During the playoffs last season. I was rooting for the Mavericks, but then midseason my loyalties shifted to the Spurs." She glanced my way with an imploring look. "Please don't tell Brady, okay?"

Maybe there was some comparison there. Not that I really knew or cared much about basketball. Still, with my heartstrings suddenly twisted up in a knot around Brady James, maybe I'd better start caring about basketball.

Aunt Alva started humming as she turned her attention back to the dishes. Eventually she looked at me again. "I like having you here, Katie, and not just because of your help with the dishes."

"Aw, thank you. I like being with you too."

"I know it's not like Fairfield."

"I can't believe I'm admitting this, but I'm glad it's not. I came to Dallas to clear my head. You know?"

"I do. More than you know. That's the same reason I came to Dallas—to clear my head. I've been here ever since."

"I get that. I'm not saying I'm ready to move here, but it's been nice to get away from things for a while. It's a whole new world in the big city."

"One with handsome basketball players." She winked. "Hey, speaking of Brady James . . ."

"Were we talking about Brady James?" I felt my face heat up, and that weird heart-racing thing started again.

"Yes, speaking of Brady, I wanted to tell you my theory on why he's scared to get back to the business of playing ball."

"Oh, it's because of his knee," I said.

"It's true, his knee needs more time. But there's more going on than that. People think that guys don't get scared, but they do." Alva gave me a knowing look. "Brady's scared."

"Of?"

"Letting his team down, plain and simple. He's scared to get back in the game because he's afraid he won't be able to play like he used to. So he'd rather risk not playing at all. When you don't play, you don't fail."

"You're right."

"Of course I'm right. Remember that scene in *Coal Miner's Daughter* where Loretta had to stand in front of a crowd and sing for the very first time? She was terrified. It takes courage to do the one thing you're most terrified to do, but it's always worth it in the end."

"I understand being afraid," I said. "I've been a little scared of letting my family down."

"Letting your family down?" Alva pursed her lips. "Why let them control your destiny, kid?"

"Oh, I'm not saying it's like that. Just saying that I hate to disappoint them. So I totally get what you're saying about Brady being afraid of disappointing his fans."

"Ah." A cloud seemed to settle over her. "Well, maybe we

all need to get over this feeling of being a disappointment to others and just get on with the business of living."

I thought through her words. "You're a smart cookie, Aunt Alva."

"Ooh, cookies." She nearly dropped the dish in her hands, but the most delightful look came into her eyes. "I was thinking of making some oatmeal raisin cookies in the morning. Do you like those?"

"They're my favorite. Queenie's too. She makes the best in town." I bit my lip, knowing there would be a reaction from my aunt. Why had I mentioned Queenie again? Somehow I just couldn't help myself when I was around Alva.

An awkward silence grew up between us. She wiped her hands on her apron and leaned against the counter. Her thoughtful expression caught me off guard. "Katie Sue, let's get one thing out in the open, if you don't mind."

"Sure, Aunt Alva."

"Despite what you might be thinking, I really don't hate my little sister," my aunt said. "You need to know that."

Relief flooded over me as I realized she wasn't upset with me. "You don't seem the sort to hate anyone, Aunt Alva. I just don't know what to think about the situation between you and Queenie. It's so . . . odd. I'm looking at it from the outside in, and you know the story from the inside out, so our perspectives are different."

"It's kind of a long story, too long for your first night here. But it all goes back many, many years, long before you were even born."

"I see."

"I wonder, Katie . . . do you happen to know a man named Paul Bradford?" My aunt's eyes misted over as she mentioned his name.

"*Reverend* Bradford? At the Presbyterian church?"

Her gaze narrowed as she shifted her attention to the dishes once more. "Yes, do you know him?"

"Of course. I've grown up knowing him. In fact, I saw him recently at my parents' anniversary party. Great guy." But what did he have to do with Aunt Alva and Queenie?

I gasped as the realization hit me.

Oh. My. Goodness.

Queenie's heart had been broken when Reverend Bradford showed an interest in another woman. Now I knew *who* that other woman was. She was standing next to me, washing dishes.

"Do you want to tell me the story?" I asked.

She sighed and passed me another plate. "Not yet. Maybe one day I'll explain it all. Or write it all down in a letter. You can read it after I'm dead. It'll be less painful that way."

"I have to wait until you're dead to know the details of what happened between the two of you? Er, the *three* of you?"

"Maybe." Her eyes filled with tears. "I'll think on it. Perhaps there's a way to get things out in the open without hurting folks all over again. I'll have to pray about that. In the meantime, let's just have a good time, you and me. It's wonderful to have someone from the family spend time with me. That's all. Wonderful."

I had to admit, it felt pretty wonderful from my perspective too. In fact, only one thing had felt more wonderful tonight . . . that awesome moment when my heart skipped to double time as Brady James pulled me into his arms.

23

Two Steps Forward

Everyone feels like family and I am back in the city that I love.

Chris Noth

I got the best night's sleep I'd had in ages in Aunt Alva's guest bedroom. I didn't even mind the 1970s paintings on the wall or the harvest gold carpeting. And the silk nightgown she loaned me—circa 1968—made me smile. But the room felt just right for me, including the down comforter on the bed. Since she kept the house as cold as a refrigerator, the comforter came in handy. I loved snuggling under the covers when chilly.

When I woke up the following morning, the smell of bacon gave me more than enough reason to get out of bed. I found one of Alva's robes hanging on the hook at the top of the bedroom door. I donned it and headed to the kitchen, where

I found my aunt in a floral dressing gown. She stood at the stove, cooking up a storm.

"Good morning, sunshine." Alva gestured with her head to the refrigerator. "There's milk in the icebox."

Icebox?

"Might as well pull out the butter too. It needs to soften a bit before we can use it. We're gonna need it for the flapjacks. They'll be done in a few minutes."

"Wow, you're cooking for an army over there."

This whole breakfast reminded me of another one several weeks ago. I'd sat at Queenie's table on a random weekday morning, talking about my relationship with Casey.

Casey.

Hmm.

For whatever reason, thinking about him didn't bring as much pain as it had that day. Maybe my heart really was starting to heal. At any rate, a plate of pancakes smothered in butter and yummy syrup would certainly help.

Our conversation shifted, and Aunt Alva went off on a tangent about how she was a week behind getting her hair done. How we'd transitioned from flapjacks to hair, I could not say.

"Just wanted to make you aware of my schedule, honey bun," Alva said. "I've got my weekly appointment at the hair salon a couple of days from now, on Friday."

Interesting. Queenie always went to Do or Dye on Fridays to get her hair done. The similarities between the two women grew stranger and stranger.

"Why Friday?" I asked.

Alva gave me a "surely you jest" look. "Silly girl. So it'll still look fresh for church on Sunday. Wouldn't want to show up for Sunday service with bed head, you know. Gotta put my best foot—er, curl—forward." This led to a lengthy conversation about what her schedule looked like the rest of the week. "I come and go from the house quite a bit," she said. "I might be in my golden years, but I'm still very active. And a good driver too. Those people at the DPS might've questioned it last time around, but I proved 'em wrong. Sure did."

Just like Queenie.

"Now, let's eat." She lifted the platter of flapjacks, nearly dropping it. "I'm starving."

"Me too."

I'd just taken my seat at the table when my cell phone rang in the living room. I sprinted to find it and answered when I saw my mother's number. I could tell from the sound of her voice that something was troubling her.

"Mama, you okay?" I asked.

"Well, I suppose I'm all right physically, but if you're asking about my mental and emotional state, I've been better. Things have been rough at the store without you, honey."

"Ah. I'm sorry, Mom."

"I don't mind admitting we're getting worried about you, Katie Sue."

"Worried? Why?"

"Well, for one thing, your brothers came home with the strangest story yesterday. Something about some girls they've met at a store in Dallas, thanks to you. Didn't make a lick of sense. Why in the world are the boys meeting girls at some sort of store? Have you been shopping a lot while you're there?"

"Well, not really. I—"

"I know some girls like to go on shopping sprees when they get their heart broken, but it only leads to ruin in the end. You'll run up credit card debt and end up in debtors' prison."

"Mama, I don't have any credit cards. And I haven't been shopping." Not really.

"Well, color me confused."

I didn't know what to say, but it didn't really matter anyway, because Mama did all the talking.

"Your brothers insist you've been spending time with a ball player. A pro ball player, no less. Now, I know my girl really well. She's never kept any secrets from me. So I told them it couldn't possibly be true or she would've told me."

Oh dear.

"Actually, Mama, I have met someone who plays for the Mavericks. Brady James. Have you heard of him? We've struck up a friendship."

"A . . . friendship?" She grew silent.

"He's very nice. I think you would like him."

"Well, I must say I'm a little surprised. Your brothers aren't giving me much information, and I for one am feeling a little left out. I don't know what in the world you're up to in Dallas, but Pop and I want you to come home now. He needs your help at the hardware store, and the choir's just not the same without your voice. I had to give Bessie May the solo in last Sunday's special, and you know she can't hold a candle to you when it comes to singing."

"Mama, that's not true. She has a lovely voice." Shaky, but lovely.

"It's just not the same." Mama sighed. "Nothing's the same since you went away."

"I've only been gone three and a half weeks."

"Seems like three months. I just don't understand why you need to spend so much time with Lori-Lou. Aren't those children about to drive you bonkers?"

"Actually, I spent the night with Aunt Alva last night. I'm in her living room now." I lowered my voice so as not to be heard.

"Aunt Alva?" Now Mama sounded interested. "Seriously?"

"Yes. We had a slumber party."

"Well, if that doesn't beat all." I could almost hear the wheels turning in her head. "Queenie's liable to have a conniption."

"Only if she knows, Mama." *So please don't tell her.*

"Well, what in the world are you and Alva doing? Can't you stay connected through the internet or something? Come back home and send her emails. Ask her to friend you on Facebook. There are plenty of ways to stay connected to people these days without actually having a slumber party. We need you here. Nothing's the same."

Hmm. If I didn't know any better, I'd say Mama was a tad bit jealous of my blossoming friendship with Alva. And Lori-Lou.

"I told you, Mama. I'm getting away for a while. Since Casey left, well, I just needed to think things through." I couldn't mention the upcoming photo shoot, obviously, but it weighed heavy on my mind. I couldn't go back to Fairfield for good until the dress was finished and the photo shoot was behind me. Now that Brady knew about my situation, I owed it to him. I would carry through with this, if for no other reason than to make things easier on him.

Mama cleared her throat. "I'm pretty sure I've got this figured out, Katie Sue. I know a little something about broken hearts."

"Huh?"

"I know why you're staying away so long. It's a tactic, isn't it?"

"A tactic?" Okay, now she really had my attention. I took a seat on Alva's paisley sofa. "What sort of tactic?"

"It's a ploy to bring Casey back home. Stay away and make him wonder what you're up to."

"That makes no sense at all, Mama."

"Are you thinking that he'll come back because he's worried about you being gone? I'm not sure that's the best strategy."

"Strategy? You really think I'm doing this to draw attention to myself? To make Casey come looking for me? That's . . . crazy."

"I'm clueless, if you want the truth of it." Mama's voice shook. "Honestly? I don't care if we ever see Casey Lawson again."

"What? Really?"

"Really." Her voice continued to tremble with emotion. "He can move away to Tulsa and stay there, for all I care. I'd rather see you end up with someone who deserves you, someone who won't leave you dangling for years on end. Someone who makes you feel the way your father makes me feel." Her words grew more animated by the moment. "Someone who'll go the distance with you. Someone who cares about family and sees your potential. That's the kind of guy I see you with." She released a long breath. "There. I got it out in the open."

I half expected her to leap into a sermonette about Levi Nash, but she refrained, thank goodness.

"You know what, Mama? That's exactly the kind of guy I see for me too." I rose and paced Alva's spacious living room, my gaze landing once again on the photograph of Queenie and Alva as young girls. "And you're right . . . that guy isn't Casey. Giving me time away in Dallas has put all of that into perspective. I've needed to completely step away to see that. You know what I mean?"

"I guess. But you've picked a doozy of a place to go. If you knew the story about Queenie and Alva, you'd understand."

"Oh, I think I'm beginning to understand." I lowered my voice. "We, um, had a little conversation last night. I'm starting to see what happened . . . from both sides."

"Did she tell you that she's the one who broke up the relationship between Reverend Bradford and Queenie?"

"Well, it wasn't phrased exactly like that, but I sort of figured it out on my own."

"Alva was behind it. She instigated the whole thing. Flirted with the poor fellow and got him all confused. Totally ruined any chance Queenie had. I don't think the good reverend was really interested in Alva, but she wouldn't give up on the idea. You want my opinion?"

I had a feeling Mama was about to give it, regardless of my answer.

"I think Alva didn't care about Paul Bradford. She just didn't want him to marry her sister."

"Why?"

"Because she didn't think he was good enough for her."

Whoa. I lowered my voice to a hoarse whisper. "You're telling me she arranged for Queenie to have a broken heart . . . to somehow protect her?"

"She didn't want her sister to end up with a man who didn't deserve her. That's the long and short of it," Mama said. "But Queenie went on to meet your grandpa Joe when his family moved into town. They had a whirlwind courtship and—on the heels of Reverend Bradford's wedding—she decided to marry him. From what I was told, Alva wouldn't even come to her wedding."

"No way."

"It's true. Bessie May spilled the beans. And it wasn't much longer before Alva moved away to Dallas."

And Alva had never married. Sad.

I felt like a real heel talking about the woman behind her back in her own home. Not that I'd brought up the subject, but I needed to put a cap on it before it got out of hand.

"Mama, I really don't think we should be—"

"The worst part is, she could've been surrounded by family

all of these years if Queenie had been willing to forgive and forget. I think Alva pulled away to keep the peace. This ridiculous separation has affected the whole family. You can call it whatever you like, but in the end, bitterness has grown up between them, and the devil thrives on bitterness."

At that very moment, Aunt Alva popped her head in the living room door and gave me a cute little wave. "Yoo-hoo, kiddo! Your pancakes are getting cold. Better come and eat while the eatin's good! And I haven't forgotten about those oatmeal raisin cookies. I've already got the dough started."

"Okay, I heard that." Mama sighed. "She actually sounds pretty chipper."

"You're right." I waved at Aunt Alva and gave her a thumbs-up.

"Go eat your pancakes," Mama said. "But promise you'll come back two weeks from Friday for Queenie's birthday party. She'll never forgive you if you're not here."

"What date is that?"

"The seventeenth."

Perfect. Two days after the photo shoot. "I'll be there. Where is it?"

"At Sam's, of course. The whole family will be there."

Not the whole family. Alva wouldn't be there, would she?

Or maybe she would. Maybe I could begin to work on her now, to see if I could talk her into going with me.

I said goodbye to Mama and ended the call. I thought about her words all morning long as I ate my breakfast, then dressed in the same clothes from the day before. In spite of my blossoming friendship with Brady, I still held some bitterness in my heart toward Casey. I didn't mean to. But in the quiet moments, usually before getting out of bed in the morning, I still seethed on the inside over his decision to leave me behind.

All right, so his decision to leave had forced me to move on.

And yes, being forced to move on had led me to Cosmopolitan Bridal.

And okay, my decision to move forward with the wedding gown had led me to Brady James.

And sure, my heart fluttered whenever he glanced my way.

When I saw it all in perspective, the bitterness faded away. In that very moment.

Brady showed up around eleven in his truck. Alva greeted him with as much enthusiasm as she had the first day she'd met him and offered to feed him a late breakfast. Brady thanked her but declined.

"Sorry, Alva," he said. "I've got to get back to the shop. I've left Jasper and Dewey working on Katie's car."

"Wait." I put my hand up. "My brothers are back in Dallas . . . again?"

Brady nodded. "Yeah, Jasper said something about needing to shop for supplies for the store."

"He did that yesterday."

"I think maybe he got distracted yesterday and forgot? Anyway, he and Dewey are working on the car. Putting in a new battery. You'll never believe what Beau is doing."

"Try me."

"Last time I saw him, he was working the cash register at the store."

"Are you serious? We couldn't get the boy to work at the cash register at the hardware store if we tried all day."

"Yep. Twiggy was busy with a customer and they needed the help. He stepped right up."

"Whoa. I think we're witnessing a real live miracle, folks."

Brady and I talked about the changes in my brothers all the way back to the bridal shop while we nibbled on some of my aunt's oatmeal cookies. I also opened up and spilled the whole story of Alva and Queenie. Why I felt so comfortable talking to Brady James, I could not say. But he had great insight, particularly when it came to my grandmother and aunt.

"Time has passed, Katie," he said. "And hearts change. Some grow harder. Some soften. But God can still mend relationships, even after all this time."

"Would you pray about that? I'd love to invite Alva to Queenie's birthday party."

"When is it?"

"Two weeks from Friday. In Fairfield."

"I'll pray, I promise." He gave me a thoughtful smile. "The way you talk about Fairfield makes it sound so great. One of these days I'll have to go there myself. Meet Queenie in person."

"I'd like that." I found myself smiling as the words came out. "A lot."

I snuck a peek at him out of the corner of my eye. He gave me a little wink and my heart did that fluttering thing again. Gracious. If this kept up, I'd have to go find a cardiologist.

Right in the middle of my heart palpitations, Brady switched gears, talking about the one thing I'd avoided all morning: his call to his mother.

"I think she was surprised," Brady said. "But I explained the whole thing and told her that Madge didn't want you to say anything."

"We can totally cancel the dress order, Brady. I don't mind."

"No, it would break her heart. She loves that design. And she still wants to go through with the photo shoot. She's just trying to come up with a new angle for Jordan's article. She said something about calling you the Someday Bride."

"The Someday Bride?"

"Yes, the bride who's been dreaming of her big day all her life. The one who plans everything in advance."

"That would be me."

"Yep. You and thousands of other women. She thinks it'll make the article more interesting that the girl who won the dress doesn't have a fixed date. Or a fixed groom."

"Or a fixed *anything*." I sighed.

"Oh, I don't know about that. I think you've got a fixed attitude. You're a hopeless romantic." His convincing smile won me over.

"Well, true. And I guess there are a lot of other hopeless romantics out there," I said.

"Yep. And they're not all women either." A playful smile tugged at the corners of his mouth.

Gracious. Was this sweet guy flirting with me, or what?

Before long we were engrossed in a lengthy conversation about the photo shoot.

"Because Mom can't come back for the shoot, she wants me to go along and represent the bridal shop," Brady said. "You okay with that?"

"Of course. Sounds like fun."

"Dahlia will come too. She'll take care of the dress and make sure it looks great. And I'm sure Madge will be there. We'll make a party out of it."

"Dahlia?" My thoughts reeled backwards in time to the conversation I'd overheard in the fitting room, the one where Twiggy said she felt sorry for the poor, pathetic brides who didn't yet have a groom. "Do . . . do Dahlia and the others know? About my situation, I mean?"

"They do." He gave me a tender look. "But you won't be hearing a word about it. Mom made a point of telling them to handle it like the pros they are."

"Do you think it changes their opinion about me?"

"Not a bit. Now stop fretting, okay?" He started talking about the various photo op places we'd seen at the stockyard. That conversation somehow shifted to goats, then to horses. This provided the perfect segue to talk about my life back in Fairfield, which I did with abandon. Brady seemed to hang on my every word, genuinely interested in what I had to say.

When we arrived back at the bridal shop, I found Dewey and Dahlia in the parking lot working on my car. Now, I'd seen Dahlia at work behind the sewing machine. I'd watched her pin and tuck hems. But I'd never seen her under the hood before. With my brother speaking so enthusiastically about all things mechanical, the girl practically swooned. Go figure.

We joined them, but only for a moment. I could tell from my brother's crooked smile that he wanted to be left alone with the Swedish beauty. Okay then. I'd give him some space, especially if it meant he would fix my car.

"See now why I left it in his capable hands?" Brady said as we walked toward the store. "I think he's trying to impress Dahlia."

"No joke. Well, if he keeps on impressing her, I might just get an oil change and tire rotation out of it, so don't bother him."

Brady laughed and opened the door to the shop. True to his word, Beau was behind the counter, working the cash register. He punched a few keys and then spoke to the young woman standing on the other side of the counter. "That will be $695.14, ma'am." His Texas drawl sounded even thicker today.

"My goodness, with such a handsome fella waiting on me, I'll happily spend that much and more." The girl smiled. "Thanks for the recommendation about the shoes to go with my bridesmaid dress. I think they're a perfect match."

"Yer welcome, ma'am." He took her credit card and rang up the transaction, then closed the drawer and handed her a receipt. "Have a great day."

"Oh, I have already." She winked.

This didn't appear to go over well with Twiggy, who approached at just that moment. She glared at the young woman and showed her to the door. Wow. Looked like things were really stirring at the bridal shop today.

Beau looked my way and his cheeks flushed. "Well, hey, Katie. Didn't see you come in."

"Mm-hmm."

"I, um, well, I'm helping out."

"So I see."

"He's had a hankerin' to work in a bridal shop for years." Jasper's voice sounded from behind me. "I guess it's been a secret desire none of us knew about."

Beau gave him a warning look. Just as quickly, his expression softened. I noticed his gaze shifting to Twiggy, who greeted an incoming customer at the door. "I have secret desires, all right." He sighed and took a few steps toward us, away from the counter. His next words came out sounding a bit strained. "Houston, we have a problem."

"What's the problem, little brother?" Jasper elbowed him in the ribs. "Can't choose between the satin and crepe for your gown?"

"It's Mama."

"Mama's never been a problem for you, little brother," I said. "She thinks you hung the moon. You're her baby."

"Mama's *always* been a problem for him," Jasper argued. "He just never saw it till now. The apron strings are choking the life out of him."

"I'm not really saying Mama's the problem," Beau said. "I

guess I'm the problem because I've let her pretty much rule my life. I'm just saying there's going to be a problem with Mama when she finds out that, well . . ."

"You've fallen and you can't get up?" Jasper gave him a look.

He nodded. "Yeah." A broad smile lit his boyish face. "And I don't wanna, either. Get up, I mean." Another lingering gaze at Twiggy followed. From across the room she turned away from the customer and gave him a little nod.

Jasper whacked Beau on the back. "Don't you worry about Mama. She wants her boy to be happy. She always has. It'll be hard to hear that you've developed an interest in a girl, but she'll get over it."

"She wants me happy, sure, but she also wants me close to home. Now that I . . ." He scratched his head. "I'm just confused."

"When she meets Twiggy, she'll love her." Something occurred to me in that moment. "Hey, I have an idea." I snapped my fingers. "You guys should invite the girls to Queenie's birthday party. Seriously. It's two weeks from Friday, at Sam's. That's the perfect opportunity to introduce them in a friendly setting. Everyone will be in a celebratory mood."

"Take Twiggy to Fairfield?" Beau looked more than a little concerned.

"I'm trying to picture Crystal hanging out at Dairy Queen." Jasper shook his head. "Nope. Just ain't happening."

"Well, how do you know unless you take them there? At the very least, you can introduce them to Mama and Pop. It's the right thing to do."

"Kind of like you introduced them to Brady?" Jasper gave me a knowing look. "Like that? I mean, you two are an item, right? I'm not blind."

"We're not an item, Jasper, and you're completely changing the subject." I swallowed. Hard. "Anyway, I think it's a good idea."

"For you to introduce Brady to the folks?"

"No, for you guys to introduce the girls to the folks."

He shrugged and we ended the conversation, but I couldn't stop thinking about what he'd said. Sooner or later we would all have to cross the great divide between Fairfield and Dallas. Between now and then, however, I'd have to figure out a way to invite Alva to go with me to Queenie's party. And I might—just might—work up the courage to invite a certain basketball player to join us too.

24

Tomorrow Never Comes

Hope is a gift we give ourselves, and it remains when all else is gone.

Naomi Judd

Just two days before Queenie's birthday party, I tried on my finished dress in preparation for the photo shoot. I could hardly believe how wonderful I felt with it on. Dahlia got so excited that she decided to Skype the whole event with Nadia.

"Turn around, Katie." Nadia's voice sounded from the speaker on Dahlia's laptop.

I complied, showing off the mid-length train on the back of the dress.

"Great job, Dahlia." Nadia sounded impressed, but she didn't gush. Maybe it wasn't in her nature to gush. "It's going to be perfect for the photo shoot. Now, Katie, I don't want to tell you how to pose for the photos, but do your best to show off the dress if you can, okay?"

"I will."

"Since we're billing you as the Someday Bride, I thought it would be nice to give you a stand-in groom. You okay with Brady playing that role? I think his basketball fans would eat it up, and it would certainly increase the sales for the magazine."

"Brady?" I felt my cheeks grow hot.

"Sure." Nadia's businesslike voice clipped along at a steady pace. "Ask him to put on a tuxedo and go along for the ride, okay? If the photographer asks for a groom, he'll be ready to go."

"You don't think that'll confuse his fans?" I asked.

"We can explain that he's a good sport." She grinned. "Get it? Good sport? It'll show that he's a team player, and that should make Stan happy."

"I doubt it," Madge called out. "That old coot's never happy."

Nadia laughed. "True. But let's just play out this day like the fairy tale it is. And remember, Katie, you represent every someday bride. I ran the idea by Jordan Singer and he thought it was perfect. His readers will eat it up. You've spent your whole life dreaming of the perfect dress, the perfect wedding . . ."

"The perfect groom." Madge elbowed me but I shushed her.

"Well, do your best not to get the dress too wrinkled on the ride over there, okay? Are you riding in Brady's truck?"

"Yes ma'am. My car would never make it."

"You don't have to call me *ma'am*, Katie. Just Nadia will do."

"Yes ma'am." I put my hand over my mouth and giggled. "Sorry!"

"Dahlia, go ahead and bustle the gown now," Nadia said. "When you all get to the stockyard, keep the dress bustled until the last minute. God forbid you should drag that train in the mud or"—she shuddered—"anything else. There are animals everywhere, after all." She paused, but before anyone could get a word in edgewise, she added another thought. "When you're ready for the first shot, unhook the bustle and let down the train, but be very careful."

"Will do, Nadia," Dahlia said. She went to work bustling the back of my gown, carrying on all the while about the embellishments on the bodice and the gorgeous ruffles on the skirt. "I daresay even Ms. Loretta Lynn herself would be happy to wear this dress."

"We might just have to ask her that question," Nadia said. "I'll ask Jordan to try to contact her."

Wow. I could hardly believe it. Maybe Queenie's favorite singer would put her stamp of approval on my wedding dress. The one I wasn't getting married in . . . at least not anytime soon.

When we ended the Skype session with Nadia, Crystal and Twiggy went to work doing my hair and makeup in preparation for the event.

I noticed Crystal's silence while the other ladies gabbed. "Are you okay?" I asked.

"Hmm?" She shrugged. "I guess. Days like this are hard."

"Why?"

She sighed. "I sometimes wonder if I'm ever going to get married. I guess I'm just one of those someday brides that Nadia talked about."

"Aren't we all?" Dahlia asked.

"Count me in," Twiggy said. "I'm a someday bride too."

"Looks like we're all in the same boat," I said.

Crystal took a seat on the bench. "By the time I'm engaged, I'll be an old woman."

"Like me?" Madge's voice sounded from behind us.

"You're not old, Madge." Dahlia walked over and gave Madge a kiss on the cheek. "You're forever young."

"And you're still a someday bride too." Crystal gave Madge a knowing look and then giggled.

"With hips like mine, I'll never fit into an A-line gown," Madge said.

"When the time comes, you're going to be a beautiful bride, Madge," Dahlia said. "I'll make your dress myself and you'll look like a million bucks."

"Whatever. I was never meant to be a beauty queen. And the only thing polished about me is my wit. No one can argue that point." Madge winked. "Truth is, I'm doing the best I can. All women my age are. And if we don't look the part—if our makeup isn't perfect, if our figure isn't the same as it was when we were teens—then the world will just have to go on spinning anyway. I have it on good authority that we all age. Our bodies change. Don't believe me? Look at Robert Redford."

"True." Crystal's nose wrinkled.

"And Jamie Lee Curtis. She's never been one to disguise her age."

"I'm going to age like Dolly Parton," Crystal said. "That woman is per-*pet*-ually thirty-nine."

This led to an interesting discussion about country music, which led them back to talking about my gown. I swished and swayed, checking out the dress from every angle, and gave a blissful sigh. I caught a glimpse of Madge in the mirror, staring at me like a proud mama hen. I couldn't help but smile.

Several minutes later, Brady appeared at the fitting room door. I hardly recognized him in the sleek tuxedo, but he took my breath away. Literally. "Whoa." I didn't mean to say the word aloud, but who could blame me?

"Wowza." Madge whistled. "You clean up nice, boss."

"You can say that twice and mean it." I bit my lip to keep from saying anything that might embarrass either one of us. "You really do look great, Brady."

"I look like a cake topper." He checked his appearance in the mirror and groaned. "Don't I?"

That got me tickled. Before long I was laughing so hard the girls had to stop working on my makeup. I promised Crystal that I'd double-check my appearance before the shoot began and take care of any necessary touch-ups.

"Trust me, you're the prettiest bride to ever grace the cover of a magazine." Brady gave me an admiring look. "You won't need to change a thing."

"Aw," all of the females said in unison.

"Thank you, Brady." I gave him a smile and then tried to look as if his words hadn't affected me. The heat in my face gave me away, though.

Dahlia's eyes narrowed. "Boss, are you flirting?"

"Me? Flirting?" He cleared his throat.

"Well, it's time to get this show on the road." Madge put her hand on Brady's back and nudged him out the door. "We've got a full day ahead of us. C'mon, folks."

Brady extended his arm. "Are you ready, Katie?"

"As ready as I'll ever be."

I held tight to his arm as we walked through the shop, so as not to get tangled up in the cumbersome ruffled skirt. Several people stopped me to comment on my gown. I felt like a princess wearing it.

Just before we reached the door, a young woman entered. Madge reached for her walkie-talkie and whispered, "Incoming Joie de Vivre."

"Joie de Vivre?" I stopped in my tracks, intrigued by this one.

"Rediscovering life after a recent catastrophe," Madge explained. She gestured to the woman, who stood off in the distance, examining a gown. "Her name is Penny Jones. And she's our most recent Joie de Vivre Bride."

"I'm not sure I understand," I said.

"Notice the smile on her face? It's as broad as the sun up above. But the mist of tears in her eyes? They tell a different story. This is a young woman whose first husband passed away in Afghanistan. She didn't think she would ever remarry. But then she met her current fiancé, and hope, once dead, sprang to life."

"Joie de vivre. Hope springs to life." I whispered the words, realizing how closely they matched my situation, then threw my arms around Madge's neck. "Madge, you're a remarkable woman. So intuitive."

Brady let out a snort. "You mean nosy?"

"No, I mean intuitive." My heart flooded with joy for her. "She sees things that the rest of us don't see. She even notices the little things."

"In spite of all my flaws?" She quirked a brow.

"I see no flaws in you. In fact, you're the most beautiful woman here," I said. "And I really mean that. Your heart makes it so."

"I might have to argue that point." She leaned over and kissed me on the forehead. "I would argue that you're the most beautiful. I haven't known you long, kid, but I can say in all honesty that they grow 'em sweeter in Fairfield."

"And I might just have to agree." Brady placed his hand on my back and smiled.

"Yep." Madge nodded. "Now listen up, you two. Once we get to that photo shoot, I'm counting on you to knock 'em dead. Take the best possible pictures for *Texas Bride* and show the world that Cosmopolitan Bridal is the best place on earth to buy a wedding gown." She glanced at the Joie de Vivre Bride. "I've got a customer to take care of, but Dahlia and I will meet you there in a few minutes, after I make sure the other girls are okay to manage the store without us. Now scoot."

Brady kept his hand on my back, gently guiding me out the door. In that moment, with the eyes of everyone in the store on the two of us, I felt like a bride. I felt lovely. It had nothing to do with the makeup or the hair, though those things certainly didn't hurt. No, what I felt came from a deeper place than that. Madge had touched a nerve with her joie de vivre comment. With those words, hope sprang to life. I would one day wear this dress for real. It would be more than just a pipe dream. In the meantime, Brady and I would play the role of cake toppers, giving the photographer all of the pictures he needed for the magazine, even if we had to playact to do it.

25

Hello Darlin'

I have an affection for a great city. I feel safe in the neighborhood of man, and enjoy the sweet security of the streets.

Henry Wadsworth Longfellow

Perched in the passenger seat of Brady's truck, all adorned in white, I felt like a bride. Well, a pretend bride on her way to a stockyard for a photo shoot, anyway. My tuxedo-adorned groom glanced at me and laughed. "I'm sorry, but something about the way you're sitting cracks me up. You're like a stone. A white stone."

"I'm terrified to move."

"Because of the dress?" He tugged at his collar. "Afraid you'll ruin it?"

"I'm just a klutz. Knowing me, I'll spill coffee all over it."
I sat perfectly still, afraid to breathe.

"There's no coffee in my truck."

"Right. Well, maybe motor oil."

"I don't think you'll be touching any of that." He grinned and then eased on the brake to stop at a light. He gave me a comforting look. "Just rest easy, Katie. And if you do run into any problems, don't worry. Dahlia will have an emergency kit with her."

"Emergency kit? Huh?"

"Yep. Instant stain remover. Needle and thread. Mini scissors. You name it, she'll have it."

"Good." I nodded and did my best to relax. "Is it hot in here?" Ribbons of sweat trickled down my back.

"I'll adjust the AC." He turned the fan directly on me and increased the flow of air. I tried to settle against the seat, but my sweaty back made it impossible. Instead, I closed my eyes and tried to imagine what Queenie would do if she saw me like this. She'd call for the WOP-pers to pray, naturally. And if Alva saw me sitting here in a wedding dress next to Brady? Well, she'd go on assuming the two of us were a couple.

Out of the corner of my eye I watched Brady drive the truck. He talked about nonsensical things, everything from the weather to the photo shoot. Something about his voice—that soothing, comforting voice—calmed my soul. It also gave me the tingles. Or maybe the dress gave me the tingles. The taffeta parts were a little itchy, after all. Still, being here with him, all six feet four of him, made me happier—no, giddier—than I'd been in ages. I couldn't help myself as the giggles bubbled up.

Brady looked my way and grinned. "You okay over there?"

"Peachy. Just peachy." Saying the word *peachy* reminded me of the night I'd been crowned Peach Queen back home in

Fairfield. As wonderful as I'd felt that night, sitting here with Brady, dressed in wedding duds, felt even better.

We arrived at the stockyard at exactly five minutes till three, just in time to meet with Jordan and the photographer, who'd wanted to capture the shots mid-afternoon due to the setting of the sun. Brady pulled the truck into the parking lot and tried to strategize the best place to park.

"I don't want you to have to walk far in that dress." His nose wrinkled. "On the other hand, I don't want to be near the front of the parking lot because the ground is still wet from the rain we had yesterday. No point in getting muddy."

No, indeed. If I got this gorgeous Loretta Lynn gown muddy, Nadia would never forgive me.

He parked in the middle, in a spot with enough open space on either side to accommodate my full skirt. Then he placed a call to Madge, who had gotten tied up at the shop with a bride.

"Looks like Madge and Dahlia are going to be a little late," he said. "Think you can make it to the shoot without them?"

"I'll do my best, boss." I laughed. "Sorry, I think I've just heard the others call you that so many times it stuck."

Brady came around to my side to help me out. When he took hold of my hand, it felt perfectly natural. I couldn't help but smile.

"You ready to do this?" he asked.

"As ready as I'll ever be."

The moment we stepped out of the truck, we drew a crowd. I'd worried about how people would respond to seeing a bride walking down the main street of Fort Worth, and I prayed that they wouldn't get the wrong idea about Brady. With someone as well known as Brady James, the risk of media showing up was very real. Why hadn't I thought of that?

"Oh, Brady." I shook my head and took a few steps away from the crowd. "We can't do this. People are going to think . . ."

"Don't worry about the fallout, Katie. I've already put Stan to work on a story for the media so people don't get the wrong idea. If I know him—and I do—he'll come up with some slant to get me back on the court."

"No doubt." I giggled.

He leaned over to whisper, "If anyone asks, we'll explain that I'm just a prop."

"You could never be just a prop." My words came out sounding a little too passionate.

He smiled. "Well, thank you for that." He held out his arm and I slipped mine through his. "We're going to march down Main Street like we belong here. Let the chips fall where they may."

"Speaking of chips . . ." I pointed down to the road, where the cattle drive had taken place a few hours prior. "Watch your step, cowboy."

He laughed.

And off we went, the happy bride and groom, arm in arm. A crowd continued to gather around us, and people pulled out their phones to take pictures.

"Hey, Brady!" an older fellow called out. "You gettin' hitched?"

"Nope," he called out. "I'm just a prop, folks. Just a prop."

"You look like a cake topper," another man hollered.

"Told you." Brady looked my way and rolled his eyes.

"A very handsome cake topper." I gave his arm a little squeeze. "Chin up, Brady. We'll get through this."

"No wonder your head hasn't been in the game," the older fellow added. "You're distracted."

Great. Someone else who thought I was a distraction in Brady's life.

Thank goodness Brady didn't feel the need to respond to that last comment. He just held his head up and guided us through the crowd to the spot near the museum where the photo shoot would take place.

Jordan met us there, a broad smile on his face as he saw us coming toward him.

"Well now, I get two for the price of one—a bride and a groom."

"We aim to please." Brady grinned and released my arm. "Hope you don't mind that I'm playing the role of groom."

"Don't mind a bit, if the Someday Bride doesn't."

"The Someday Bride doesn't." I giggled.

"Show him your dress, Katie," Brady said with a smile.

I did a little twirl and showed off the ruffles in the skirt.

"Looks great." Jordan smiled. "And it's going to photograph well, I'm sure. We've got a spot all set up for the first shot." He pointed at the area, which had been taped off to keep the crowd away. "Perfect background, right?"

Perfect was right. Underneath the mid-afternoon sun, the area felt like a scene from the Old West. In a few hours, if this photo shoot lasted that long, Brady and I would be riding off into the sunset. For some reason that got me tickled. That, and I couldn't stop thinking about the fact that he'd called himself a prop.

Jordan introduced us to the photographers—a married couple, Hannah and Drew Kincaid from Galveston. Turned out they had done a lot of photo shoots involving brides, so they knew just how to ask me to pose. Good thing too, because I froze up the minute I stepped into the spot they'd prepped for me. The first couple of shots were rough at best. And it didn't help that total strangers were watching, whooping and hollering, and asking Brady about the big day.

Madge and Dahlia finally showed up, but their presence didn't serve to calm my nerves, especially with Dahlia fussing over the wrinkles in the dress. Only when the photographers decided that Brady should join me in the photos did I begin to calm down.

He stepped into place next to me and slid his hand on my back. "The prop has arrived."

"You're no prop," I whispered. "And I'm no model."

"Oh, I don't know. You're prettier than a picture, that's for sure." He gave me a little smile and I calmed down immediately.

"Okay, you two." Hannah gestured with her hand. "I hope this doesn't make you feel too awkward, but you're going to have to give us some up-close and personal poses. Can you do your best to get cozy?"

Oh, I could definitely get cozy with this guy. On the other hand, he was a full head taller than me. Maybe more so. Hannah saw my plight right away and brought me a wooden crate to stand on.

"Try this." She put it in place and gestured for me to make use of it.

With Brady's help I climbed up onto the crate, nearly falling in the process. He caught me around the waist, and the cameras started snapping. I settled into place and gave them a funny pose, one that sent me toppling right into my groom. The cameras kept snapping. Brady, in an impulsive move, grabbed me around the waist and lifted me into the air. The crowd roared with delight.

"Three-point shot!" someone hollered.

He laughed and set me back down on the crate.

"Let's try some sweet poses now," Hannah instructed. "Cheek to cheek. That sort of thing."

"Happy to oblige." Brady gave me a little nod.

"Face each other and put your palms together," she instructed. "And then lean in."

"Lean in, eh?" Brady quirked a brow as he placed his palms against mine. "Don't mind if I do."

My heart skip-skip-skipped as I leaned against his cheek for several photos. I felt his breath warm against my face. Hannah and Drew took several shots from a variety of angles while the crowd continued to whoop and holler.

"Okay." Drew put his camera down and walked toward us. "We'll do a few shots of Katie with Brady looking at her."

"Adoringly," Hannah added. "Can you look at her adoringly, Brady?"

"Won't take much effort." He gave me a little wink.

Madge let out a whistle and the crowd responded with another whoop.

"Katie, we'll do a bunch of different poses," Hannah said.

And we did. I loved the ones with my back to the camera as I looked over my shoulder. I even loved the ones where I sat on the crate, sort of hunched over, like an exhausted bride after a long day. My favorite, however, was the one where I caught a glimpse of Brady looking at me from a distance, his eyes brimming with affection.

Wow, could this guy act, or what?

Hmm.

Hannah and Drew instructed us to take a break while they readjusted the sun deflectors, and Brady walked my way. He slipped his arm around my waist, and I gave him a curious look.

"They're not shooting right now," I whispered.

"I know," he whispered back. He stared into my eyes and I felt myself melting, kind of like the Wicked Witch after being hit with a bucket of water. I couldn't seem to control the emotions that washed over me as he pulled me closer still. "Can I be honest here?" he whispered.

I nodded. "Honesty is good. Take it from someone who's been afraid to be honest—with herself and with you."

"I'm going to be perfectly honest." He brushed a loose hair out of my face, and I thought I heard the click of a camera but ignored it, too drawn in by this handsome prop of mine. "This news of yours, about not being engaged?"

"Made you want to jump off a bridge?" I tried.

He shook his head. "No. Not even close."

"Made you wonder how you were going to handle the press once the word got out?"

"Well, there is that. But that's not what I was referring to." He gazed into my eyes with such tenderness that I felt like swooning. Not that I'd ever swooned a day in my life, but I suddenly understood what the term meant. The cameras continued to click, but I found myself completely ignoring them, enraptured by this awesome man in front of me.

I sighed. "Made you wish you'd never met me?"

"Good try." He reached for my hand and gave it a squeeze. "But you're 100 percent wrong on that count." He laced his fingers through mine. "Your news about the wedding being off is actually the best news I've heard in a long, long time."

"It . . . it is?"

To my left, the cameras continued to click.

"Mm-hmm." He leaned in close to whisper in my ear, "Because I don't mind saying I can't stand Casey what's-his-name."

"Lawson."

"Lawson," he echoed. "Never met the guy, but I can't stand him."

"Oh?" My knees went weak as Brady pulled me into his arms.

"Yep," he whispered. "I'm not like other guys I know—playing the field. I've been hanging on for the ride, waiting for God to zap me with someone who made my head spin."

"O-oh?"

"And you?" He brushed his cheek against mine, words soft in my ear. "You made my head spin."

I couldn't help but giggle. "And that's a good thing? Or are you saying I make you dizzy?"

"You make me dizzy, all right." In a typical impulsive move, he grabbed me by the waist and spun me around. The cameras continued to click, click, click.

"Whoa." I laughed so hard and so long that the crowd joined in. Before long they were all cheering.

Brady put me back down and took hold of my hands. "I don't mind admitting that I was half crazed, thinking of you marrying that Casey guy."

"The one you hate." I bit back the smile.

"Well, *hate* is a strong word. I strongly disliked him."

"Because . . ."

"He had what I wanted."

"What. You. Wanted." I repeated the words but didn't have time to think them through before Brady's soft kiss on my forehead caught me off guard.

Oh. My. Goodness.

I stood there melting in his arms. Okay, maybe the ninety-degree heat had a little something to do with the melting, but still, I felt myself lost in a haze—a wonderful, romantic haze, one that included a crowd of onlookers and a couple of photographers who seemed to be enjoying this.

Oh boy, you make a great prop.

I gazed into his eyes and whispered, "Are you saying all of this so we'll get a great shot?"

He shook his head. "I couldn't care less about the photos, Katie."

Jordan held his hand up and cleared his throat. He took a couple of steps in our direction. "Sorry to interrupt, but we're nearly ready to wrap up. Just a couple of shots left."

"Give her a kiss, Brady!" someone in the crowd hollered out.

"Yeah, every bride needs a kiss from her groom," Madge said with a wink.

"A kiss, eh?" Brady grinned that boyish grin of his. "I'd be pleased. If the lady doesn't mind."

I giggled and my heart started that crazy skittering thing again. "The lady doesn't mind."

Nope. She didn't mind one little bit. And she had a feeling—call it a bride's intuition, call it whatever—this would be the first of many, many kisses yet to come.

Brady lifted me back onto the crate so we could stand face-to-face, and then, with cameras clicking all around us, he gave me a kiss sweeter than all of the peaches of Fairfield combined—one worthy of a magazine cover.

26

Before I'm Over You

A city is a place where there is no need to wait for next week to get the answer to a question, to taste the food of any country, to find new voices to listen to and familiar ones to listen to again.

Margaret Mead

By the time the sun had fully gone down, Brady and I had finally managed to sneak away from the crowd and have some alone time. With Madge and Dahlia's help, I managed to change out of my wedding gown in the restroom and back into my jeans. Dahlia went on and on about the photo shoot, then helped me get my dress onto a hanger and back into a zipper bag.

"Can I ask you a question?" She looped the bag over her arm, fussed with it for a moment, and then passed it to me.

"Sure." I did my best to juggle the bag so as not to harm the gown inside.

"You two weren't acting out there, were you? I mean, I've known Brady for years and I've never seen this side of him before."

I shook my head and draped the bag over my left arm. "I honestly don't know how to answer that question." Little giggles followed.

"Oh, girl . . ." Madge shook her head. "You can't deny the obvious. And maybe it's not as complicated as you've made it. Maybe it's very, very simple." She walked out of the restroom, carrying on about how life was just like that—full of surprises.

It was full of surprises, for sure. I couldn't help but smile all the way back to the store, where I left the dress so that it could be cleaned. Brady and I said our goodbyes—very generic, since we happened to be in front of the ladies at the shop—and I headed off to Aunt Alva's house. She peppered me with questions. When I couldn't answer them without blushing, she pursed her lips and smiled.

"I see how it is."

Yep. She saw, all right.

I hated to ruin anyone's good mood, but I needed to talk to her about Queenie's party. After I explained that I would be leaving for Fairfield on Friday afternoon, she wrinkled her nose.

"I'll miss you, girlie. I'm getting used to having you around."

"Well, that's the thing," I said. "You don't have to miss me at all, Aunt Alva. Come with me."

"To Fairfield?" Her eyes widened in obvious surprise. "Over my dead body."

"It's time, Alva. You should come. It's Queenie's birthday."

"I know when my own sister's birthday is." She released a sigh. "But no thank you. You go on and have a good time. I'll be here waiting when you get back. Maybe I'll paint the guest room while you're gone." She went off on a tangent about how she'd been thinking of painting that room a lovely shade of rose, but I knew she was just avoiding the obvious. Maybe I'd been wrong. Maybe this wasn't God's perfect timing to take Alva home again. Oh well.

I tumbled into bed that night, the scenes from the photo shoot still fresh on my mind and the scent of Brady's cologne lingering in my imagination. I replayed that awesome moment when he'd given me such a sweet little kiss on the forehead, then that lovely point where his lips had touched mine. Who would have guessed the day would go the way it had, and yet . . .

I slept, dreaming of Brady, then awoke all smiles. I thought of him all day Thursday, though I didn't see him once, since Alva and I spent the day resting. I replayed the moment of our kiss over and over as I slept Thursday night and awoke Friday morning in a joyous mood. In fact, I kept on smiling until noon, when Lori-Lou called to tell me that she and Josh had been approved for the house and had a lot of packing to do.

"You sound out of breath, Katie," she said.

"Oh, I'm just putting my suitcase into my car. Going home for Queenie's party. You coming?"

"No." Lori-Lou sighed. "Josh is working extra hours, so I'd be by myself with the kids."

"I could help."

"You're sweet, but it's too much to handle if he's not with me. Besides, we're down to one car right now. Mine still isn't working. Before you go, though, I need to talk to you about something."

"What's that?" I hefted my suitcase into the backseat.

"Did you know that Casey's back home?"

That stopped me dead in my tracks. "Casey's back home?"

"Yeah. Beau called Josh yesterday."

"Casey's in Fairfield?"

"I think maybe he didn't like the job in Tulsa? Or maybe it wasn't a good fit? I don't know. I just know he's back home. Beau said that everyone's walking on eggshells around him."

Casey. Back home. Crazy.

My heart flip-flopped all over the place at this news. I vacillated between anger, hopefulness, and a variety of other emotions that ping-ponged around my heart. Most of all I wondered why he hadn't called me.

Then again, why would he? We weren't a couple anymore, after all.

Lori-Lou went on to ask about the photo shoot, and I told her about the shot of Brady kissing me.

"Wow." She giggled. "Wow, wow. Now there's a plot twist. What are you going to do if they choose that one for the cover? Your family is bound to see it. And Casey too, right?"

"He doesn't read bridal magazines, but I suppose it's inevitable. Who knows, maybe the people at *Texas Bride* won't choose that picture for the cover, right?"

"True. They might want one of you in the dress. By yourself, I mean. But still . . ." Lori-Lou started scolding Mariela for coloring on the walls. She returned breathless. "Sorry about that."

"Don't ever be sorry about your life, Lori-Lou," I said. "You've got a great life. Great husband. Wonderful children."

"If you don't put those colors down right this minute, you'll never use them again, young lady!" Lori-Lou's voice faded and then she returned again. "What were you saying?"

"Just saying that life is good. It's full of twists and turns, but it's good. And I'm not really worried about the magazine cover. My parents—and Casey—will find out in a couple of months, but I'll have to cross that bridge when we come to it."

"In the meantime, don't do anything rash."

"Like appearing on the cover of a national magazine kissing a pro basketball player?"

"I thought you said he was kissing you?"

"Right. I think I kissed him back, though."

"Hey, no one would blame you. The guy's great. Tall, handsome, suave, but kind too. And he's a Christian."

"And he's been waiting on the perfect-for-him girl. I heard all about it."

"Does he realize the perfect-for-him girl still hasn't quite let go of the not-so-perfect-for-her guy back in Fairfield?"

"I've let go of him, trust me." The truth of those words settled over me. "So, Casey's really back in Fairfield?"

"Mm-hmm. Just try to avoid him this weekend."

"Oh, I will."

I thought about my cousin's words as I headed back inside. Before leaving, I gave Aunt Alva a hug and tried one last time to talk her into going with me. She shook her head and told me to have a good time.

"But we're having the party at Sam's," I said. "That's your favorite restaurant, right?"

"You'll have to eat a double portion of barbecue for me," she said. "I just can't do it, honey. Not yet, anyway."

I wondered when—if ever—she would work up the courage to go back home again. Still, it wasn't my business.

I made the drive back to Fairfield, a thousand different thoughts flying through my head. Brady. Kissing. Photos. Casey. Newspaper. Mama. WOP-pers. Queenie. Birthday. Alva.

It all rolled together in my brain.

I arrived at Sam's about twenty minutes early and checked my email on my phone. My heart jumped when I realized Jordan Singer had sent me a link to the photos from Wednesday's shoot. I clicked the link, and picture after picture greeted me in living Technicolor.

Oh. My. Goodness.

I rolled the window down on my car to keep from getting overheated, then flipped through the pictures, mesmerized by how great the shots were. Hannah and Drew had done a spectacular job of capturing not just the ambience of the setting, not just the amazing Loretta Lynn gown, but the emotions on my face.

And Brady . . .

Whoa. My heart quickened as I saw picture after picture of Brady gazing at me with pure adoration in his eyes. Either the guy was a terrific actor, or . . .

"Katie?"

Mama's voice came from outside the open window. I minimized the photo on the screen and turned to face her. "Yes?" I did my best to steady my voice. "You scared me."

"Katie, what was that?" She pointed at my phone. "What were you looking at?"

"Oh, some pictures. Wedding gowns. You know how I am."

"Well, yes, I know you like wedding dress photos, but that almost looked like . . ." She shook her head. "I could've sworn I was looking at a picture of you in that wedding dress. Pull it up again so I can see it. Strangest thing ever."

Thank goodness I didn't have time to do that. Queenie pulled into the spot next to us and needed help getting out of her car.

"Why in the world they don't have more handicapped spots is beyond me. There are never any available, no matter what time of day I come."

Like she had ever come at a different time.

I noticed that my grandmother was having more trouble

with her knee than usual and asked her about it. "Oh, this old thing?" She pointed down. "It gives me fits, but I keep going. I'm still a spring chicken, you know."

"Well, happy birthday, spring chicken." I gave her a kiss on the cheek.

"You back for good?" Queenie asked. "Or just home for the weekend?"

"I came home to spend time with you, but I might go back for another week or two." Or longer. Somehow the thought of spending more time with Brady held me in its grip.

"Guess you heard that you-know-who is back." Queenie gave me a pensive look.

"Yeah, I heard he was home." I sighed. "That might be a good reason for me to stay put in Dallas a little longer, if you want the truth of it."

"You can't avoid the inevitable forever," she said. "And I don't know how in the world you're handling staying with Lori-Lou. All of those kids would drive me bonkers. How are you managing?"

Oy vey. There it was. The dreaded question. "Well, actually, it's pretty crowded at Lori-Lou's place, so I found someone else to stay with."

"Someone else?" Queenie's gaze narrowed. "You have other friends in the city?"

"Not friends exactly, Queenie," I said. "More like . . . family."

"Family?" She tilted her head and I could read the confusion in her expression. Until the light bulb went on. Then, in an instant, confusion morphed to anger. "Oh no. Tell me you haven't made amends with Alva."

"Made amends? Queenie, I never had a falling-out with her. In fact, I've never had much of anything to do with her, good or bad."

"How in the world did you end up at her place, anyway? Did she track you down?"

The timing certainly wasn't right to tell Queenie the whole story.

"Well, I think it's time to change the subject." Queenie squared her shoulders. "We gonna stand out here in the heat or go inside? Where is everyone, anyway?"

Mama gave me a wink. "They're inside."

They were inside, all right. The whole Fisher clan was seated at the usual table holding signs that read "Happy birthday, Queenie!"

She shook her head and grumbled that we shouldn't have gone to so much trouble, but her attention was quickly diverted to the three strangers at the table. I was a little diverted too. Looked like my brothers had talked Dahlia, Crystal, and Twiggy into coming to the party.

Oh boy.

Was this going to be fun, or what?

27

You Wouldn't Know an Angel (if You Saw One)

Change is the one thing we can be sure of.

Naomi Judd

Mama stared at the girls, her eyes narrowing as she noticed Twiggy sitting next to Beau. And Crystal sitting next to Jasper. And Dahlia sitting next to Dewey.

"Well, who do we have here?" My mother took a seat and looked all around the table, her brow knitted.

"Mama, this is Dahlia." Dewey looked a little scared, but Dahlia didn't seem to notice.

She offered Mama a broad smile. "Nice to meet you, Mrs. Fisher. I've heard so much about you. And Queenie . . ." She looked at my grandmother, who took her usual seat at the head of the table. "My goodness, I feel as if I already know you, I've heard so many fun stories."

"All good, I hope." Queenie gave my brother a concerned look.

"All good." Dahlia smiled.

Mama seemed to be having a hard time with our guests. She narrowed her gaze as she looked at Dewey and his guest. "Dahlia?" Mama spoke the word, then repeated it slowly, as if trying to make sense of it. "Dah-li-a."

"It's Swedish," Dahlia explained, her accent sounding even heavier here in Fairfield than it had in Dallas. "It means *valley*."

"Well, my goodness." Mama fanned herself with her hand. "Down in the valley, the valley so low."

Dahlia's countenance fell at once.

"Mama!" Dewey groaned. "It's a beautiful name for a beautiful girl."

"Well, she is lovely, isn't she?" Mama pointed at Dahlia's hair. "Is that real?"

"Mama!" I gave her a scolding look.

Dahlia didn't seem bothered by my mother's hair question. "Actually, they're extensions. I got them at a salon in Dallas a few months ago. I think they work for my face shape, don't you?"

"Did she say *salon* or *saloon*?" Mama whispered.

I gave her a warning look.

"I need to take you to meet Nancy Jo at Do or Dye." Mama turned her attention back to Dahlia. "She's new in town and is really hip. Like you. I'd bet you two would be terrific friends. What did you say those things in your hair are called again?"

"Extensions."

"Extensions." Mama mulled over the word and shrugged. "Need to get me some of those, I think. This current Diane Keaton 'do' is turning out to be more of a 'don't,' don'tcha think?" She fussed with her hair.

Jasper, perhaps nervous by our mother's odd welcome to Dahlia, decided this would be the perfect time to introduce Crystal.

"Mama, I want you to meet someone. This is Crystal. She's from Georgia. Where they have peaches."

Like that would help.

The petite blonde flashed Mama a broad smile. "Oh, Miz Fisher, I've heard so much about you!' Her Southern drawl seemed more pronounced today. "Jasper here tells me you're the *purr*-fect mama, and that's just *purr*-fect with me, because my mama and daddy are singing with the angels right about now. I miss 'em *so* much." She rose and walked to my mother's chair, then wrapped her in a big hug. "I hope we'll be *free*-unds. Can we?"

"Well, shore, honey." Mama's own accent thickened. "I have a feeling we're two peas in a pod."

"Mmm, peas." Crystal giggled. "I haven't had a good bowl of black-eyed peas since I left Georgia."

"Then you have to come to our house when we're done. I made a big pot of black-eyed peas just yesterday."

"Ooh, I'd love that. Yum." Crystal gave Mama another hug, told her that she felt sure they'd be best friends, and then headed back to her chair.

Beau, perhaps encouraged by this scene, cleared his throat. Mama shifted her attention his way, her gaze landing on Twiggy, who sat beside him in complete silence.

"Beau? Who have we here?"

The whole table grew silent. You could've cut through the tension with a knife.

Beau took a swallow of his sweet tea, then released a slow breath. "Mama, I'd like you to meet Twiggy."

"Twiggy?" Mama's brows scrunched. "Like the model from the sixties?"

A delightful smile lit Twiggy's delicate face. "Yes, that's right."

"Is she your mama or something?" Before Twiggy could respond, my mother gave the young woman a closer look. "I do think I see a family resemblance, especially in the calorie department. You look as if you could stand some padding, girlie. We'll have to load you up with carbs. It'll do you a world of good."

Twiggy paled. "Oh, no thank you. I'm off of carbs. In fact, I'm gluten-free. Well, mostly."

"Gluten-free?" My mother's eyebrows shot up so high I thought they might take leave of her face. "Well now."

Oh. Dear.

Mama couldn't abide anyone who hated bread. Bread was a staple in our world, kind of like air or water. Or lemon pound cake.

Beau's sweetie lit into a dissertation about some diet plan she'd found online. Before long she and Dahlia were engaged in a conversation about it. Mama, on the other hand, refused to play along.

"The only diet I've been able to stick to is the one where you cut back at the buffet."

"Or eat your weight in lemon pound cake," Beau whispered to me.

"I heard that." Mama gave him a sour look. She pointed at Twiggy's short bob. "Now that's a haircut! I think I saw this once on a TV show. Did you pay money to have that done or cut it yourself?"

"I-I paid money." Twiggy squared her shoulders. "I've never cut my own hair. Well, not since I was three, anyway."

"I've cut Herb's hair for years," Mama said. "And my boys' too, though frankly, most of the time they just shaved it all off in the summertime, due to the heat. I always say a woman who can cut her man's hair is of great value. She saves him the $6.99 at the barber shop."

"Oh, I *ahl*-ways cut my brothers' *hay*-er too," Crystal said. "I'm *real*-ly good at it."

Mama turned her gaze to Crystal and smiled. "Good to know. Why don't you and I go have a look at the buffet, Crystal? In fact, I'll show you around the restaurant so you'll feel right at home."

"Oh, yes ma'am." Crystal rose and joined my mother. "I'd love that."

"When we're done, I'll come back and feed that skinny one some bread." She pointed at Twiggy, who sat in stony silence, glaring at Beau.

Mama and Crystal headed off arm in arm to take a little tour of the restaurant. Dahlia engaged my grandmother in some conversation about the weather. And Twiggy—God bless her—reached for a slice of bread from the basket in the center of the table.

Beau offered a little shrug, then passed her the butter. "And there you have it," he said with a smile. "That's our mama."

Yep. That was our mama, all right. Nothing we could do about that, at least at the moment. Queenie switched the conversation to the recent drought, and Pop joined in, talking about how he'd seen an upswing in the sale of garden hoses.

Less than five minutes later Mama and Crystal returned to

the table, all smiles. I couldn't help but notice my mother was carrying a large slice of lemon pound cake. Strange, since we hadn't eaten any real food yet.

"You'll never guess, Katie. Crystal's from Georgia." Mama took her seat once again and set the pound cake down.

"Well, yes, I know. She's—"

"From Atlanta. She was Miss Peaches two years in a row. Isn't that a fun coincidence? I told her that you were Fairfield's Peach Queen your senior year and she can totally relate." Mama gave Crystal an admiring look. "She even loves peach cobbler, my all-time favorite."

"Well, Mama, you didn't think I'd bring home a gal who didn't like peaches, did you?" Jasper looked offended. "I know a good girl when I see one."

"I believe you do." Mama shook her head and looked at all of the girls. "I still can't get over the fact that all of you met in a bridal shop. Doesn't make a lick of sense to me."

"Well, that's kind of a long story," I said.

"No time for that now." Mama shifted her gaze to Twiggy. "I daresay we get busy feeding this one something before she wilts away to nothing. Oh my goodness. Why, you're eating the bread."

"I am." Twiggy took another bite. "It's good."

"Well, for pity's sake. I hope we don't have to call 9-1-1," Queenie said. "I once heard of a gal who had to be hospitalized after eating bread."

"It's a very real problem," I said. "People who are overly sensitive blow up like balloons when they eat bread."

"Good thing I'm not overly sensitive then." Queenie gave me a wink.

"It's not really like that, anyway," Twiggy said and then took another nibble. "I'm not hypersensitive to gluten or anything like that. Mostly I just don't like the carbs, so the gluten-free diet works for me. Really, it's more Paleo, if you want the truth of it." She took another big bite of the bread.

"Paleo?" Mama's nose wrinkled. "Are you an archaeologist or something?"

"No. It's a kind of diet."

"Well, I understand. The doctor put me on a diet once too. Didn't really take, but I gave it the old college try." Mama took a nibble of her lemon pound cake. "I think mine was called the California diet. No, maybe it was the Arizona diet. Anyway, it was named after some state. Never heard of the Paleo thing. I'll have to look it up on the internet."

Queenie sighed. "I'm terrible on the computer. Things are whirling so fast on that machine, I just can't keep up. To be honest with you, I'd be just as happy if there was no such thing as the internet. I liked things the way they were before we were all in each others' business on those crazy social media sites."

"Oh, but if we didn't have internet, our whole business would collapse," Pop said. "We're dependent on networking, you know."

"Well, all this talk about bread has me hungry," Queenie said. "Does anyone mind if I get some food? It is my birthday, after all."

"Yes, we wouldn't want the birthday girl to starve." Pop chuckled.

Everyone rose and made their way to the buffet. Mama caught me in front of the salad bar and leaned down to whisper in my ear, "Dewey's got his eye on that tall girl with the platinum hair, does he?"

I nodded. "Dahlia's very nice."

"I don't trust anyone whose name I can't pronounce."

"Like Mayor Luchenbacher?" I asked.

"Well, of course I can pronounce Luchenbacher. I grew up with Karl Luchenbacher. That's not foreign to me. Delilah is foreign."

"Dahlia."

"Exactly. Foreign. And I can't understand half of what she says. Do you think she's trying to impress us with that accent of hers?" Mama's eyes flashed with suspicion. "Maybe she's really from California or someplace like that, and she's just acting. Putting on a show so people think she's all hoity-toity when she's just a regular small-town girl like us."

"I don't think there's much that's regular about us," I said.

"I'm definitely not regular," Pop said as he stepped into the spot next to me. "Haven't been for the past four years, but I think it's got something to do with male menopause."

This led to yet another bizarre conversation with my parents.

"That Twiggy girl is the last person on earth I'd picture with my Beau." Mama reached to fill her plate with lettuce. "Such a skinny little thing."

"Mama, why do you care if Beau has a girl?"

Mama turned back to look at me. "I don't expect you to understand, Katie. You're not a mama."

"But even if I was, I'd want my kids to be happy. It's obvious Beau is very happy with Twiggy."

"He can be happy with someone closer to home. When the time is right."

I pulled her off to the side, away from the others. Time for a heart-to-heart with Mama. "What if the time is right now?" I asked. "And what if the place really is Dallas? Would that be so awful?"

A painful silence followed my words.

"What if this is God's answer to Beau's prayers for someone to love?" I continued. "Would you argue with him? The Lord, I mean."

"She lives in *Dallas*."

"If we could put that part aside and focus on the look of happiness on Beau's face, then wouldn't you agree this is for the best?"

Mama said nothing. She shifted her salad plate from one hand to the other.

"Point is, she brings out the best in him," I said.

"In Dallas."

"That's where her work is, sure. But Dallas isn't exactly Timbuktu, Mama. It's only an hour or so away."

"Conversation over." Mama headed back to the salad bar. "My goodness, it's crowded in here tonight. We have to fight for food."

Among other things.

We filled our plates and headed back to the table. Before long everyone but Mama settled into comfortable conversation. We even had Queenie laughing on more than one occasion. When it came time to open gifts, she turned her attention to the packages, obviously intrigued. She had just ripped the paper off of a gift from Mama when something—or rather, some-one—caught my attention from the other side of the room.

Walking toward us, albeit hobbling a bit, was Aunt Alva . . . on Brady James's arm.

28

Who's Gonna Take the Garbage Out

My plan is to have a theatre in some small town or something and I'll be manager. I'll be the crazy old movie guy.

Quentin Tarantino

I couldn't say which shocked me more—seeing Aunt Alva or seeing Brady. Not that I was unhappy to see either, mind you. Just stunned.

The moment Queenie laid eyes on her sister, she stopped unwrapping the gift and froze in place, eyes wide.

Pop rose and moved toward his aunt, then swept her into his arms. "Well, as I live and breathe. So good to see you, Alva. Wonderful of you to come. God bless you for that."

This got a "humph" from Queenie, who went back to her gift.

"I'd know this face anywhere." Pop gestured to Brady. "One of my favorite basketball players ever."

"Thank you, sir." Brady smiled, but I could tell he was a little nervous.

I rose and made introductions. Pop seemed pretty flabbergasted to find one of his favorite Mavericks players standing next to him at Sam's. Across the room, a couple of other customers whispered to one another as they stared at Brady.

"It's so nice to meet you, sir." Brady extended his hand.

My father shook it and then looked at me. Then back at Brady. "I'm sorry . . . where did you say you two met?"

"My mom owns a store in Dallas," Brady said. "Katie is . . ." He gazed at me with tenderness in his eyes. "A customer."

"A customer." Pop looked at Brady. "Our family owns a store too. Hardware. What sort do you have?" Brady had just opened his mouth to respond when Pop interrupted him. "Let's pull up a couple of chairs. You two hungry?"

"Starving." Alva nodded. "Haven't had Sam's barbecue in years."

Pop, God bless him, put Alva and Brady on the far side of the table from Queenie.

Alva shifted her gaze to the table, where Queenie continued to work on the gift from Mama. "Hope you don't mind that we've come without an invitation."

"Oh, they had an invitation." I flashed a warm smile. "From me."

Another "humph" followed from Queenie.

When my aunt lit into a lively conversation with Twiggy, Dahlia, and Crystal, Mama looked aghast.

"You know these gals, Alva?" she asked.

"Well, sure. We're all friends. People in the city are very friendly, you know. Not like here."

This garnered another grunt from Queenie, who'd managed to get the gift from Mama opened at last. It turned out to be a devotional about the power of positive speaking. Ironic.

From across the table Brady looked my way and shrugged. I did my best not to let the joy on my face show, but Mama must've picked up on it. She gave me one of those "we're going to talk about this later" looks.

He offered to fix Alva's plate and disappeared to the buffet. I caught up with him in front of the barbecue.

"I can't believe you're here," I said.

"Me either. Alva called me right after you left. Said she'd had a change of heart. But she knew she couldn't drive all this way, so she asked me to play the role of chauffeur."

"You've been doing a lot of role-playing lately."

"No." He smiled. "Not role-playing at all. It's the real deal, every bit of it. And I'm glad to be here."

He might not have been so glad a minute or so later when the locals swarmed him, asking for autographs. After delivering my aunt's plate to the table, he graciously signed all sorts of things—from menus to church bulletins. By the time he arrived at the table with his own food, my aunt was nearly done eating.

Brady took a seat and gave me a little wink. Alva must've picked up on this and smiled at me. Then she looked at my mother. "Marie, you look even younger than the last time I saw you."

Mama looked stunned by this, but a smile turned up the edges of her lips. "Well, thank you, Alva. That's very sweet."

"It's the hair. Why, you look just like Diane Keaton in that movie she did with Jack Nicholson."

"That's what Katie said when she saw my new do." Mama

fussed with her hair and then reached into her purse for her lipstick compact. "Maybe I'll keep this hairdo after all."

"Katie's a smart girl." Alva winked at me. "Pretty sure it runs in the family."

"Lots of great things run in the family," Pop said. "Right, Mama?"

He looked at Queenie, who never lifted her gaze from the pile of presents in front of her. She'd opened them all and looked as if she wanted to bolt.

I had a flashback to a particular Friday night when I'd gathered around the table with my family at Sam's. This very table, in fact. My brother had joked about hernias and hemorrhoids that evening. I'd dreamed of a day when I'd grow old with a fella who didn't mind such bizarre conversations around the dinner table. Now here we sat—Brady James and the whole Fisher clan. Strange.

A few minutes later we wrapped up the party—if one could call it a party—and my brothers headed out with the girls. Mama had somehow coerced them all into going back to our house for coffee and birthday cake. Pop carried Queenie's gifts out to her car and she followed on his heels, still not speaking to her sister. I found myself alone with Alva and Brady.

"Well, that was awkward." Alva's nose wrinkled. "Sorry, kiddo. I thought maybe the timing was right."

"No, it's my fault. I'm the one who encouraged you to come. Queenie is just so . . . ."

"Stubborn. Always has been." Alva shrugged. "Runs in the family."

We walked out to the parking lot, where Pop was still loading presents in the back of Queenie's car.

I looked at Alva and released a breath. "What do you say we nip this in the bud, once and for all?"

"You think?" She looked nervous.

"This is as good a place as any." I looked up at Brady for some encouragement, and he gave me a confident smile.

"You ladies do the talking. I'll do the praying."

"He's closer to heaven all the way up there." Alva gave a slight chuckle. "Okay. Let's get this over with."

We walked over to Queenie's car just as Pop opened the front door for her. My grandmother glared at me as we drew near, as if to say, "Back off, people."

I didn't back off. Neither did Alva, who stood to my left.

"Queenie, we need to talk, and I think it's better done before we get to the house."

"No talking necessary," she said.

"Queenie, please . . ." Alva's voice sounded shaky. "Can't we just say a few words?"

"Nothing to say."

"But you two used to be really close." I posed this more as a question than a statement, but I could tell Alva was a nervous wreck.

"We were." Alva nodded. "Very close."

"And then?" I asked.

My aunt's eyes misted over. "And then . . . life happened."

"Life happened?" Queenie finally looked at us. She rolled her eyes. "*You* happened. Life didn't happen."

"Queenie . . ." A lone tear trickled down my aunt's wrinkly cheek.

"Conversation ended, please and thank you." Queenie turned the car on.

"Oh no you don't." My father, never one to argue with his mother, reached inside the car and turned it off. "We're going to deal with this right now, Mama, whether you want to or not."

"Humph."

"Jealousies are jealousies," he said, "but sisterly love lasts forever."

"Sisterly love?" Queenie huffed. "Don't talk to me about sisterly love." She looked over at Alva, her eyes brimming with tears. "All these years, and you come back now? Why?"

"Because I love you."

"Love? Where was your love five years ago when I had my gallbladder out? I was sick in the hospital and you didn't come see me."

"I had surgery on my knee six months ago and you didn't even pick up the phone," Alva countered.

"I lost my husband and you didn't so much as send me a note or card."

A painful silence hung over us at that proclamation.

"I . . . I didn't know what to say." Alva's gaze shifted downward.

"Wait." I put my hand up. "This could go on for hours. Point is, you two haven't spoken in years. We get that. What I want to know is, why? Can you just get to the root of the problem, deal with it, and move on?"

"She. Knows. Why." Queenie's jaw clenched.

"And I told you back then that I was sorry. You wouldn't have it. You've never had it." Alva pointed an arthritic finger at her younger sister. "You've never forgiven me, and it's eaten you alive all these years."

"Time to get things out in the open," I said.

My grandmother gave me a warning look, but I wouldn't be shushed. We'd spent too many years in this family keeping things under wraps.

"Confession is good for the soul," I said. "So c'mon, Queenie. Why can't you let go of what happened all those years ago?"

She shook her head. "If Alva wants to tell you, she can. I . . . I just . . . can't." My grandmother paled and looked as if she might be sick.

"Queenie?"

She leaned forward and gripped the steering wheel, her breathing unsteady.

"Mama? You okay?" Pop leaned in the car. "Are you getting overheated?" He reached around her and put the key in the ignition.

"I'm . . . I'm not feeling well."

"Queenie, I'm so sorry," Alva said. "Really, truly sorry."

My grandmother nodded and then slumped over the steering wheel. My heart rate doubled as I called out her name and then turned to Brady.

"Call 9-1-1!"

I tossed him my phone. Queenie lay completely still. Alva crouched over her, tears flowing.

"Sister!" she called out. "Sister, look at me. You wake up right this minute!"

"I don't think she can, Alva." My father checked his mother's pulse. "Everyone back away. She needs air."

"But she needs me," Alva said. "I've never been here for her." Her voice elevated. "But I'm here now, Queenie. I'm here now."

"She's got a pulse. I think she just passed out." Pop pointed the air vents at her. "I pray that's all it is."

Several minutes passed, but they felt more like hours. The wail of a siren in the background eventually alerted me to the fact that the ambulance had arrived. Less than a minute later a young paramedic was working on my grandmother. Pop made a quick call to Mama, who turned her car around and headed back to Sam's with my brothers and the girls right behind her.

"What happened?" the paramedic asked as he checked her pulse.

"She was in the middle of an argument with me," Alva said.

"Next thing you know, she was having trouble breathing," Pop said. "Then she passed out."

"Was she in pain?" The paramedic listened with his stethoscope to Queenie's chest.

"I . . . I don't know." Pop shook his head.

About the time Mama and the others arrived, the paramedics had Queenie loaded up on a stretcher. We all gathered around her in a circle. If there was one thing we Baptists knew how to do, it was pray.

Turned out the Presbyterians were pretty good at praying too. Reverend Bradford showed up at that very moment. He rushed to my grandmother's side. "Queenie? Queenie, I'm here. Hang on now, you hear me? Hang on."

She seemed to rally at the sound of his voice and gave a slight nod. Still, her eyes never opened.

"What happened here?" He looked at Alva and his eyes widened.

"It's my fault." Alva began to cry in earnest now. "Everything is always my fault."

"No. No one is pointing fingers," Reverend Bradford said. "Right now, the only one we need to be focusing on is Queenie. So let's pray."

The Presbyterians and Baptists all joined hands in a circle and prayed the house down. Er, the parking lot. Reverend Bradford apparently had a slightly charismatic edge to his praying that seemed to get Mama more emotional than ever. Her tears flowed as he interceded on my grandmother's behalf.

And when Brother Kennedy, a local Pentecostal deacon, joined in, we really had a prayer meeting. We didn't get a lot of "Amen!" and "Hallelujah!" action in the Baptist church, but I certainly didn't mind it today, not with my grandmother's life hanging in the balance.

By the time we finished, I had no doubt in my mind the Lord had heard our multi-denominational prayer. I had a feeling Queenie had heard it too, based on the half smile that appeared on her lips as they lifted the stretcher into the ambulance.

"Is she coming to?" Mama asked.

The paramedic nodded. "I think so, but let's keep her calm, okay? Not saying you folks shouldn't pray, but that was a little loud."

I watched as my grandmother disappeared into the ambulance, then I felt Brady's arms slip around me. Nestling into his comforting embrace, I wept.

"She's going to be okay, Katie. I just know it."

I nodded and gazed up into his eyes filled with compassion. In that moment, I knew he was right. She was going to be okay. In fact, everything was going to be okay.

29

If Teardrops Were Pennies

There are things about growing up in a small town that you can't necessarily quantify.

Brandon Routh

The whole incident with Queenie shook me up so badly that Brady offered to drive me to the hospital. My parents and Alva followed behind us. Then came the various boys and their respective girls, who'd all decided to stay until we knew for sure that Queenie was okay.

Turned out she was.

It took Doc Henderson a few hours to come to his conclusion, but he shared the news sometime around midnight. "It wasn't a heart attack, folks. Just a case of angina, possibly brought on by stress. Has she gone through anything stressful today?"

"You could say that twice and mean it." Pop sighed. "Yes, she's had a stressful day."

"My fault," Alva whispered, her eyes flooding for the hundredth time. "Always my fault."

"*Not* your fault," Reverend Bradford said. He turned to the doctor to ask if he could go into the room to visit with Queenie and was told to keep the visit short. Seconds later he disappeared.

Pop shook his head. "It'll be interesting to see how that one pans out."

"Well, we've got her on medication that will keep her very calm while she's here." The doctor turned to look at Brady. "Don't I know you?"

"This is Brady James." Pop squared his shoulders and made the introduction, clearly proud to be doing so.

"I thought so." Doc Henderson chuckled. "Hey, how's the knee?"

Brady shrugged. "It's on the mend. Had my first surgery four months ago. They're talking about a second one, but I'm not sure yet when that will be."

"Take it slow and easy," Doc Henderson said. "I've known many a knee surgery that didn't take because the patient tried to move too quickly. Tricky business, these knee problems."

"Try telling that to my agent." Brady rolled his eyes.

"Give me his number and I'll be glad to." The doctor nodded and then faced my dad. "Now, about your mom. I'll probably release her tomorrow afternoon. I like to give these things time—usually twenty-four hours or so. But when she goes home it'll have to be to a stress-free environment."

"Guess that means I'll be going back home," Alva said.

"No way." I rose and walked over to take the seat next to her. "You're coming back to our place, Aunt Alva."

"I insist," Mama added.

"But Brady . . ." She gave him a hesitant look. "He came all this way just for me."

"And I want to stay until I know for sure Queenie's okay." He glanced at me. "Is that all right?"

"Of course." Relief flooded over me at this declaration.

"I saw a hotel up near the freeway. I'll stay there."

"You'll do no such thing," Mama said. "You should come to our place."

"I don't think there's room, Marie," Pop said.

"Well, let's do this. I'll send all of the boys—you included, Brady—to Queenie's place. And the girls"—she glanced at Dahlia, Twiggy, and Crystal—"can stay with us."

Beau looked at her with widened eyes. Likely he thought our mother would murder Twiggy in her sleep. "You sure, Mama?"

"I'm sure, baby boy. We all need some rest, and it's too late for anyone to be driving back to Dallas tonight. The girls and I will get along just fine, I promise."

Everyone stood at the same time, several in attendance yawning.

"Madge is gonna have her hands full tomorrow if none of us show up for work." Dahlia slipped her arm around Dewey's waist. "But I'd hate to leave until I know for sure your grandmother is okay."

"I'm happy you're staying." He planted a kiss in her hair. Mama watched this from a distance and then announced that she was heading back home.

Brady took me back to my car, and I gave him instructions for how to get to Queenie's house. Before we parted ways, he pulled me close and gave me a little kiss on the cheek. "I'm praying for her, Katie."

"I'm grateful." The words were more than just a platitude. Knowing that he was praying for my grandmother meant everything to me.

When I got back to my house, I saw that Mama had already settled our guests in the various bedrooms and the boys were nowhere to be found. I tumbled into bed and slept like a rock. When I awoke the next morning I found Mama and Pop in the kitchen, visiting with Dahlia, Twiggy, and Crystal. Turned out Mama and Crystal both liked to cook. And when my mother plopped a huge stack of pancakes down in front of Twiggy, she never said a word about gluten. Instead, she just dove right in, a delirious smile on her face.

"We'll get 'er fattened up yet," Mama whispered. "Then just see if my baby boy finds her so beautiful."

I rolled my eyes but said nothing. What would be the point?

Afterward we headed up to the hospital, and the boys met us there. My heart did that usual pitter-pat thing that it always did when I saw Brady. He smiled and extended his arms. I gave him a warm hug.

The three girls said their hellos and goodbyes pretty quickly, then Dewey announced that he was driving them all back to Dallas. Jasper and Beau offered to go to Queenie's house to pick up a change of clothes. I had just stepped out of my grandmother's room to say goodbye to everyone when I saw a familiar face. Bessie May. She came tearing around the corner, fear in her eyes.

"Katie Sue! I'm so glad you're here. How's Queenie?"

"Better," I said.

She grabbed my hand. "Your father says there's a pro basketball player in Queenie's hospital room."

"That's right."

"*Why* is there a pro basketball player in her hospital room?

300

Don't you find that odd? The woman never watched a basketball game in her life, other than the ones at the high school, and she wasn't terribly fond of those. In fact, she's not fond of sports at all."

"True. It's kind of a long story, Bessie May."

"I have plenty of time for a long story. I always get a little dizzy when I go into hospital rooms, so I'll just sit right here and you can tell me all about it."

"Isn't this Saturday? Don't you have a rummage sale at the church this morning?"

Her eyes widened and she gasped. "For pity's sake! Yes!" She rushed into the room to say hello to Queenie, then quickly tore out the door, headed to the church.

"She's very fast for someone her age," Brady observed as I came back into the room. "Was she a ball player in a former life?"

"Hardly. The woman knows nothing about sports, as was probably evidenced by the fact that she didn't know who you were. Er, are."

We visited with my grandmother for a while. She seemed genuinely embarrassed that people had created such a fuss. On and on she went, talking about what a goober she felt like. Until Mama happened to mention that Alva had spent the night at our place.

"O-oh?" Queenie sat up a little straighter in the bed. "Is she still there now?"

"Yes, she's resting up. I think last night was harder on her than she wanted to admit."

"Ah." Queenie shook her head. "Well, how's the weather out there?"

Nice diversion.

My father glanced at his watch a couple of times, and

Queenie finally took the hint. "I know what you're fretting about, Herb. Just go open the store. It won't hurt my feelings in the slightest. I'm about ready for a nap anyway." She yawned to prove her point.

"Well, if you're sure, Mama." My father stood and walked over to his mother's bed and gave her a kiss on the cheek. "Glad you're going to be okay. You gave us quite a scare."

"Sure didn't mean to." My grandmother shrugged. "Now, get on out of here. You've got work to do. They're gonna spring me loose soon, so I'll call you when I need to hitch a ride."

My father nodded and then said his goodbyes. The rest of us decided to leave a short while later when Queenie dozed off. No point in sitting there staring at a sleeping woman.

"Want to go to Dairy Queen for lunch?" I asked Brady.

"Dairy Queen?" He stretched and glanced at his watch. "Haven't been to one of those in ages."

"Well, you don't know what you're missing. If we leave now, we can get there before the lunch crowd."

"Sounds great."

We stepped outside of my grandmother's room, and I gasped when I saw an old friend in the hallway. He was approaching with a concerned look on his face.

"Levi Nash."

His handsome face lit with recognition when he saw me. "Katie. I just stopped by to check on your grandmother. We've been praying for her. How's she doing?"

"Better, actually. I heard you were going to be coming back to Fairfield for the summer. It's good to see you."

Levi's attention shifted to Brady and he smiled. "Well, I guess the rumors are true. I heard there had been a sighting of Brady James." He stuck out his hand.

"In the flesh." Brady shook Levi's hand.

"Good to meet you." Levi turned back to me, which made me feel honored. Most folks made such a big deal about Brady that they hardly seemed to take notice of me. "To answer your question, I'll be back and forth from Dallas to Fairfield. I'm interning at the church, but I'm still leading a Bible study on campus in Dallas too."

"That's wonderful."

"I think my mom's glad to have me home, even if it is just for the summer."

"The WOP-pers are glad too."

"Those WOP-pers." He laughed. "They're something else. They sure prayed me back from a rough place. I'm thankful for that."

"You seem so happy, Levi," I observed. "Peaceful."

"Does it show?" He grinned. "Still can't believe I'm the same guy."

"You're not, actually."

"Guess you're right. My whole world has changed."

"It's obvious. This new life seems to really agree with you."

"Thanks. I'm just so grateful." He turned to give Brady a nod. "Great to meet you. Think I'll go in and visit Queenie now."

"She's asleep," I said. "So you might need to wait a bit."

"No I'm not." Queenie's voice rang out from inside the room. "All that chattering outside has me wide awake again."

I clamped a hand over my mouth. "Oops."

"Send that boy in here," she said. "I need some Levi time."

He laughed and stepped inside the room with a wave of his hand.

"He seems like a great guy." Brady slipped his arm over my shoulders as we walked down the hospital corridor together.

"My mother wanted me to marry him," I said.

Brady stopped and looked at me. "Wait . . . she wanted you to marry Levi? Or Casey?"

"Levi." I laughed. "It's complicated."

"Well, do me a favor and don't marry either one." He gave me a little wink and pulled me close.

I agreed, without any hesitation at all.

Less than five minutes later we pulled into the parking lot at Dairy Queen. As I stared through the plate-glass windows, I had a flashback to a day not so many weeks ago when I'd sat in this very same place, ready to go inside to meet Casey for an Oreo Blizzard. It felt like a million years ago.

Or not.

Brady and I stepped inside the restaurant, and I thought my heart was going to sail right out of my throat when I saw Casey sitting with a couple of his friends in our old booth.

Oh. Help.

"You ready to order?" Brady turned his attention to the menu. "I'm starving."

"Mm-hmm."

He ordered a burger and I got the chicken fingers basket, then we headed to a table near the back. As we passed by Casey, he glanced up at me, his eyes widening. They grew even wider when he saw Brady. I gave him a little nod and kept walking, but I felt like I might faint.

"You okay?" Brady asked. "You look like you're not feeling well all of a sudden."

"Yeah. I'll explain when we get to the table."

I didn't get a chance to explain. The other patrons at Dairy Queen gathered around us, gushing over Brady like a celebrity. He took it in stride, but I could tell he really wanted to just fade into the woodwork. Or eat a cheeseburger in peace.

We did manage to eat . . . finally. "You sure you're okay over there?" he asked after several moments of silence on my part.

"Yeah. I, um . . . there's someone here that . . . well . . ."

"Someone in Dairy Queen?" He looked around at the various booths, stopping when he got to Casey's. I didn't have to explain, because Casey was staring at us as if he wanted to take Brady down. I had the strangest feeling it would only be a matter of time before the Oreos hit the fan.

30

If You Were Mine to Lose

We cannot direct the wind, but we can adjust the sails.

Dolly Parton

B rady stared at Casey and then looked back at me. "I'm guessing that's the person you're talking about."

"Yeah. That's the one."

"Casey?"

"Yeah." I sighed. "Sorry."

"Don't be." Brady glanced his way once again, then reached for my hand. "Should I say something to him? Is he making you uncomfortable?"

I was uncomfortable, all right, but didn't want Brady to draw attention to the fact. I didn't have to fret over Casey for long because my former almost-fiancé and his friends left the restaurant a few moments later. No doubt all of the attention on Brady was more than Casey could take. I finally breathed a sigh of relief. Well, until Mama walked in with Aunt Alva. They waved and came straight toward our booth.

"Well, hello, you two." Mama plopped down and fanned herself with a church bulletin. "We just stopped in for a bite. Didn't think you would be here."

"Your mama was kind enough to come back to the house to fetch me," Alva said. "I had a hankerin' for a burger and some ice cream."

At that moment, the manager of the restaurant showed up with two M&M Blizzards in his hand. "For our special guest." He smiled as he handed one of them to Brady and the other to me. "Welcome to the Fairfield Dairy Queen, Mr. James."

"Well, thanks." Brady took his Blizzard and swallowed down the first mouthful. "Mmm. If I keep eating like this, I'll never play ball again."

"Ooh, someone take that ice cream away from him!" Alva laughed. "It'd be a crime if Brady James stopped playing ball." She pointed her finger at him. "Ice cream is hard on the joints." She looked at the manager and said, "Can you bring me one too?"

"You a friend of his?" the manager asked.

"You betcha. We're practically family. If I have my way, we actually will be." She gave Brady a playful wink.

The manager nodded, then headed off to fix a Blizzard for Aunt Alva.

Ophelia Edwards, one of Mama's more troublesome choir members, sat in the booth behind us. She joined in the conversation without invitation. "Marie, who is this handsome young man sitting with our Katie Sue?"

"Now, Ophelia, you know Brady James, surely." Mama continued to fan herself. "Everyone knows Brady."

"Can't say as I've seen him before." Ophelia took off her glasses and wiped them with her chocolate-smudged napkin, then put them back on, covered in streaks. "Nope. He doesn't look familiar."

Alva rolled her eyes. "Surely you've seen him on television."

"Oh, is he that new fella on *Guiding Light*?" Before any of us could answer, Ophelia slapped the table with her hand. "I can't believe I'm admitting right here in Dairy Queen that I watch that show. I've tried to give it up, but it just keeps hanging on. Like a bad cough."

"No, ma'am, I'm not on *Guiding Light*," Brady said. "In fact—"

"Well, I don't blame you for quitting. All of those nasty bedroom scenes." Her face reddened. "You're a good man to give it up."

"Oh, I'm not saying I gave it up. I'm saying—"

"Well, make up your mind. Either you're on *Guiding Light* or you're not."

"He's not, Ophelia." My mother made a "she's crazy" sign behind Ophelia's back. "*Guiding Light* hasn't been on since 2009. Please don't ask me how I know that."

"Well, for pity's sake. I could've sworn I watched it yesterday." Ophelia's nose wrinkled.

"This is Brady James," Alva said. "Point guard for the Mavericks and a good friend of the family."

"The Mavericks? Don't think I've seen that show. When does it come on?"

"It's not a show, Ophelia," Mama said. "It's a . . . never mind."

"Well, why did you say the boy was on television? I swear,

308

people are so hard to follow sometimes." Ophelia took a bite of her chocolate-covered dip cone, which left a smudge of chocolate on her cheek. She then turned her attention to Alva. With narrowed gaze, she pointed to her and said, "You look familiar. Do I know you?"

The manager arrived just then with Alva's Blizzard. He passed it off to her and she took a bite, then gave Ophelia a knowing look. "Well, you should, Ophelia. We graduated from Fairfield High the same year. In fact, we were pretty good friends back in the day."

This apparently led to some confusion on Ophelia's part. She couldn't quite place Alva. Not that my aunt seemed to mind. She turned her attention to her ice cream.

Out of the corner of my eye, I watched Brady. Such a great sport. I couldn't picture him living here, in Fairfield. Couldn't see him having lunch at Dairy Queen every day. Still, he seemed to fit in just about every place he went.

When we finished our Blizzards, I asked Brady if he wanted to take a drive around Fairfield and he agreed. We said goodbye to Mama and Alva, then headed out of the restaurant. Getting out took awhile, what with all of the people stopping us along the way.

Finally cleared from the traffic, Brady reached for my hand and squeezed it. When we got to the door, I realized that Casey was sitting outside at one of the tables on the patio. He glanced up at Brady. And me.

Mostly me.

"You're Brady James." Casey's opening line wasn't very well thought out, apparently, since he wasn't actually looking at Brady when he spoke the words.

"Right." Brady slipped his arm over my shoulders.

Casey looked back and forth between Brady and me, and

I could read the confusion in his eyes. Now he homed in on me, giving me a penetrating gaze. "Katie, we need to talk."

"Brady and I were just headed out for a drive. Can it wait?"

"I, well . . ."

Brady cleared his throat and then announced that he would be waiting in the truck. I nodded and told him I'd be right there. Once he disappeared from sight, Casey tried to take my hand, but I wouldn't let him.

"Katie, I'm confused."

Well, duh.

"I mean, I'm confused about what you're doing in Dallas. This is out of character for you to go away."

"Ah. I see. So, it's okay for you to go to Oklahoma, but I can't go see my cousin in Dallas? If we're not a couple anymore, then why do you care where I go?"

"It's just not like you to go away."

"I happen to like Dallas. I've met a lot of nice people there."

"Okay, I have to ask—what's the deal with Brady James? How in the world do you know him? When I talked to you about him during the playoff game, you didn't even know who he was. Now you're dating him?"

"Who said Brady and I are dating?"

"It's obvious you have feelings for him. And vice versa. You were holding hands."

"Brady and I are in the getting-to-know-you stage. And to answer your question, I met him at a store where he's working."

"Wait. A pro ball player works in a store? What kind of store?"

"It's kind of a long story, Casey, and I don't have time for a long story. That's what I was trying to say before. We're headed out for a sightseeing trip and then back to my parents' place to have dinner. I'm leaving to go back to Dallas tomorrow after church, so you won't be seeing me around." I took a step away and then turned back. "So, what happened in Tulsa?"

"Nothing." He shrugged. "I'm going back. Just came home to pack up my stuff."

"Queenie thought you were back for good."

His eyes widened. "Oh, I see. Is that what you thought?"

"I didn't know what to think. I still haven't quite figured out the part where you left in the first place, so seeing you come back again is even more confusing. It's all so strange."

"Kind of like you staying in Dallas and buddying up with a pro basketball player at some store."

"We're changing. Both of us." *Obviously.* "We're not the same people when we're away from Fairfield."

He shrugged. "Guess not."

"And that's okay. Maybe we needed this to discover who we really are." I glanced toward Brady's truck and saw him standing next to the door on the passenger side. I wouldn't keep him waiting any longer. "Anyway, have a nice trip back to Tulsa, Casey. Give your mama my love before you go. Oh, and if you happen to see me on the front of a bridal magazine wearing a really awesome dress, don't panic."

"What?"

"Just don't read too much into it, okay? It's not a ploy to get you back. In fact, I seriously doubt you'll ever see me wear that dress in person. So rest easy."

"O-okay." He paused. "Have fun in Dallas."

"I will," I said. And I meant it. I gave him a little wave and walked toward Brady, all smiles.

"You okay?" he asked when I drew near.

"Oh yeah. Better than I've been in a long time. Feel like I've lost a hundred pounds."

"Katie, if you lost a hundred pounds, you'd be the size of a toddler."

That made me laugh. He pulled me into his arms and gave me a kiss on the forehead. "That's just a sampling of what's to come," he whispered.

"Mmm." Sounded good.

We spent the next few hours on a lengthy drive through the country. I showed Brady everything. The property my great-grandparents had owned. The high school. The lake. I took him by every place that had ever meant anything special to me while growing up, including the ballpark where my father coached Little League.

As we stood at the edge of the ball field, Brady pulled me close. "I can see why you love it here, Katie. This is very . . . quiet. Peaceful." After a moment's silence he added, "Quaint."

I couldn't tell from the way he used the word if he really meant it as a compliment. "You mean small?" I asked.

"I think it's just right. There's enough of a town to offer the things you need, but not enough to overwhelm you. It's nice."

"Well, speaking of town, there's one place I haven't taken you yet. Would you like to see our family's hardware store?"

His eyes sparkled as he answered, "I thought you'd never ask."

"Pop's already gone home by now, I'm sure," I said. "But I have a key."

We drove to the store and found it empty, as I'd said. That turned out to be a very good thing.

I never thought I'd be kissed by a pro ball player in the lawn and garden section of my family's hardware store, but that was exactly what happened. Brady caught me somewhere between the fertilizer and the sprinklers and gave me a kiss so sweet that I almost tumbled straight into the insect repellent display. When we came up for air—and it took awhile—I felt a little woozy.

He caught me and grinned. "Easy now."

I giggled.

"I guess I should've asked your permission before doing that."

"Doing what? Kissing me? Who asks permission?" I gave him a wink. "I'm not sure I really got the full effect. Would you mind trying again?"

And so he did. He kissed me again in the lawn and garden section. And twice in housewares. And three times in hardware. By the time we reached the electrical department, I'd pretty much made up my mind that we had already generated enough electricity to light the city of Fairfield for a month. He must've realized it too, because he took a giant step backwards and mouthed, "Wow."

"Yes. Wow. That's—that's the word I was thinking." Wow. Wow to the moon and back. Most of all, wow to the idea that I'd waited until the age of twenty-four to really, truly have that sort of reaction to a kiss from a boy. Correction—a man. Yes, Brady James, all six feet four of him, was more than enough man to knock a girl off her feet in the hardware store.

"You're quite a kisser," I said.

"Well, I should be. I've had a lot of practice on *Guiding Light*. But don't tell Ophelia."

We both laughed until tears came.

Then, in an instant, I remembered something. "Brady, it's almost six thirty. Mama's expecting us home for dinner."

"What about Queenie? Should we go back up to see her before visiting hours are over?"

"I'm sure she's already been released, actually. I'm guessing Pop is there now, ready to drive her home. I'll stop by her house tomorrow after church. Besides, I have a sneaking suspicion she'd want the two of us to spend more time together. She's a romantic at heart, even though she doesn't always come across that way."

"You think?"

"Yes." I thought about what I'd just said. "I'm pretty sure Alva would too. You know, those two sisters are more alike than they are different. And I think they would both be tickled pink that you and I are . . ." A girlish giggle escaped. "Well, you know, that we just . . ."

"Kissed in the family hardware store?"

"Yes. Kissed in the family hardware store."

"Well, anything for the family," Brady said. He reached down and gave me a little kiss on the tip of my nose. "Anything for the family."

31

There Goes My Everything

Stand straight, walk proud, have a little faith.

Garth Brooks

On Sunday morning we all attended church together. Brady left immediately after the service so that he could call his mom and update her on the photo shoot.

I managed to talk Alva into staying in Fairfield and riding back to Dallas with me. If she'd known that I planned to take her to Queenie's house after church, she probably would've bolted. Still, with nowhere else to go, she reluctantly tagged along. My parents led the way in their car, and we followed behind them in mine, knowing we would have to leave for Dallas by four o'clock.

When we arrived at my grandmother's house, I could tell Alva was hesitant to go inside. In fact, I wondered if I would be able to talk her into getting out of the car at all.

"Couldn't I just wait here?" she asked.

I gave her a sympathetic look. "Alva. C'mon in. Let's get this over with."

She sighed and followed me to the door. My dad gave the usual three-rap greeting, then opened the door and led the way inside. Queenie was all smiles until she saw Alva. Then her smile quickly faded. She said nothing to her sister at all. Not "Thanks for coming." Not "Get out of my house." Nothing. It was as if Alva hadn't come at all.

Mama and Pop did their best to make small talk, asking Queenie how she was feeling.

"Oh, I'm fine," my grandmother responded with a wave of her hand. "Fit as a fiddle. Not sure what happened the other night. Just got worked up, I guess."

"Well, I'm glad you're okay now, Queenie," I said. "You scared us to death."

"Didn't mean to do that." Her nose wrinkled. "In fact, I didn't mean to draw attention to myself, period. That's the last thing I wanted to do, especially with all of the young folks showing up with dates."

"It was an interesting evening, for sure." Pop shrugged. "Not exactly our usual Friday night routine, but I kind of liked the changes."

"You liked seeing your mother passed out in a car in the parking lot of Sam's?" Queenie asked.

"Of course not, Mama," he said. "Just saying that I'm coming to the realization that breaking from the norm can be a good thing. And I'm really glad you're better now."

"Thank you. I'll be back up and running soon. Tell me

what I missed at church this morning. Did Bessie May sing the solo again?"

Mama rolled her eyes. "Yes. And speaking of Bessie May, I'm not going to be able to stay very long. I have to be at the church at four o'clock for a meeting. We're getting new choir robes, and Pastor needs me to be there to settle a dispute between Bessie May and Ophelia about the color. Can you believe Ophelia wants to go with purple? I mean, seriously. Purple?"

"I like purple," I said. "It might shake things up a little."

"But . . . purple?" Mama looked aghast.

"Alva and I need to leave by four o'clock too," I said. "We've got a drive ahead of us."

"I still can't believe you're going back," Mama said. "Are you moving away for good, Katie?"

"Would it be so awful if I did?"

She paled. "What are you saying?"

"I don't know. I love it there, Mama. I really do. I mean, I love Fairfield too, but there's something about Dallas . . ."

"It's that boy."

I didn't know quite how to respond to that one. After a moment, I finally decided that I needed to come clean and tell my parents the whole story about the contest, the dress, the photo shoot . . . everything.

And so I did.

My father sat with his jaw hanging down as I relayed the story, and Mama . . . well, she looked as if she might be sick.

"You're telling me that you're about to be on the cover of a national magazine wearing a wedding dress that was made just for you?"

I nodded.

"So, those pictures I saw you looking at on your phone the other night . . . ?"

"Were from the photo shoot. Would . . . would you like to see them? They're really good."

It took her a minute, but she finally agreed. I pulled them up on my phone and then passed it her way. Though she refused to admit it aloud, I could tell she thought the pictures were beautiful. Pop certainly did. He whistled when he got to the picture of Brady kissing me.

"Guess it's a little clearer why you're set on going back to Dallas."

"Yeah." I sighed.

"So this is how it is." Mama gave me a pensive look. "One minute you're marrying Casey Lawson, the next you're kissing a baseball player."

"Basketball player," Pop, Alva, and I said in unison.

"And Mama, just for the record, you were ready to marry me off to Levi Nash the minute you heard that Casey had left town."

"True." My mother fanned herself with her hand. "I never felt that Lawson boy was good enough for you, just so you know."

Her statement seemed to strike a chord with Alva, who squirmed in the seat next to me. "Is it getting warm in here?" she asked.

"No, it's just fine." Pop settled back in his chair.

"I for one think it's good for Katie to get away and experience new things," Alva said. "To have new adventures."

"You would." Queenie's first words to her sister were short and to the point. "Which is, I suppose, why you've convinced her to stay with you."

"W-what? You think that's why I asked her to stay with me—to separate her from her family?" Alva looked shocked by this.

"Well, isn't it?" Queenie placed her hands on the arms of her chair.

"Of course not." Alva shook her head. She glanced around the living room, and I could tell she wanted to get up and look at a photograph she kept eyeing on the mantel. I'd never noticed it before, but it was the same photo that she'd framed and put on display in her own living room. Ironic.

Queenie directed her next sermonette at me. "Well, I suppose there's nothing I can say to keep you here. It's not like this is the first time someone's taken off for Dallas and left me in the lurch."

As those words were spoken, I realized exactly why Queenie didn't want anyone to move away from Fairfield. Why she'd fought so hard to keep Jasper here when he'd wanted to move to Houston. Why she'd talked Dewey into going to the local junior college. Why she'd encouraged Mama to hold so tightly to Beau.

She'd already lost her sister to the big city. She didn't want to lose anyone else.

In that moment, the revelation came swift and sure. Queenie didn't hate Alva at all. She loved her so much that she kept a tight rein on everyone else so as not to lose them as well.

Alva cleared her throat and I turned to her, seeing the tears trickling down her cheeks. We had to put an end to this.

"You two need to talk, Queenie," I said. "Get things out in the open."

"Nothing to talk about."

"Sure there is, Mama." My father stood. "Marie and I will go in the kitchen and make some coffee."

"When you come back, bring me one of those little sandwiches Bessie May brought over last night," Queenie said. "I haven't had lunch."

"Sure," Pop said. He and Mama scurried from the room.

"You want me to stay or to leave?" I asked.

"Stay," Alva and Queenie said in unison.

"Okay, stay it is." I settled back against the cushions on the sofa. "Who wants to go first?"

I noticed that Alva's hands were trembling. "Queenie, I . . . I owe you an apology."

Queenie huffed but didn't say anything.

"All those years ago, I got in the middle of your relationship with Paul. I led you to believe that I had feelings for him, but it wasn't true."

"Wasn't true?" Anger flashed in my grandmother's eyes. "You're telling me now that you didn't try to break us up because you cared for him?"

"I liked him fine as a person, but I didn't think he was right for you. I didn't think he was good enough for you, if you want the truth of it." Alva sighed. "I was young and foolish. But I'm older and wiser now."

"Older, for sure." Queenie gave her a sideways glance. "But I'm not buying that story, Alva. Not one bit."

"Well, that's your loss, because it's the truth. I didn't want to give up my sister to just anyone. Paul was a fine boy—man— but I didn't think he deserved you. I didn't really consider what it would do to you if he broke your heart."

Queenie's eyes flooded with tears. "You don't know what you're talking about, Alva."

"Yes I do."

"No you don't. You think that Paul broke my heart?"

"Well, sure. You two broke up, didn't you? I assumed . . ."

"You assumed wrong. I turned him down." When Alva didn't respond, Queenie raised her voice. "Alva, do you hear me? Are you listening? I said that I turned him down."

"What do you mean?" Alva looked stunned.

Tears ran down my grandmother's face. "Paul Bradford proposed to me the summer after I graduated from college, but I turned him down."

Alva scooted to the edge of the sofa. "Why would you do a fool thing like that? If you loved him, why not marry him?"

Queenie swiped at her cheeks with the back of her hand. "Because as much as I cared about him, I cared about my sister even more. Even if she wouldn't speak to me all these years."

"Are you saying you turned the man down because of me?"

"Of course I did. I thought you had feelings for him, and I didn't want to hurt you. You were the last person on God's green earth I'd want to injure."

"Were?" Alva gave her a hopeful look.

Queenie sighed. "Are."

"All these years I didn't know what to think." Alva rose and paced the room. "I wondered why you didn't marry him. Wondered if he'd broken your heart."

"Well, you can rest easy on that count," Queenie said. "He didn't break my heart. I broke his. And I'm not sure he ever got over it."

At that, the room went silent.

"You're just plain crazy, you know." Alva stopped at the edge of the fireplace and looked at the photograph on the mantel. "You always have been, but this really takes the cake."

"Thanks a lot." Queenie squirmed in her chair.

"No, I mean it. Paul Bradford was in love with you and you let him slip through your fingers because you were more worried about me? I'd say that's the definition of crazy."

Queenie bit her lip. "You might be right."

"Maybe it's not too late, Queenie." I gave her a hopeful look.

"What do you mean?"

"I mean, he's a widower. You're a widow. Maybe you two should . . ." I left the sentence open-ended.

"Not. Going. To. Happen." Her jaw clenched.

"Because he's Presbyterian?"

"No." Pain flashed in her eyes. "Because too much time has passed. It's water under the bridge now."

"But I want you to be happy." Alva walked toward her sister and took a seat in the chair next to her. "You still can be."

My grandmother's eyes filled again, and she swiped at them with her hand. "Alva, I had the best husband a woman could ever ask for. Joe meant the world to me. I'm sorry you never really had the chance to know him. You would have loved everything about him. So don't worry about my happiness. God turned my broken heart into the most wonderful experience of my life."

"So why the tears?" I gazed tenderly at my grandmother. "Is it possible you're starting to have feelings for Reverend Bradford again?"

"I let go of those feelings years ago."

"But Queenie, no one would blame you if they . . . resurged. You know?"

"I'm too old for feelings."

I shook my head. "No one is too old for feelings."

"I am. I'm eighty-two. Eighty-two-year-olds should be more practical, less emotional."

"If anyone has earned the right to be emotional, it's someone your age. So don't apologize if you are smitten. And by the way, love knows no age limits. Is it possible—even a teensy-tiny bit possible—you've got some feelings for Reverend Bradford?"

"His name is Paul." Her words came out as a whisper.

"Paul." I gave her a bright smile. "He showed up at Sam's the night you collapsed. Did you know that?"

She shook her head. "No, but I'm not surprised."

"I'd venture to say he's in love with you now." I don't know where the words came from, but I'd obviously spoken them aloud, based on the look of shock on my grandmother's face. "Isn't he?"

Her gaze shifted downward and then back up to me. "Yes. He is."

"Really?" I got it right!

"Yes, I have it on good authority he is crazy about me." Queenie sighed. "Head-over-heels, can't-sleep-nights, can't-walk-straight, can't-remember-if-he's-fed-the-cat crazy."

"How do you know that?" Mama asked as she walked back into the room with a tray of sandwiches in hand.

"Because he told me." Queenie tried to stand, nearly stumbling in the process. "Yesterday. And the day before. And the day before that." She finally managed to stand upright. "He's told me every day for the past six months. Every single morning there's a note on my front door that says, 'You are loved.'"

"Are you serious?" I asked.

"Want the proof?" Queenie hobbled over to her desk and opened the drawer. She reached inside and came out with a folder stuffed full of handwritten love letters, which she pulled out and showed us. My father happened in at that very moment with several cups of coffee on a tray.

"This," my grandmother said as she clutched the letters to her breast, "is all the proof anyone will ever need. Paul Bradford is head over heels in love with me."

32

Let the World Keep On A-Turnin'

It's important to give it all you have while you have the chance.

Shania Twain

My father very nearly dropped the coffee tray when he heard his mother's impassioned speech about Reverend Bradford.

"W-what did you say, Mama?" The cups on the tray rattled this way and that.

"I said that Paul Bradford's head over heels in love with me. And if you need any proof, this is my July folder of love notes. Would you like to see June? May?"

"Are you serious?" My father set the tray down on the coffee table and stepped toward her.

"They go back for several months." She pointed at the drawer. "The man's been driving me out of my ever-lovin' mind telling me how much he adores me. I thought I'd go insane if I didn't tell someone."

I couldn't help the laughter that escaped. "Oh, but Queenie! This is the stuff romance novels are made of. Wow. Double wow. That's so cool. And so . . . romantic."

"I know." She sighed and took a seat once again, still holding on to the letters. "He's always been the romantic sort. Time hasn't changed that."

"Then why not put the poor man out of his misery once and for all and marry him?" Alva asked.

"I can't." Queenie shook her head. "I just can't."

"Why?" Mama asked.

"Ooh, let me guess." I put my hand up. "It's because he's Presbyterian?"

Queenie laughed. At first it came out as one of those light-weight chuckles, but eventually it morphed into a full-fledged belly laugh. "Oh, good grief, no. I have nothing against the Presbyterians. Nothing whatsoever. I never have."

"You don't?" Mama and I spoke in unison.

"No." Queenie's face turned the prettiest shade of pink. "I just stayed away from the Presbyterian church—especially for prayer meetings—because I knew he was there, slipping love notes into my purse when no one was looking. I couldn't think straight when I was around the man. I just wanted to toss caution to the wind and run straight into his arms." She fanned herself with one of the love notes.

"Then why didn't you?" I asked.

"Because I worried about what people would think." She looked at her sister. "I worried about what you would think. Even after all these years, your opinion matters most to me."

"I think you're nuts, but I've already said that." Alva slapped her hands down on her knees. "Listen, if I ever turn down a perfectly wonderful man, it won't be to save face with you or anyone else. It'll be because he's not the right fella for me. And by the way, I might've convinced you that I had an infatuation with Paul Bradford, but trust me, we would've been miserable together."

"Really?" A hopeful look crossed Queenie's face. "You mean that?"

"I do. For one thing, I can't abide a man in a robe."

"A bathrobe?" I asked.

"No." Alva shook her head. "That robe he preaches in. Reminds me of a woman in a dress. Seems kind of strange to me."

"Seriously?" Queenie said. "I think he looks perfectly wonderful in it. I feel closer to heaven when I see a reverend in a robe."

"And there you have it. He makes her feel closer to heaven." I laughed. "Write that down, Queenie. Leave it on his door tomorrow morning, and just see how he responds. I have no doubt in my mind you'll end up making his day. His week. His year. He's been waiting for this and deserves to hear it straight from the horse's mouth."

"Oh, I don't think I could. I just don't."

"Why?"

"Because . . ." She paused, and I could almost read her thoughts. They were the same thoughts Mama had expressed every time she feared one of us kids might be moving away.

"You're afraid of change," I said.

She nodded. "Everything is running smoothly right now. If I interrupt the flow of that, who knows what'll happen."

"So what?" Pop shook his head. "Seriously. So what? That's what I was saying before about Friday night at Sam's being a blessing in disguise. We're stuck in a rut and I'm tired of it."

Queenie looked startled, but Mama even more so.

"Stuck in a rut?" she said.

"Yes, Marie. Stuck, stuck, stuck." He paced the room, clearly agitated.

Mama shook her head. "But Herb, I like things to stay the same. I thought you did too."

"There was a time when I did, yes. But something's stirring inside of me and I can't seem to stop it. I'm . . . bored."

"Bored?" Mama paled. "But consistency is a good thing. I like to know that you're coming home from the store at 5:05 p.m. I like to know that Katie and the boys are tucked into their beds at night."

"You do know we're all in our twenties, right, Mama?" I said.

"Of course I know. I gave birth to you. But that doesn't make the changes any less painful. In fact, it makes them worse." She sighed. "Is it really so awful to know that everything around here moves like clockwork? Friday nights at Sam's. Thursday evenings in choir. Sunday morning and evening at church."

"She likes routine," Pop said.

"And control," Mama said. "I like to be in control of it all. So when things happen that are out of my control—"

"Like Queenie being hospitalized or Beau falling for a sweet gal who lives in Dallas?" I offered.

"Yeah, like that. It rocks my boat."

"Your mother has never cared to have her boat rocked." Pop gave me a knowing look.

Ew.

"Point is, all of these changes of late have upset my apple cart, and it's really got me rattled."

"Peach cart might be a better choice of words," Pop said. "But you know what? Forget the apple cart."

"W-what?" Mama looked stunned. "What did you say?"

"I said forget the apple cart. Kick it over. Embrace change." He gave my mother a funny look. "I think I have the answer, Marie. It's been staring me in the face all along. You and I . . . we're going to do something different. Something totally unexpected."

"We . . . we are?"

"Well, sure. If the kids can all accept the changes that life has to offer, then so can we. I say we get on that big ship—the new one in Galveston—and go to the Cayman Islands."

"The Cayman Islands?" Mama's eyes widened. "Herb Fisher, we rarely leave Fairfield except to run to the mall in Dallas, and that's only a couple of times a year. How can we go to the Cayman Islands?"

"That's my point. That's exactly why we must go there. And Cozumel. I understand the ship makes a stop there. We'll go to one of those private islands and go snorkeling."

"Snorkeling?" Mama looked aghast. "I've never snorkeled a day in my life."

"Then you're long overdue."

Queenie rose from her chair and announced that she had to make a run to the bathroom. As if the woman could run. "My goodness, this is all so exciting," she said. "You've got me so worked up that I hope I make it to the powder room." She gave me a little wink and added, "Fill me in when I get back."

My father took a few steps in my mother's direction. "Don't you get the point, Marie? It's time to break with tradition. Do something new. Adventurous." A dreamy look came over him. "Shoot. Maybe I'll sell the hardware store."

"What?" Mama and I said in unison.

"Why not? A man can't work forever."

"But you're only fifty-seven," Alva said. "Too young to retire."

"So what?" He shrugged. "There's no law that says a man has to work until he's sixty-five. I've got some money put away. And if we sell the store, we'll be set for our golden years. Maybe we can jaunt around the country in an RV like my old friend Buster Haggard."

Mama leaned over to whisper, "You might recall that Mr. Haggard lost his marbles at about this same age. Bought an RV and hit the road. We haven't seen him or his wife Mabel since. Last I heard, they bought a little cabin in the mountains in New Mexico." She shivered. "Can you imagine?"

"I can!" Pop clasped his hands together. "Let's follow in Buster's footsteps."

"You want to hit the road and never come back?" Mama looked floored by this. "You want people to say we've lost our marbles?"

"No. But doggone it, Marie, I love the idea of doing something different. Let's skip Sam's this coming Friday night."

"Skip Sam's?"

"Sure. Let's drive to Dallas and eat a steak. A giant, juicy steak at one of those big, fancy steakhouses. And afterward we'll go to that cheesecake place and spend eight dollars on a slice of cheesecake."

"Surely you jest."

"Surely I don't." He waggled his thick brows. "Try me."

"But I can get lemon pound cake at Sam's for a fraction of the cost," Mama said.

"And you do. Every week. But when we're in Jamaica—"

"Wait." She put her hand up. "Who said anything about Jamaica?"

"The cruise I was talking about. It stops in Cozumel, Grand Cayman, and Jamaica."

"You've really been researching this?"

"For three months. Even talked to a travel agent."

"We know a travel agent?"

"My third cousin twice removed. She lives in Waco and I sent her an email. Anyway, when we're in Jamaica we'll eat jerk chicken and drink virgin piña coladas."

"I'll die of botulism."

"But what a way to go, Marie." He grinned. "Can you imagine the stories our kids—and grandkids—would tell? Grandma and Grandpa went to Jamaica and breathed their last breath on a tropical island, drinking piña coladas and eating contaminated chicken. It'll be great."

"Herb, you've lost your mind."

"Maybe. But it's about time, I daresay."

Now Mama started pacing the room. "I don't think you understand. If I go on a vacation to Jamaica, who's going to take over the choir while I'm gone? Everyone knows the choir is my domain."

I raised my hand. "I have a suggestion. Let Bessie May do it."

"Bessie May?" Mama's cheeks flushed pink.

"Sure. She's been dying to take over for as long as I can remember."

"But she has arthritis," she argued. "She couldn't possibly lift her arms to direct. Not long enough to get through three verses and a couple of choruses."

"Then let them sing one of those praise choruses the kids sing," Pop said. "They don't have a lot of words. Surely she could last that long, arthritic joints or not."

Mama looked as if she just might faint. "Herbert Fisher, are you actually suggesting that I let Bessie May lead a contemporary worship song while I'm gone?"

He nodded and looked as calm as if he'd just said, "Hey, let's eat grilled cheese for lunch."

"But Herb. Surely you don't mean that." Mama's eyes reflected her complete shock at this idea. "A praise chorus?"

"I do mean it. And if you feel like arguing with me, I'm up for it. I can think of all sorts of other suggestions to change things up. At the church. At the store. In our . . . private life." His eyes sparkled with mischief. "That reminds me, I've been thinking about changing the color of the paint in our bedroom. That tan color is so depressing. What about something in a great shade of red? Not a bright red, but more of a wine color. Doesn't that sound romantic?"

At that, Mama had to sit down.

My father took a seat next to her. "Marie, the point is, I'm ready to do something different. Unusual."

Mama turned to me, her hands trembling. "It's finally happened. Your father has snapped. I've heard of this in men his age but never dreamed it would happen to him. To us." She shook her head. "I don't know what to say. I'll miss you after they take you away to the padded room, Herbert."

"Don't be silly. Say you'll dance with me, Marie." He rose and grabbed her hand. "We might need to take salsa lessons before we get on the cruise ship. I hear they've got dance competitions, and I'll want to enter."

"He's running a fever." Mama rose and felt his head. "I'm sure of it. He's delirious. Someone needs to call 9-1-1."

"Delirious, yes." My father chuckled. "Feverish, no. Unless you mean feverish for you." He planted a huge kiss on her, dipping her à la *Dancing with the Stars*.

Mama came up from the kiss, her cheeks blazing red. "Well, if that doesn't beat all."

"What did I miss?" Queenie asked as she hobbled back into the room.

"Pop's lost his marbles," I said.

"They're going on a cruise," Aunt Alva added. "To Jamaica."

"Does that mean they won't be here to eat dinner at Sam's Friday night?" Queenie asked.

"We're not leaving that quickly," Pop said. "But you people can expect some changes around here, that's for sure."

"Fine by me. I'd like to go to Lonestar Grill on Friday. I hear they've got great chicken-fried steak."

"Or maybe you could come to Dallas for a few days and stay with Katie and me," Alva suggested.

"I just might." Queenie nodded. "I just might."

"See there, Marie?" Pop plopped back down in his chair and leaned back, crossing his arms. "That's what happens when you kick over the apple cart."

"Apples, mmm." Alva giggled. "Apple pie sounds really good right about now. Katie, do you have any interest in stopping by Sam's for some pie on our way out of town? We can skip the meal and get right to the good stuff."

"Skip dinner?" I said. "Go straight to dessert?"

"Sure. I do it all the time."

"We don't," I said. "We eat at the same time. Same place. Same meals. Same . . . everything."

"Did you not just hear my passionate speech about kicking over the apple cart, kiddo?" My father laughed. "Go to Sam's. Eat pie. Skip the meal. Do a dance in the middle of the restaurant. Let the people talk."

"Amen!" Alva chuckled. "What he said. Let's get some pie. And maybe some ice cream too. A girl only lives once. She might as well enjoy herself, don't you think?"

"I do."

Before we left, Alva walked over to Queenie and the two embraced. Genuinely, truly embraced. I gave Queenie a kiss on the forehead, then walked over to her desk and pulled out her stationery and a pen. Without saying a word, I laid both on the desk in plain view. She looked up at me and I gave her a wink. No doubt she'd be writing Reverend Bradford a note shortly after we left. I hoped.

Alva and I landed in the parking lot at Sam's at 4:17 p.m. I'd never been to Sam's at 4:17 before. The hostess looked confused, but she walked us to our usual table.

"I don't want to sit here," Alva said. "Too sunny. Let's go in the front room."

That just about caused the waitress to call for backup. "O-okay."

Minutes later we were chowing down on huge slices of apple pie. Then I had a brownie. And just to top it all off, I ate a piece of lemon pound cake. No doubt the rumors would fly once Alva and I left. Gretel Ann would call Frenchie at Do or Dye. She'd tell her that "that Fisher girl" had gone crazy. Before long the whole town would be buzzing that I'd had my dessert before my dinner. They'd blame it on my breakup with Casey. They might even speculate that I was losing my marbles like Pop. But I didn't care. Maybe I was losing my marbles. Or maybe, as Mama said, my apple cart had tipped over.

Mmm, apples.

Just for fun, I headed back up to the buffet for a second slice of apple pie. If I was going to be the topic of conversation in Fairfield, Texas, I might as well go for the gold and really give 'em something to talk about.

33

Heart Don't Do This to Me

A city becomes a world when one loves one of its inhabitants.

Lawrence Durrell

The week before *Texas Bride* released their October issue, Nadia flew back to Dallas so that she could attend her charity event. We spent the next several days dealing with the media while preparing for the magazine to hit the newsstands. I'd never seen the folks at the bridal shop so excited.

I'd been nervous about seeing Nadia in person, ever since the day Brady told her about my broken engagement. Still, with my heart becoming more entangled with her son's every day since, I had no choice. I finally broached the subject the night before the magazine released. We all met up at Alva's house for dinner.

Over a yummy meal, we shared details about several upcoming press engagements and a visit from a high-end buyer from out of state. The rest of the meal was spent talking about the dress itself and how much Nadia loved the final product.

She used her napkin to dab at her lips, then pulled it down and looked at me. "Katie, I'm going to need to go soon. I really need some sleep. But before I do, I want to talk to you about something. Would you walk me out to my car?"

I nodded, feeling my heart slither up to my throat. "Sure. I've been wanting to talk to you too."

I followed her out of the house to her car, and she opened the driver-side door. Before she got inside, she faced me and placed her hand on my arm. "I need you to know something, Katie."

"Y-yes ma'am."

"Before I ever design a gown, I pray and ask the Lord to show me not just the design but the fabrics, the textures, everything."

"I think that's great."

"Sometimes I have a real sense about things. Other times, not so much. But in your case, I knew without a shadow of a doubt just what sort of dress would be perfect. I didn't know anything about your fiancé, nor did I need to. The dress I designed was for you. And it was heaven-inspired. I need you to know that in case you have any doubt in your heart about whether or not that Loretta Lynn gown was meant for you."

"Oh, Nadia." I threw my arms around her neck. "You aren't mad that I didn't let you know right away? I wanted to. I really did. But everyone seemed to think I should keep it to myself so that you wouldn't be hurt. Please forgive me."

"Well, of course I forgive you. I was never mad, just a little perplexed. I was sad that you didn't think you could tell me right off the bat, but I'm definitely not hurt that you're not marrying the wrong man. That would have been catastrophic."

I felt the edges of my lips curl up in a smile.

"I knew the minute Brady picked me up at the airport the other day and from the smile on his face every time he mentioned your name—he's fallen . . . again. Only, this time he didn't break anything." She grinned. "If you know what I mean."

I pressed back a giggle. "If anyone had told me I'd end up falling for a pro basketball player in Dallas, I would've said they were crazy."

"So you do have feelings for my sweet boy?"

"Do I? He makes it so easy. I've never met anyone like him. These last couple months have more than convinced me that my heart is tied to Dallas."

"Well, speaking of which, I wanted to talk to you about the dress, but something else too. Madge tells me that you've been a huge help around the shop. She's really impressed with your design skills."

"I've enjoyed helping rearrange the layout and the window displays. And I'm so grateful for the income. It's been a fun way to freelance."

"Well, we've seen an upswing in sales since those displays have been redesigned. Not only that, she said that you're the one who came up with the national ad that's going in the *In Flight* magazine next month. Is that right?"

I nodded.

"From what I can tell, you've got a penchant for PR. You see what it takes to draw people in. That's why the windows go over so well with the customers."

"You think?"

"Well, sure." She smiled. "Katie, I want to make this official. I want to offer you a full-time position at the shop."

"Really?"

"Yes. Your dedication over these past several weeks has convinced me that you are more than just a customer. You have a natural talent, and I'd love to see it cultivated."

"Oh, Nadia. I'd be honored. You have no idea."

"I think I have some idea. I was young once too, and needed a break. I hope you enjoy being with us at Cosmopolitan." She reached over and gave me a motherly hug. "I know it's not the same, being in Dallas. But it's not really that far from Fairfield."

"I know. And my parents are going to be coming back and forth more often now. In fact, they're coming tomorrow so they can be here for the big day."

"So they know about the dress now?"

"Yes ma'am."

"Wonderful. I can't wait to meet them." She yawned and then slipped into the driver's seat. "Give that boy of mine a kiss from me and tell him not to stay out too late. We have a big day tomorrow."

"Will do." I gave her a little wave and watched as she pulled away. My heart was so full I could hardly stand it. When I turned around, I saw Brady standing in the open doorway of my aunt's house. I sprinted to him.

"What did she say?" he asked.

"She offered me a job."

He smiled. "I had a feeling that was coming. Madge has been singing your praises."

"Just Madge?"

"Well, the girls put in a good word for you too." He pulled me into his arms and gave me a little kiss on the forehead.

"Just the girls?" I gazed up at him and caught a glimpse of the moonlight above.

"Well, maybe someone else. But he's a little biased, so I'm sure the decision wasn't based on anything he had to say."

"Surely not." I gave Brady the sweetest kiss, and then we stood in a comfortable embrace.

After a few moments, Brady loosened his hold on me. I could tell he had something on his mind. "I, um . . . I saw the orthopedist this morning."

"You did?"

"Yeah. He wants to do another surgery on my knee."

"Why didn't you tell me, Brady?"

He shrugged. "I've been thinking about it. Praying about it. Hadn't really decided until tonight, so I didn't bring it up."

"Well, now I can pray too. Are you going to do it?"

"I am." He nodded. "It still bothers me . . . a lot. I know that Stan thinks I'm ready to play again, but I'm not. And my mom still needs me at the shop. And now that you're there, well . . ." He pulled me close again. "Just one more confirmation that it's okay not to return to the game just yet. I've got to be healed up before I get back on the court."

"Getting healed up is for the best." Alva's voice rang out from behind us. "Sorry to be a nosy poke, but I had to come out to, um, take out the trash."

"Sure you did." I laughed and then extended my arm so that she could join us in a hug.

After Brady left that night, I settled into bed but had a hard time sleeping. With so much stirring, the sense of anticipation kept me wound up tighter than a clock. When the alarm went off at 6:30 I'd only had three hours' sleep, but I had to put on my game face.

Game face. Ha. Those words made me think of Brady, and

thinking of Brady made me want to get to the shop as quickly as I could. I had to wait on Aunt Alva, of course. She moved a lot slower than I did but still managed to be ready by eight.

We arrived to a flurry of activity. The girls were all dressed to the nines. Well, all but Crystal, who was noticeably absent. I asked about her, but Brady just shrugged. "I get the feeling she's going through a transition of some sort."

"Transition?"

"I'm not sure. Did you know that you have guests?"

He pointed to some customers on the far side of the shop who were busy looking at gowns with Nadia and Madge. Only when they turned to face me did I realize I was looking at my parents. Not that I would've recognized Mama. She'd had her hair colored, a lovely honey shade. And the makeup . . . wow. I'd never seen her look so polished and professional before.

I rushed to greet them and wrapped them in a warm embrace. "You've met Nadia?" I asked.

"Yes, and Madge too. They're even sweeter than you described them to be."

"She called me sweet?" Madge put her hands on her hips and laughed. "Go figure."

"We were just telling the ladies what a beautiful shop this is." Mama pointed to the gown on the mannequin near the front of the store. "And your dress! Katie, it's fabulous. Looks just like something Loretta Lynn would wear, but it also reminds me so much of you. It's perfect!"

Nadia beamed. "That's the idea. But we have Dahlia to thank for that. She's been a big help to me while I've been in Paris."

"That Dahlia is the sweetest thing," Mama said. "She was such a comfort to us on the weekend that Queenie was hospitalized. Oh, and speaking of Dahlia, did you know Dewey drove us here? He's been dying to come for a visit. And thank goodness too! If it hadn't been for him, we would've gotten lost."

"Not me," Pop said. "I've got that newfangled GPS thing on my phone. Now that we're out and about more, it's come in handy."

"Where is Beau?" I asked. "And Jasper? Are they both coming?"

"Well, it's the strangest thing." Mama wrinkled her nose. "Beau is coming in his own truck. But Jasper said he'd rather stay at the hardware store. Pop offered to shut it down for the day, but Jasper wouldn't hear of it."

"Very strange."

"You can say that twice and mean it," Mama said.

"Very strange," Pop and I said in unison.

That got a laugh out of Mama and Nadia. Mama stayed in good spirits until Beau arrived a few minutes later. When he entered the store, he went straight to the counter to visit with Twiggy, only giving the rest of us a little wave.

"Well now, that boy of mine." Mama clucked her tongue and took a step in his direction.

"Marie." Pop rested his hand on her arm. "Let it be."

"Let it be? But I just want to say hello to my son."

"Marie."

Turned out Beau wanted to talk to Mama more than any of us knew. After saying a few words to Twiggy, he headed our way and announced that he'd loaded his truck with all of his belongings from home and planned to stay in Dallas, starting today.

"Wait, w-what?" Mama looked stunned.

Pop, on the other hand, looked relieved.

Dewey, who'd just joined us, didn't say a word.

"I've got a new job, Mama," Beau said. "Making good money too."

"There is a God and he loves me!" Pop raised his hands to the sky.

Mama's eyes narrowed to slits as she looked at Beau. "You took a job . . . where?"

"Well, it's the craziest thing," he said. "I think you're going to laugh."

"Try me." Mama crossed her arms at her chest. "And please don't tell me you've developed a penchant for dress design. I'm not sure my heart could take it."

Dewey slung an arm around Beau's shoulder. "Now there's a brother I can be proud of."

My father pinched his eyes shut and shook his head. "It's my fault. I should've been a more manly influence. I let your mother coddle you, and now look at what we've created . . . a wedding dress designer."

"No, Pop. It's nothing like that." Beau rolled his eyes. "It's something completely different. I'm going to get to use my God-given talent to help others. It's a great feeling."

"Talent?" My father looked stumped by this. "You have talent?"

"Easy, Pop." I gave him a stern look.

"Yes," Beau said. "It's a great opportunity, and I can say without any hesitation that I already love it."

"And what he really, really loves," Dewey interjected, "is a certain little gal who's no longer gluten intolerant."

"He's in love with her?" Mama turned and glared at Beau. Her tightened expression softened after a moment. "Well now, I have an idea. Why don't you work from home in Fairfield? People do that all the time these days. And if that little skinny gal is truly interested in you—and who wouldn't be interested

341

in this handsome face?—she would come to Fairfield. She has to know that you live there, after all. And a woman's place is with the man she loves."

"Well now, maybe it's the other way around," Pop said.

We all stared at him.

"What do you mean, Herb?" Mama asked.

"Maybe, just maybe, a man's place is with the woman he loves."

You could've heard a pin drop at that statement.

"Don't you remember when we were dating?" he said. "I wanted to move away to Waco? I had a great job offer."

"I remember the job offer, but I thought you turned it down because you really wanted to stay put in Fairfield."

"No, you wanted that. And I loved you, Marie. Still do. So I stayed in Fairfield and took over my father's hardware store. I'm not saying I regretted that decision, but I will say that I just wanted to see the smile on your face every morning. Being where you wanted to be made my heart happy enough to stay put."

My mother put her hands on her hips and for a moment looked as if she might cry. "Herbert Fisher, why didn't you ever tell me this?"

He shrugged. "I got over it."

"Got over it?"

"Well, you know what I mean. I grew to love our life in Fairfield and hardly ever thought about that job again." He slipped his arm over Beau's shoulder and gazed at Mama. "But Marie, maybe our boys need the same consideration."

"Are you saying . . ." Mama flinched as she glanced at Beau. "Are you saying that my baby boy should really move far, far away from home, from those he loves, to enter into a relationship with a gal from someplace we don't even know?"

"Precisely." Pop nodded. "And I'm also saying that he's not a baby. He'll figure that out when he has to show up at work every day and pay rent on an apartment. In Dallas. Which, by the way, isn't far, far away from home."

"Technically it's a house," Beau said. "I'll be living in a house with a guy named Stan."

"What?" I said. Now here was an interesting piece of the puzzle.

"Yep. He's great. And that's what I was trying to say earlier. I'm going to be working for Stan, not the bridal shop. He's a sports agent and he needs someone to assist him. You won't believe the big-name players he represents. I've met so many cool people."

"Oh, thank the Lord." My father slapped Beau on the back. "I couldn't quite picture how I'd go about telling my friends that my son designed wedding gowns for a living."

Beau rolled his eyes. "Stan's been agenting for years, and he's going to teach me the ropes."

Stan chose that very moment to enter the front door.

"Oh, great," Madge said as she and Brady walked our way. "Look who's come for a visit."

"C'mon, admit it, Madge," Brady said. "He's growing on you."

"Like a fungus." She rolled her eyes.

The door opened again, and this time Lori-Lou entered with Josh and their girls. Alva followed behind them holding baby Joshie.

Madge flew into gear at once, reaching for her walkie-talkie. "Incoming Mama Mia!" she said. "Incoming Mama Mia!"

"Whatever does she mean?" my mother asked.

"It's code for . . . oh, never mind." I laughed and walked over to greet Lori-Lou, who fussed at Mariela.

Less than a minute later Lori-Lou looked as if she might be sick. She managed to say, "I-I don't feel so well," before bolting from the room.

Josh watched her leave and then turned back to me with a sigh. "It's always like this."

"Always like what?" Alva asked as she shifted Joshie in her arms. "She gets sick a lot?"

"Yes. When she's . . ." He pointed at the girls, who'd taken to crawling under one of the clothing racks.

"Josh? Are you saying that Lori-Lou is . . . expecting?" Alva let out a little squeal as he nodded. "Seriously?"

"Oh, it's serious, all right. And trust me, it was quite a shock. She's been in tears for weeks. I can't believe no one's noticed."

"So, that day at the stockyard," I said. "Lori-Lou was having morning sickness?"

"Right. I think she was actually relieved that you thought it was the stomach flu."

"This is a particular strain of the flu that lasts about nine months." Mama laughed. "Caught it a few times myself."

I wanted to run after Lori-Lou and apologize for not paying more attention, for being so distracted with my new life at the shop. But just as I turned to do so, the door opened again and the shop filled with reporters and photographers from all of the local news stations. I watched as Nadia greeted them, and then the real fun began.

Our copies of *Texas Bride* were hand-delivered by Jordan Singer, who arrived moments later. I couldn't believe my eyes when I saw the quote from the queen of country music herself—Loretta Lynn. Turned out she loved the dress and gave it her stamp of approval. I loved it too. And when I saw the photo that had been chosen for the cover, I couldn't help but laugh. There I sat, plopped down on a wooden crate, in that gorgeous Loretta Lynn gown. Its ruffled skirt spilled out beautifully around me, as if I'd somehow planned it that way, and the details on the bodice shimmered underneath the afternoon sunlight. All in all, a perfectly wonderful photo.

Best of all? The handsome fellow in the tuxedo. He stood just a few feet away, gazing at me with a smile ten thousand times sweeter than all of the peaches in Fairfield.

Epilogue

Less than two weeks after the magazine cover went live, my parents left for their first-ever Caribbean cruise. Mama called me from the port in Galveston just as I arrived at the shop on a Saturday morning. We hadn't opened yet, so I had plenty of time to talk.

"Katie, can you hear me?" She spoke a little too loud for comfort.

"Sure, Mama." I pulled the phone away from my ear. "What's up?"

"Listen, we're leaving on this ridiculous cruise right in the middle of hurricane season, so if you never see us again, just know that I love you and I wanted the chance to see you walk the aisle in that beautiful Loretta Lynn gown."

"Mama, I'm not engaged."

"Well, I know, but someday you will be. If we're swept away by a hurricane, please bury me in my blue dress. You know the one, with the pretty collar?"

"Mama, if you're swept out to sea, we won't need to bury you."

"True." She sighed. "Well, don't miss me too much. Oh, and check on Jasper while we're gone. You do know what's happening back home, don't you?"

"What do you mean?"

"You're not going to believe it," Mama said. "You're just not."

"Oh, I don't know. These days I'd say my mind is opened to believing all sorts of new and interesting things. What's up?"

"Call him when we hang up. He'll tell you. But in the meantime I have some news about Queenie."

My heart skipped a beat as fear settled over me. "What happened to her? Is she sick?"

"No."

"She fell and hurt herself?"

"No. Not even close. Brace yourself, Katie."

"O-okay." I drew in a deep breath, unsure of what to expect.

"She's. Become. A. Presbyterian."

I couldn't say why those words struck me like they did, but I laughed so hard I almost dropped the phone. Then Mama started laughing. After a while we simply had to end the call because we couldn't get it under control. Brady heard me all the way from the workroom and came out to the front of the store, filled with questions. When I told him, he started laughing too.

I spent the next few minutes trying to picture my grandmother in the Presbyterian church. Watching the man she adored preach . . . in a bathrobe. Okay, not a bathrobe, but a robe. Feeling closer to heaven.

Funny how life turned out.

A quick glance at the clock let me know we still had fifteen minutes before opening, just enough time to call Jasper. He answered his cell phone on the second ring with a brusque "Hello?"

"Mama said I should call you. What's up?"

"She told you about Queenie?"

"Yep. I hear she's a Presbyterian now."

"Yes, but wait . . . there's more. There's been a sighting."

"A sighting?"

"Queenie. And Reverend Bradford. Sitting in your spot at Dairy Queen, eating Oreo Blizzards."

"Whoa. I thought Queenie was borderline diabetic."

"Katie, be serious. I'm trying to tell you they're a couple."

"Queenie and Reverend Bradford. Out in public. Eating ice cream." I thought about that and smiled. "Which explains why she's become a Presbyterian. But she really is borderline diabetic, Jasper. She's kept it under control with diet and medication. You didn't know that?"

"I guess I'd forgotten." He sighed. "It's true what they say . . . people will sacrifice just about anything for love."

"Even their health." I laughed, then grew more serious. "Or the desire to move to the big city."

"Yeah, and that's probably the real reason Mama told you to call me. Crystal has moved to Fairfield."

"What?"

"Yep. I, um . . . I'm going to ask her to marry me, Katie."

"Oh, Jasper." I felt the sting of happy tears in my eyes. "I'm so happy for you."

"I'm pretty happy for me too. And you know what? Now that Crystal's here helping out at the hardware store, I don't feel that same pressure to get out of town. In fact, Fairfield is looking better by the day."

"I'm so glad. I'll bet Pop was surprised, though."

"He was. Did you know he was actually talking about selling the store? Can you believe that?"

"Yeah, he mentioned it awhile ago."

"Well, I think I've talked him into letting me take over as

manager instead. That way he and Mama are free to gallivant around the country."

"Now that they've lost their marbles," I said.

"Yep. And speaking of which . . ."

Off in the distance I heard the sound of a customer's voice. Sounded familiar.

"Is that Bessie May?" I asked.

"Yes." He chuckled. "Arguing with Crystal about the price of a garden hose. You know how she is. Always wanting to barter."

"Let me guess. She's offering her two jars of peach preserves in exchange for the hose."

"One jar. Her prices have gone up. But Crystal's taking the bait," Jasper said. "Sorry, but I'm going to have to intervene before things get out of control. Gotta go, sis. Take care of yourself in the big city."

"And you take care of yourself in the small town."

We ended the call and I couldn't help but smile. I pictured it all—my brother in a small town with the woman of his dreams at his side, me in the big city. I sighed, thinking about how good God had been to us.

"You seem kind of dreamy over there." Madge's voice startled me back to reality. "If I didn't know any better, I'd say you were in love."

"Oh, I'm in love, all right." A giggle followed. "With this place. With my new life. With . . . all of it."

"All of it?" She jabbed me with her elbow and gestured to Brady, who fastened a veil loaded with Austrian crystals onto a mannequin.

"Well, it might be a little soon to say." I'd never admit my feelings aloud to Madge, but right now they had me smiling from the inside out. I continued to gaze at Brady, emotions overtaking me. I felt my cheeks grow warm as he looked my way and gave me a wink. In the process of flirting with me, he nearly tumbled from the ladder. Poor guy.

"See the effect you have on him, girl?" Madge groaned. "It's the only downfall to you working here. Now he'll never get any work done." She mumbled something about how he'd never worked very hard in the first place, but she lost me after a line or two. Brady James was the hardest-working man I'd ever met, and the most dedicated team player. No doubt about that.

He climbed down from the ladder, extended his arms, and gave me a "come hither" look.

I glanced up at the clock and took note of the time. Only two minutes until the store opened. Just enough time for one final play from my end of the court. With a spring in my step, I raced across the bridal shop and flew straight into the arms of the man I adored.

Acknowledgments

A huge thank-you to my agent, Chip MacGregor, who not only represented this story but also gave me the idea. I'll confess, I wasn't sure I could pull off a story about a guy running a bridal shop, but Brady ended up being the perfect hero!

As always, I'm grateful to my editor, Jennifer Leep, and to my awesome marketing team at Revell—Michele Misiak, Erin Bartels, Lanette Haskins, and many others.

I have come to depend on my line/copy editor, Jessica English, on every Revell story. I can't fathom publishing a novel without her. What a blessing she is in my life.

More than anything, I must give thanks to Eleanor Clark, one of the finest ladies I've ever known. I loosely patterned the character of Queenie after her, but only the good parts. She's truly one of the godliest women on the planet—an author, grandmother, mother, friend, and true patriot. What a blessing she's been in lives of so many. She showed me her town—Fairfield—in all of its glory. Through her, I learned that quaint, small-town living is a lovely way to spend your life.

To the people of Fairfield, thanks for letting me poke fun at you. I haven't been to any of your churches and took quite a few liberties with the denominational jabs, but they were all in fun. I know that you are all working hard for the cause of Christ and celebrate your efforts. Even the Presbyterians.

To my wonderful proofreaders who read the book from cover to cover before I turned it in, bless you. I rarely see my own errors, so having your eyes on the story helped . . . a lot.

To my Lord and Savior Jesus Christ, thank you for one more opportunity to share a fun story with a faith message. I count it a privilege.

COMING OCTOBER 2015

Every Girl
GETS CONFUSED

BOOK 2 *in the*
BRIDES *with* STYLE
SERIES

1

Hoop-Dee-Doo

If anyone had told this small-town, freckle-faced girl that she'd end up gracing the cover of a big-city bridal magazine wearing the world's most beautiful wedding gown, she would've said they were crazy. But that was just what happened.

Through a series of unfortunate—er, fortunate—events, I found myself plucked up from my predictable life in Fairfield, Texas, a quaint little town where Pop ran the local hardware store and Mama led the choir at the Baptist church. In less time than it took to say, "Hey, let's all go to Dairy Queen for a Blizzard," I found myself transported to a whole new world in the Dallas–Fort Worth metroplex, that of Cosmopolitan Bridal.

From there, I somehow landed on the cover of *Texas Bride* magazine wearing an exquisite gown that had been specifically designed for me by none other than Nadia James, Texas's most renowned dress designer. All of this because of a contest for brides-to-be, a contest I had no right entering in the first place since I wasn't exactly engaged. I'd come close to having a ring on my finger, but my now ex-boyfriend, Casey Lawson, had left me high and dry in the eleventh hour. My ringless finger still ached, and I shuddered whenever I thought about the pain and embarrassment our very public breakup had caused back in Fairfield.

Not that anyone at Cosmopolitan Bridal seemed to care about my lack of a groom. They were far too busy celebrating the upswing in sales after the October issue of *Texas Bride* hit the stands. I found myself firmly planted in the happiest place on earth. Or at least the happiest place in the state of Texas. Groom or no groom, I was destined to be surrounded by gowns, veils, and bridesmaid dresses every day. Goodbye, Dairy Queen. Hello, big-city life.

Settling into my new job turned out to be easier than I'd imagined once Brady James, the shop's interim manager, welcomed me with open arms. After a brief getting-to-know-you season, he also welcomed me with a few sweet kisses. But my budding relationship with the pro ball player turned bridal shop manager didn't necessarily mean I'd be wearing that gorgeous wedding gown for real, at least not anytime soon. But a girl could still daydream, right?

That was exactly what I found myself doing near the close of day on the first Monday in November. A firm voice brought me back to reality.

"Katie, did you place that ad in the *Tribune*?"

I startled to attention as our head sales clerk's voice sounded from outside my office door. Before I could respond, Madge entered the room, her arms loaded with bolts of fabric—tulle, lace, and the prettiest eggshell-hued satin I'd ever laid eyes on. The bolt on top started to slide, so I bounded from my seat to grab the slippery satin before the whole pile went tumbling to the ground. I caught it just in time and secured its spot atop the others.

"Thanks." Madge shifted her position, nearly losing her grip on the bolts once more. This time she managed to hang on to them. "So, did you place the ad?"

"I did." I gave her a confident smile. No one could accuse Katie Fisher of falling down on the job. No sir. I aimed to please.

"Ah. I see." Madge's nose wrinkled. "Well, Nadia wants to talk to you about that. She's on the phone."

"O-oh?" I still flinched whenever my boss's name was spoken. Working for one of the country's top designers still made me a tad nervous. Okay, a *lot* nervous. "It's almost midnight in Paris. Why is she calling so late?"

"It's important."

I gave Madge a nod and reached for the phone. Seconds later, I was engaged in a lively conversation with Nadia. I assured her that the ad had been placed in the *Tribune*, as per her earlier instructions.

Instead of celebrating that fact, she groaned. "Oh no. I was hoping you hadn't placed it yet."

"Why?"

"Because we're backlogged. Madge says we've taken over sixty orders for the Loretta Lynn gown just since I left the Dallas area. They've come in like a flood, and I'm not there to build a dam."

"I see." Although her dam analogy left images of beavers running through my mind.

"I didn't think about what this would do to our business, to be honest. I mean, I expected sales, of course, but we'll have to mass-produce to keep up with the demand. We've been busy in the past, but never like this."

"What can I do, Nadia?" I reached for my pen and paper.

She hesitated and then released a little sigh. "That's the problem. I don't know."

My pen hovered above the paper, awaiting its cue.

"I've talked to Dahlia. She's hired three new seamstresses, but they just can't keep up." The exhaustion in Nadia's voice rang through. "It's a happy problem, I guess. Growing pains. But I truly don't know what I'm going to do. There's no way we can continue taking orders for dresses if we can't fulfill those orders."

I set my pen down, ready to offer all the assurance I could. "Don't worry, Nadia. We'll figure it out, I promise. I'm sure Brady has a plan in mind."

"I hope so. That boy of mine is a whiz—on and off the court."

"Yes, he is." Only, he wouldn't be on the court anytime soon. With his knee injury requiring a second surgery, Brady would miss out on the first half of the season. The very idea broke my heart.

"When you see him, please give him my love." Nadia released a yawn. "I'd better hit the hay. Long day tomorrow."

"Of course."

I'd just started to say goodbye when she jumped back in. "Katie, in case I haven't said it often enough, we're tickled to have you on board at Cosmopolitan Bridal. I credit our recent successes to you."

"To me?" I was just the one who'd pretended to be engaged so I could enter a contest.

"Yes. I truly believe God brought you to us. And you're doing a fantastic job with the marketing end of things."

"Maybe a little *too* good?" I countered.

She chuckled. "Never thought I'd say so, but yes. Do you think you can pull the ad from the *Tribune* before it goes live?"

I glanced at the clock. Five minutes till five. I'd have to get right on it. "I'll give it my best shot, Nadia. I'll shoot you an email after I find out."

"Thanks, hon. Talk to you later."

"Bye."

I put in a call to the advertising rep at the paper and asked him to pull the ad. No telling what he would put in its place, but that wasn't my concern. I needed to keep my focus where it belonged—on the shop.

And on the handsome fella now standing in the door of my office. I felt the edges of my lips turn up when I saw Brady standing there. Mr. Tall, Dark, and Handsome took a couple of steps in my direction and I rose to meet him. He extended his arms as if to offer me an embrace, but I shook my head and whispered, "We're on the clock."

"It's six minutes after five." He gave me a knowing look and then pulled me into a warm hug. "And you . . ." He kissed me on the cheek. "Need . . ." He gave me two more kisses on the other cheek. "A break." Those words were followed by the sweetest kiss on the lips. I found myself transported to a happy place.

Well, until Madge cleared her throat from out in the hall.

Brady brushed the tip of his finger across my cheek and then took a step back just as she entered the room, clucking her tongue in motherly fashion.

"Are you two at it again?" Madge rolled her eyes. "I thought we agreed to no PDA."

"PDA?" Crinkles formed between Brady's dark brows.

"Public displays of affection," Madge and I said in unison.

"Makes the customers nervous," she added.

Brady crossed his arms at his chest. "Let me understand this. You're telling me that the sight of a man kissing a woman makes happy-go-lucky brides-to-be nervous?"

"Well, in the workplace, I mean." Madge shook her head. "Anyway, I suppose it's really none of my business."

"Yep." Brady pulled me back into his arms. "And we're off the clock. So you just tell any nervous bride to worry about her own love life, not mine."

Love life?

Did he really just say *love* life?

I gazed up, up, up into Brady's gorgeous blue eyes, my heart soaring to the skies above—okay, the ceiling above—as he gave me a kiss that erased any doubts.

Madge left the room, muttering all the way, but I couldn't seem to rid myself of the giddy sensation that threatened to weaken my knees. Just about the time I'd leveraged the distance between heaven and earth, my cell phone rang. I hated to interrupt such a tender moment, but it might be Nadia calling again.

Strange, though, that she would call me on my cell and not the office phone.

Brady stopped kissing me and gave me a little shrug as I reached for my purse. Seconds later, as the phone rang for the third time, I finally held it in my grip.

Only, it didn't stay in my grip for long. When I read the name *Casey Lawson* on the screen, it took everything inside of me not to toss the foul thing into the trash can on the far side of the room—a perfect three-point shot.

Instead, with my heart in my throat, I pushed the button to answer the phone and tried to offer the most normal-sounding hello that a once-jilted girlfriend who'd just been caught kissing a new fella could give.

Award-winning author **Janice Thompson** enjoys tickling the funny bone. She got her start in the industry writing screenplays and musical comedies for the stage, and she has published over one hundred books for the Christian market. She has played the role of mother of the bride four times now and particularly enjoys writing lighthearted, comedic, wedding-themed tales. Why? Because making readers laugh gives her great joy!

Janice was named the 2008 Mentor of the Year for American Christian Fiction Writers (ACFW). She is the incoming president of her local (Woodlands, Texas) chapter and is active in that group, teaching regularly on the craft of writing. In addition, she enjoys public speaking and mentoring young writers.

Janice is passionate about her faith and does all she can to share the joy of the Lord with others, which is why she particularly enjoys writing. Her tagline, "Love, Laughter, and Happy Ever Afters!" sums up her take on life.

She lives in Spring, Texas, where she leads a rich life with her family, a host of writing friends, and two mischievous dachshunds. She does her best to keep the Lord at the center of it all. You can find out more about Janice at www.janiceathompson.com or www.freelancewritingcourses.com.

Come Meet

Janice Thompson

at www.JaniceAThompson.com

Read her blog, book information, and fun facts!

Follow Janice on Facebook and Twitter

Be the First to Hear about Other New Books from REVELL!

Sign up for announcements about new and upcoming titles at

RevellBooks.com/SignUp

Don't miss out on our great reads!

Revell

a division of Baker Publishing Group
www.RevellBooks.com